LAYERS

LAYERS OF DECEPTION

Leo James

Copyright 2019 Leo James.
All rights reserved.

ISBN: 978-1-9164049-0-8

10 9 8 7 6 5 4

For Mom & Dad

Acknowledgements

I would like to thank all the folks for the advice and assistance that shaped and improved my story during the writing process. In particular, I'm very grateful to Mike Hawkes, Joe Nugent, Dr. James Chan, Annie-Rose Bostock and Howard Brown for their editorial guidance; Deb Burke, Pete Barrett, Julie King, Angela Tucker, Lauren McHugh, Petra Rohr-Rouendaal, Liam Burke, Sheila Williams and Sebastian Karig for reading the novel as it progressed and providing crucial feedback.

A special thank you to Mary Thompson - an amazing editor!

The cover was developed at www.essence-design.co.uk by the very talented Regine Wilber.

PART ONE

SATURDAY 11TH APRIL

The unprotected driveway offered zero cover as hard raindrops ricocheted like pellets off David's car. Orange-lit street lamps illuminated the downpour. The cyber security expert yanked the collar of his three-quarter length coat over his head. It was either a soaked head or backside – easy choice. Lola, his yellow Labrador, reluctantly traipsed behind. She hated being wet and once sheltered behind the vehicle, gave herself a hearty shake. David opened the tailgate of the Renault Estate and the pooch jumped in.

'Good girl.' David smiled as Lola settled on her blanket. He threw his coat into the back of the car and slid quickly into the driver's seat.

Trish emerged from the house carrying a bow-wrapped box. She closed the front door, tested it with a push and a pull, then rushed towards the car in a futile attempt to dodge the downpour. Once seated, it took a while to wipe her blinking eyes and dry her glasses.

'I'm bloody soaking.' Trish twisted and stretched to place the present on the rear seat.

'Let's get moving... party'll be over.' David checked Lola in the mirror. 'Good girl. Lie down now.' David pulled the estate off the drive and headed to the party.

'Spend time with me tonight. Don't leave me talking to your sister... or Tim.' Trish wagged her index finger. 'Focus on me for a change. Most of the time you're absent. If you're not working, you're thinking about work.'

'Tim's all right. He's harmless.' David glanced at Trish and smirked.

'All arms more like. Bloody octopus. Any chance to grab my backside or have a fondle.'

'He's no Hardy What's his name — just friendly.'

The Renault's headlights pierced the cloudburst as the traffic slowed.

'Yes, too friendly. I'm sure June must know.'

'She'd defend him to the hilt.'

'Letch. Any chance to grope, especially when he's had a few drinks.'

'If he does anything that makes you uncomfortable, let me know and I'll speak to him about it,' David glanced at his wife. 'You're beautiful. My lovely Trish. Are you surprised?'

'Ah. You realise it. Funny. You married me remember, not your job.' She pushed his shoulder.

'You are so funny and so lovely.' He looked at her again and smiled.

'If I'm so delectable... why do I always have to grab you for a hug or a kiss? You're married to your phone and that company. You should be careful. I'm a great catch. If you're away I don't see you, and when you're here, you have your head down looking at your phone or your bloody laptop.'

'Don't go on. It's a difficult time. You know I need to keep things going.'

'Let the other directors take some pressure. It's not all down to you. Have some home life.'

'For God's sake. Let's have a good evening.'

'You've just got back and you're off away again. How does that make me feel?' She bowed her head, letting her hair screen her face.

'It won't be for long...Steady!' David felt the car slide a little, so he straightened it and gripped the steering wheel tighter. 'Christ, these tyres are wearing thin already!' The wipers were at full velocity yet were struggling to keep the deluge off the screen; he kept his speed well below the limit.

'I'm not going on the M25 in this... we'll take the A10.'

'OK. You know best as always.' Trish looked away.

'Let's just have a nice evening. It's Dad's seventieth.'

Trish did not respond.

The shower was easing.

'You're a good girl Lola.' Trish turned around in her seat, she nudged her glasses with a fingertip, and smiled. 'Not far to go. Treatie time when we get there.' Lola wagged her tail expectantly.

The downpour reduced to a drizzle.

A black Audi pulled alongside them and slowed instead of overtaking. David looked across at the two men in the car. The passenger stared back and surveyed the pair with a half-smile.

'What's he want?' David glanced several times whilst trying to focus on the road ahead. 'He's driving too close. Nutter.'

The Audi hovered a little longer. David checked again. The passenger averted his stare and looked down. The Audi's engine revved and it sped away. David stroked his beard and shrugged. 'Strange—.'

The explosion caught him mid-thought. It was deafening and quick. He felt numbness and tingling but didn't know the detail - Good job. Both of his eardrums had burst in the blast. The Renault's airbags activated with twin bangs and filled the car with acrid smoke. He lost his grip on the steering wheel as the bag forced him backwards before jolting him forward again into the cushion. His seat belt locked up to reverse the action. Trish's head lurched forward, causing her spectacles to propel into the air, before her skull cracked against the passenger window. The car slid sideways along the wet road, narrowly missing a van as a white minibus braked hard behind it. The Renault finally lost all traction on the sodden surface and began spinning. Lola yelped in her rear compartment prison. The poor thing was being thrown around like washing on a full spin cycle.

The car crossed a grass verge, and smashed into a street light, its doors buckling inwards. The momentum carried it still further into a tailspin, then a flip, before propelling it backwards into some bushes. Upturned and stationary, a further explosion punctuated its demise as flames consumed the chassis, tyres, and all.

Traffic ground to a standstill and onlookers spilled out of their vehicles. They did it in freeze-frame. There was little point in rushing to this one.

CHAPTER TWO

Sunday 8th February

The distinctive silver plaque and embossed gold lettering above the receptionist's head welcomed visitors to Tan Koh Chong Group. This was the company headquarters, based in the penthouse of the Tun Sambanthan building, central Wilayah Persekutuan district of Kuala Lumpur. The receptionist bowed. 'Good afternoon, Mountain Master.'

Mountain Master, head of Kongsi Gelap thirty-one - the Triad gang controlled the centre of Kuala Lumpur, upheld the traditions of extortion, drugs, smuggling, and prostitution, and had ambitions to expand activities on an international scale. Despite his slender frame, he exuded confidence: tailored suit, dark brown eyes, tanned complexion, and jet-black hair. Flanked by one of his foot soldiers, a huge man resembling a sumo wrestler wearing a black suit, they walked straight past the receptionist and into the boardroom.

When his father died, Mountain Master's life became focused on building wealth, status and power. Ever since university he wanted to be a successful businessman, to influence politicians, gain vast wealth, and be admired by the Islamic elders at the local mosque. As the proud head of the organisation, he ordered his subordinates to carry out deeds to accumulate riches and power. The gang's rank names referenced controlling comrades of the organisation. At the lowest level were the probationary affiliates – often drawn from local youths, these so-called Blue Lanterns became rank and file members after an initiation ceremony. Above them were the key leaders: White Paper Fan, the money man; Red Pole, the Enforcer; and Straw Sandal, the strategist. At command level came Vanguard, Deputy Mountain Master, Incense Master and the Mountain Master himself.

The opulent boardroom's striking marble floor lay in a synergy of black, white and brown squares. At each corner stood stone pillars reminiscent of a Roman temple. A single large fan circulated, and air boomed out of the conditioning unit. Mountain Master sat at the head of an oval table, and his hench man stood motionless in front of one pillar.

Incense Master, also known as The Commander, arrived next. Born in Malaysia of Chinese origin, he radiated a quiet stillness. They nodded to acknowledge each other. Mountain Master clicked his fingers. 'Two oolong.'

The huge man bowed and left the room to organise the tea.

Incense Master leaned forward in the chair. 'We are completing on the purchase of the New York condo next week.'

'Good. Is the rental organised?'

Incense Master smiled and crossed his legs. 'Two options, one is a US law enforcement agency. No details of which agency though.'

'Do we need to be cautious?'

'No, not in the US.'

'Good.'

A petite woman entered the room, carrying a tray with a pot of oolong tea, teacups and saucers. She bowed, laid the contents on the table, bowed again, tiptoed backwards and left the room.

Other gang members arrived and sat around the table on wingback chairs. Vanguard, Head of Operations, had a skinny, weasel-like face and a slight frame. Accompanying him was White Paper Fan, a plump man with glasses and greying hair. Last to arrive was Red Pole who had many years' experience in the Malaysian army and police force. The assembled men met once a month to discuss progress, including revenue earned from protection agreements and prostitution at the Beach Club and Cuban Latino bars.

Red Pole stood up and saluted. 'Straw Sandal cannot attend the meeting. He sends his apologies.' Straw Sandal's position was liaison officer for the group. Red Pole sat back down.

White Paper Fan, the money man, summarised income for the month.

'What are we doing about Kongsi seventy-seven?' Vanguard asked, 'They're trying to take over the Ampang District, though they already own the northern suburbs.'

'The police are patrolling Ampang. A large district; difficult to cover the whole area at all times.' Red Pole opened his arms wide to emphasise his point.

Mountain Master stood up, walked over to the window and looked out at the city skyline. 'Let's move on. I will speak with Mountain Master at Kongsi twenty-six. They also want them stopped.' He turned and looked at Vanguard. 'Where are we with Q7?'

'They arrive today for the final presentation. Farid will award the contract this week.'

Mountain Master sat back down. 'Any problems?'

'No, we are ready. The girls are at Cuban. Briefed and given photos,' Incense Master said.

'Hotel rooms set up, Vanguard?'

'Yes, all four wired for video and audio.'

'Good. We need to move fast and ramp up the offshore flow. Are we all agreed?'

They nodded and carried on with the rest of the agenda.

# # # # # #

"Ten minutes to landing" buzzed the plane's tannoy system as British Airways Flight BA33 approached Kuala Lumpur International Airport (KLIA), passing over masses of neat rows of oil palms interspersed throughout large areas of woodland.

Steve sat cramped in the aisle seat. He stretched, peered with heavy-lidded eyes, and forced a smile at the flight attendant as she strolled along the aisle. The Valium tablet did not have the desired effect as he had slept on and off during the journey; grogginess made him uncertain how much sleep he'd got. Either way, the Q7 deal played on his mind throughout the journey. He had forgotten Mark, sitting nearest the window, separated by a vacant middle seat. His lanky frame was not engineered for long-distance plane journeys in coach class. He would not have blamed Mark if he'd got a regular job anytime over the past three years, Steve pondered. *The last year has been tough. I must keep him onside.* Determined to show confidence, he needed him more than ever for the final push. Although Mark loved Kuala Lumpur, Steve wanted to make sure that Mark, being a gay man, remained discreet and didn't attract unwanted attention when visiting a Muslim country.

Steve always made sure they checked the latest data and advice before entering any country. Malaysia still upheld the British Penal Code of 1871 making it illegal for men of any age to engage in sexual intercourse with other men. The level of tolerance for homosexuality differed from its neighbours in South East Asia. In addition, the Islamic Sharia laws forbade sodomy and cross-dressing. Same-sex handholding occurred often, although conservative Malaysians frowned on all displays of public affection.

The plane touched down and once they had passed through passport control and retrieved their suitcases, they emerged from the arrivals' exit, then headed towards the Information Point. Steve spotted a sign displaying, 'Steve Roussos, Mark Farrell, Seguro Limited', held up by a well-dressed chauffeur who relieved them of their baggage.

Mark smiled. 'No matter how many times we use the hotel limo service, I love it.'

'The only way to travel,' Steve said.

They followed the driver and moments later emerged from the air-conditioned coolness of the terminal into the sweltering tropical heat. Although shaded by the airport canopy, the blast of year-round heat and humidity caused Steve to experience an immediate flow of sweat from every pore of his body, even though he removed his jacket. Many visits to Kuala Lumpur and he still found it difficult to get used to the hot, oppressive climate. They strolled past the massed ranks of Mercedes Benz and the Malaysian-manufactured Proton limos. The chauffeur led them to an elegant, long wheelbase Proton. They jumped into the back of the car, and were greeted by an array of drinks, papers and magazines provided as part of the service; the driver turned on the engine and a welcome stream of cool air greeted them

As they drove along the toll road into Kuala Lumpur, a heavy thunderstorm reduced traffic to a walking pace despite it still being early evening. The rain descended, creating flash floods and gridlock, slowing their progress.

Steve stretched and yawned. 'This may take some time. We'll meet Glen and David in the morning for breakfast to run through everything.'

'Great. We're in good shape,' Mark said.

Steve smiled. 'Yes, we're gonna win the deal.'

I hope so! Three years of hard work. Shit or bust.

Mark nodded.

The car crawled along the road; the downpour now beating off the windscreen, causing the wiper blades to work overtime. Steve peered out of the window. Kuala Lumpur had turned into a construction site as high cranes loomed from what seemed every available space, interrupting the skyline like giant Transformers. He reflected on the good times working for large companies: living the dream, on excellent salaries, great commission and more than generous expenses. There were the stresses of meeting targets for sure, but they had left the financials, fundraising, board meetings and staff issues to the management.

Happy days.

Steve reflected on the company's current situation and knew they had got nowhere near the capital needed to carry on. The company had raised millions in contributions and loans, but still struggled to break even, because they did not get the full amount promised from any of the shareholders. Three years of lack of financial backing caused lots of problems. They assumed all the money would come in; but Steve accepted how naïve they had been, generating only a fraction of the amount they needed. They hired all the staff, started the software coding and kicked-off the product development plan. He regretted not taking the Valido offer to buy Seguro. There had been four months of painful and costly legal wrangling before Roger and the lawyers made them walk away from the deal, followed by over eighteen months chasing money. He would bite their hand off now if Valido made the same offer.

# # # # # #

The looming cranes looked unstable in every direction. One of them took a direct hit from a bolt of lightning. In the illuminated skies, the jagged half-built skyscrapers looked like twisted ruins. Steel pillars to carry automated trains, the latest undertaking to deal with traffic congestion, stood at regular intervals, like giant sentries petrified by a powerful enemy. They travelled underneath a massive six-lane flyover which caused a temporary lull in the rain drumming down, sheltering the car. Motorbikes jammed both sides of the road, their riders wearing makeshift plastic jackets, taking refuge from the rain under the concrete structure. Vehicle lights glinted on their shiny transparent coats, many revealing Arsenal, Man United and Chelsea soccer shirts. The rain eased, and the traffic moved forward at a stop-start pace as the bottleneck unfolded.

After seven PM, local time, the Proton pulled up at the Concorde Hotel Kuala Lumpur. The bell boy greeted them as they stepped out of the car, gathered their suitcases from the trunk and moved them into the hotel lobby featuring a vast marble floor, pillars and a reception desk. Even the walls and ceiling were set in expensive marble. They booked into the premier level as usual with a view of the Petronas Twin Towers. As they had done many times previously, they walked straight over to the elevators, and ascended to their rooms.

CHAPTER THREE

Monday 9th February

Steve got to sleep before ten PM, woke at two AM, and again '
just before four. Rubbing the rheum from his eyes, he pulled
two pillows together to prop up his head, then stretched,
leaned over and grabbed his MacBook, placing it on his
stomach. He set up Wi-Fi and went online before he started
FaceTime and called Beth. 'Hiya, can't get much shuteye.'

She smiled. 'Hi love, what's the time?'

He brushed his hand through his hair whilst the other
covered a yawn. 'Four in the morning.'

'Oh dear. You'll be exhausted.'

'I'll adjust over the next few days. The adrenaline will keep
me going.'

'You poor thing.' Beth leaned forward to stroke the image
of Steve on the screen.

'Wow, I need you now.' He smiled.

'I bet you say that to all the girls.' Beth blushed. 'You
should do some of the Tai chi and yoga I taught you.'

'I'm sure that would help. But I'm exhausted.'

'I know. Once you adjust, it's the best thing you can do. I
love it.' She smiled.

'You get the kids off to school OK?'

'Yes, Jake's got hockey practice, so I got his kit ready. He
didn't tell me until this morning. Ellie and Kate are missing
you. Millie is missing her walks.'

'Ahh.'

'I'm taking Kate to Doctor Harris.'

'What's wrong? Is she OK?' He felt his shoulders tense.

'A wheezy chest, I'm taking her just in case.' Beth looked
tired.

Steve rubbed his eyes with the base of his palms and pushed them deep into his sockets. 'Poor thing. Give her a big kiss for me.'

'I will – oh, and we got another letter about the mortgage. They want us to meet about the arrears.' Her eyes rolled skyward.

'Can you ring and tell them I'm away? If they're awkward, I'll call them tomorrow. OK?'

'Should we cancel the holiday?' Her expression slid into a frown.

'No, its cash flow.' *Jesus Christ. I don't need this right now.*

'OK.' She sighed.

'Thanks love, you're a rock.'

'Just win the contract.' Beth's brow puckered.

'Plan is to meet the guys in the hotel lobby to get prepared for the presentation tomorrow. I suppose I better try to sleep.'

'Yes, you should get some sleep.'

'OK, I'll ring tomorrow and talk to the kids. Love you.'

'And you,' Beth smiled.

# # # # # #

Steve took another Valium and drifted into a deep sleep after five AM. At eight AM the boom of his iPhone alarm woke him. His head felt heavy and pain shot from the bridge of his nose across both eyes. He stopped the beeping sound, picked up a bottle of the complementary water from the bedside cabinet and drank the contents. He liked the familiar layout of the room: queen-sized bed, black leather lounge chair and a large TV. It all made him comfortable, despite being six thousand five hundred miles away from home.

Refreshed after using the powerful rain shower, he put on a T-shirt and boxer shorts, and opened the French doors onto the balcony where an uncomfortable dearth of fresh air greeted him. Thanks to Kuala Lumpur's location on the equator, the city experienced some of the most intense heat and humidity the earth offered. The bustle of cars, trucks and mopeds spewed out carbon monoxide, hydrocarbons and nitrogen oxides created by the extreme temperatures, as they crawled along the road in both directions, with the metro sandwiched in between like the filling in the middle of a cake. *This would be no good for Kate's poor chest. I hope she is OK. That's all we need.*

Once Steve got dressed, he facetimed Glen Lewis, Seguro's Sales Manager for Asia.

Glen filled Steve's screen with the proximity of his face. 'Namaste.' He bowed his head. 'Farid Razak wants us to go to dinner tomorrow evening after the presentation.'

Steve raised his eyebrows. 'Sounds promising if the CEO wants to take us out. If we don't balls-up the presentation, we'll nail this deal.' *We must nail this!*

'Hope so.'

'Did you speak to Farid?' Steve rubbed his chin.

'No. Anil sent me a message.' Glen lit a cigarette.

'David OK?'

'Yeah, he got in two days ago and has spent most of the time in his room. Ordered room service for breakfast. Mind you he can set up and configure the Q7 demo from the hotel. Mad, eh?'

'I'm gonna get dressed and check emails. So, let's meet in the hotel lobby before breakfast. Nine o'clock. The four of us. OK?'

'I'll ping David and Mark. Namaste,' Glen replied as he closed the call.

# # # # # #

The Hotel lobby was bustling with people: guests and visitors queueing at the reception desks, waiting in line for taxis, or generally milling around. Steve headed across the magnificent marble floor, past the elegant staircase and into the atrium. He spotted Glen waving to him.

Glen leaned back in a leather lounge chair, hands behind his head. Although he lived in the UK, he had invested most of his working life living in Asia. He had embraced the continent over the years and he loved Malaysia and Singapore. A stocky figure, carrying too many extra pounds, his short brown hair and clean-shaven square jaw made him stand out in Malaysia. Glen's casual trousers and shirt displayed the labels of the fashion conscious. "Gadget man" as he was known, having two phones, an iPad, MacBook, and his treasured Breitling timepiece to name but a few.

Steve, feeling a little light-headed, tried to relax in the armchair next to Glen. He put his notepad on the table and smiled as he stretched. 'How's Alice?'

'Don't care.' Glen grimaced.

'Is she gonna be OK with you spending time over here?'

'Not bothered. Been two years since we've been in any sort of relationship. My uncle Patrick told me she has a boyfriend. He's welcome to her. Good luck to him. More worried about Harry and Lauren. I Skype them every morning before they go to school.'

'How are the kids?' Steve gave him the thumbs up.

His eyes brimmed with warmth. 'Harry loves his football. He's playing for the school and doing well. Lauren is Lauren. She's delightful. Alice is a wonderful mum but after eight years together, we've both moved on, so no relationship anymore.'

Steve yawned. 'You're gonna be spending a lot of time over here if all goes well tomorrow. Are you going to be OK?'

'I love Kuala Lumpur – the buzz, the people, the food, the bars, the sun, the women and the nookie. Everything except for the traffic. It's mad.' Glen smiled at a waitress as she delivered the drinks.

'You make me laugh,' Steve smirked.

'Makes sense to rent an apartment. No brainer. The Concorde Hotel rates are much higher. We can get a two-bedroom apartment in downtown Kuala Lumpur for less. Lloyd's pad is fantastic, bloody great value. Mad eh? ' Glen had met Lloyd Dodd at Goldman Sachs in Chicago a few years previously. He sold a solution to Lloyd's company. Goldman Sachs had transferred him to a new role in Kuala Lumpur, six months before, as part of a new investment fund.

'I tell you what.' Steve raised his cup. 'If we get revenue in the next few months from Q7, we can go for a two-bedroom apartment near Petronas Twin Towers. Deal?' *He can have what he wants if we get out of this mess.*

'Yes. Deal! No brainer.' Glen clicked his glass against Steve's cup. 'Cheers... Ah, hi Mark.' Glen looked up as Mark strolled into the lobby. He ordered a drink at the lounge bar, shook Glen's hand and sat next to him.

'Are we ready for tomorrow?' Steve said, segueing out of the small talk.

Glen looked to the floor. 'We still need to fix a glitch with the demo.'

Fucking Hell! Why didn't he tell me straightaway? Glen, you're such a tosser. 'What the... We've only got until tomorrow morning to get ready.' Steve felt sick.

'We know that. Chill.' Glen laid his laptop on the table and opened the lid.

'What the hell's wrong? We've spent weeks preparing for this. Over three years' effort, creating the solution. The investors pumped millions into the company.' Anger churned in Steve's chest. *Keep calm. Need them on my side. Keep calm.*

'We'll sort out the problem before the meeting. Cool.' Glen spoke into his coffee cup before taking a sip, his voice suddenly lower.

'This is the big break we've been waiting for with one of the major companies in Asia. We're all in deep shit if we don't get this deal.' Steve pulled himself to his feet.

'So, no pressure eh? Chill.' Glen threw up his hands in resignation. 'Calm down, calm down, we'll fix it.' He lifted his shoulder in a half shrug.

Steve sat back down. 'What's the problem?' Vomit bubbled inside Steve's stomach. *We don't need this.*

'We're waiting for the right parameters to work with the Q7 system for the live demo. Anil will email the information this morning.' With a flick of Glen's wrist, he waved away the question.

You tosser. 'What caused it?' Steve glared at him without blinking.

Glen shifted in his seat, eyes fixed on the laptop screen. 'Q7 upgraded their software. Old settings on our commerce system. We'll set-up the right data today and test the demo again before we arrive. I'm sure we can show complete demo of both the smartphone payments app and the smartphone loyalty app. We'll use an Android phone.'

Steve sighed. *Calm, confidence, encouragement. Stay calm.* 'Let's push Anil to get the info as soon as possible. Make sure he understands we are not at fault.'

'I'm sure he understands. He's working with us. No probs.' Glen tugged at his earlobe.

'What about the presentation? You added the new images of the Payments Gateway and included the patent references?' Steve said.

'Yes, I loaded them over the weekend. Cool.' Glen nodded.

'Good.' *Need to make sure Farid knows it is not our fault.*

Glen pointed to the slides on his laptop as he flicked through them. 'It's over eighty meg. I can't email the slides to you, the bandwidth on the hotel Wi-Fi is shit. Drops in and out. So I'll copy the presentation to a USB stick.'

David joined the group and sat down next to Steve. His casual fitting shirt and trousers covered the majority of his pale skin, and a bushy beard emphasised his geeky appearance.

'Ah, David.'

'Sorry, I got caught up with emails.' David chewed on a cuticle.

'OK, we're waiting for info from Anil at Q7,' Steve said.

'Yes, I know.' David shoved his hands in his pockets.

'We'll do a fantastic job tomorrow.' Steve slammed his hand on the table.

David jumped and smiled. 'We will.'

Steve opened his notepad. 'Mark, you got your mind map completed?'

'Yes, I'll cover the patents and vision.' Mark folded his hands in his lap.

'For you David, technical and support questions.'

'Fine by me.' David nodded.

'What about the competition?' Steve pointed his pen towards Glen. 'Did Farid or Anil give you any hints?'

Glen breathed in deeply. 'No real hints. Nought really.'

'What do you mean? Not really?' Steve tapped his pen on his pad.

'I can usually find out something. Some hints. But in this case, nothing. It'll be fine on the day.' Glen slouched.

Steve wrote a quick note. 'Can you listen to their private discussions during the meeting? Might get a few clues. Probably Malay?'

'Should be. Depends on who attends. I'll keep my ears open,' Glen said.

'Malay for sure.' Mark raised his eyebrow.

Glen waved at him dismissively. 'In government circles sure, Malay. Otherwise could be Tamil, Cantonese, Hokkien, Hakka, Teochew or Mandarin.'

'Sounds complicated.' David frowned.

'I'm looking forward to knocking them dead tomorrow. Let's grab breakfast. Then we'll do a dry run of the agenda for tomorrow.' Steve thrust his chin forward. *Calm. Stay calm, tired.*

'Let's use the business centre on the twenty-sixth floor. We can run through the presentation.' Glen pointed to the mezzanine.

'Great. Give Anil a call. Push him along. We're fucked if this doesn't work,' Steve said.

'Will do. Cool' Glen nodded.

CHAPTER FOUR

Tuesday 10th February

The Seguro team arrived ten minutes early to Q7's air-conditioned head office on Jalan Tun Samahon, in the centre of Kuala Lumpur. The tall building which Q7 occupied, Wisma Bernama, was as impressive as the adjacent building, The National Theatre, but both were dominated by the famous Petronas Twin Towers. They moved from the taxi straight into the building, with no adverse effects of the humid climate.

Great. Anxious but not too bad. The double hit of Valium is working. Let's hope the rest of the day goes well.

Anil Krishnan greeted the Seguro team in the lobby. Above average height for someone from Malaysia, his thinning, dark hair and tanned complexion made him appear much older than his mid-thirties.

Steve's hands were sweating and shook as he signed in at Q7's reception. He took a deep breath and followed Anil.

Calm, relaxed, assured.

An elevator arrived, and they bustled into the confined area. After a short period of silence, Anil announced, 'Farid will not be attending the meeting today, but will join you for dinner later.'

Steve figured Farid would need to go through the Seguro presentation and demo before they could reach any decision. Farid made all the decisions in Q7. *Another month's delay at least.* He feared the end for Seguro and his marriage.

Disastrous! He felt his sweaty neck with a clammy hand.

They got off at the thirty-fourth floor and Anil escorted them along a lavish corridor which led to the boardroom. David set up the connection between the laptop and the projector. Glen connected both the Samsung Android mobile and the Apple iPad to the Wi-Fi in readiness to show the Seguro system.

Various members of the audience arrived until Steve counted eight people from Q7 and four from Seguro. Once everyone was seated, Anil announced, 'Everyone is here. Shall we start?'

Steve raised the palm of his hand. 'Yes, we're ready to go, Anil.' He gripped the arm of the chair.

'OK, I am Anil Krishnan, Chief Operations Officer at Q7, and this is Anthony Suppiah from Finance.' He pointed to Anthony, a large man with glasses and greying hair, who nodded in response. 'From our Marketing team, Kim and Hapsah, the Technical team, Boon and Rakesh, and from Logistics, Suni and James.'

'Thank you, Anil. Thank you to you and your colleagues for shortlisting Seguro. Team introductions: I'm Seguro's Chief Executive and Founder, Steve Roussos. Over twenty years' successful track record in the financial services and mobile telecoms industry.'

The door opened, three men came into the room and sat in the audience. Anil said something to them in Malay. They stood up, bowed and left the room.

Anil nodded towards Steve. 'Carry on, please.'

Steve shot up an eyebrow and smiled. 'I love new and emerging technologies, specialising in digital and mobile financial services. We as a team have a strong collective history of successful implementations of large, complex programmes. In summary, our mobile app is a secure wallet to send money to friends and relatives, pay online or quick and easy international payments to merchants. It can store credit cards, debit cards and bank details protected. Simple, safe, and quick.' He coughed, his throat dry. 'Glen.'

Glen smiled, cleared his throat and said, ' Namaste.' He nodded. 'Glen Lewis, Sales Manager for Asia. My career started in banking, based in London. I'm now focused on Telecoms, Internet and Media sectors in Asia Pacific. Many years' experience working in East Asia, South Asia, South-east Asia and Oceania.'

'David.' Steve said. He tried to ignore the distractions of the phone beeps as the Q7 audience received messages.

'David Morris, Chief Technical Officer. Overall responsibility—'

Suni's phone rang. David paused. Suni answered the call. He talked in the local language. David waited. Suni finished the call.

David continued. 'Overall responsibility for software development, engineering, implementation and support. Many years' experience working on life-critical and projects including Trident Nuclear for the UK Ministry of Defence and NATO. Focus over recent years has been sonar systems and security infrastructure.'

Steve nodded to David, then Mark.

'Good morning everyone.' Mark smiled as he scanned the audience. His usual trick to engage their attention.

Suni and James chattered to each other.

Mark hesitated.

The noise level annoyed Steve. Other Q7 people received pings on their phones. A few of the team typed and sent messages. Suni stood up, followed by James. They bowed and left the room.

'Mark Farrell, founder and author of our worldwide patents. As Chief Scientist, I bring the vision and strategy to Seguro. I headed up m-commerce and security for the Mobile Data Association, creating the initial framework to address specific issues around application deployment, privacy and content management. Also, in the early days, I headed up the "mobile-futures" activities for the Mobile Association's Security Forum.'

'Thanks, Mark.' Steve stood up. 'Some examples of our collective achievements over the years...Worked on the ApplePay programme within a large bank's digital division, leading to a successful launch; Helped produce digital payments product strategy for one of the largest credit card issuers; Defined the mobile wallet product suite for a European mobile operator's financial services; Part of the design and launch team for one of the world's first mobile wallet and micropayment systems with another large European mobile operator; Created a large mobile commerce account, generating millions in revenue.'

Steve coughed and swallowed hard. 'We are going through the UK certification process. Our certification gives companies and the UK Government an absolute line of defence against cyber-attacks and data breaches for financial transactions. You know what government agencies are like. We are unique, so it takes time, but we are very confident.'

Mark looked away and delicately pinched the bridge of his nose as he closed his eyes.

Steve spotted Anthony reading something and yawning. This deflated Steve. Kim and Boon peered at their phones. Hapsah sported a fixed smile and Rakesh peered at his laptop. 'Mark, can you talk about our vision?'

They should switch their mobiles to "Do Not Disturb". Sitting on their arses playing with their phones. Give me a break.

Mark leaned forward, his fingers laced before him on the table top. 'Thanks, Steve. Seguro's mission is to become a leader in secure mobile online payments, Wallet Transfer and Forex Integration. Our expertise lies in the ability to help Q7 create a true mobile commerce and payments' ecosystem. Users can send amounts either online or from a mobile phone to anyone, anywhere in the world, using only their phone number. Seguro solutions will enable Q7 to generate mobile financial transactions and payment services from electronic top-up to airtime share to wallet-based fund transfers. Within and across international borders to a variety of players including mobile operators, banks, micro finance institutions, retail merchants and international remittance agencies.'

Steve stood up, walked to the head of the boardroom table, hands at his side in clenched fists of tension. He turned on the projector and used the presentation as a prop to deliver many compelling reasons for Q7 to award the contract to Seguro. He hated the fact that he depended on this deal happening, certain he would do a much better job if this deal did not matter so much.

Glen and David showed the system on an Android mobile phone, tablet and PC before passing the devices around the audience to try for themselves. The demos worked well. The Q7 team showed great interest and asked many questions. Although deflated by the constant chattering and interruptions, common experiences in Asian culture, somehow Steve was consoled.

Let's hope they give Farid the thumbs up so we can move fast.

# # # # # #

Steve and Glen arrived at the restaurant. A friendly waitress escorted them to a group of tables on the veranda, overlooking the busy street. Although after seven PM the evening air was almost tropical with a pleasant breeze; the two men sat and ordered two beers, followed by a further two beers.

'I'm tired, hungry and the drinks are going to my head.' Steve pressed his palms against his cheeks, elbows on the table.

Glen's large frame relaxed back into the chair. 'I'm fine. This is so nice. Chill.'

Steve rubbed his eyes. 'Did you pick up any comments in the meeting?'

Glen shook his head. 'Nah. No helpful comments. The three guys who came into the room and left had already booked the room. Also seemed to be a problem with their Wi-Fi hub. DDOS problem, hence the constant interruptions.'

'I hate interruptions. Anything about us?' Steve's jaw clenched.

'No, but they all liked the demos. Worked well. Cool.' Glen ordered two more beers.

'Are they messing us about?' Steve proclaimed and stood up. 'He's late. Where the hell is he?'

'He'll be here. Chill.' Glen ushered Steve to sit back down.

Steve reached into his pocket, pulled out a strip of pills, popped one into his mouth and swallowed it.

'What you taking mate?' Glen said.

'Just something to calm me. Doc gave me some Valium. Just to calm the stresses, you know. Just temporary.'

'I can get you something stronger than that. If you want. You can get anything here. It's mad.' Glen smiled.

'No, just temporary. I haven't told Beth. Or anyone. Just need something to de-stress me. So keep this to ourselves,' Steve said.

'Cool mate.'

'We need this deal. We're fucked if we don't close this,' Steve said.

Glen jolted upright. 'Now you're worrying me. We've won small deals with NetTel and Airnetiq. The Monetary Authority of Singapore shows promise, or at least the trials do.'

'Still not enough money to grow the company. We've raised our own money and taken family loans to keep the company afloat. So, it's dire.' Steve shook his head. *Fuck. Confidence. Don't panic. Shit.*

Before Glen had a chance to ask any more questions, Farid Razak arrived and sat down at the table. Although wearing his usual expensive suit, shirt and tie, his small frame supported a large gut due to many extravagances over the years. The thinning hair on the crown of his head and dark black stubble made him appear much older.

'Sorry, I'm late gentlemen. Women problems,' Farid said with a wry smirk.

Steve wanted to wipe the smile off his face but held his nerve. 'Hi Farid, how are you?' *Fat, bald bastard. Give us the deal!*

'Good meeting today?' Farid ordered a large whisky from the waitress.

'Yes, although you need to ask your guys to give their feedback,' Steve said.

'Do not worry. I always do.' He took a sip of his drink. 'Time for food. Let's order, I am famished.'

Farid ordered a selection of Vietnamese dishes for the table, without asking what Steve and Glen preferred to eat. Since Farid was their potential customer, Steve showed lots of enthusiasm for his food choices. They smiled and nodded through the various business and social exploits Farid described in great detail. They added inane laughter on cue to support his pathetic locker room stories.

Farid paused for a few moments, studied the amber liquid rolling around his glass as he swirled it. 'You are our chosen partner.'

Startled for a moment, Farid's words brought up the hairs on the back of Steve's neck. He glanced over at Glen, who smiled from ear to ear. 'Forgive me Farid, but did you say we are your new partner? Are we successful in winning the contract?'

His eyes narrowed as his eyebrows pulled together. 'Yes, but I am telling you now, this must be a success as I overruled my Finance Department. You are high-risk. I like you guys but if you fuck up, I will come down on you like a mountain of stones and I will make your lives a misery. Are we clear?'

Steve's palms became damp, his mouth dry, his stomach tight, and his throat clogged. 'Yes, Farid. You made the right choice. We will not let you down.' He stretched his hand towards Farid, to seal the deal with a handshake.

Thank God, thank Allah, thank everyone!

Farid clasped Steve's hand. 'Enough of this for tonight. Let's get the paperwork completed in the morning.'

'Bloody marvellous!' Steve's cheeks blushed. He could see the attempted upper-class accent amused Glen.

Farid made a call on his mobile, then placed the phone in his inside pocket. 'OK gents, meet at my offices at noon tomorrow to complete the agreement. I bid you good night.' He shook hands and left, leaving Steve to pick up the restaurant bill. They waved as he departed in a waiting limo.

Glen shook his head and breathed out deeply. 'Boy, does he love the sound of his own voice. Mad, eh?'

'Yes, and he has left me with the bloody bill.' Steve unclenched his fists.

But who cares.

'We've got the deal.'

'Yes.' Steve lurched to his feet and thrust his fists in the air. 'Another beer.'

Two beers later, Steve relaxed for the first time in many months.

Glen beamed. 'Let's go celebrate. Hanky Panky.'

'I'm shattered. Let's get the contract signed and then we can celebrate.' Steve clasped his hands behind his neck and leaned back.

'I'm going to the Beach Bar to meet up with Lloyd Dodd. Come along, you deserve a good time. No brainer.'

'No, Glen. You go, but don't forget we meet at Q7 at noon tomorrow. Let's meet in the lobby at ten-thirty. We can grab a coffee and prep before we head over.' Steve yawned.

CHAPTER FIVE

Wednesday 11th February

The following morning, Glen snapped awake. 'What's the time? I don't remember coming back to my room,' he said aloud.

A petite oriental woman lay on her back next to him in the bed, still asleep, with the absolute relaxation of a small child. Her long, jet-black hair rested on the pillow. Her features were small: tiny ears, dainty nose, and sharp glossy cheekbones. The white bedsheet revealed delicate shoulders and one small breast, its pastel pink nipple in view.

The woman opened her eyes, squinted at her surroundings and stretched. 'Mr Glen, did you sleep good?'

'Who are you?' he said in a crocked voice.

'Do you want to go to breakfast?' She rested her head on his shoulder and moved her hand across his bare chest.

'Who are you?' Bug-eyed, he rubbed the sleep from his face.

She smiled and drew nearer.

'Oh yes, I remember. Ah, at the Beach Club Bar last night. Great stuff.' Glen hopped out of the bed, stepped back, and stood naked whilst pulling the sheet to cover his crown jewels.

She slipped out of the bed and walked towards him, naked other than a lotus flower clipped to her hair. 'I am Mai which means "Angel" in English. Lovely time together, Mr Glen. You want me to shower you?'

'Shit. No, No! Get dressed, please. I must go. Right now.' His voice spiked. He was in a rush to make the pre-meeting with Steve to discuss the signing of the Q7 contracts.

She nodded. You want me to come back later?'

Her pale blue silk dress and white panties lay in a heap on the carpet. She walked over to retrieve her clothes, dressed and pulled on her white knee high patent leather boots.

'Yes. I'll call you. Cool. Got to run to an important meeting.'

'I love to meet you later, Mr Glen.'

He fiddled with his trousers. 'Here, take this to buy breakfast and something. I'll meet you tonight. What about the Cuban Bar? No brainer.' He handed her a five-hundred-ringgit note retrieved from the wallet in his trouser pocket. As he pulled on the first leg he almost fell over trying to put his trousers on.

Mai accepted the note, bowed, opened her bag and handed Glen a piece of paper. 'I give you my number. You call me.'

He ushered her out of his hotel room and grabbed his iPhone to facetime Steve. 'Hi mate,' Glen said with a hoarse voice.

'Where are you?' Steve barked.

'Sorry, delayed. I'll take a quick shower and meet you downstairs. I won't be long. Cool. Say fifteen minutes?'

'Mark and David are here with me in the hotel lobby.'

'OK, meet you downstairs.'

# # # # # #

Steve remained pensive, desperate to get the contract agreed and start the money flow.

'Come into my office. Take a seat.' Farid beckoned the Seguro team. They sat opposite Farid. Anthony Suppiah from finance sat alongside the large desk.

'Help yourself to drinks,' Farid instructed as he swivelled around in his plush leather chair. His office window afforded a superb frame around the iconic Petronas Towers with a good view towards the SkyBridge which spanned the forty-first floor between the Petronas Twin Towers.

He pressed a speed dial on his desk phone. 'Hi Anil, can you bring the specification and the Seguro order to my office?

Steve and his team are here.' Farid stood up, then paced back and forth from his desk to the large office window opposite. 'We are under a non-disclosure agreement so what we discuss and agree today is confidential. As a leading electronic payment service for online goods and services in Asia, we serve over one hundred thousand retail locations across six countries, with mobile payment and electronic delivery channels which accept major credit cards. Now, this feature is important. We plan to extend our services to grow into a global technology leader for smartphone and PC transactions. Users will send amounts to anyone anywhere in the world, with their smartphone. We want to launch mobile top-up, a wallet for fund transfers within and across foreign borders to mobile operators, banks and retailers. We are aiming for two hundred and fifty million subscribers using Q7 and to develop into the world leader in mobile online payments. Can you implement and handle the volume required, using your solution, within the next two months?' He stopped pacing, turned and looked straight at Steve.

Holy shit, WOW!

'Yes, we can roll this out within two months. David, OK?' Steve looked for support.

After a short silence David lifted his hand. 'As long as we receive maximum cooperation from the Q7 team, and our full in-house team to implement the system and process. Yes.'

Right answer. Thank God David is at the meeting. Relieved, Steve wanted to jump up, shout "Yes!", and phone Beth, but instead he tried to stay calm and collected. Steve shot a look across towards Glen, David and Mark, who remained very calm under the circumstances.

Anil entered the room, shook hands with each member of the Seguro team, and handed the documents to Farid. 'I guess the specification is for you David?' he said as he handed him the implementation document.

'Yes. Mark and I discussed the specification with Anil and his team. We can complete the programme requirements with minor modifications to our standard solution,' David responded.

Anil and Mark nodded in agreement.

'Now for the commercial terms.' Farid's eyes squeezed into thin slits. 'Q7's responsibility for the project includes computer hardware, network, resources, and roll out of the solution across our infrastructure. Your responsibilities include delivery and installation of the payment software, configured to our requirements and twenty-four by seven support. Are you in agreement?'

'Yes.' Steve nodded.

'Our proposal is to share the revenue between us. You get zero-point-two-five of a percent per transaction. Are you happy with shared revenue?' Farid bowed and smiled.

Steve shuffled in his seat. 'Our standard contract terms include a licence to use our software, but we are open to share the revenue as we grow. In addition, detailed timelines, modification and implementation costs for the project.'

Farid leaned forward and set his hands on the table, palms up. 'No, no, Steve, you misunderstand me. This is a shared risk venture. We are a success and you are a success. You offer the software and the support. Q7's infrastructure and resources are in place, and we share the risk.'

Although the air conditioning boomed out cold air, perspiration caused Steve to reach for his handkerchief to mop his forehead and neck. They needed money now to help keep the company in business. 'Can we agree on a basic cost of modifications paid by Q7 for the work completed?'

'If we cannot partner in the way I described, we cannot move forward. I am taking a huge risk on you. Our financial credit checks show problems with Seguro finances. I overruled our financial director because I like you, and I believe in you. Our plan is to grow to over one billion transactions per month by the end-of-year three. You can do the maths. I am sure we will buy your company before you reach this target.' Farid paused. 'Show commitment, Steve. Show backbone. I like you.'

Anil leaned back in his chair, crossed his legs and pointed his pen towards Steve. 'Even if transactions average only one US dollar, you will receive two and a half million dollars per month, and transactions should be much higher.'

That's thirty million dollars a year. It would value us at over three hundred million dollars based on the price-earnings ratio for the IT industry. Fucking hell! Q7 would pay half a billion for us. Roger will kill me, but we must complete the deal.

He wanted to phone Beth – now. 'Deal. We are looking forward to making this an international success.' He tried to stay as calm as possible.

'Excellent, my friend.' Farid grinned. 'Anthony will draw up a basic contract.' Anthony nodded. He continued, 'I am sure our trust in you will make us successful together. Now the real work starts. Two months to get this show on the road, as you say in England.'

Farid shook hands with each of the Seguro team as they followed Anil out of Farid's office to the elevators and down to the lobby. They handed over their badges to security and exchanged pleasantries with Anil before leaving the building.

'Over here.' Steve motioned as a taxi pulled up alongside. They jumped in and he instructed the driver, 'Concorde please, Concorde Hotel.' He sat back in the seat, laid the back of his head on the headrest, raised his arms, took a deep breath in and out, then said, 'We did it! We did it! Q7, eh? We did it!'

# # # # # #

Once they got back to the hotel, Steve returned to his room to call Roger Slater, Seguro's Financial Director, Company

Secretary and first significant investor. Roger retired in his early fifties after selling his engineering business. Successful over the years in various industries, he was happy to come out of early retirement to embark on the adventure of making one last attempt to impact the world. He was overjoyed to hear they had won the deal.

A relieved Steve continued, 'Yes, they want to share the revenue. We get zero-point-two-five of a percent per transaction.'

Roger paused for a moment and said, 'So, we get paid for the software licence and a revenue share on top?'

Steve drew in a long breath. 'No, pure revenue share, using Q7's hardware and resources for the implementation and roll out of the solution across their infrastructure.'

Roger paused again. 'We need to negotiate this further. We must get money up front. What are the timescales for revenue?'

Steve hesitated, his breath quickened. 'No, this deal or nothing. Farid has put his neck on the line for us. We should generate revenue within two months, or sooner if Mark and David can work their magic. Q7 want to increase to one billion transactions per month, two and a half million dollars per month to Seguro.'

Roger sounded concerned. 'The overheads and loan repayments are over ninety grand per month. And don't forget expenses. Are we going to ship part of the team to Malaysia? Another twenty grand at least for flights, hotels, and keeping them fed. If we take two months before launch, and another month to generate revenue, we are looking at a further two hundred and ninety grand needed for the three months before we get any revenue.'

'Yes, but the revenue opportunity is huge.' Steve twitched his right eye.

'But not guaranteed? We must get extra funding from Antonio Zefron and Cliff Lin.' Roger groaned.

Steve shook his head. 'If we'd funded the company in the first place, we wouldn't keep diluting the hell out of our shares to keep the business going. We win a contract which will ramp up to two point five million dollars per month, and we are disappointed.'

'Not guaranteed, Steven.'

'Don't call me Steven. You sound like a headmaster.'

'I'm concerned.'

'You didn't deliver. Your investment ended up going pear-shaped, so you didn't invest what you promised.' Steve rubbed his forehead.

Roger raised his voice. 'Nobody predicted the investment would get tied up in US lawsuits and corruption by a few bastards.'

'We found new investors who made crazy demands and didn't give us a fraction of the money pledged. And now you're putting pressure on me. Big time,' Steve shouted.

'We've been over this many times, Steve. I got Antonio's investment. No excuses.'

'This is a concrete signed contract.' Steve raked his fingers through his hair.

'You can guarantee nothing. I need to sell this to Antonio and Cliff. Meanwhile, we need the staff in the UK and Malaysia to be behind this push.'

'I'll scan and email the order over to you. Farid is producing a simple contract which he will send over for review,' Steve said.

'OK, I'll ask the solicitor to review it and we'll get it signed.'

'I'll send out an announcement to the staff on email today. It's positive and timely. Listen... sorry, I've got to go. I'm meeting with Mark and David. Talk later.' Steve ended the call before Roger replied.

Fuck you, Roger!

Steve stripped naked, switched the air conditioning to maximum setting and jumped into the shower. He needed to calm down.

Refreshed, he slipped his shorts on, sat back in the black leather lounge chair and called Beth on FaceTime from his iPad.

'Hi,' Steve smiled.

'Hello love, everything OK?'

'Yes, my darling. Great news. We've won the deal with Q7,' Steve announced wearing a huge grin on his face as he puffed out his chest.

'Oh, that's great for you.' Her voice broke lower.

Beth looked tired. 'You OK?' Steve could see her hair was untidy. Her gaze seemed unfocussed, perhaps preoccupied by something.

'I'm fine love. Things are getting me down. I can't wait to relax on a sun-lounger. Just tired. I'm fine. Oh…I've painted the old charm dining table.'

'Painted it?' Steve smiled.

'Yes, I've upcycled it using chalk paint. A lovely creamy grey. I'm pleased. Just need to paint the chairs.'

'No wonder you're tired, love. You amaze me,' Steve said,' Can you ping me over a picture?'

'Yes. It transforms the table. I'm really pleased with the new look,' Beth said.

'We'll be on that beach soon. Only need a few months to get money rolling in and we can pay everything off and more.' Steve smiled.

'Oh. So not yet. A few more hurdles?'

'Have I ever let you down?' He tried to make light of the conversation.

'Yes! Do you want a list?' she said in a mocking voice.

'We can send a copy of the order to the bank and I'm sure they'll hold off on the house and let us delay the mortgage until the money comes in from the deal.'

'Oh, good. Hope so.'

'I'll sort out everything. Miss you and the kids. Oh, and Millie. How's Kate?'

'She has asthma.' Beth wore a sad and tired expression.

'Asthma. Is she OK? What did Doctor Harris say?'

'Inhalers and he referred her to a consultant.'

'How long is the wait?'

'National Health Service list. Pity. Remember when we took private health cover for granted? Not now.' Beth slouched.

'I'll get the money. We'll go private.' Steve tried to sound as positive as possible.

'Doctor said the inhalers should help.'

'Is Kate OK using them? What if she gets an attack?' Worry lined his forehead.

'She knows what to do if she gets chest tightness or shortness of breath.'

'Will she carry an inhaler at school?'

'Yes, and the office store them for emergencies.'

'Poor love. Give her a big kiss for me. Can't wait to get back home on Friday. I don't enjoy travelling alone and waking up in a strange hotel bed without you.' Steve lowered his head.

'Well done on the new deal.'

'Thanks, Beth. I hope you can get some rest and feel a lot better. I'll ring tomorrow and talk to the kids. Love you.'

'Love you,' Beth said before Steve ended the FaceTime call.

# # # # # #

Steve met David, Mark and Glen in the hotel bar. They gathered around the complementary buffet and devoured a few beers, except for David who sipped Pepsi. Steve thrust his arms into the air. 'We should celebrate. We're heroes! Where shall we go?'

'I'm meeting Lloyd at the Cuban Bar tonight and going on a date. You know what I mean?' Glen had a mischievous look plastered on his face.

Mark winked. 'You and Lloyd, I would never have guessed.'

Glen smiled. 'Yes funny, mate. He's more your type.' He scoffed.

Mark smirked. 'Yes, he is. For sure. Just my type.'

Steve persuaded Glen to go and eat first. They agreed to go to Chinatown.

David looked bemused. 'We've eaten.'

Glen stood up, put his two mobiles, cigarettes and lighter in his pockets. 'That was only a snack. Come on David, let your hair down. Cool.'

When outside the hotel, Glen gestured to the bellboy to order a taxi that dropped them outside Hutong on Petaling Street. Steve loved the allure of the night market, as they wandered along enjoying its sights, sounds and energy. Not an easy task, given the humidity and local passion for cars and motorbikes. They strolled along the busy street in Kuala Lumpur's Chinatown, pavements covered with ubiquitous plastic tables and chairs, the illuminated Chinese lanterns overhead and the road filled with stalls selling every type off Malaysian cuisine imaginable. As they passed the Sri Maha Mariamman Temple, the stalls selling garlands of sweet smelling jasmine, and the strong aroma of Chinese traditional herbs wafted through the air from across the street. All this was at odds with the backdrop of modern skyscrapers dominating the capital's skyline.

They arrived at Wong Ah Wah, a restaurant covering five shop fronts along Jalan Alor, a short walk from the shiny heart of the city's shopping district. In one corner, a man presided over a charcoal-heated grill, preparing Wong Ah Wah's celebrated chicken wings. Nearby, a young woman produced lamb, chicken and beef satay. Glen ordered for the group: a meze of roast stingray; tangy, sour chilli sambal; chicken wings; dry mutton; peratal curry; tangy, citric fish curry and a round of beers.

After several beers Steve was a little light-headed, but comforted himself that the large quantity of food consumed would soak up the beers. And anyway, he deserved to celebrate the big win at last.

'Cheers guys. We did a great job!' Steve raised his glass.

Glen raised his glass. 'Cheers.'

The rest of the guys responded.

Once they finished eating and a few more drinks, they joined Glen in a taxi destined for the Cuban Latino bar.

The taxi drew up outside the bar on Jalan Bukit Bintang. Steve paid the cab fare. They strolled past the patio tables positioned across the front of the bar, occupied in the main by young Asian women who smiled at them. The men congregating around the entrance to the bar itself, most of whom were ex-pats enjoying the balmy night air, beer and studying the array of pretty ladies.

They walked inside, then approached a square-shaped bar area manned by several tenders. The interior depicted the design elements of a real Cuban restaurant: frescoes and peeling paint on the walls, giving an authentic Havana look. An exuberant DJ was playing the latest salsa, jazz and Latin music. Beyond the metal balustrades, upstairs they could glimpse an intimate lounge, furnished with comfortable leather sofas.

Ordinarily, Steve would have expected to be struggling by now, but he suspected that the good food and adrenaline were helping to keep him buoyant. He ordered a round of drinks. Glen nudged him and pointed across the bar to Lloyd. 'He's over there, mate, chatting to those birds.' Glen shouted. 'Hey Lloyd, how's the wife? Cool.'

They approached as Lloyd was in deep discussion with two women. He did not acknowledge them until Glen pushed his palm against Lloyd's shoulder.

'Hey guys, meet Perla and Alya. They are my new friends from the Philippines.' Lloyd winked. 'Perla is a pearl all right.' He raised his glass.

Glen made a zigzagged beeline, beer in hand, towards Alya. 'Namaste, I'm Glen, how are you?'

A confident woman with an American accent stepped forward. 'I am Alya.' She bowed her head and brought her palms together.

Glen moved closer to Alya and brought his palms together too. 'Namaste. Alya is a lovely name. Mad, eh?' He winked at the onlookers.

Lloyd put his arm around Perla as though protecting her from the predatory advances. 'You're such a cool operator.' He ordered another round of drinks, having to shout above the noise of the crowd and thumping music.

Overhearing David and Mark talking about cyber security attacks by the Chinese and Russians, Steve smiled. *Look at David sipping a soft drink! Typical. Those two talking shop when they should be enjoying themselves.*

The bar was packed wall-to-wall with women, ex-pats and locals congregating around the perimeter of the square-shaped room. A Filipino salsa band replaced the DJ on stage and soon played UK and American cover songs.

Mark ordered more drinks, prompted by Glen.

Steve suddenly felt intoxicated. *What the hell? The relief of the deal was encouraging him to let go.*

'Don't forget our lovely ladies, mate,' Glen said. Mark nodded as he pushed past a number people to get closer to the bartenders, whilst holding up a five hundred ringgit note to get their attention. His imposing stature allowed Mark to tower above others waiting to be served, as the nearest barman struggled to deal with the throng of people.

A man standing next to Mark beckoned on of the staff. 'Hey, he's next.' The smiling bartender obliged, and Mark reeled off his order.

Mark turned to the man who had helped him and nodded. 'Cheers.'

'No problem. Adam. My name is Adam Jothi from Malaysia.' They shook hands.

'Good to meet you, Mark Farrell from the UK.' He handed the round over to Glen and David, who in turn handed them out. 'Can I buy you a drink?'

'No, thanks.' Adam raised his glass. 'Maybe later.'

'OK, great.'

'Where are you from in the UK?'

Mark leaned towards Adam and cupped his ear. 'Sorry, say again?' He pointed towards an area away from the bar.

They moved away. 'That's a bit better,' Mark said.

Adam repeated the question.

'Manchester.'

Adam smiled. 'I lived in Birmingham. I attended the University of Birmingham.'

The group cranked up the sound: two percussionists, one keyboard player, two singers and two dancers packaged into a seven-piece Colombian band played sets of salsa, bachata and merengue music.

Mark leaned forward towards Adam's ear. 'Music's loud.'

'Yes, shall we go to sit out on the terrace? We can talk,' Adam said.

'OK.' He followed Adam through the crowd, and they sat at one of the few free tables outside on the terrace. The sound of the music hit every corner of the seating area, but the volume was low enough to chat. Soft blue lighting spanned the awning covering the complete length of the terrace. Waitresses stalked the tables, eager to take drink orders.

Back in the bar, Steve struggled to focus as he looked around. 'Where's Mark gone?'

'On the terrace.' David pointed towards Mark and said, 'How are you?'

'Fine,' Steve responded, 'Who is his friend? Can't see his face.'

'Not sure.' David scratched his beard.

Steve put his arm across David's shoulders. 'How's Trish?'

'Fine thanks. She doesn't want me to spend too much time over here, but she's fine.'

'How's- Oh no, look at the state of him.' Steve spotted Glen walking towards them. Leading Alya by the hand, he knocked into a few people in his path as he made his way over.

Glen moved from side to side in time with the music. 'Come on guys, let's dance. Hot babes on stage and on the dance floor. Let's show our moves. Come on.' He grabbed David's hand and pushed it back and forth in a mocking imitation of dance.

Steve steadied himself by holding on to the stool just behind him. 'I think I'll just watch thanks. I'm… You know.'

David pulled his arm away from Glen's grasp. Glen shook his hips, this time grabbing Alya's hand and waving his arm in a clumsy parody of a dancer. 'Come on, we've had a few beers and we're celebrating the big win. It's time to party. Great stuff.'

Steve shook his head and smirked. 'You're a party animal.'

'I'm going back to the hotel,' David said, 'to call Trish.'

Glen gulped back the rest of his drink. 'You pussy! Help, help, I'm stuck under Trish's thumb,' Glen mocked.

Steve put his hand on David's shoulder. 'Don't listen to him. I'll be following you.'

'Good night.' David left.

Glen stood stationary for a moment. 'Bloody hell mate, it's Mai from the other night, coming over.' She was heading right towards him with a friend following on.

'Quick, you talk to Alya. She's with you. Cool,' He motioned Alya closer to Steve. His gaze caressed Mai's painted-on red dress and matching knee high patent leather boots as she approached.

'He's got a new friend?' Alya's eyes shifted straight to Steve.

He struggled to think for a moment. 'Just an old friend.'

'I'm Alya, what's your name?' She said.

'Steve.' He held the bar stool to steady himself. 'I'm Steve.'

Alya sat on the stool and rubbed the back of her hand down Steve's arm. 'Where are you from?'

His gaze lingered over her. He sensed the danger she might pose. 'The UK.'

She smiled. 'You are. Where in the UK?' she said in a soft voice.

Steve coughed. 'Fareham.'

Oh, woozy now. Beer has gone to my head.

She cupped her hand around his bicep. 'Are you going to buy me a drink?'

Although his focus was impaired, he could not divert his eyes. Her white dress caressed her dark skin. The top cut low, just covering her breasts, and a slit to the waist exposed the top of her leg as she sat cross-legged on a bar stool. Steve took a seat on the stool next to her.

'OK, just one. I've had enough already.' He shifted his gaze away from Alya towards the band.

As he waited for his beer, a dull, nervous throbbing in his stomach caused him to contemplate walking to the restrooms and then leaving the bar. They watched the band playing whilst Lloyd ordered more drinks and then passed two over to Steve and his new friend. Glen, Mai and Mai's friend Tien joined them. Alya linked Steve's arm, tugging him closer, making him feel even more uncomfortable, although the beer reassured him. *She is harmless.*

Lloyd made sure Perla and Tien closely flanked him. Steve smiled to himself as Glen towered over Mai. He glanced at his watch, struggling to focus on the exact time.

Alya studied Steve with a wry smile. 'You're handsome.'

This is unravelling. Keep calm. She looks so good.

Her eyes held him hostage. 'Are you a sportsman?'

Shit. 'No, but I try to keep myself as fit as possible.' *What the fuck am I saying?*

'You look like a sportsman. You're muscular and firm.' She squeezed his biceps. This made his stomach flip again. He admired her body and tried to think of something less suggestive but could think of nothing else.

Steve paused. *Think. Think.* 'Where do you work?' He was feeling very anxious and wondered if he should take another Valium.

'A fashion shop, here in Kuala Lumpur. Rich people buy expensive clothes. It's called Bon Bon Boutique. Do you know it?'

Lloyd interrupted. 'Let's go back to your hotel.'

'Great stuff. Cool. Hit the bar,' Glen slurred.

Steve shook his head. 'I'm ready to go back, but it's straight to bed for me.'

Lloyd laughed. 'You're keen.'

CHAPTER SIX

Thursday 12th February

The walk back to the Concorde Hotel in the humid night air, made Steve even more light-headed. Lloyd marched Tien and Perla into the bar. Glen and Mai embraced as they entered the lobby and again began to caress each other when they reached the bar. Steve and Alya followed. Mai looked like a little girl next to Glen, Steve thought.

Lloyd reeled off another drinks order and pointed to Steve. 'Put the bill on his room.'

Steve swayed and plonked himself onto a nearby dark blue leather armchair. 'OK, one more beer.'

Lloyd sat on a matching sofa and pulled his two new friends onto his lap. It was a symphony of colour: Tien in a bright orange Kimono-style dress, Lloyd in a tan linen suit, and Perla in a jade-green, strapless number. Lloyd laughed. 'The walk of shame, the looks from the cab drivers. Who gives a shit?'

On the adjacent couch, Glen and Mai settled into the plush leather seats. Glen pulled Mai even closer. 'No one cares after midnight. No one cares, and hey, what goes on tour stays on tour. It's mad.'

Steve sat cross-legged, shaped in a way to stop Alya from getting too close while Lloyd gave equal attention to his two friends, caressing their thighs, and alternating between petting and kissing.

The resident Filipino band was playing the hit song "Waterloo". Steve cringed and finished his drink, stood up, staggered, walked a step, then turned, and stumbled a little. 'I'm off to my bed now guys.'

Alya jumped up, smiled, then tried to steady him with both her hands on his waist.

Lloyd raised his glass. 'Enjoy. Both of you.'

Glen smiled. 'Yes, enjoy mate. '

Steve held the palm of his hand towards Alya. 'I'm fine. You stay here.' He looked at the rest of the group. 'Goodnight.'

He walked in a zigzag motion across the lobby towards the elevator. He pressed the call button, and the doors opened. Alya ignored Steve's instructions and followed him in. She already knew the exact floor and room. He struggled to press the floor number, so Alya stepped forward to help him. As they ascended, Steve found it difficult to avert his gaze from Alya's petite frame, jet-black, shoulder length hair, piercing blue eyes and dark tanned skin.

# # # # # #

As they left the elevator Steve said, 'I will sleep now, you should join your friend. Nice to meet you'.

Alya smiled and moved closer. 'I'll walk you to your room.'

The fragrance of her perfume reminded him of fresh jasmine. *Smells wonderful, and I'm horny. She looks so good.* Drunk and nervous, he fumbled with his key card. 'You are a lovely woman Alya, but I must go to sleep now.'

Again, Alya helped the swaying Steve to open the room door. 'Am I beautiful?' They entered the room together.

'You are a beautiful woman, but I will sleep now. I'm so jet-lagged.' He felt a rush of butterflies in his stomach.

'I need to sleep, too. A nice time together.' Her face lit up.

Steve sat on the leather chair and Alya on the side of the bed. The split in her silk dress parted, and the dimmed lights reflected off her shining legs.

'Where are you from?' Steve tried a little small talk. Consumed by the scent of her perfume, he struggled to keep his eyes off her.

'Davao in the Philippines.'

'Why are you in Kuala Lumpur?' Thinking about her gave him sharp palpitations.

'I can get work here to make money for my family.'

'A big family in Davao?' His brain fizzled.

'Yes, mother, father, two brothers, my sister and my son.'

'Your son, how old is he?' His thoughts wouldn't line up. Every time he tried to align one, it tumbled down, scattering the rest. He wondered for a moment if one of his drinks had been spiked?

'He is six.'

'Oh, dear. How old are you?'

'I'm twenty-three.'

'Twenty-three, wow. When did you last spend time with your son?' *Holy shit.*

'I send him money, and I go home once a year.'

'Who looks after him?' His mind was turning to mush.

'My sister and mother.'

'You miss your son?' His cheeks flushed.

'Yes, I miss him.' She leaned across the bed to open her little pink handbag and get a picture of her son to show him. The slit in her dress widened as she did this, increasing the difficulty for him to focus on the photo.

'He's a handsome little fella. Where is his father?' His cheeks burned hot.

'His father has gone.'

A moment of silence. Inches away, Alya gazed into his eyes, her knees now touching his. In slow motion, she stood up and reached behind her neck, unhooked her strap, and her dress fell to her feet. No bra. Hard pink nipples topped her firm breasts. Steve remained motionless, unable to look away.

His heart pounded furiously as she stood before him, inches from his face. *Oh, my God. She's gorgeous. Fucking hell. I'm hard.*

She sat back down on the edge of the bed and moved both her hands over his thighs, leaned forward, put her head on his shoulder and her breath tickled his ear. Paralysed, breathing heavy and laboured, an avalanche of launched missiles tearing through his mind: *twenty-three, twenty-three, son, hard for her, I'm hard, I'm gonna puke, too much beer, she looks lovely, Beth, horny, shame, the guilt.*

'I can't do this,' Steve muttered through clenched teeth.

'What did you say Steve?'

'I can't do this!' He said.

'But I want you.' Alya placed a gentle kiss on his ear.

'I can't.'

'We both want this, and no one will ever know,' she whispered.

No one will ever know.

There was a slight nervous hesitation before he pulled her towards him.

No one will ever know.

# # # # # #

As the sun rose, a shaft of light beamed through the parted curtains of Glen's hotel room. Waking, he stretched and looked over towards Mai's delicate frame lying next to him. Already awake, she stared back at him.

'Hello, Mr Glen. How are you today?' Mai's face lit up as she spoke.

'Hung-over. Not sure how we got back to the room.' His voice was husky from the previous night.

'Would you like me to help you with anything?' A sheet covered her from below the nipples of her breasts.

'My head hurts. You're gorgeous. Beautiful skin. I'm horny. Do you want me? Hanky Panky eh? ' Glen smiled.

'Yes. I make you feel wonderful.' She tracked his gaze.

He gestured her to move nearer, whilst he pushed the bedsheet down with his hands and legs, far enough down to cover only his feet. She smiled and moved forward to caress his midriff, kneeled beside him on the bed, moved her palms across his chest, his stomach, and then back to his chest in a circular motion. Her hands moved softly towards his legs to caress the insides of his thighs.

She looked at him and smiled. 'It is very nice, Mr Glen?' Her dainty hands moved across his willing body. He leaned over, opened the bedside drawer, fumbled around, and found a single wrapped condom. She smiled and took the packet from him, opened the wrapper and pulled the condom down over his erect penis. She straddled his thick-set body and moved into position.

He gave a gentle sigh as he closed his eyes, and pressed his head back into the pillow, consumed by the emotion. 'This is paradise.'

Mai smiled and shook her long, black hair as she moved up and down on top of him. Glen groaned as he climaxed in record time, even for him. He pulled her towards him and put his arms around her.

Glen was already looking forward to how he would enjoy a "girlfriend experience" with Mai. He loved to find a woman for the entire length of his visit and treat her like his girlfriend. As his companion and guide, to go to restaurants together, take day trips and act like a couple. He always paid for everything. In the past, two romances blossomed from his "girlfriend experience" into the "wife experience", but he soon discarded them once he got bored. He loved the fact that he not only got a sex partner, he got a friend with benefits. Mai would become his new temporary girlfriend, his sleeping partner, and his lover.

Afterwards, he breathed deeply, relaxed on the bed and stretched across to reach for his cigarettes and lighter. He offered Mai one.

She shook her head. 'I love you, Mr Glen.'

'Bet you say that to all the boys. Mad eh?'
She smiled.
'You hungry?' Glen picked up the room service menu.

CHAPTER SEVEN

Friday 13th February

A huge man, who seemed to collect tattoos, opened the door of the old shophouse. Vanguard entered carrying a soft leather briefcase.

Mountain Master was expecting him. 'What did we get Anil? Sit.' He pointed to a chair.

Vanguard sat down at the desk and placed the case on the floor, next to his chair. 'Audio and visual are in all the rooms.'

Mountain Master looked up. 'Two oolong.' The huge man bowed and left the room. He turned to Vanguard. 'Show me.'

Vanguard pulled his computer out of his bag and placed the laptop on the desk. He moved his chair closer and clicked on an icon. A video played. 'Steve Roussos and Alya.' He pointed to the laptop screen. 'She is a real pro, showed her sister's boy's picture. Like putty in her hands.'

'Make a copy for me?'

He retrieved a storage stick from his briefcase, placed it in the USB slot of his laptop, and copied the video. 'For the other rooms. Glen Lewis. Mai. Good shots. David Morris, no useful footage. He called his wife and fell asleep.'

The huge man entered the room, followed by a slight woman wearing a head veil which extended to cover her body, except for her hands and face. The woman carried a tray with a pot of oolong tea, teacups and saucers. She bowed, laid the contents on the table, bowed again and left the room walking backwards.

Mountain Master gestured towards the huge man, who promptly poured the fragrant tea which had a hint of honeysuckle. 'Glen Lewis has many girlfriends. Make sure Mai gets as much information as possible.'

Vanguard copied another video to the USB stick. 'Yes, Mai will tell Tien everything. They are clear.'

'Good.'

Vanguard coughed and shuffled his shoulders with a sheepish expression. 'Look Prem,' he said, 'We have footage of Mark Farrell.' He coughed again. 'With a man who looks like your brother. This is not your brother, but we need to be careful.'

'Take all the parts out of the video footage that show the face of the other man, leaving enough evidence of illegal contact and take some screen shots which clearly identify only Mark Farrell? Our business is not with the other man. Give me a copy of the new video.'

Vanguard nodded as he ejected the USB stick and handed it over. Mountain Master unlocked his desk drawer and deposited the USB stick before locking the drawer.

'I will make the changes.'

'And give me a copy.'

'Yes.' He bowed his head. 'We will also monitor all conversations.'

Mountain Master nodded.

When they had finished the tea, Vanguard closed his laptop, placed it back into his briefcase, stood up, bowed, and walked to the door. The huge man opened the door and nodded to Vanguard as he left.

CHAPTER EIGHT
Monday 16th February

In the Q7 boardroom, Steve shook hands with Farid and each of the Q7 staff in turn as he walked the perimeter of chairs positioned around the boardroom table.

Farid leaned forward, placing his elbows on the table, and then pointed his pen in mid-air. 'Let's start the meeting. Present are Steve, Glen, David and Mark from Seguro. From Q7, Anil, Anthony, Kim, Hapsah, Boon, Rakesh and myself. Who is on the conference call?'

The Seguro team announced themselves.

After a short pause Steve said, 'Everyone present from Seguro.'

Farid cleared his throat. 'To save time please introduce yourself when you first talk. Farid Razak, Q7's Chief Executive. Anil, can you start?'

Anil stood up. 'Thank you, Farid. Welcome. Malaysia has a population of over thirty-one million people. There are eighteen million internet users. Q7 offer services from local venues across Malaysia, such as retail stores, petrol stations, coffee shops, cybercafes and bookstores. We plan to add the Seguro Payment Solution. Our services are certified by the Malaysian Electronic Clearing Corporation, part of Bank Negara Malaysia. Bank Negara is the Bank of England of Malaysia. Oh, I forgot, Anil Krishnan, Chief Operating Officer at Q7.' He sat back down, crossed his legs, and made a note on his pad.

Steve welcomed the lack of noise and interruptions from the Q7 team. *They must be serious now. Brilliant.*

Farid drummed his pen on the table. 'One of the main areas I wish to discuss is our relationship with Axiatel. They are one of the major telecommunications operators in Asia.'

Steve smiled as he had already spent two years of effort trying to sell the Seguro solution to Axiatel with little progress.

Farid explained in more detail. 'Axiatel total one hundred and seventy million customers in five countries across Asia; Malaysia, Singapore, Indonesia, Cambodia and Sri Lanka. We start with Malaysia and Indonesia which is over sixty million customers.'

Steve glanced at Glen and tried to keep calm. 'Sounds good, Farid.'

Farid nodded. 'Kim, can you go through the services we will move to the Seguro System?'

A petite woman with very short black hair, stood up. 'I am Kim Tan, from marketing at Q7 and I manage the Seguro launch.' She bowed. 'The m-commerce services launch will be the mobile phone top-up, person-to-person money transfer and customer loyalty.' She bowed again. 'In the next phase we launch the following quarter: mobile commerce and mobile banking. The following quarter: international and domestic money remittance. Hapsah, can you talk about publicity?' She bowed and sat down.

This time a tall woman with striking dyed pink hair and pink-rimmed glasses stood up and bowed. 'Yes, I am Hapsah Yung. I work with Kim in Marketing. We will create news and announcements on the Q7 portal, Facebook Fans' page and Q7 Twitter page. Q7 runs Wi-Fi at many coffee outlets. Every time users log on to Wi-Fi at the outlets, we play a video.' She bowed. 'The trailer is mandatory and ensures the largest exposure. We will place posters at all Q7 affiliated cybercafes.' She bowed again and sat.

Steve looked at Farid. Farid nodded. 'Steve Roussos, Chief Executive Officer at Seguro. Thank you. So, let's understand. You will offer the services Kim described to the sixty million customers of Axiatel and they will use the Seguro solution to process the charges using various payment instruments.'

Anil uncrossed his legs. 'Yes, don't forget we already run these services on our physical distribution network. We accept major credit cards and online banking.'

Steve's body thawed as the stress drained away. *This is so positive. Calm, confident, relax.* 'Sounds good, Anil.'

'Glen Lewis, Sales Manager for Asia. Namaste. David or Mark, can you explain to the Q7 team, our suggested configuration? If Q7 agree with the configuration, we can set up the solution.'

David looked towards Mark, and Mark nodded. 'David Morris, Chief Technical Officer at Seguro. Our worldwide patented solution provides a powerful but simple solution. Our system converts the payment to the chosen currency. So, we authenticate both ends of any transaction and exchange neither the payee or recipient's details.'

Steve interrupted. 'Take us through in more detail David.'

David nodded. 'So, a person – let's call him John, wants to pay let's say, Harry. Our solution sends the payment through both our Payment Service Grid and Platform Routing Charge Handler. An example: John chooses how he pays from his bank, bitcoin, cash to top-up centre, or stored on the platform in a wallet. Harry decides where he wants the payment to go: to a bank, bitcoin, or Q7 who hold the funds in an in-platform wallet. The Payment Service Grid gets the fund routing data and forex exchange for John and Harry. John is not aware of any account details about Harry or what currency Harry wants to receive. We calculate the optimal route for the funds. Most important for Q7 and Seguro are charges, payments or commission to us. Mark, can you run through the escrow mechanism and charging mechanism?'

'Sure,' Mark said. He sat back in his seat, smiled, paused and looked around at the audience. 'As you know, I'm Mark Farrell, Chief Scientist.' He smiled. 'The Input Conversion Charge takes a fee as commission on the amount sent. We can also make money on currency conversion with a simple setting using the Licence Fee Handler. A notification charge to the person receiving the funds is also an option, via text message-'

Steve nodded. 'And peer-to-peer escrow.'

'Ah, yes,' Mark said, 'Our system holds the funds until the merchant delivers the physical or digital goods. And vice versa. We use a blockchain escrow system to make sure the contract between the buyer and merchant is upheld. We can also apply this for person-to-person payments.'

'Thanks, Mark.' Steve smiled.

Boon and Rakesh asked a number of technical questions about monitoring, reporting, compliance and territories. The Seguro support team answered questions about compliance and project management. The meeting progressed to cover the dates and actions required to meet the tight deadlines imposed by Q7.

Farid and Anil exchanged nods, both looking very smug.

Steve was feeling super positive, like all his dreams were coming true. *This could be it. The breakthrough. Finally, the luck we deserve.*

CHAPTER NINE

Saturday 21st February

An Exhausted Steve, arrived back in the UK. He had spent fourteen hours on a Malaysia Airlines flight from Kuala Lumpur which touched down at London Heathrow after midnight, forty minutes late and greeted by typical cold English weather. Once home he crept up the stairs, peeked into the bedrooms to look in on the kids before going to bed himself. In silence he took his clothes off and placed them on the chair, making sure he did not wake Beth. Once in bed, he soon fell straight to sleep.

# # # # # #

He woke to the sound of his kids playing on the landing as the Grandfather clock in the hallway chimed eight times. Steve looked at Beth, who was fast asleep.

What an idiot!

What a stupid fucker!

Why did I get so drunk?

Any man would take the opportunity, wouldn't they?

Why didn't I leave the bar, run like hell?

But I didn't.

Idiot!

So guilty, it's killing me.

It's the curtain call for me. If she found out what happened.

It's bad enough, Beth's family are sure they won't get their money back.

Those unspoken words, those looks.

You can tell they regret investing a penny.

How many holes do I need to dig?

If she found out about the loans from my brothers.

Sure to be the end.

Q7 has to be a big success.

It has to be.

I need to kick the Valium. It's turning into a habit.

On the plane, he had laid out his plans. First, he would tell her the truth. He would not lie and had no wish to live a lie, he convinced himself. The plan was to admit all, explain what had happened and pray she would understand and forgive him. His next move would depend on her reaction. He would tell her he was sorry and would do nothing to hurt her again. If she fell to pieces, he would beg for her forgiveness on bended knees. Either way, he would show how much he loved her, worshipped her, and would ask her for one more chance.

Beth woke. 'Morning. How are you, my love?'

'Morning. Knackered, but great to be home, I missed you so much.' He put his arm around her, kissed her forehead and held her close. Steve wanted to celebrate the deal with Q7, and hoped she did not expose his guilt, just by looking at him.

Beth stretched, and leaned forward, looked into his eyes and gave him a welcome kiss. 'This is so nice.'

He held her even closer and kissed her ear as he caressed her hair. 'I love you. I'm only back for two weeks, but it's great to be home.'

Beth smiled. She tapped a finger on his lips and then their lips met. She placed her head on his chest and Steve put his arm across her shoulders and caressed her arm.

Steve gazed up to the ceiling. 'How's Kate?'

'She's OK, but she had a bad asthma attack at school the other day.'

'How's her chest? Does she need an X-ray or something?'

'The consultant will tell us what to do.' Her face scrunched up in worry.

Steve caressed her shoulder. 'Let's go private.'

She raised her head from his chest and looked up at him. 'Where's the money?'

'We'll get money soon from Q7.' His stomach tightened.

'So? What about the mortgage arrears. Credit cards. We need a family holiday. How can we pay for a consultant?'

'I'll get the money.' His stomach knotted.

'One of the inhalers includes steroids.'

'Steroids! Are you sure?'

'Yes, stops the attacks, but the effect is gradual.'

'Poor Kate.' Panic jabbed hard at his stomach.

'She needs her dad. We all need you.'

'I'm back for Jake's birthday and here for the next two weeks to get the Q7 project underway.'

They kissed and embraced. Steve smiled at the sound of laughter coming from the landing. It mixed with loud shouts as their daughters, Kate and Ellie teased Jake about his newfound interest in girls. The twins, three years older than Jake, considered themselves much wiser. Steve heard Ellie tormenting her brother. 'How many girls will give you a birthday kiss?'

Then it was Kate's turn. 'They will all be chasing him around the school on Monday.'

Steve laughed when he heard Jake running downstairs. 'No, they won't, you silly girls, they're not like you.' Steve thought Jake must have reached the front room because he heard: 'Brilliant!' Followed by 'Wow! A PlayStation. Mum! Mum!'

Beth smiled. 'Daddy's here. Daddy's home.'

The twins cheered and ran into the bedroom. They jumped on the bed and embraced Steve. Beth looked at Steve, smiled and shrugged her shoulders.

'Dad! Mom! Come here please,' Jake shouted.

Beth slid across the covers to sit on the side of the bed. 'Saturday, thank goodness. Let's go downstairs.'

'OK coming, give me a minute son. Happy Birthday!' Steve shouted.

Beth slipped on her dressing gown and put on a pair of specs. 'Come on dad and girls.'

The twins rushed out of the bedroom and down the stairs. 'Daddy's home, Daddy's home.' Ellie shouted excitedly.

Steve smiled. 'Kids, eh? What's with the specs? Sexy.'

'Problems with my contact lenses.'

'Oh, you are my sexy personal assistant.'

She slowly blinked her eyelids. 'Hopefully a temporary thing. Come on, get up, let's go.'

Steve whispered, 'Did you put the other thing in the utility room?'

Beth nodded.

He put on his dressing gown, and followed Beth downstairs, accompanied by the family's brown Labrador. 'Good girl, Millie, where's Jake? Good girl.'

'Happy Birthday, Jake.' Steve hugged him and swung him around the living room. Millie joined in by grabbing Steve's string rope in her mouth. She shook the rope as if it was the final kill of a rabbit.

Jake jumped up and down whilst clapping his hands. 'Thanks, Dad. Thanks, Mom. PS4 games. Brilliant. I got FIFA and NetSpeed. Will you play NetSpeed with me, Dad?'

'Let's play after breakfast. Come and let me show you something else.' Steve hugged Ellie and Kate. 'Are you girls looking after Mom?'

'Yes, Daddy,' they said in unison.

Steve took Jake's hand and led him, followed by Ellie and Kate. Millie was trying to muscle towards the front of the entourage. They congregated in the kitchen. 'Come on, Mum, follow us.' They marched past her in the kitchen headed towards the utility room. She followed. Steve opened the utility room door.

Jake rushed past him. 'A BMX bike. Hey, Dad, alloys!' He got onto the bike still wearing his pyjamas.

Beth reached out and grabbed the bike safety helmet she had placed on side board. 'Here, make sure you wear this when you ride your bike. Let's get dressed, breakfast and then go to the park.'

Steve put his hand on Kate's head. 'Can my lovely Kate come to the park?'

Beth crouched in front of Kate and held her hand. 'Yes, she'll be fine. You'll bring your inhaler, Kate, won't you?'

Kate smiled, and Steve picked her up and held her. 'My lovely girl.' Ellie put her hands around Steve's waist. He bent forward to pick Ellie up and hold her in his other arm. 'My lovely girls' You're getting bigger and lovelier every day.'

# # # # # #

After breakfast, the family gathered in the hallway. Beth helped Jake with his coat, fixing his coat buttons. 'Come on Jake. Make sure you don't forget your safety helmet.'

Steve wheeled the BMX whilst trying to find his car keys. 'Girls, can you get Millie's lead and bring along her towel? They're in the utility.' The family marched out to the car making lots of noise. Millie jumped into the car. She shared the boot of the Estate car with the BMX but did not seem to mind. 'Good girl.' Millie settled on her favourite rug. *Good job the Estate is big enough to get the whole family in, including the wife, the kids, the dog, and the bike.* He smiled to himself.

After a short journey, they entered the park at Holly Hurst Gate. Once everyone was out of the car, they set off for their walk, with Jake wheeling the bike, and Millie trotting happily behind the group. Steve loved the bright, brisk day, a complete contrast to Kuala Lumpur.

Millie ran down the path towards the trees at Holly Hurst. Equipped with the helmet, Jake rode on ahead. Steve and Beth smiled. Jake shouted with joy as he took off towards

Westwood Coppice. They lost sight of him for a moment. He emerged further along where Millie had to dart away to avoid the speeding bike. Ellie and Kate held hands as they walked. Just before Holly Hurst, they veered off towards the Titchfield Stone.

'Big week ahead at work.' Steve strolled along.

Beth took Steve's hand as they walked. 'Yes love. I hope the project goes well for you and we can try to get back to normal again…I'm going to re-decorate the lounge.'

'Are you sure? You've got a lot on your plate,' Steve said.

'Yes. It's hard managing the girls, Jake, Millie and work. It's only part-time but we need the money. I'll do the decorating on my days' off.'

'I don't know how you do it.'

'We'll be fine… And anyway, I love DIY.' Beth smiled.

God, I love her. I can't tell her what happened. It would hurt her too much. Beth's supported me all along. Time to put things right. They'll all get their money back. I'll clear the mortgage arrears and clear everything, now we've won the deal. Everything will be OK. I'm sure.

Millie led the way along their usual dog walk route. At the Titchfield Stone, they carried straight on towards Hill Head Wood before arriving at Bracebridge Pool. They circled the edge of the pool and headed past Upper Nut Hurst before reaching Keeper's Pool and back to the edge of Holly Hurst.

Steve put the muddy bike in the back of the car, whilst Millie waited to jump in alongside the BMX. 'Do you like your bike, Jake?'

'I love it, thanks Dad, thanks Mom.'

CHAPTER TEN

Monday 23rd February

The Seguro team gathered at the Institute of Directors, also known as the IoD in Pall Mall, London. Steve had been a member of the prestigious organisation for many years. He was proud to belong to a club which had gained the UK Royal Charter in 1906.

Steve grabbed a coffee and sat down. 'OK, guys, help yourself to a drink and biscuits. They'll bring along sandwiches at 12:30.' He kicked-off the Q7 project.

The Seguro team in Malaysia and two of the Wales-based UK developers, who did not travel down, connected into the meeting using Skype. Once the rest had taken their seats around the large oval table, Steve started the meeting. 'OK, I wanted to get us off-site, so we can plan the implementation at Q7 with no interruptions.' He smiled. 'David will oversee everything. A great job - he has agreed to stay in Malaysia until the project is underway. David can you talk about last week's meeting with Q7?' *Keep him sweet and in Kuala Lumpur as long as possible until the money flows.*

'Sure,' David announced via the Skype connection. He outlined the aims, timescales, requirements of the project, and updated the team on the personnel involved from Q7. 'They want the standard SeguroPay authentication solution based on registration using hash key and email address or mobile phone number. They are working with Axiatel in Asia supporting millions of mobile phone devices. They want the SeguroPay Secure Payments software for all devices. Mark, can you expand on the configuration?'

Mark took his Skype connection off mute. 'Yes, we'll route all payments from the customers' bank account, pre-paid cards, loyalty points, and our secure wallet. All the payment routing and notifications will use the Payment Service Grid software. They want to support crytocurrencies, starting with Bitcoin and then adding others, including Ethereum, Litecoin and Tether. Standard system configuration along with notification preferences such as text and email. Q7 want to allow people to change mobile devices without losing their account settings. Input or output accounts can be a bank, bitcoin, top-up, or wallet. Q7 want variable charge rates for bitcoin, bank, wallet, airtime and vouchers. We'll hook into their existing forex and financial structure.'

'And KYC,' David butted in.

'Oh yes, know your customer. Q7 have their own KYC validation, so great for us.'

They assigned the group to various roles in the project, including overall operations, development lead, implementation, and configuration.

The team spent the rest of the meeting going through the detailed plan, in readiness for the next two months.

Steve felt the stress easing and a more positive outlook was emerging. *We're getting there. Thank goodness.*

CHAPTER ELEVEN

Sunday 1st March

Mai sat beside Glen in the taxi as Glen instructed the driver on approaching Jalan Ampang road. 'It's Somerset Wisma, Ampang, Kuala Lumpur.'

'Yes sir,' said the taxi driver.

'Number 187, 50450, Jalan Ampang.' Glen embraced Mai. 'We'll find the perfect place for us in the Golden Triangle.'

The famous Golden Triangle main shopping and entertainment district was on the north side of Kuala Lumpur. At the centre was the busy shopping area of Bukit Bintang. The office towers of Raja Chulan, the five-star hotel strip of Sultan Ismail, the party street of Jalan Ram – all attracted many people day and night. Soaring scrapers, huge shopping malls, nightclubs, and top-notch hotels pierced the entire landscape.

'Listen to this,' Glen read from the brochure. 'The stylish Somerset Ampang Kuala Lumpur features an ideal serviced apartment, within the prestigious Embassy Row area. Ideal for executives and families on business and leisure travel. That's you and me, Mai,' Glen smiled.

He continued, 'We furnish each spacious residence with designer fittings and modern amenities, including an integrated kitchen, an iPad dock and Wi-Fi. The amenities, services and facilities make you comfortable no matter how far away from home. After work or shopping, work out in the gym or relax in the rooftop infinity pool and jacuzzi. Lovely jubbly.'

Mai kissed his cheek. 'Hope we find somewhere. This area is great for us.'

The new romantics arrived outside the building, and were greeted by Aisha, who was wearing a purple floral gown and a pink headscarf covering her head, neck and shoulders. The headscarf concealed her hair but showed an attractive woman with dark eyes, and pale orange lipstick.

'I do not like her; she looks at me like I am nothing,' Mai said in a whisper.

'No probs,' Glen said.

Glen and Mai followed Aisha up to the sixteenth floor and into one of the show apartments.

'Our apartment is a superior residence, close to business offices, embassies and shopping centres,' Aisha said. 'For all destinations within the city, the light rail from Ampang Park LRT station is ideal.'

Glen wandered around the accommodation. 'What do we get?'

Aisha read from a list. 'Equipped gymnasium, residents' lounge with games console and board games, rooftop infinity pool, jacuzzi, twenty-four-hour reception and security, plus closed-circuit TV surveillance.'

'So, this is a one-bedroom suite?' Glen asked.

'The room is big, and the bathroom has a nice shower and bath. A queen-sized bed. And a walk-in closet,' Aisha said.

'Can we walk to KLCC train station?'

'Yes, less than a five-minute walk to the KLCC.'

Glen turned to Mai. 'Do you like it? No brainer.'

'I like it very much, but not her.' Mai pointed at Aisha.' I not care for her, now she ignores me, I am not invisible,' she whispered to Glen.

'You're with me. No probs.'

# # # # # #

They celebrated finding a dream home by visiting their new favourite restaurant at Kin Kin, a hole-in-the-wall establishment in the Chow Kit area of Kuala Lumpur. No one visited for the extensive menu. Kin Kin was famous for one dish only, and it was always Mai's first choice: chilli pan mee made from minced pork, poached egg, dried anchovies and homemade noodles. It was spicy and delicious but served with no frills. Likewise, there was no fancy decor, just lots of plastic chairs, tables, and bowls.

CHAPTER TWELVE

Monday 9th March

Steve spotted David standing outside the coffee shop, focused on his iPhone. He smiled to himself. Typical David, wearing a business shirt and trousers, but balanced on his head an old canvas hat to protect him from the sun. Steve had arrived back in Kuala Lumpur earlier that day. 'Hello stranger.' Steve hoped the message David had left earlier about some concerns at Q7 was nothing that would hold up the project.

David looked up. 'Hi Steve, how are you?' They shook hands.

Steve shrugged his shoulders. 'I've checked into the Concorde. Arrived two hours ago. Knackered, but the shower has woken me up for now. Still sweating like a pig though.'

David pointed towards Starbucks. 'Let's go in.' They joined the short queue.

Steve shook the collar of his shirt. 'Air-con is great. Two weeks of crap weather back home and now I'm sweating as much as before my shower.'

'Been bloody hot. What are you having?'

'An iced tea, thanks. Cliff Lin is meeting me here in an hour. You're welcome to stay and chat.'

David nodded.

'I'm intrigued. What's wrong?' *I hope he's not going to be a pain.*

David looked down at his trainers. 'I've found a serious problem. Our system has become an onion router, along with all the computers on the Q7 network.'

Steve struggled to hear him over the noise of the coffee shop chatter. 'What have you found?'

Once they had collected their drinks, David looked around and found a table in the corner of the cafe. 'We're the payment point; part of a dark net.' He stroked his beard.

It concerned Steve how worried David looked. *Bollocks! Bollocks!* 'What do you mean? Payment point for the dark net?'

David whispered. 'It's the onion router. Online anonymity invented by the FBI in—'

'I know what the bloody dark net is for God's sake.' Steve shook his head. 'That's where you can buy credit cards and hire contract killers. So where does the router fit?'

David sat back in his chair. 'Sorry. Onion routing is a way for computers to communicate across a network anonymously, peeling off a layer of the onion to reveal the next computer along the path to receive the information.' David had an anxious look on his face.

This can't be happening. Fucking hell! We're getting out of the shit. I'm not diving back into it. No way!

Steve feigned calmness. 'Who set this up?'

Oh shit. Let me think what to do!

'Has to be someone within Q7,' David said, 'or a back-door set-up for an outside organisation.'

Can't be right. Q7 are big. 'An inside job?'

'Could be. Also, transactions on our system start and finish on the Onion…' David stroked his beard.

Steve interrupted, 'So, you mean people are paying for stuff and receiving payment for stuff on our system across the dark net? What on earth would they be selling?'

'Drugs, laundering money, card fraud, you name it.'

'What services have Q7 launched so far?' Steve said.

'Top-up, person-to-person payment, mobile commerce and loyalty points.'

'So, they could use these services to launder money.' Steve brushed his hand through his hair, feeling increasingly concerned. *For fuck's sake, David. We don't need this.*

David increased the rate of stroking his beard. 'Yes, but it gets worse. One of the commission payment instruments, uses our solution—'

'So, let me get this right,' Steve interrupted.' Q7 split the commission? So, money is being syphoned off from Q7 to illegal outfits?'

But, Steve reassured himself. *We can't be sure it's illegal stuff.*

'Yes, that's right. The system accepts bitcoin as input and wallet as output. That's where the dark net may come into play as Q7 purchasers can be anonymous.'

'So, we may have a money laundering racket going on here? Could be an inside job? I need to talk to Farid. Leave it with me, I'll meet with him.'

This needs to go away!

They then huddled over Steve's laptop and worked through a series of issues, plans and strategies.

# # # # # #

Steve spotted Cliff as he entered the coffee shop. 'Here he is, we can talk more later.' He stood up to shake Cliff's hand. Cliff Lin was a gentleman with an optimistic outlook on life. His fine grey, shoulder length hair clashed with his smart black trousers and tailored white shirt, which caressed his small-boned frame. He was a strong supporter of Seguro, even making a financial investment in the company.

Cliff shook hands with David. 'Good morning, gentlemen.'

'Do you want a drink?' Steve asked.

'No thanks. I need to go to a business meeting at my golf club this afternoon.' Cliff took a sip from his water bottle.

'Are you still enjoying your golf?'

'I love it. Roger tells me you won the Q7 deal.'

'Yes, it's immense and the timescales are short, so we will grow the revenue.'

Cliff looked at David. 'Are you confident?'

'Yes, confident. We agreed to go live within two months.'

Right answer. We need to keep him on our side. He is important to us.

Cliff smiled. 'I am looking forward to revenues and dividends soon!'

Steve nodded. 'Have you met Farid Razak, Q7's CEO?'

'Yes, I have seen him at the club, but I don't know him well.'

Steve and David talked further with Cliff about many subjects including Manchester United winning the league, unreliable London buses, great food on Emirates Airlines and the price of gold, before Cliff had to leave.

Steve turned to David. 'Cliff's a great guy. We're so lucky he's a supporter. He knows Malaysian business and customs. If it gets sticky at Q7, I'm sure he'll help smooth things out.'

David nodded but looked uneasy and distracted.

CHAPTER THIRTEEN

Tuesday 10th March

Mai arrived at the dormitory building wearing a short white dress that Glen had bought her the day before. She wore her pink high heel boots accompanied by a matching patent leather handbag. Although early evening, the sunlight beamed onto the building. The video cameras and motion sensors tracked her progress. She pressed the buzzer entry on the metal door, entered and walked up the stairs to the third floor.

# # # # # #

She spotted a man lying in a doorway, beer can in hand, slumped against the door. Mai immediately thought of her father. The memories were not happy. She had spent the past two years in Kuala Lumpur after moving from Vietnam to find work and send money back to her family. Mai grew up in the countryside near Hanoi where her parents worked as farmers. They had been a poor family, but got by, even though her father always drank. His behaviour spiralled downwards when he lost his job at a local farm. He became violent. The family fell apart. Her mother, sister, and Mai moved out. Mai studied to become a nurse when she finished school, but when her parents split up the funds ran out, so they forced her to leave nursing and find work as a day labourer, harvesting crops for local farmers. She hated it; her dreams ended.

Her good friend, Tien, moved to Kuala Lumpur a few years earlier. When she came back to visit, she told Mai she had earned a lot of money as a waitress. Gossip in the village presumed she did something other than waitressing; which she always denied. Tien asked Mai to come with her, but at the time the suggestion scared Mai. Two years later, when Mai gave birth to a son, she changed her mind. She told her mother she needed to earn money in Malaysia, so left the baby with her. Mai wanted a decent future for her son. She did not tell her mother what she intended to do.

Everyone in Mai's village suspected how young women made good money in tourist towns. Families maintained face in the village by saying their daughters worked in a hotel or restaurant. Women found their way into the sex industry where, if attractive, they earned many times more money than working on a farm. They thought of them as good daughters doing their duty; as long as they sent back enough money to support the family.

When Tien took Mai to a bar in Kuala Lumpur for the first time, Mai walked out - she could not cope, so she got a job serving drinks, earning a fraction of what Tien earned. If she could make enough to start a new life, she could finish her training and become a qualified nurse. Mai wanted to make her son proud of her. After many restless nights, she talked herself into sleeping with men for money. She convinced herself that this was a means to an end.

Her first customer, a western man in his thirties', terrified her. She hated her job but consoled herself with thoughts of her family and the money. When he left, she showered for a long time. She cried and worried about what her mother would say. None of her customers ever asked her about her life. Mai supposed they did not care.

Mai wanted to achieve a level of financial security she could not dream of in Hanoi. She hoped, after two years in the industry she would save enough money to return to the village and raise her son.

# # # # # #

Mai walked along the corridor to the cramped dormitory where she had lived with Tien before moving in with Glen. It was a squalid area shared by four other women from Vietnam, above one of the establishments where they worked. They looked out for each other. Whilst she stayed there, Mai always kept her phone near her and called her best friend if she experienced problems with any of the men she satisfied. Tien would drop everything and come to help her. Deep down Mai dreamed of earning enough money to allow herself to move somewhere where she could study and then set up her own business. Financial security was what she wanted, and she could get that for herself.

A prominent gang owned bars and ran a series of criminal activities such as drugs, extortion, and prostitution. They controlled the women by confiscating their passports. The clan fined and beat them if they tried to escape and dished out threats against the women's families. If the girls sought help from the authorities, they risked being deported.

# # # # # #

Mai entered the room and Tien embraced her. They sat on the floor, opposite each other; a small grey mat separating them. They shared a plate of noodles and talked to each other in their local Vietnamese dialect. Tien placed her chopsticks on a side plate. 'How is Xuan?'

'He is growing fast. I would love to go back to be with my boy.' Mai looked to the floor. 'I miss him.'

Tien leaned forward and placed her hand around Mai's wrist. 'They grow so quickly. Is Glen treating you well? Does he hurt you?'

Mai looked up and smiled. 'He is a good man. I like him very much. He treats me very well. I like being with him.'

'How long can you stay with him?'

'I am with him at the Concorde Hotel. He wants me to live with him. We looked at apartments in the centre of Kuala Lumpur.'

'Did you find out anything?'

Mai shrugged. 'No, he has said little. He seems happy. Work is good. So, no problems.'

Tien squeezed her wrist. 'Did he talk about Q7?'

'No, nothing.'

'You must find out any information. Mountain Master wants you to keep him happy. Listen and talk to Glen, tell me what you can find.'

Mai pulled her wrists out from Tien's grasp. 'I can dream.'

'We must do our job. We don't want to make them angry.'

'Glen is strong, and gentle. He can help me start a new life.'

'They will hurt our families. Please do your job.'

'I will try.'

Tien made oolong tea, and they talked about work, clothes, their friends and what was happening back home in Hanoi.

They left the dormitory together, both going to work. Mai headed back to the Concorde and Tien set off for the Beach Club.

CHAPTER FOURTEEN

Tuesday 24th March

They gathered in the boardroom of Q7 for the weekly project update. Steve hoped for positive news.

Farid called the meeting to order. 'Welcome to the progress meeting. Let's begin. We scheduled two months to get the services underway. Q7 generated its first income only five weeks into the project. Correct Kim?'

Kim stood up. 'Yes, we completed Phase one.' She bowed. 'We moved Axiatel online and retail services to the Seguro system. The marketing launch has started with our retail distribution and TV coverage.'

Glen interjected, 'I'm very happy to join you at any meetings with Axiatel.'

Kim bowed again. 'Axiatel distributed outlet literature, TV and radio advertising.' She bowed and sat down.

Farid smiled. 'Very pleasing. Anil, are the payment tariffs in place and the bank links?'

'Yes, Farid. We are generating money from the services.' Anil nodded towards Anthony.

Anthony responded, 'Yes, just under twenty thousand transactions in the first three days since launch. I will produce a full report at the end of this month.'

Farid leaned across the table and shook Steve's hand. 'Congratulations. We are generating revenue three weeks earlier than expected.'

Relief cascaded across Steve's shoulders.

Thank fuck.

'Are the servers installed with the latest Seguro software?' Anil asked.

Mark coughed. 'I'll answer that. Yes, we installed version 1.26 which includes the latest rules engine for payment processing. We need to complete the final load testing and rules compliance this week. We'll then hand over first line support to Boon and Rakesh.'

David raised his hand. 'We found one concern when we ran the compliance checks.' He read notes from his iPad. 'Unknown IP addresses on the servers, and an unknown licensing payment setting for a bank account belonging to a company called Grithos PTE Limited.' He stroked his beard.

Not now! I don't want you involved. Shut the fuck up, David. Steve spotted Farid and Anil exchanging a glance.

Anil responded. 'Yes, a partner commission. No problem.'

Farid stood up. 'If there is nothing else to cover today, let's call the meeting to a close. Well done everyone.'

As they left the room, Farid called Steve aside and gestured to the rest of the group to continue. 'I want to speak with you.'

Steve nodded.

# # # # # #

Once the others had left the room. Farid said, 'Grithos is a Q7 partner, so we share the transaction commission. A long-standing arrangement. It is not David's business. You get a share of the revenue. Do you understand?' He stretched out the last word for emphasis.

Phew, I'm glad Farid and Anil explained away the commission. End of the problem, I hope. Who cares what's going on, as long as we get paid. 'Yes Farid, sorry, I understand, I'll talk to David.'

'Good. Why don't you come over to my club, we can talk?' Farid smiled.

'OK.'

'Let's meet at Tegu Gentlemen's Club, six-thirty PM, on Thursday.'

Steve nodded. 'Great. I'll be there.'

Steve headed back to the hotel in a taxi. He answered a Skype audio call. 'Hi Roger.'

'Hi, how are we getting on at Q7?' Roger sounded optimistic.

'Superb. Just had a progress meeting with Q7. We launched within five weeks and twenty thousand transactions in the first three days. Anthony, their accountant will publish figures every month.'

'We need to get a forecast of transactions and details of our revenue share. The launch is excellent, but creditors are chasing me, including Nigel from Applegate to renew the Asia Patent filings.'

'A forecast?' Steve forced his eyes to pop wide.

'Yes. Cameron Kelp are chasing payment for the quarterly accounts. The hosting company are threatening to cut off the servers. Antonio has transferred the salaries and payroll taxes for this month. We need to pay Glen's expenses.'

Give me a break, we're working at lightning speed here.

'I'll need my expenses paid. Struggling to pay for this trip, never mind costs at home.' He ground his knuckles against his forehead.

'It's difficult, Steve.'

'Yes. Mark, David and I are living on fresh air. It doesn't work.' Steve slowly shook his head.

'Once we receive enough revenue, we'll all get our back pay, expenses and dividends. It's hard at the moment.'

'Doesn't fucking help now though. Anyway, Q7 agreed to pay into our bank account as the transactions happen. They agreed we can configure a Seguro payment instrument. The financial guy from Q7, Anthony Suppiah, wants our bank details to set up the payment.' Steve wanted to vent his frustration.

'Oh, wonderful. Phew, we needn't wait thirty days as per the contract. Excellent Steve.'

'I negotiated with Farid last week as we are a month ahead.'

'I'll send over our bank account details,' Roger said.

Screw you.

Steve ended the call.

CHAPTER FIFTEEN

Wednesday 25th March

The following morning, Steve visited Glen's hotel room.

Mai opened the door to greet him. 'Hello, Steve. Glen on the phone. Come in, please.' She held the door ajar and bowed as Steve entered the room. He sat at the desk, and Mai offered him a cup of tea.

Glen sat back on a black leather chair and waved towards Steve.

Steve smiled. *I hope he's focusing on winning new business rather than entertaining Mai.*

'Is everything good at Q7,' Mai asked, 'Glen tells me they are a big customer.'

Steve nodded. 'Yes.'

'Do you like the people?'

'People? Err, Yes.' He wondered why Mai had asked such an odd question. 'Do you know anyone at Q7?'

Mai bowed. 'No, I ask because if good at Q7 then good for you and Glen. Then I am happy as well.'

'How are you getting on with Glen? Are you putting up with him?'

She smiled. 'Yes, I like him very much.'

Glen looked happy. Steve figured he had found an apartment.

'Fine,' Glen said. 'I will come to you tomorrow to sign the contract.' He nodded. 'I'll bring along my ID and bank details.' He punched his fist into the air and smiled. 'Yes, in the company name, yes put Seguro Limited, but payment will be from my personal account at CIMB Bank.' Glen waved to Steve again as he ended the call. 'Thank you. Bye.' He put the mobile phone in the top pocket of his shirt. 'Hi, Steve.' He threw his arms into the air. 'Yes! Our own apartment. We can get the keys tomorrow. Cool mate.'

Mai handed Steve a cup of tea and sat beside Glen, on the arm of the leather chair. 'Oh, my love.' She kissed him on the neck, below his ear.

'I can't wait. Cool.' He unmuted the TV and continued watching the English Premier League football match highlights. 'Great game. ManU are winning.'

'Quick chat about Q7?'

Glen pressed the mute button on the remote control. 'Q7 is a goldmine. Might even get my expenses paid!'

'Yes, brilliant. Huge opportunity at Axiatel.'

Glen lit a cigarette. 'I've been trying to get into them for years, mate.'

'Hey. The UK banned cigarettes indoors, so why smoke here?' *You're such an idiot sometimes.*

'This is a smoking room. No probs.' Glen stubbed the cigarette out on the ashtray. 'What did Farid want?'

'He's not too happy with David and he has asked me to meet him at the Tegu Gentlemen's Club tomorrow evening.'

Glen smiled. 'Wow. You're privileged. I've only been invited once. The Singapore Raffle's equivalent in Malaysia. I'd be happy to come along mate. Mad, eh?'

'No, he wants a private word.'

'Cool. Goal! Yes.' Glen turned the sound back on. 'Get in ManU.' He muted it again as Steve continued to talk.

'He didn't like the way David raised the issue and wants us to discuss any concerns we may have direct with him or Anil first in future.'

Glen shook his head. 'Tell the bearded geek to shut his mouth and get on with the project. We do our job. Whatever they do, it's up to them. No brainer.'

Steve leaned forward, rested his elbows on his knees, and held his head in the palms of his hands. 'David's like a terrier when he gets onto something.'

'He shouldn't put his nose into stuff outside the project. Anyway, he's an old woman. He worries about everything. It's mad.'

'He's a good guy.'

'Yes, he is,' Glen relented, 'but he needs to focus on our stuff.'

'You're right.'

'I'm starving.' Glen looked at Mai.

She handed him the menu. 'You want room service?'

He looked at the menu. 'Yes, burger and fries, you want chicken noodles?'

'Yes, my love.'

'Steve?'

'No, I'm fine.'

Glen called the hotel restaurant and reeled off a list of items from the expensive hotel menu.

Good job you're a good salesman but you piss me off, idiot. 'Are you making headway with other opportunities?'

'Yes. I'm putting together a forecast for Monday's call.'

'While David, Mark and I are here, you should use us. Get us in front of prospects.'

Glen's phone rang. 'Ah, it's my son.' He answered the call.

'Hi Harry. Are you OK? – How's the footie? – Good, did you score? – two goals. Fantastic and you won the Man of the Match. Brilliant. Well done... You doing your homework? – Good. Can your sister come to the phone? – Love you, Harry. Speak tomorrow. Enjoy school... Hello Lauren. Are you doing what mummy says? – Ah, good... Oh lovely... You are a good girl. Daddy's girl... OK. I'll ring you tomorrow. Bye. Love you, Lauren. Bye.'

Room service arrived, and Steve decided to leave. 'Catch you later.'

I'll leave him to his food and footy. Not a care in the world. Fat bastard.

CHAPTER SIXTEEN

Thursday 26th March

The taxi arrived outside the Tegu Gentlemen's Club; Steve paid the fare and adjusted his tie. He wasn't sure if he should feel this nervous. The concierge opened the door and bowed as Steve walked past him into the club.

A male receptionist greeted him. 'Good evening, sir.'

'Good evening. Steve Roussos. Farid Razak, please.'

He nodded to acknowledge Steve and then talked on his walkie-talkie. A few moments later a man appeared wearing a formal dress suit. 'Mr Roussos to see, Mr Farid.'

'This way, Mr Roussos,' the man said. A mixed aroma of stale cigars, smoke, and wood polish hit him as he walked through the lobby. *All very old-school English.*

Steve was led into a regal sitting room with leather chairs, coffee tables, and gilt-edged mirrors hung against ruby red walls.

As soon as he spotted Steve, Farid stood up and shook his hand, ushered him to sit on the plush red leather seat opposite, and then ordered drinks. He nodded and sat back down.

Steve took this to be his cue to skip the usual smalltalk and express his concerns. 'I'm worried about David's findings. One of our guys has completed the audit and David has found several discrepancies which we will need to declare in the report. He has also found some serious issues.'

Farid rested his elbows on the arms of the chair, and interlacing his fingers, he looked at Steve. 'There are certain ways of doing business in Malaysia.'

Steve folded his arms. 'I'm worried about a payment made to a company called Grithos, for every transaction. Q7 has configured the Seguro system with a royalty payment of two cents per transaction. David checked their website and found an offshore company based in Singapore. He also found several onion router servers on the Q7 network. The onion router sets up a dark net, so payments and commerce are anonymous and used for illegal means.' His throat felt dry.

Farid looked down. 'Thank you for bringing this to my attention.'

'I'm sorry, Farid. I hope we can sort this out.' Steve's breathing quickened.

'Who knows of this?' Farid leaned forward.

'David and I.'

'Anyone else?'

'No one else.' Steve shook his head.

'Have you mentioned this to Anil?'

'No, apart from what David said at the team meeting I decided to talk to you first.'

We need to cover this up. Who cares if it's illegal. We need the money.

Farid smiled. 'I like you, Steve. I will talk to my people. Can you send the report and leave it with us?'

'I'll let David know.'

'Steve, the management team at Q7 asked me to express our gratitude for the speed at which you launched the Seguro solution. You and David have proven yourselves, so we want to reward you both.' He reached into his inside pocket, pulled out two plastic cards and held them up.

Steve could see the words "Maybank Man of Steel" prepaid card etched across the top, and the word "VISA" in the bottom right-hand corner.

Steve leaned back and held up the palm of his hand towards Farid. 'No. You needn't do that.'

'We deposited fifty thousand ringgit on each of the cards and here are the PIN numbers.' Farid handed Steve the two plastic cards. 'A token of our appreciation.'

'There's no need for a reward.'

'Please accept them and please keep your findings confidential. Ask David to do the same.'

'OK, Farid. Thank you.'

# # # # # #

When Steve got back to the hotel he met David in the lobby. They sat near the entrance on one of the leather settees. Steve put his laptop on a small table. 'I told Farid. He asked me to keep this confidential whilst he investigates. Wants us to keep this between the three of us until he finds out what's happening.'

David opened his laptop and made notes. 'Was he shocked?'

'No reaction. A Malaysian thing, maybe? We didn't talk about who he suspected.'

'I don't like this.' David shook his head.

'Get one of the guys to run the compliance report and send it without analysis. OK? I want you to drop the investigation.' Steve raised his voice.

David stroked his beard.

'Farid is so pleased with our progress he has given me these prepaid cards as a reward. He has given them to you and me. Fifty thousand ringgit on each card. That's ten grand on each for you and me.'

David looked horrified. 'What! What's the catch? No, I really don't like this. We need the money, but we can't take them. We have to tell Roger.'

'It's a prepaid card from Maybank. No name registered and it's a Visa payment which debits the card when you use it at any store. You can even draw cash out at any ATM in Malaysia. Can't we use them to fund expenses?'

'I'm concerned, Steve.' By this time David was continually shaking his head. 'Every system connected to our network is on an onion router which creates a dark net, and they are splitting the revenue with a dodgy company.'

'Relax, David. You'll give yourself an ulcer.' *Gotta keep him calm. And relax, breath. Calm.* 'Q7 is a big company in Malaysia. I'm sure Farid has nothing to do with onion routers and dark net. Grithos might be his cousin. Who cares?'

'No, there's something fishy going on here. If I'm honest, the situation makes me even more suspicious when Farid gives us ten grand each. How can we be certain they won't blackmail us later if we expose this? No, I suggest we spend nothing on them no matter what,' David said.

David was adamant that there were serious issues at Q7 and the fact that they had been given the debit cards seemed to him to be a bribe to cover up these issues.

Steve needed the project to continue, so conceded to David. 'Yes, we need to be careful. I agree. I've already accepted the cards from Farid, so I'll put them into the hotel deposit, and not touch them.'

David's head moved from shaking to nodding. 'Yes, makes sense. Let's add to our defence on this to make sure we cover ourselves. I suggest you send me an email which states: As discussed, we received the Maybank debit card from Farid at Q7, and as agreed we will not use them but keep them in a safe place. I will respond to you with my agreement and a note about my suspicions.'

'Great idea. Don't want this to come back and bite us.'

'I'll check a few more things and shout if I can find anything.'

For fuck's sake, David.

'No. No, David. I already said. Leave Q7 alone. Focus on getting the project under way. We'll chat with Mark tomorrow. Clear?'

'Yes.'

CHAPTER SEVENTEEN

Friday 27th March

The following morning, Steve stepped out of the elevator on the ground floor of the hotel. He spotted Mark talking to a hotel receptionist and wandered over to him.

'Problem with my shower. They'll sort it today.' Mark frowned.

They strolled towards the restaurant, hampered by the bustling lobby with many people in the way.

'What do you reckon?' Steve said.

'You mean about David?'

'I'm worried. He's found problems at Q7. Puts us all in the shit.' Steve tried to put on a brave face.

'We'll sort the issue, whatever it is,' Mark said confidently.

A waiter greeted them at the entrance to the restaurant and ticked off their names. The front of the restaurant had bi-fold doors, which were open to the bright sunshine, warm air and a shimmering swimming pool. The whole landscape was bathed in the warm glow of the rising sun.

Steve ordered his customary eggs over easy and bacon from the cuisine chef dressed in a white uniform and hat. Mark helped himself to a choice of local delicacies from the buffet. After a short while, they joined David at his table.

'Bring Mark up to speed,' Steve said.

Mark nodded. 'Fire away.'

David put his cutlery down beside his plate and sipped from his water glass. 'I'm concerned about Q7.'

Mark carried on eating. 'Why? Looks as if the project's going well. We launched ahead of time. Performance and scalability are great.'

David continued in a hurry, 'No, our system is fine. The problem is with Q7's network. I've been using the Linux penetration system security tools to help with testing. It's set up to scan all devices that have been on the Q7 network for the past few weeks, collecting forensic info. I used a wireless device for sending malicious traffic across the Q7 network, gathering raw packet streams to get data. Wireshark to find plain text passwords, websites visited, and other application data. I've captured packets on the network, searched through database files and extracted the data sent across the network.'

Mark looked at Steve. 'Jesus. If Q7 find out. It's illegal, David. They'll kick us off the project. They could arrest us.'

Steve had not started his breakfast. He held his cup of jasmine scented green tea in his hand. 'Hold on Mark. David is not digging any further, let him explain.'

David picked up his knife and held it upright on the table. 'Someone should be arrested. The servers are all configured as an onion router and there's a pool of bitcoin mining servers, most are high-capacity rack-mounted computers.'

Mark stopped eating. 'You're joking? Is our system secured?'

David tapped his knife on the table in rhythm. 'The onion router has multiple touch points on the network and runs lots of e-commerce sites. The dark net is controlling millions of anonymous bitcoin transactions, and a licence payment per transaction to a company called Grithos. Their website is on the Q7 network, so they are getting royalty payments.'

Steve put his hand towards David's knife. 'You'll kill someone with that.' *Or I'll kill you if you don't stop that tapping.* 'I met with Farid and told him we have found suspicious transactions. He is investigating and asked us to leave it to him and keep this confidential.'

David put his knife down. 'The Seguro solution protects both the sender and receiver. Trouble is we protect the bad sender and the bad receiver of payments. Who knows what's going on, money laundering, selling drugs. A money launderer's dream. If this got out in the UK, every government agency would breathe down our necks to either close us down or issue notices demanding we name the parties. God knows what they can get away with in Malaysia.'

Steve leaned back on the chair and brushed both hands through his hair. 'What's the difference between the standard wallet and dark net wallet?'

Mark laid his palms flat on the table, paused and said, 'dark net is a bitcoin application which protects its users' identities, much stronger than the normal privacy protections. Keeps the user anonymous by encrypting and mixing its users' payments. So, money can flow untraceably online.'

Steve needed to drill down further. 'Technically, how does the dark net protect the identity more than a standard wallet?'

Mark explained, 'A standard wallet records every bitcoin payment in the blockchain. So, any corporation or government agency can trace bitcoiners' spending using their bitcoin addresses.'

David interjected. 'But on the dark net, every time a user spends bitcoins, their transaction combines with another user chosen at random who is making a payment around the same time. If, say, Fred is buying a computer from an online seller and Harry is buying LSD from an illegal marketplace, dark net will combine their transactions so the blockchain records only a single movement of funds. Bitcoins leave Fred's and Harry's accounts to pay to the computer seller and the dark net market trader, but only the legal transaction is shown'

Mark added, 'They encrypt everything. So, it's an anonymous chat with your illegal market vendor. They use PGP software which makes the sending of information over the web more secure by using public and private keys. Both sides need to have the PGP programme installed on their computers for generating keys and for encrypting and decrypting messages. They use a feature called the digital signature to send an encrypted message, unique to the sender so no eavesdropper on the network can decipher whose coins went where. They hide payments.'

Steve felt unwell, his head bursting, and although the weather was hot and humid, his hands were cold and clammy. *I need to contain this. Confidence, calm, relax.* 'What should we do?'

To Steve's annoyance, David picked up the knife again. 'We should cut off the links between the Seguro system at Q7 and their dark net. Go to the police.'

'No, not yet,' Steve interrupted, 'Keep this confidential as Farid has asked us to do. Mark and I will meet with Farid again and tell him more about your findings. I'll call him today.'

Mark nodded in agreement.

CHAPTER EIGHTEEN
Monday 30th March

Prem Jothi arrived at the Tegu Gentlemen's Club. Despite his slight frame, he exuded confidence, enhanced by his striking brown eyes and a tanned complexion. He wore a tailored suit complemented by his dark hair, which showed no hint of greying. The concierge and his assistant bowed exaggeratedly, to recognise Prem Jothi's importance. He walked past, without acknowledging them, and into the lounge.

Prem spotted Adam sitting in the lounge and walked over to him. He leaned forward and tried to hug Adam, who turned away.

Adam Jothi, a year younger than his brother, had very similar features, but Adam was taller and had a much more colourful and outgoing dress sense. 'When is Farid due here?'

Prem sat opposite Adam and ordered drinks. 'Relax, we have plenty of time to talk.'

Arms crossed, Adam sank back in the chair. 'I want you to get off my back. I don't work for you. Back off.'

'You are my brother. I will protect you.'

Adam stood up. 'I want to live my life.'

Prem leaned to one side and placed his elbow on one of the chair arms. He cradled his head. 'Kuala Lumpur is not a good place. For people like you.'

Adam opened his arms. 'People like me! People like me?' He sat down, leaned forward and pushed his face towards Prem. 'I can look after myself. You're not protecting me, you're controlling me.'

Prem held both his palms towards Adam. 'It is dangerous for you.'

'You try to control Mama, Dewi, and me. You treat us like slaves.' He pointed his index finger at Prem.

'No.' Prem shook his head.

'You control us. You have changed since father died,' Adam said.

'Our father didn't know about you. Islam does not allow people like you. But you are my brother and I love you.'

Adam stood up again. 'People who are gay.'

'Be quiet,' Prem whispered.

Adam raised his voice, 'Yes, gay.'

Prem tried to cover Adam's mouth with the palm of his hand. 'Do you want the police to arrest you? Do you?'

Adam pushed Prem's hand to one side. 'You only care about your reputation. You do not care about us! I want to leave here and live somewhere else. I only stay because of Mama and Dewi. You are a bully!'

'I love them both,' Prem said.

'You think only of yourself.'

Prem drew the conversation to an abrupt end. 'Ah, here is Farid, we can talk later.'

# # # # # #

The taxi arrived outside the Tegu Gentlemen's Club. Steve turned to Mark in the back seat. 'Farid will be with a colleague called Prem Jothi. He wants to introduce us to him. You never know, might be a business opportunity. Not sure what business he's in, but Farid might put a good word in for us to push the Seguro solution.'

Mark nodded. 'This haze is getting worse.'

'Yes. On the news last night. It's smog.'

'Smog?'

'Yes, I'll ask Farid.'

Steve paid the cab fare, and they went into the club.

'Good evening, Mr Roussos. Good evening, sir,' the concierge said. Steve let him know they were meeting Farid. A smartly dressed man arrived at the desk and he escorted Steve and Mark into the lounge, and over to where Farid was sitting.

Farid shook their hands. 'Gentlemen, take a seat.' He pointed to one of the leather settees. 'I would like to introduce you to Prem Jothi, a close friend and adviser. Also, let me introduce you to Prem's brother, Adam.'

Steve shook Prem's hand. Prem did not speak. He looked good in his smart suit, jet-black, and longish hair. His blue eyes were staring at Steve. Mark fixed his stare on Adam.

They sat down.

Mark, drop the Gaydar antenna! 'Good to meet you both. This fog is dense today.' Steve tried to break through Mark's fixation.

Farid nodded. 'Yes, terrible. Forest fires from Indonesia.'

Mark re-engaged in the conversation. 'Is the cause a drought?'

'No, happens every year in Indonesia. Palm oil producers in Indonesia set land on fire as a cheaper way to clear it for new planting. It is illegal,' Farid said.

Steve had not seen this before in Malaysia. 'So, this hits Kuala Lumpur every year?'

'No, this year the wind has blown northwards so acid haze from the fires are moving across Malaysia, Singapore, and have reached southern Thailand.'

'Ah. I wondered why I hadn't seen it before. Let's hope it disperses soon.' Steve nodded. 'I'd like to talk to you about our findings at Q7. Can I arrange a time with you?'

'We can talk now. Prem is my closest friend. Don't worry, I have investigated the issue, and I have it under control, so no problem.'

'It's a delicate situation.' Steve looked at the floor. 'David has found more evidence. Mark, can you explain?'

'I understood David agreed to leave the investigation to Q7?' Farid said.

'Yes, but I wanted to update you on all his findings.'

Farid nodded.

Mark shifted upright in his chair. 'David has found many computer servers on the Q7 network running an illegal network of onion routers. He's found a dark net controlling anonymous bitcoin transactions. Who knows what could be going on? Money laundering, selling drugs, could be anything.'

Steve reinforced Mark's point. 'We are concerned.'

Farid looked to Prem. 'I am investigating the problem. Keep this confidential between the five of us. Prem knows of this.'

Steve turned to Farid. 'What do you want us to do?'

'Leave this with me. Do nothing more. Do you understand?'

'But this situation is serious,' Steve said.

Farid gestured to Prem. 'Yes, I understand. This is why I have asked Prem to be here. He will look at this issue and bring in the Malaysian police when he has more information.'

Prem nodded.

'This may become a police matter, so I ask you again to keep this between us five. Understood?' Farid said.

Mark and Steve nodded.

Farid raised his voice with authority. 'Mark, tell David not to do any more network testing, and thank him for bringing it to our attention. An internal issue. Is that understood?'

Mark shifted in his seat, glanced at Steve, paused then nodded, before looking at the floor.

# # # # # #

They returned to the hotel and met David in the cafe to update him.

'Mark discussed your findings with Farid, and they have started an internal investigation. If they discover anything, they will contact the police. They want us to stop our investigation. A guy called Prem Jothi is looking into it. OK?'

'I see.' David closed his eyes, shook his head, then opened his eyes.

Mark leaned towards David. 'We should leave it to Q7. It's their problem, not ours. Farid said it's an internal issue. Let's leave it to him and this Prem Jothi to hunt the bad guys. We're just the secure payment piece. We are not responsible for illegal stuff on their network.'

David shuffled in his chair. 'This all sounds dodgy' He gulped his coffee. 'Could be anything illegal. Who knows! And a syphon company milking a cut of every transaction. If this was in the US or UK, they'd either close us down or issue notices demanding we name all parties.'

'We don't know for certain.' Steve pointed towards David. 'You are seeing an onion router and dark net. Yes, a payment to a local Malaysian company. So, what? It's an anonymous network so you can't be sure it's illegal.'

'We should segregate the Seguro server on their network,' David said.

'OK, if that change makes you both happier,' Mark said, 'Seguro only processes the payments across the Q7 network. If it's used by the bad guys doing illegal stuff, it's Q7's responsibility.'

'Something fishy going on.' David shuffled again in his chair. 'Steve, Farid tried to bribe you with the prepaid cards. Who is Prem Jothi? I don't like this. We should report this to the Bank of Malaysia.'

'Bank Negara. Let me talk to Farid,' Steve offered.

'Is Farid part of this?' David asked.

'He is the chief executive of a large and respected company in Malaysia. Why would he need to do this? Makes little sense.'

'David, can you set up a firewall behind our server at Q7? We should ask the guys to hand over the system to Q7 as soon as possible.' Mark said.

'I hope it's not too late. We should go to the authorities now. We should hold an emergency board meeting,' David stroked his beard.

'How would that help?' Steve leaned back. *I need to get David off this project altogether. He needs to shut it and get on with something else.*

David stood up. 'We are a secure transactions company for God's sake. We can't be seen to be involved with illegal transactions.'

Mark stood up and put his hand on David's arm. 'It's Q7's responsibility, not ours. Sit down.'

David shrugged, pushing Mark's hand away, and sat down. 'As directors, we have a responsibility to the board.'

'Let's get the system handed over, so we're not involved,' Steve suggested.

David raised his voice. 'We're already involved.'

Steve shouted: 'David, for fuck's sake, we need the revenue. We need money. We are directors. Our responsibility is to grow the company and grow the revenue. We're dead without Q7. For crying out loud! We can't fuck this up! Do you hear me?'

David breathed in heavily and continued, 'We'll go to prison if we get tied up in this fraud, illegal stuff, or whatever it is. It stinks. This could—' David said before Steve interrupted.

'Look. I will take care of this. You move on to other projects. Mark can complete the handover to Q7.'

'Fine by me.' Mark raised his shoulders up and back down.

'I'm not happy. But if you as a director take full responsibility then it's on your head, not mine,' David said, 'I'll book a flight back to the UK at the weekend. Been here for ages. Could do with getting back. Trish is complaining. I miss her and Lola.'

Great idea. Get him out of the way. Whilst this settles down.

'Great, sounds good. Is Trish OK?' *Try to lighten this up. Calm.*

Concern marred David's features. 'Trish is still fretting. I'll book a flight.'

Steve put his hand on David's shoulder. 'It'll be fine here David. Don't worry. Get your flight booked.'

And off this project altogether. I don't give a fuck what they are doing. We need to get paid. Get out of this shit!

Mark nodded. 'The project is under way. We'll sort out any issues.'

Steve glanced at Mark and smiled.

CHAPTER NINETEEN

Wednesday 1st April

Mark studied his watch as he waited in the lobby of the Mandarin Oriental hotel. A waiter offered him the opportunity to order a drink, but he declined.

A few minutes later Adam glided on shiny shoes out of the hotel elevator. 'Hi.' He wore a loud blue suit and white shirt. A designer's dream. They shook hands formally and sat down.

'Hello. Surprised you were with Farid,' Mark said.

'Surprised me as well.'

'So, you know Farid Razak, and Prem Jothi is your brother, eh?'

'Yes, I have known Farid all my life, and yes Prem is my brother.'

'Do you work with him?' Mark asked.

'No, I have in the past. He is the big cheese now, since our father died.'

'So, you know we are working with Farid at Q7?'

'Yes. Floor thirty-two, room 3206.' Adam put the Malaysian Times newspaper on the chair next to Mark.

Mark tried to rationalise Adam's action.

'Floor thirty-two, room 3206, come up in ten minutes. Key is under the paper.' Adam stood up, bowed and walked back to the elevators.

# # # # # #

Mark counted down the ten minutes, checked email on his iPhone, then sent Jamie, his latest boyfriend back in the UK, a text. 'How are you cutie <smiley>.' No reply, so he sent another - 'I need you now <smiley>.'

The time seemed to pass slowly. On the dot, he strode to the elevators, ascended to the thirty-second floor, then moved briskly along the corridor to room 3206.

# # # # # #

With the curtains closed, a single bedside lamp lit the room. Adam sat cross-legged on a mat on the floor in a Buddhist pose, with his hands cupped together, his eyes closed, chanting, '*Om Tare Tuttare Ture Soha.*' He was naked, sporting a supple body. His back was erect, and his head fixed straightforward, as he sat motionless in the traditional yoga pose.

Mark whispered, 'Hello.'

'*Om Tare Tuttare Ture Soha*, I am asking Green Tara, the Buddha of enlightened activity to make our hearts one, and our love forever. *Om Tare Tuttare Ture Soha,*' Adam said in a soft tone.

Desire burned a hot spot in the pit of Mark's belly. He kicked off his shoes, took all his clothes off and laid them on the chair, eyes fixed on Adam. He tiptoed over and knelt beside him. Adam repeated his mantra, '*Om Tare Tuttare Ture Soha.*'

Mark caressed Adam's back, shoulders and arms. With Adam's eyes still closed, Mark moved his hand to caress his smooth, clean shaven chest. Every part of Adam's body remained relaxed.

Mark's phone beeped. He ignored it. It did not matter. Nothing else mattered.

Adam moved his hands onto the floor then arched his back, now on all fours. His head faced forward, still with closed eyes, whilst he pivoted back and forth on his knees and hands, allowing Mark to take him. Adam's smooth skin, gentle features and warm body consumed Mark. Nothing else mattered

# # # # # #

Afterwards, they moved to lie together on the bed. Adam's body sank into Mark's instantly, the hard planes of his muscles enfolding Adam. Adam caressed Mark's chest and his lips brushed Mark's ear, raising goose bumps across his skin. Mark looked at his phone and spotted a text from Jamie in the banner across the screen: 'I need you now too. Come quick. <smiley>'

Mark quickly replied - 'I just come <smiley>.'

He leaned forward and kissed Adam on the cheek before gently sliding over to get out of bed, walked across to the window and pulled back the curtains. Mark gazed at the Twin Towers. So close, he felt he could just lean out and touch them. The reinforced glass pane would not open even if he wanted to; the proximity was an illusion created by the sheer size of the buildings opposite.

'The Towers are immense.' He turned to face Adam.

'Yes, you are a tower.' Adam smiled, and held out his arms.

'It's amazing.' Mark's eyes bored into his.

Adam smiled, stretched and said, 'Yes, you are amazing. Come here.'

Mark felt the heat of a blush on his cheeks.

CHAPTER TWENTY

Monday 6th April

'Hi David, how was the trip back to the UK?' Steve had expected the call.

'Long flight. Nice to be home with Trish though.'

'It's still muggy here, very oppressive today. We need an English man praying for rain!'

'Ha-ha, it's freezing here, but great.'

Steve laughed. 'Now you're rubbing it in.'

David gave a nervous giggle. He paused and coughed. 'I've been researching Grithos.'

'I thought you'd dropped the investigation?' Steve's breath audibly stalled in his throat.

'Listen to this. The Malaysian New Straits Business Times said that over one hundred companies are under investigation by Bank Negara Malaysia for money laundering activities. It's got me wondering.'

Steve's neck was flexing. 'Now look... You don't want to be causing trouble... This situation is dangerous, I'm serious.' *Please don't fuck this up now. We need the revenue. This is Malaysia. Nothing to do with us. For God's sake.*

David coughed again. 'I had to do more digging. I looked up Malaysian and Singapore company records. This Grithos is a dodgy company with a pretty website, but nothing else. I know it's got to be a front for something. It's an offshore company registered in Singapore, so they get a cut for every transaction on the Q7 system as a legitimate company receiving licence payments. That's the bogus bit, but it looks kosher to the accountants and auditors, I'm sure. So, the Finance guy, Anthony Suppiah from Q7 is not aware of any issue. I traced the payment on our system for Grithos to a bank account in Singapore. It stinks.'

Steve responded, 'Anthony drew up the agreement with only Farid and Anil involved at their end. I wondered why the procurement people were not all over this. Odd.' *Shit, did I say that out loud? Bollocks! I must keep this quiet.*

'I knew it.' David raised his voice. 'Next step is to use the ethical hacking tools to find out what the illegal stuff is and then trace the...'

Steve interrupted, 'Don't do that yet. I'll discuss your findings with the police over here in Kuala Lumpur. Leave it with me. Understood? You need to trust me to do the right thing.'

David coughed and then coughed again to clear his throat. 'I've loaded an image of the Q7 system onto a mini drive. We can go much deeper into the forensics. It's an ultra mini drive - straightforward to use, compressed and encrypted. Weighs next to nothing, fits into your MacBook's card slot, and is invisible once it's plugged in. The image is of the system network across most of the Q7 servers for about eleven weeks of data. I'm sure by using forensics I can trace the transactions. I've made two more mini drive copies of the image.'

'So, that's offline. Good. So, you won't need to access Q7?' *I need to stop this now. Stop him meddling.*

'Not yet.'

At least it keeps David busy for the time being whilst we get the money rolling in. Hopefully isolates the problem.

'I'll courier the copies of the drive over,' David said, 'Can you and Mark take a look? For security, I'll send part one of the secure vault password by text to you, and part two by text to Mark.'

'OK, I'll let Mark know. So, you don't need to spend any more time on this,' Steve said, 'You can focus on new projects. I'm sure Farid will sort out any internal problems he may have. Let's talk again at the next update meeting. Cheers.'

'Thanks Steve.' David sounded tired.

# # # # # #

Steve arrived at Q7's offices ahead of the next meeting and an assistant escorted him to Farid's office. Farid beckoned Steve to sit, pointing at a plush swivel chair. Steve could smell whisky. The room had a stale, pungent aroma. Farid's desk was cluttered. He pushed some files and a bound leather book to one side and then pressed the speakerphone button. 'Mr Roussos is here.'

'Thanks for seeing me before the meeting, Farid.'

'Not at all.' Farid placed his elbows on the desk.

'David has checked further into Grithos.'

Anil entered the room, rustling papers as he closed the door behind him. He walked over, and shook hands with Steve, then sat next to him. They faced Farid across a large desk.

Farid turned to Anil. 'Steve has concerns.'

Steve explained that David had found more information. 'It's owned by offshore companies based in Singapore, and it's on the Q7 system, so Grithos receive licence payments.

Anil bowed his head. A nervous smile broke on his face. 'Thank you for bringing this to our attention. I will talk to Anthony.'

Farid smiled. 'I can take you and David to meet with the Malaysian police to let them know about David's findings. I will call them now. If they are available, we could go today after the meeting.'

'Thanks. David is back in the UK now, but I'm happy to go with you.'

'Leave it with me.'

'David has a complete trace of the Seguro servers at Q7. We can run the analysis without accessing the Q7 installation as you have requested.'

'Look, Steve, I have told you - We will investigate, not David. Are we clear?' Farid's expression seemed carefully controlled.

'We are just trying to help.'

'Please control David. It has nothing to do with Seguro. We investigate our own issues.'

Steve nodded. He figured, or at least hoped that Farid was a good guy doing his best to make Q7 a success.

Farid stood up. His hands pushed against the table as he got up, and Steve felt the vibrations of the movement. 'Anil, can you bring the guys into the boardroom? We are ready now. I need to make a call and will follow shortly.'

# # # # # #

They gathered in the boardroom. The ceiling fan whirred. Steve could just hear it above the chatter.

A few minutes later Farid hurtled in with all the momentum of a tidal wave, slamming the door behind him. The room fell silent. 'Let's begin. Kim, can you update us please?'

Kim stood up and bowed. 'We are eleven weeks since the launch. Phase one is going well. Axiatel- customer base top-up is growing, and person-to-person value transfer, mobile commerce, plus customer loyalty and retention. Q7 and Axiatel marketing launch has started.' She bowed again and sat down.

'Thank you, Kim. Anthony?' Farid nodded.

Anthony coughed, opened his box file and took out two sheets of paper. 'I reported over one point six million transactions in the first two months since launch.'

Anil turned to Steve. 'Is everything going well with the Seguro implementation?'

'Yes. David and his team have handed control over to Boon and Rakesh in Q7 Technical Services.'

Farid barked: 'Good. Q7 will run and manage the system.'

Steve's stomach growled in protest.

The group covered the rest of the agenda and actions.

Farid bellowed, 'If there is nothing else to cover today, let's call the meeting to a close.'

# # # # # #

Farid and Prem accompanied Steve to Bukit Aman, a suburb of Kuala Lumpur, home of The Royal Malaysia Police headquarters. They had picked up Prem en route.

Farid made the introductions. 'Superintendent Anwar Tempawan of the Royal Malaysian Police. Superintendent, Mr Steve Roussos.'

The number of badges on the officer's black police shirt struck Steve. His shoulder lapels supported many silver stars and crowns, which Steve figured signified his rank. There were also silver studs on his collar, shirt and pocket buttons. They shook hands and exchanged pleasantries before sitting down.

'Nice to meet you, and thank you for seeing me,' Steve said.

'Mr Jothi and Mr Razak told me you have some concerns.' The superintendent's neat but bushy, black moustache obscured the view of his lips moving.

'Yes, my colleague, David Morris is an industry expert in online payments and internet security. He has found a network which could be selling drugs, laundering money, committing card fraud. You name it.'

'Do you have any evidence, Mr Roussos?' The superintendent asked, whilst glaring from under thick, black eyebrows. 'Of any crimes?' He pressed home his point with a penetrating gaze that probed Steve's face.

'No, but anywhere these networks appear there's usually illegal stuff going on,' Steve glanced away.

'But do you have evidence?'

Steve tracked the superintendent's gaze. 'No, not of illegal services. It requires deeper forensics and data to investigate any suspicious transactions. Although, I'm sure David will uncover more information – sellers, purchasers and payment trail. David can find the evidence you need.'

Farid put his hand on Steve's arm. 'Steve, my friend. We will assist the police. I don't want to trouble David. Is that clear?'

'I understand, Farid. Superintendent, David has investigated a company who are receiving licence payments for each transaction on the Q7 payments solution. Offshore companies own Grithos PTE Limited, based in Singapore. They receive payments into a Singapore bank account—'

'I talked to Anil, Steve,' Farid interrupted. 'We have suspended payments to Grithos pending investigations. I will ask the superintendent to investigate the company and their dealings.'

'Given time, David will find the evidence,' Steve said.

Farid smiled. 'Please let the police investigate.'

'He is keen to stop any criminal activities.'

'Mr Roussos,' the superintendent intoned, 'thank you for making me aware of your findings. I will take over from here. As you have no actual evidence of wrongdoing, we will investigate whether there are any illegal activities. The Royal Malaysia Police fight online crime in Malaysia. If a crime exists, we will uncover it and bring the criminals to justice. Thank you for bringing this to our attention.'

'Please listen to the superintendent,' Farid said.

Prem, Farid and Steve shook hands with the superintendent and said their goodbyes.

# # # # # #

Once they had left the police station, Farid let Steve know that Prem and he had a meeting they needed to go to, otherwise they would have offered him a drink at the local coffee bar.

Prem said, 'Thank you. Are you available to meet tomorrow?'

These were the first words Steve had heard from him. *Why is he here?*

'There is something I want to discuss with you,' Prem continued.

'Sure, Prem. Where shall we meet?'

'At this address, eleven o'clock.' Prem pencilled on the back of a business card and handed it to him.

'Tomorrow.' Steve nodded. He hailed a taxi and left.

\# \# \# \# \# \#

Steve arrived back at the hotel. He really wasn't sure whether he should feel relieved or frustrated. He just knew that the project must be a success. Steve spotted Mark in the lobby.

'Farid arranged a meeting at the police headquarters this afternoon. Prem Jothi tagged along. We met with Superintendent Anwar Tempawan of The Royal Malaysia Police.'

'Any progress?' Mark hung a lopsided grin on his face.

'I told him everything. He seemed to understand. But with no concrete evidence, other than a group of networks, which might be hiding illegal goings on.' Steve tailed off, uncertain how to put his frustrations into words.

'Was Adam there?' Mark asked.

'Adam, no, should he have been? He's Prem's brother. I don't think he's involved in Q7.' Steve wondered why he would ask about Adam. There were other, more important things on Steve's mind.

'Oh, just checking if he was with Prem.'

'You got your gaydar antenna up again? Remember, Malaysia is an Islamic country and all that.' Steve smirked.

'I couldn't resist.' Mark cocked his head.

'Keeping up appearances is important in Malaysia. Please be careful. You know I'm concerned about you.'

'You're not my mother.' Mark smiled. 'In Kuala Lumpur as long as I'm discreet, it's fine. Don't worry. Blue Boy in Bukit Bintang is a gay club. The Pavilion shopping centre is gay-friendly. There's more. I'll be fine.'

'It costs nothing to look. Guess you won't get arrested for looking.'

'It's more than looking, Steve.' He had a mischievous look plastered on his face.

'You're joking. Be careful.'

For God's sake. I need you to focus on making sure we control David.

'Where did you find a willing participant? The Blue Boy?'

'Err…. Adam,' Mark said sheepishly.

'You're joking. Prem's brother. Is he gay? Adam. No!'

Shit. Let me think.

'Yep. Oh, so gay.' Mark's cheeks flushed.

'But…When did you meet?'

'We've hooked up a few times. Again, next week.'

Bollocks!

'Mark! Mark!' Steve shook his head, 'You don't do things by halves. Does your latest boyfriend, err, John know about this?'

'It's Jamie, and yes he knows. Not everything, but yes, he knows. He's sorry he can't be here.'

'Is this a quick fling? Be careful, don't upset him. We don't want to cross Farid, or this Prem.'

'I can't get enough of him. He's keen. So, no problems.'

'Fucking hell, Mark. This is dangerous.'

'Don't worry, Steve.'

I should ship him back to the UK.

Steve's heart rate kicked up a notch. He was feeling dizzy, and overwhelmed.

CHAPTER TWENTY-ONE

Tuesday 7th April

Steve arrived to meet with Prem Jothi, at the address on the business card Prem had given him. It was a small office on the second floor of an old shophouse near Chinatown. The room housed various types of chairs, randomly positioned across the wooden floorboards. A single large fan circulated the air. Prem sat on a leather Chesterfield chair, flanked by a large man who seemed to collect tattoos. Another man, tiny in stature, stood motionless as he looked out of the shutters. The windows overlooked a red pagoda roof entrance to the bustling and crowded Petaling Street. The room was filled with the sounds of horns blaring, and engines revving. Steve felt uneasy at the sight of tattoo man, who watched his every move.

Prem shook Steve's hand and pointed to another leather chair. 'Take a seat, Steve. Oolong tea?'

'Yes, please. Thank you.'

Prem nodded to tattoo man, who left the room and returned with a tray containing a pot of tea and cups. He laid them out on the table. Steve thought it funny seeing the huge man daintily serve the tea. He smiled to himself; Mark would find tattoo man attractive.

Prem sat back in the chair and crossed his legs. 'Farid has great admiration for you, and I trust his judgement.'

'Thank you.' Steve smiled.

'He likes your team and you have a good family. Elizabeth.' Prem nodded. 'David and Patricia. Glen and Alice. And Mark yet to find his wonderful wife.' He smiled.

Steve nodded. He thought it odd that Prem would mention Beth and the other wives.

'Farid and I have known each other since we were children. We met at school when we were five years old. We are like brothers.'

'That's great.'

'Farid and I even began our graduate education together at the University of Malaya. It is Malaysia's oldest university. I graduated with a degree in International Business Studies and started my first distribution company at the age of twenty-two. Then I started a Malaysian company in the media industry. Three years later I founded a new group, specialising in commercial services. I have a strong influence at the ministerial federal level and international partnership, in many areas of business.'

Steve figured Prem wanted to impress him, so played along with the monologue.

'Thank you. Very impressive, Prem.'

'Yes, I carry influence with the Malaysian government ministers, major companies here in Kuala Lumpur and banks, including Bank Negara. I can help you, Steve.'

'Wow, great. We can use our success with Q7 as a platform to persuade other companies to adopt our secure payment solution in Asia. It would be fantastic to get Bank Negara to adopt our solution.'

'If they declare policy, then every bank in Malaysia has to do the same. My close friends are ministerial officials with direct responsibilities for the banks in Malaysia. Let me make a few calls,' Prem said.

Promising, if he can open a few doors for us.

'Excellent. I'll send you our information,' Steve said

'No, I have the basic information. I will arrange the introductions for you. Happy to help you my friend.'

'Do you want to sign an agreement with us?'

'No, we help each other. I am sure we can call on you.'

Steve was happy to have Prem as a prominent figure supporting them; combined with the Q7 success this could open several new opportunities and grow the business. He felt a little uneasy; could not understand why Prem wanted nothing in return and wondered what he was after. He was also troubled by what "call on you" meant.

'OK Prem, let me know if Seguro can help?'

CHAPTER TWENTY-TWO

Saturday 11th April

David sat at his desk, reading a document on his MacBook. Lola was curled up next to his chair. He heard Trish calling from upstairs.

'Shit. Is that the time already?' He patted his dog on the head and stood up. 'Better get ready, Lola.' He walked into the kitchen, grabbed an apple out of the fruit bowl, tossed it into the air, caught it, and strolled into the lounge.

He watched Trish come down the stairs, carrying her coat. 'Come on, David. What are you doing? I'm ready.'

'Fine. It'll take me ten minutes, that's all.' He took a bite out of the apple and sat down. Trish brushed her coat.

'Listen.' David scrunched his face into its serious look. 'I've found a problem with our customer in Malaysia.' He watched Trish put her coat on the banister and walk back into the room.

'Does that mean it will delay you getting any money?' Trish enquired.

'Please sit down for a minute. I don't know. It's going well, but I've found a serious fraud.' He felt a little rush of butterflies in his stomach.

Trish sat down opposite David. 'Fraud?' Her eyes widened.

'Yes, we could get pulled into it.' David stroked his beard.

'How serious is it?'

'I'm worried. I have to go back to Malaysia.' His forehead creased with concern.

'You've only just got back. You said the other directors would take over the project. Isn't that what you said?'

'But there's something going on.'

'Let the others sort it out.'

Lola jumped onto the couch beside David. 'There's a good girl.' He rubbed his hand across her head. 'Let's get ready, Lola.' He stood up.

'Don't change the subject. Wait. You promised.'

'The other directors will need my help.'

'When are you going?' She questioned.

'In the next couple of weeks.'

'You said this was the last time. I hate it when you go away.' She pulled at the threads on the sofa arm.

'This situation is serious. I need to go back.' He fidgeted with his beard again.

'You don't have to do anything. You're a director for God's sake. Delegate. Get someone else to do the work and manage them from here.' A groan accompanied the roll of her eyes.

'I asked you to come with me, but you don't like Asia.'

'We can't leave Lola. Someone has to look after her.'

'You don't understand. It's important. And anyway, it doesn't help matters if you keep moaning. I'll be back as soon as I can.'

'You know I don't like you to go away.' She looked away.

'I don't want to go back. Do you think I need this? Come on, we'll be late.' David left the room and went upstairs to get ready.

# # # # # #

The unprotected driveway offered zero cover as hard rain bounced off David's car. He yanked the collar of his three-quarter length coat over his head. His backside was getting wet. Lola, reluctantly traipsed behind. She hated rainwater and once sheltered behind the vehicle, gave a hearty shake. David opened the tailgate of the Renault Estate and the pooch jumped in.

'Good girl.' David smiled as Lola settled on her blanket. He threw his coat onto the back of the car and slid quickly into the driver's seat.

Trish emerged from the house carrying a bow-wrapped box. She closed the front door, tested it with a push and a pull, then rushed towards the car in a futile attempt to dodge the rainfall. Once seated, it took a while to wipe her blinking eyes and dry her glasses.

'I'm bloody soaking.' Trish twisted and stretched to place the present on the rear seat.

'Let's get moving... party'll be over.' He looked in the mirror. 'Good girl. Lie down now.' David pulled the estate off the drive and headed to the party.

'Spend time with me tonight. Don't leave me talking to your sister, or Tim.' Trish wagged her index finger. 'Focus on me for a change. Most of the time you're absent. If you're not working, you're thinking about work.'

'Tim's all right. He's harmless.' David glanced at Trish and smirked.

'All arms more like. Bloody octopus. Any chance to grab my backside or have a fondle.'

'He's no Hardy What's his name — just friendly.'

The Renault's headlights pierced the cloudburst as the traffic slowed.

'Yes, too friendly. I'm sure June must know.'

'She'd defend him to the hilt.'

'Letch. Any chance to grope, especially when he's had a few drinks.'

'If he does anything that makes you uncomfortable, let me know and I'll speak to him about it,' David briefly turned his head. 'You're beautiful. My lovely Trish. Are you surprised?'

'Ah. You realise it. Funny. You married me remember, not your job.' She pushed his shoulder.

'You are so funny and so lovely.' He looked at her again and smiled.

'If I'm so delectable... why do I always have to grab you for a hug or a kiss? You're married to your phone and that company. You should be careful. I'm a great catch. If you're away I don't see you, and when you're here, you have your head down looking at your phone or your bloody laptop.'

'Don't go on. It's a difficult time. You know I need to keep things going.'

'Let the other directors take some pressure. It's not all down to you. Have some home life.'

'For God's sake. Let's have a good evening.'

'You've just got back and you're off again. How does that make me feel?' She bowed her head, letting her hair screen her face.

'It won't be for long...Steady.' David felt the car slide a little, so he straightened it and gripped the steering wheel tighter. 'Christ, these tyres are wearing thin already!' The wipers were at full velocity yet were struggling to keep the deluge off the screen; he kept his speed well below the limit.

'I'm not going on the M25 in this... we'll take the A10.'

'You know best as always.' Trish looked away.

'Let's just have a nice evening. It's Dad's seventieth.'

Trish did not respond.

The shower was easing.

'You're a good girl Lola.' Trish turned around in her seat, she nudged her glasses with a fingertip, and smiled. 'Not far to go. Treatie time when we get there.' Lola wagged her tail expectantly.

The downpour reduced to a drizzle.

A black Audi pulled alongside them and slowed instead of overtaking. David looked across at the two men in the car. The passenger stared back and surveyed the pair with a half-smile.

'What's he want?' David glanced several times whilst trying to focus on the road ahead. 'He's driving too close. Nutter.'

The Audi hovered a little longer. David checked again. The passenger averted his stare and looked down. The Audi's engine revved and it sped away. David stroked his beard and shrugged. 'Strange—.'

The explosion caught him mid-thought. It was deafening and quick. He felt numbness and tingling but didn't know the detail - Good job. Both of his eardrums had burst in the blast. The Renault's airbags activated with twin bangs and filled the car with acrid smoke. He lost his grip on the steering wheel as the bag forced him backwards before jolting him forward again into the cushion. His seat belt locked up to reverse the action. Trish's head lurched forward, causing her spectacles to propel into the air, before her skull cracked against the passenger window. The car slid sideways along the wet road, narrowly missing a van as a white minibus braked hard behind it. The Renault finally lost all traction on the sodden surface and began spinning. Lola yelped in her rear compartment prison. The poor thing was being thrown around like washing on a full spin cycle.

The car crossed a grass verge, and smashed into a street light, its doors buckling inwards. The momentum carried it still further into a tailspin, then a flip, before propelling it backwards into some bushes. Upturned and stationary, a further explosion punctuated its demise as flames consumed the chassis, tyres, and all.

Traffic ground to a standstill and onlookers spilled out of their vehicles. They did it in freeze-frame. There was little point in rushing to this one.

# # # # # #

The Audi continued into the distance as the passenger sat upright, stared back out of the window and made a call. 'It's done.'

The driver reached across and switched on the radio. 'I'm starving.'

PART THREE
PRESENT DAY

CHAPTER TWENTY-THREE

Monday 13th April

Steve woke to the sound of his iPhone ringing. Blurry-eyed, he looked over at the digital clock on his bedside cabinet and answered the call. 'Hi Roger, it's just after three AM here.'

'Steve, I have bad news.' Roger coughed. 'I got a call this evening from David's dad and the police.'

'David?'

'I'm sorry to tell you David died in a road accident. He and his wife Trish passed away at the scene.' Roger's voice cracked.

'No! What happened?' Steve's heart stuttered, and he experienced a falling, spinning down feeling. He jumped out of bed and covered his mouth with his hand.

'On Saturday evening, David and Trish were travelling along a dual carriageway on the outskirts of London. They were heading to David's mum and dad's house for his dad's birthday. They never arrived.'

'Oh no, I'm so sorry. His poor mum and dad. Devastating! And Trish, David loved her so much.' A dull headache formed behind his brow.

'No mother wants to bury their child,' Roger said, 'And also Trish's mother, devastating. There's nothing we can say to them other than we will help them in any way we can with arrangements. No other cars or people involved. There's a police investigation. The petrol tank exploded as they drove along the dual carriageway.'

'Explosion? How could that happen? David only bought the car two years ago, brand-new. I'm devastated.' A million thoughts rushed into Steve's mind, though he couldn't snatch and hold on to any single one.

'There will be an inquest. The police need to establish what happened. So, his dad has no idea when they will release David's and Trish's body for their funerals. It's devastating for the families.'

'I can't believe it. We talked the other day. I can't fucking believe he's dead.'

'Leave it with me to tell the team over here,' Roger said.

'OK,' Steve said, 'I'll talk to Glen and Mark later this morning. I'll let Q7 know.'

'OK.'

'I'll fly back to the UK in the next few days.' Steve's shoulders dropped with a sigh.

'Take care.'

# # # # # #

Even though Steve had taken another Valium, he could not get any sleep after Roger's call. So many thoughts going around in his head. He was feeling even more anxious.

Did I push him too hard?

Have I caused it?

How did the car explode?

Too focused on the dark net?

I can't understand.

I'm devastated.

Is Farid involved?

Surely not.

Not in the UK.

As soon as he had pulled himself together he called home, 'Look, Beth.' He cleared his throat. 'Sad news. David and Trish died in a car crash on their way to David's mum and dad's house near London. It's just dreadful.'

'Oh no. Not David. David's poor parents. And Trish. Oh her mom.' Beth sobbed. 'Very sad. David and Trish were devoted to each other.'

'Roger sent flowers and a card from us all to David's parents and Trish's mom. I'll really miss David,' Steve said.

'I know. And poor Trish, I'll miss them both.' Beth sobbed and Steve did his best to console her.

As soon as eight AM arrived, he called and asked Mark and Glen to meet him.

# # # # # #

Steve was already in the lobby area when Mark and Glen arrived together. They ordered coffee and sat down.

Steve told them the devastating news. He shuffled on his chair and coughed. 'I was sitting here in the lounge with David less than two weeks ago and talked to him on the phone just the other day. Can't believe he's dead.'

Mark's face turned pale.

Glen leaned forward and bowed his head. 'It's mad. He was a great guy. A waste of his talents, and a loss to the industry. Mad, eh? We should raise a toast to David.'

'David.' They said in unison. Mark motioned the words, but nothing came out.

Steve put his hand on Mark's shoulder. 'I'm gonna go back to the UK in the next few days. Sort a few things out.'

Glen raised his stare from the floor. 'You going to David's funeral?'

'David's dad is not sure when his funeral will take place. The police are investigating the crash. There was an explosion. It makes little sense. David's car was new. Maybe it's just a coincidence, but I've got a bad feeling about this.'

'About what? What do you mean?' Glen looked puzzled.

'David's crash. I could be wrong. It's just… What do you think of Farid?'

'Farid?'

Steve sipped his drink and paused for a moment before he answered. 'Could he get involved in illegal dealings?'

Glen shook his head. 'Illegal dealings? What dodgy dealings?'

'Look you've been selling in Asia for years. Do you know much about Farid beyond Q7?'

'He is a character. He likes women, the liqueur, and goes out most nights to the Cuban Club or his Gentlemen's Club. Women and booze on tap. I got to know him well during the time I was trying to close the deal with Q7. I guess he likes me.'

Steve widened his questions. 'You met Prem Jothi?'

'Prem Jothi, yes. Seen him around town, with Farid lots of times. He is into services and other stuff. He must be rich as he always has a minder with him. Mai knows him, but I'm not sure if there have been any goings on between her and Prem before I got onto the scene. Just like Farid, he loves the women and the booze.'

'Mai knows him?'

Glen's phoned pinged. He ignored it. 'Yes, she is in awe of him. Not Farid. Just Prem. Mai and I have seen them a few times at the Cuban bar. Looking for a bit of hanky panky.'

'Poor David,' Mark said as the words emerged.

Glen continued, 'Farid gave me a Maybank prepaid card to put stuff on the tab, and I used it for other stuff. It's got thousands of ringgit on it.'

'You shouldn't take money, Glen. It might compromise you and Seguro.' Steve said.

'Chill. No probs. He's rich Steve. It's only a few drinks. What's David's death got to do with him?'

Chill. I'll give you chill. You don't understand Glen! Steve raised his shoulders and held his palms upwards. 'Oh no. Nothing Glen. Don't worry.'

CHAPTER TWENTY-FOUR

Thursday 16th April

Although Steve tried to focus on the project, he had spent the last few days trying to figure out David's death. It was going well at Q7, but he could not get the news of the crash out of his mind. The thought of an explosion weighed heavily on him. He prepared to go back to the UK.

He had spoken to Roger several times during the week. David's dad had given the police, Roger's number and they contacted him. Steve was trying to make sense of it all. Seemed that the police were taking no chances, they assigned the Metropolitan police under the counter-terrorism command. He was astonished to hear the words terrorism and explosion. The police had sent in a bomb disposal unit to the crash scene and they searched David's home for trigger bombs.

Roger had instructed staff to work from home until further notice. The police searched the Seguro offices, looking for anything. They said they don't know what they're looking for necessarily when they go in, other than treading carefully in case the home and offices are compromised. They took everything of David and Trish's that may provide evidence, including his black leather briefcase, iPad and MacBook.

The police were also disappointed that the press had caught wind of the explosion and reported the incident. The Metropolitan Police had reluctantly setup a press briefing schedule.

CHAPTER TWENTY-FIVE

Monday 20th April

On his return to the UK, Steve was focussed on finding the reason for David and Trish's death. Once he arrived back, he went straight to Roger's house.

Roger opened his front door. 'Come in. You must be exhausted. How was the flight?'

Steve followed him and took off his overcoat. 'Not too bad. I'll be shattered later.'

Roger led him through the hall and into the dining room. They sat next to each other at the table. 'Great work by the team. Very proud of them.'

'Yes.' Steve nodded.

'How are Mark and Glen?' Roger said.

'They're OK. Both very quiet but you know lads, they don't show their emotions. Mark was close to David. We need to watch him.'

'I talked to the guys in the office. They're shocked.' Roger looked down.

'Yes, I'm going tomorrow to meet the rest of the team…. Any further update from David's dad or the police?'

'I went to see Mr and Mrs Morris yesterday. They have no news on when they'll release the remains for their funeral. They're very anxious. The police are still investigating the explosion, but not giving away any info. A frustrating and difficult time for his family.'

'Did you arrange for me to meet with the investigating officer?' Steve said.

'Yes. He is available this afternoon. Is that too early?' He copied down the contact details and handed the note to Steve.

Steve took the note and put it in his wallet. 'No, I'm fine. I'll see them today.'

'You need some rest, but if you think it's worth it, hope it helps.' Roger said.

'I'm worried.' Steve paused. 'Not sure if I'm putting two and two together and making five. David found dodgy information on the Q7 network and odd transactions going on.'

'What do you mean? It's going well, isn't it? I even received a payment today. Over eighty grand this month. At this rate, we'll get back pay and inland revenue up to date. Might even pay your expenses.' Roger looked anxious.

'No, nothing to do with us. We're not doing anything wrong. David was investigating and found our payment solution is being used for illegal, anonymous transactions and odd payments to a Malaysian company owned offshore. He found dodgy network servers using something called the onion router and a dark net.'

'How are we involved?' Roger looked confused.

'Well, if we are processing payments it could be for illegal stuff; moving money or bitcoins.'

'I think I understand. Have you spoken to anyone at Q7?' Roger asked.

'Yes, we met with Farid. He brought in a guy called Prem Jothi. They are investigating. They even took me to talk with the head of the local police in Kuala Lumpur.' Steve stared at Roger. 'Crazy, eh?'

'We should leave it with Farid.'

'But my head's in a spin. Over-thinking as I'm prone to do. They knew David was an expert in this field and told us to keep this to ourselves and not investigate further. David was pushing me to go to the police, but there's no hard evidence. I told him not to, but he insisted on digging deeper. Now, this crash has put me in a tailspin. There was an explosion! His car blew up! They could have bumped him off!' Steve shook his head.

'Sounds very far-fetched Steve. Why on earth would a successful company get involved in this? They're making money from their business. Lots of money. Why follow someone from Malaysia to murder them in the UK?' A worried expression marred Roger's face.

'You have a point. The police must have picked up the master copy of the Q7 network image. I'll talk to them.'

# # # # # #

Steve arrived at the London Metropolitan police station in Golders Green. He walked up to the reception desk, introduced himself and asked for Detective Superintendent Sproson. The desk sergeant pointed towards a row of red plastic chairs. 'Take a seat, Mr Roussos.'

A few minutes later a tall man came into the waiting area wearing plain clothes. He shook Steve's hand. 'Inspector Grimes, Mr Roussos. Come this way, sir.'

Steve spotted the officer's red and white striped trainers, and Levi's'; looking nothing like a policeman. His shirt barely reached the top of his jeans. *The police are getting scruffier, and younger every day.* Steve followed the inspector into an interview room and he was asked to take a seat. The officer sat the other side of the desk and turned on a recording unit; announced the beginning of the formal interview and asked Steve to confirm his full name.

This concerned Steve.

'Mr Roussos, this investigation relates to the tragic incident involving your colleague Mr David Morris.'

'Yes, I've known him for years. He's a dear friend. A tragic loss. I know little about his crash except what I heard from my other colleague, Roger Slater.' Steve wanted to make sure he was as clear as possible.

'We have assigned a Senior Investigating Officer, Detective Chief Inspector Sproson. The DCI will oversee the case. I'm also assigned to the case. We are working with the National Crime Agency anti-terrorist squad to assess the origin of the explosion. Any information which can help us in this investigation is welcome. Do you have any information? About the incident? Or leading up to the crash?'

'No, I was in Malaysia. I want to help, so I flew back.'

'What is on your mind?'

'Well, David is a computer geek and an expert in IT security,' Steve explained, 'Chief Technical Officer at Seguro, or should I say "was". He had many years of experience. He has published articles and books on the subject. A company in Malaysia called Q7 awarded us a contract just over two months ago. David found suspicious activity on their computer network which concerned him.'

'Can you be more specific about how this affects the investigation? He had returned from Malaysia,' the inspector said.

'He recently flew back to the UK. Just over two weeks ago. They killed David because of what he found.'

'So, you figure someone in Malaysia travelled to the UK to murder your friend? And the reason was Mr Morris found suspicious activity on the internet?'

'You have already confiscated David's MacBook. David loaded an image of the Q7 system onto a mini drive. The mini drive is a complete master image of the Q7 system. The company I mentioned earlier. The mini drive should be in his MacBook's card slot. I have the password.' Steve handed over a piece of paper containing the password. 'Please get your computer forensic experts to analyse the data. This will prove what's going on at Q7.'

The inspector put the paper into a clear plastic bag, sealed it and made a note on the label. 'Did you discuss this with Q7?'

'We brought it to the Chief Executive's attention, and he arranged for me to meet with the local police superintendent in Kuala Lumpur. Could be over-reacting.' Steve looked upwards trying to figure out what really happened.

'So, you believe someone in Malaysia may have a reason to murder Mr Morris? You think it's related to Mr Morris's findings at Q7. You informed Q7 of your suspicions and they are investigating the claims of Mr Morris. They brought in the local police to talk to you?'

'Yes, Superintendent Anwar Tempawan of The Royal Malaysia police. He said I didn't have enough evidence and told me to leave it with him and he would investigate further.' Steve raised his voice slightly.

'I will ask the National Central Bureau to contact the Malaysian police. They will get an update from the local superintendent.'

'OK, great. Maybe I'm over-thinking. Watching too many movies.' Steve collapsed back in the seat.

'Interview ended. We will be in touch with you if we need any further information. Thank you, Mr Roussos.' The inspector turned off the recorder.

'Is that it? They murdered David.' Steve gasped.

'Can you wait here please Mr Roussos? I want you to meet one of my colleagues. 'The inspector left the room.

# # # # # #

A few minutes later, two officers entered the room and sat opposite Steve. They started the recording and asked Steve to confirm his name again.

'Thank you, Mr Roussos. I am Detective Chief Inspector Graham Sproson and my colleague Detective Inspector Rebecca Power.'

The Detective Inspector nodded.

This time the officers wore police uniforms. DCI Sproson towered over the detective inspector even when they were both sitting down. The DCI's distinguished grey hair gave him an air of maturity and confidence. DI Power, was much younger; she had long ginger hair tied up in a knot and a ruddy complexion.

'We are part of the National Crime Agency, conducting enquiries into the deaths of Mr and Mrs Morris,' The DCI said, 'We have not found any more evidence to conclude that this was an act of terrorism. It is now a murder investigation under homicide and major crime command. We are following several lines of enquiry. We need to ask you some more questions.'

Steve nodded. 'Happy to help.'

DI Power explained. 'We confirmed that an explosive unit caused the car crash; planted under the petrol tank, detonated using a remote device.'

Bastards. They wanted David out of the way.

'Oh, my God. I knew it! Isn't there access to CCTV?' Steve said.

'We are investigating the footage, following up on several cars travelling in both directions, and suspect a particular car that drove at high speed away from the explosion. Someone covered the number plates. Are you aware of Mr Morris's government security status?'

'Yes, David was a security expert. He had security clearance for work he did in the nuclear industry.'

'Nuclear?' DI Power looked quizzical.

Steve explained. 'This goes back to his early days working at the Ministry of Defence VSEL submarines. He advised other government agencies, which included nuclear. David developed guided missile software for subs. So, he needed to get the OK to visit Malaysia using travel advisory notifications. It was a pain. Although I was in The Royal Signal Regiment where we specialised in providing Data Communication Services, Information Assurance and Electronic Counter Measures – that's Force Protection to support operations – I don't need security clearance any more. But I helped David to get his travel approval organised with the itinerary and letters from customers we planned to meet in Malaysia and Singapore.'

'Thank you, Mr Roussos. Was Mr Morris involved in any covert activities in the UK or abroad for any agencies?'

'Covert? Not sure what you mean? If you're asking if he was spying I very much doubt it, but I have no idea.' Steve could not stop himself from grimacing.

'Thank you. And Mrs Morris, David's wife. Did you know her well?'

'Yes, Trish. She has been David's partner for as long as I have known him. That's over ten years,' Steve shook his head, 'Have you contacted the Malaysian police?'

'We will contact the UK National Central Bureau. They will follow up on your information. Do you have any plans to leave the UK?'

'Only to go back to Malaysia. I'm arranging customer meetings. I have no confirmed travel dates yet,' Steve said.

'Can you make us aware of any travel plans? If we need you to answer any further questions, we will contact you. Thank you for your help. Interview ended.'

# # # # # #

'I'm home.' Steve shouted as he opened the door.

An excited Labrador did her usual welcome by running to fetch her favourite rope toy then barked with excitement.

'Hi love.' Beth skipped downstairs and met him at the door, throwing her arms around him. 'Hello stranger. Come here, let me give you a hug. Oh, I missed you. How are you?'

'Just sorting out more shit, but it's so good to be home.' Steve stretched his shoulders.

'Ah.'

Steve kissed her. 'How are the kids? Is Kate feeling any better?'

Beth put her hands on his shoulders. 'We have a date for the consultant. It's the middle of next month.'

'What? Will she be OK until then?' He put his hands on her hips.

'She has only had a couple of episodes.'

'That's not good,' Steve said, 'I'll come along to see him with you. I'll make sure I'm back. Jake and Ellie?' He took his jacket off.

Beth took a step back. 'They're fine, missing you. I need to tell you something.'

'What?' Steve stopped in mid-motion.

'Millie is having puppies.'

'She's pregnant, how did that happen?'

Beth smiled. 'Do you need me to draw pictures?'

He patted Millie on the head. 'Poor girl. What have you been up to?' Steve looked at Beth with a puzzled expression. 'Who's the father? I hope she didn't get out.'

'Of course not. We need the money, so I had her mated with Ron and Gabrielle's lab. The bills are stacking up.' Beth shook her head.

'Are you going to cope with Millie and everything else?'

'Do I have a choice?' she said.

He put his coat on the banister and pulled Beth towards him. 'What would I do without you?'

She rested her head in his chest. 'You owe me big time.'

'I know.' He kissed her.

'How's it going? Glen behaving himself?'

'Glen is his usual self, but it's going well. The solution is up and running. We should get some money soon.' Steve smiled.

'I'll believe it when it's in our bank. But it's great you are getting there.... Oh, I forgot to say... I've changed the downstairs loo as it was ancient. Gabrielle was throwing one away which is in perfect nick. And I did all the plumbing myself,' Beth said.

'What?' Steve took a moment for it to sink in. 'The loo. How have you done that?'

'I'm not stupid,' she smiled.

'I know. I'm never surprised by what you can do.' He held her close. 'I love you. What would I do without you?' He skimmed his lips along the sweep of her cheek ending with a peck on the lips. 'I've been to see Roger today. He is in touch with David's dad. There is an investigation. I visited the police to see if I can help.

'I can't stop thinking about David and Trish. I'll miss my girly talks with Trish. I know it wasn't often but it was great to chat about you men and work.' She sobbed.

Steve's shoulders dropped.

'And I meant to ask, what will happen to Lola? Will she stay with family?' Beth pondered.

'She was in the car,' her paused, 'with David and Trish.'

Tears welled in Beth's eyes as he consoled her.

Steve sighed, 'Can't wait to see the kids.'

CHAPTER TWENTY-SIX

Wednesday 22nd April

Steve received a call asking him to visit the London police station again. Further information had emerged. He got dressed, skipped breakfast and headed to the station.

# # # # # #

An officer escorted Steve into an interview room and asked him to sit at the table. DCI Sproson entered, shook Steve's hand and sat opposite. 'Thank you for coming in again. We appreciate your help with the investigation.' He started the recording.

DCI Sproson said, 'We have spoken to the UK National Central Bureau, and they contacted the Royal Malaysian police. They are investigating several companies who are financing illegal activities in Malaysia.'

'Illegal activities. Oh, my God. Q7 murdered David.' Steve's brow furrowed.

'We need more evidence to come to that conclusion Mr Roussos. The Malaysian police informed us that you and members of Seguro are under investigation. They asked us to bring you in for further questioning.'

'What?' Steve tried to swallow and talk at the same time but ended up choking on his surprise. 'We've done nothing wrong.'

What the hell's going on?

'We are not suggesting that, sir. We would like to discuss your dealings in Malaysia. Are you dealing with any companies in Malaysia?'

'Yes, we are.' He explained the details again of Q7, Grithos and suspicious activity and the introduction to the Malaysian police. Steve sounded like a broken record, repeating the same update again.

'So, you are receiving payments from this company?'

'My company, Seguro, installed a solution to process online secure payments and person-to-person secure transactions. We started the project with Q7 over two months ago.'

'How are you receiving money?' DCI Sproson said.

'Seguro receive a licence fee per transaction. It's a revenue share agreement with Q7.'

'Is the payment sent to Seguro's bank account?'

'Yes, Roger Slater, our Financial Director deals with all the financials. The payments arrive at the end of each month into our company bank account. We use HSBC Bank. We are a UK company with a UK bank account.' Steve let out a harsh breath.

'Have you, personally, received any payment from Q7?'

'No,' Steve said. Then thought, 'Oh wait, Farid provided David and I with a prepaid card, but we didn't use them.'

'Thank you. We will tell the Malaysian police, via Interpol.'

'Hang on. It's too much of a coincidence. David gets murdered after he uncovers suspicious stuff going on at Q7. What else could it be?' Steve said.

'We are following several lines of enquiry, including the possibility of a terrorist attack. We can't rule out other reasons such as Mr Morris's security clearance level and earlier involvement in the nuclear industry. We can't rule anything out Mr Roussos.'

'It makes little sense. Something is wrong. You should investigate Q7. There must be a connection,' Steve said.

He found it difficult to think straight. Many thoughts, some repeating numerous times.

Was it my fault?

Should I have protected David more?

What could I have done to prevent this?

Why wasn't I more assertive — telling him to stop?
If only I had kept him away from this project.
Am I responsible.
I've killed David and Trish.
I couldn't stop the project.
We need the money.
Was I too desperate to listen to David.
I have to find out who murdered him.

'Thank you. If you have any further information, please contact us. We will be in touch with you if we need anything further.'

'Can I go back to Malaysia?'

'You are free to go where you wish.'

'Thanks.'

CHAPTER TWENTY-SEVEN

Friday 24th April

Glen and Mai arrived at the Concorde Hotel. He paid the cab driver, and they walked hand in hand through the atrium lobby to the bar. The Crossroads Bar was crowded that evening as the resident band "Two BY Two" from Manila in the Philippines entertained, singing popular hits. He found a table and sat on a lounge settee then placed his two phones, phone charger, cigarettes, and lighter on the arm of the vacant chair beside them.

Leaning back in the chair, he pulled Mai towards him. 'Keep this sofa for Mark and Adam. Come here.'

A waitress approached. 'Hello, Mr Glen. How are you today? Iced tea?'

'Hello, Alyssa. I haven't seen you for a while. I'll have a beer and Mai will have a vodka and coke. Cool'

'OK, Mr Glen.' Alyssa jotted on her notepad as she retreated to the lounge bar.

Mai looked with suspicion at Glen.

Glen squeezed her playfully. 'Chill. She's the waitress who serves every day in the bar. No probs.'

'I know my love,' Mai said

Glen smiled.

Mark arrived as Alyssa brought Glen and Mai's drinks. He ordered a beer and sat down.

'Namaste. How are you?' Glen bowed his head.

'Had a sleep, and a great shower.'

'Where are we meeting Adam? The main man.'

Mark looked at his wristwatch. 'In the lobby. In seven minutes.'

Glen nodded. 'Did you clock the Ferraris parked out front? Mad, eh?'

'There's a big wedding going on. Hotel left a message in my room. Local bigwig.'

Glen smiled. 'It's mad. When the taxi dropped us off, there must have been a dozen red Ferraris lined up outside. Lucky colour in Asia.'

The resident band played their renditions of Whitney Houston's classics.

'This bears no resemblance to Whitney Houston.' Mark held his hands to his ears.

'Cool. It's great.' Glen and Mai swayed from side to side.

The noise from the band and the crowded lounge got louder and louder.

'Enjoy it mate. Come on,' Glen said.

Mark's phone pinged as a message arrived. 'Adam is in the lobby.'

'I will always love you. I, I will always love you, Glen sang.'

'Come on drink up.'

The music reached a crescendo as they left the bar. The lobby was very busy. Glen detoured to the back of the atrium to look at the huge banquet hall, full to the brim with wedding guests. At the far end of the banqueting suite, the stage held a band dressed in traditional Indian costumes playing Bhangra music. People dancing, eating and drinking. Fantastic costumes. The centre piece of the room housed a giant cake in the shape of a religious temple.

Mark walked over to Adam and they shook hands formally. Adam greeted Mai by kissing her on both cheeks.

Glen shook hands. 'Namaste. Let's go eat.'

Mark questioned Glen. 'Where is the Xin Kandar restaurant?'

'It's just over the road. We can walk,' Glen said.

Mark frowned. 'Walk. It's very humid.'

Adam smiled. 'Good for you to walk.'

# # # # # #

Even though it was dark outside, the heat and humidity made the air sticky. It had been raining, so it was even more humid than usual. They waited for the traffic lights to change to red before crossing the carriageway, weaving between the stationary cars, bikes, vans and taxis. Xin Kandar was a short walk beyond through the square, past the fountain and a small park. The restaurant was renowned for its Chinese Cantonese food. Its speciality was dim sum. One of the few restaurants in Kuala Lumpur which served authentic dim sum in pushcarts, reminiscent of old tea houses in Hong Kong and parts of China.

A waiter greeted them in Cantonese before seating the group next to the window. A man dressed in a traditional costume played the guzheng, a traditional Chinese instrument. He accompanied the chatter of customers enjoying the food.

Glen smiled. 'It's mad. I love the experience of the Orient. Many locals here tonight, so it must be a good restaurant. Shall we order drinks?'

The waitress handed each of them a menu and took their drinks order.

Mark turned to Adam and looked straight into his eyes. 'Can you recommend a good dish for me?'

Glen butted in. 'Yes, mate, and for me and Mai, as long as you include noodles.'

'Sure.' Adam gazed back at Mark.

Once the waitress returned with the drinks, Adam ordered Cantonese food choices accompanied by two noodle dishes, and congee, a Chinese broth.

Glen raised his glass. 'Great stuff. Let me raise a toast to Kuala Lumpur and our success... Cheers.'

Mark welled up, a sheen of water covered both eyes. 'And David, a great guy. Cheers.' He lifted his glass and looked towards the sky.

Adam did the same. '*Sorakan*.' The Malay word for cheers.

Mai looked to the floor for a moment, raised her glass and said in Vietnamese, '*Chuc mung*.'

Glen pulled Mai towards his side. '*Chuc mung*. *Sorakan*. Cool.'

Adam chose several dim sum dishes from the ladies in the pushcarts. He had to speak in Cantonese as that was the only language the waitress understood. Adam spoke in Cantonese to ask Mai if she had any favourites. She fixed her gaze towards the ground and did not respond.

Adam looked at Mai and talked to her again in Cantonese. 'I am your friend. You love Glen and I Mark.'

Mai looked up, nodded and looked to the floor again.

'Hey, you chatting up my girlfriend? Mate.' Glen smiled at Adam.

Mai responded. 'He says nice things.'

Glen pulled Mai even closer. 'Thought you batted for the other side?'

'Hey.' Mark pointed a finger at Glen and tilted his head towards him.

'Let's enjoy the night, mate. Chill. We are on our way.' Glen waived his empty glass, summoning the nearest waiter to bring more drinks. 'Tuck in.' He piled several dim sum onto his plate.

Mark looked at Mai. 'Are you enjoying the new apartment?'

Mai smiled at Glen. 'Yes, I love it.'

Glen beamed. 'You must come over. No brainer.'

Mai nodded. 'Yes, I cook for you.'

'Great. We'd love to.' Mark nodded towards Adam, who reciprocated.

Glen put his thumb up to gesture his agreement. 'Hotel drives you crazy, glad I got out.'

Mark nodded. 'Yes, hotel rooms! Tell me about it.'

'You could move in with Adam. You could wear a dress mate!' Glen laughed, knocked back the rest of his drink, and summoned the waiter to get another round.

More food arrived.

Mark mimicked a canned laugh. 'Ha-ha, hilarious. You're a comedian.'

Adam smiled at Mark. 'Yes, we can live together, but we should go to live in Singapore.'

Glen looked at Mai. 'In Vietnam, are they OK with gays? If you know what I mean.'

'Yes, they are.'

Glen looked puzzled. 'How come it's legal in Indonesia? The biggest Muslim population in the world. It's mad.'

'Except for Aceh province, which upholds sharia law, gay sex is legal in Indonesia,' Adam said.

'We should go to Jakarta.' Mark smiled and winked at Adam.

Glen shook his head. 'Eight times more Muslims in Indonesia than Malaysia. So why are they OK with you gays? Mad, eh?'

Adam shook his head. 'It's not simple. Bali is gay-friendly but other areas are not safe. Just last week Indonesian police arrested a group of men for holding a gay party. They said some men were watching gay porn and performing deviant sexual acts.'

Glen gulped back his drink. 'I thought you said it was legal?'

'They use anti-pornography law to arrest them. Jail sentences as much as fifteen years,' Adam said.

'It's safe in Kuala Lumpur as long as you don't flaunt it,' Mark said.

Glen looked puzzled. 'Where can you go? You know. And be yourself.'

'It's very handy to be with a local.' Mark smiled at Adam, then gestured exclamation marks with both hands. 'For people like us.'

Glen flicked his fingers towards a waiter. 'A special knock on the unmarked door. If you know what I mean.'

Mark said, 'No, not at all. At Frangipani restaurant, lots of people like us, go eat and then on to the Blue Boy Club.'

'Is that the one in Bukit Bintang?' Glen said.

Mark winked and gestured to Glen with a V sign. 'Yes, it's dark, smoky, seedy and kitsch all at the same time. Great atmosphere. I love it.'

'It gives us freedom,' Adam said, 'Sharia law forbids us. So, our lifestyle is difficult, and almost illegal, for Malays like me. It is also difficult for transgender people because sharia law forbids cross-dressing.'

Glen raised his empty glass. 'You mean ladyboys. Something wrong with them.'

Mark took a deep breath. 'They're just human beings, Glen. Grow up.'

Mai leaned on Glen's shoulder. 'I have friends who are ladyboys,' Mai said, 'Not happy people but kind. They send money to their family.'

'Yes, I have made good friends at the Blue Boy Club,' Adam said, 'Every weekend they have the same acts. And the same people go there. They are like an extended family; meet at Frangipani's, eat and go to the Blue Boy.'

'Acts, eh?' Glen said.

'Yes, same performers for a long time. Drag shows. Ladyboy, gay and lesbian acts,' Adam said.

'I love the ladyboys,' Mark said.

'Pervert,' Glen said.

'Fuck you,' Mark responded.

'Aren't you a Malay Muslim mate?' Glen pointed at Adam.

'I am a Buddhist.'

'Ye protest-eth too much.' Mark frowned at Glen.

Glen raised his empty glass. 'Chill. You're right. Look at David. We only live once, so let's enjoy it.'

'To David.' Mark raised his glass.

Mai and Adam followed.

'Maybe Steve will give us more info when he arrives on Sunday,' Glen said.

'To success, and friendship.' Mark lifted his glass again.

They followed.

Glen ordered more drinks.

CHAPTER TWENTY-EIGHT

Sunday 26th April

'Why have you stopped me? I'm in Malaysia on business.' Steve sat uncomfortably at the table.

The uniformed officer checked each page of Steve's passport. 'Malaysian border control sir.'

'I've just arrived on the London flight, knackered. What's going on? Why are you keeping me waiting?'

The officer did not look up from his task. He mouthed, 'Mobile phone?'

Steve took his mobile out of his jacket inside pocket.

The officer remained focused on the paperwork. 'Put it on the desk, sir.'

Steve complied. The officer deposited the phone into a plastic bag, sealed it, and wrote on the label which adorned the bag.

'The Royal Malaysian police have asked us to detain you. Wait here until an officer arrives.' He gathered the paperwork, the bag containing the mobile phone and Steve's passport. He left the room and locked the door behind him. They furnished the sparse room with a single table and four chairs. White walls with spotlights placed across the centre of the matching white ceiling. Steve leaned forward in the chair and placed his head in his hands, elbows resting on the table. He did not wear a watch as he relied on his mobile phone to change to the local time zone; uneasy that he did not know the time as there was no clock on the wall.

'Hello. Is anyone there?' He stood up and paced the parameter of the room. 'Hello. What's happening?'

He wondered if this had any connection with David's findings at Q7, or even David's murder.

A uniformed man entered the room. He sat at the table and pointed across to the other chair. 'Please take a seat, Mr Roussos.'

Steve sat down. 'You can't keep me. I have rights.'

'I am Sergeant TetLeong from the Royal Malaysian Police.'

'When can I go?' Steve stood up.

The sergeant gestured to him to sit down. 'We received a Red Notice International Wanted Person Alert from Interpol. So, we have detained you pending an investigation into international money laundering and illegal financing. I am from OCB – Organised Crime Bureau.'

'Why me?'

'You must understand, we work with· the Criminal Intelligence, Narcotics, Customs and Excise Department, and Immigration Department. The battle is to find and limit leaders of gangs, terrorists and the criminal network. You are under investigation.'

Steve protested. 'What's going on? I'm a UK citizen. Living in the UK. I was born in the UK. I'm not involved in money laundering or anything else. This must be a mistake. I need to get to my hotel to rest.'

'No mistake Mr Roussos. We know you are receiving money from Malaysian companies.'

'Yes, my company, Seguro, has a customer in Malaysia. We have been working with them for over three months. We won a contract to deliver a new secure online payment service for their customers. I've told the UK police. What's going on? I met with Superintendent Anwar Tempawan and told him our suspicions of a dark net. The company is Q7. Ask him.'

'The Royal Malaysian police are investigating companies who are money laundering through Malaysia to finance illegal activities.'

'I understand, and I reported Q7 to you.'

'The UK police provided information and we believe this involves you and members of Seguro. We have detained you for further questioning,' TetLeong said.

'Oh my God. What? I've done nothing wrong. This is crazy. I'm innocent.'

The officer left the room.

Steve was dumbstruck and shocked.

What will Beth think? What time is it?

# # # # # #

A short time later the officer returned to the room. 'Mr Roussos, we believe the illegal laundering and financing taking place is to finance drug trafficking. Did you know, you can get the death penalty in Malaysia for drug trafficking? If convicted you could serve a long prison sentence in a Malay prison, which I do not recommend for my worst enemy.'

'Can I call my wife? Where's my phone?'

TetLeong ignored his request. 'There is one way, Mr Roussos. If you cooperate and work with the Malaysian police to break this illegal operation, we may reduce your sentence.'

'Sentence? What sentence? What have I done? Nothing for God's sake!'

'If you cooperate with us, we will protect you.'

'Protect me. What do you mean?'

'These are dangerous people.'

'I will help.' Steve held his hands out in front of him, conceding to his fate. 'What do I need to do? Can I go now?'

'You can go for now, but you must assist us.'

Steve looked to the floor.

'Here is your phone. You can go. I will be in contact with you.'

'Thank you. I will help you, but just want to clarify that I've done nothing wrong. And anyway, what about my passport?'

'We must hold on to it for the time being.'

Steve shook his head and breathed in deeply. 'How can I check into the hotel? I need my passport.'

'I will call the hotel. They will let you check-in. Tell no one we have spoken. If we suspect anything, we will bring you in.'

'I'm innocent.'

Fucking Bastards.

'Remember, we will be watching you.'

CHAPTER TWENTY-NINE

Monday 27th April

After a restless night, Steve arrived by taxi at the opulent clubhouse of The Kuala Lumpur Golf & Country Club in Klang Valley, surrounded by manicured fairways and a scenic backdrop. He spotted Cliff Lin waiting at the entrance, chatting with the receptionist.

'Cliff. You're looking well, I guess you're playing lots of golf?' They shook hands.

'Welcome,' Cliff said. They strolled into the restaurant. 'Yes, I am well. Not much golf, but I am well.'

'Traffic is crazy this morning. Grid-locked Kuala Lumpur,' Steve said.

'It's a protest. Happens every year. Malaysian ethnic Indians claiming rights abuses which go back to colonial labour schemes. The British brought their ancestors to Malaysia as forced labour workers. They want Britain to pay damages of one million pounds to each of the two million Indians from Malaysia.'

'Will they ever get it?'

'No, they're claiming British officials didn't honour their responsibility to protect ethnic Indians when they granted independence to Malaysia in 1957.'

They strolled along to the restaurant. The back wall supported a procession of framed photographs of club committee members through the years. Steve smiled to himself as the early pictures showed only white-skinned men, then it changed to only dark-skinned men. He figured it must have been the change in 1957. 'That would create two million millionaires. Wow.'

Cliff smiled. 'They will protest for the next thousand years and the response will still be no. How are things at Q7?'

'We installed and launched within five weeks. A minor miracle. And we're already receiving payments.'

'Good. So, my investment is making good progress then. I am looking forward to dividends soon.' Cliff smiled.

'Me too,' Steve nodded.

'Dear David,' Cliff said, 'Tragic news. It is a great loss.'

'Yes, we'll all miss him, It's devastated his family.'

'Please send my condolences to them.'

'Thanks, Cliff… Have you met Prem Jothi?'

'Jothi, yes I know him, but not very well. I saw him here a few times playing golf. He is an interesting man with a strong reputation. I believe he has dealings in many areas of business and government. Great for Seguro to associate ourselves with him and his companies.'

'Ah, Prem Jothi is the reason I wanted to talk to you. As well as wanting to be in your excellent company of course! The head of Q7, Farid Razak introduced me to Prem Jothi. Farid Razak and Prem Jothi are close.'

Should I tell him? About Q7?

Might spook him. He's pumped money into Seguro.

Not sure.

'Is Prem involved with Q7?'

'No. Although he has attended some meetings we have had with Farid. Prem offered his help and introductions to companies and government agencies in Malaysia.'

No, I won't tell him yet. I will prove they murdered David. I need to think.

'It us good to get his help. That is my advice.'

'Thanks, Cliff.'

CHAPTER THIRTY

Tuesday 28th April

Steve arrived at Glen's new Somerset Wisma apartment, on the upmarket Jalan Ampang Road. He took the elevator to the twenty-sixth floor and rang the doorbell. Glen greeted him, and they exchanged pleasantries. The large living room impressed Steve, comfortably equipped with a dining table, chairs and leather suite. A large TV covered a significant part of one wall. He smirked when he spotted the fridge poised by the side of Glen's easy chair, brazenly displaying the sign "Man Cave". Typical Glen. *Idiot.*

Mai came out of the kitchen and bowed.

Steve kissed her on both cheeks. 'Hi, how are you? It's nice of you to invite me to dinner.'

Mai bowed. 'I enjoy it. I love to cook.'

'Beer, mate?' Glen mimicked drinking out of a glass.

'Yes. Thanks.'

'Take a seat. Mai will bring the food. I'm starving mate.' Glen rubbed his tummy. They sat down on the settee to watch the soccer game on TV.

'How are you doing? Nice apartment.' Steve said.

Mai is really nice. Glen is a lazy idiot! What on earth is she doing with him!

'We love it. I've been swimming every morning in the rooftop pool. It's brilliant. I can walk to the office. I love it. Cool.'

'How's Harry and Lauren?' Steve asked

Glen smiled. 'I Skype them every morning before they go to school. But I do miss them. I'm planning on going back for a couple of weeks.'

'Yes you should go back soon...How's Mai?' Steve said.

'She is great. Just lovely, and a superb cook. Mai is smart you know. She trained to be a nurse in Vietnam.' Glen beamed.

'Wow, can she get a job as a nurse in Malaysia?'

'No, she doesn't have a work permit. I'm gonna help her get one. No brainer….and I'm teaching her to use the PC and apps. She is excellent.' Glen said.

'Great. Are you managing OK with money for the kids and expenses over here?'

Glen hung his head. 'Nah not really. I'm behind on my expenses from Roger. Still waiting. It's been over six weeks since I sent him an expense claim, and I still haven't received payment. Without the prepaid card Farid gave me, what would I do?'

'I'm worried you're taking money from Farid. Could be dodgy,' Steve said.

'Dodgy. How can it be? Just don't tell Roger. I need my expenses paid.'

'I can't talk about it now. There's something going on in Q7.' Steve's forehead creased with worry.

Glen leaned closer to Steve. 'What things? It's going well. The Seguro system is up and running. Oh, and Prem Jothi, you talked about him last time. He'll introduce me to sales opportunities in Malaysia and Singapore.'

'Be careful. I don't trust him. Although Cliff Lin said we could get good opportunities from Prem through his contacts.'

'Cliff is right. Prem is going places and can help us bring in more sales to Seguro. No brainer.' Glen gave a half shrug.

'I don't like it. What if Farid and Prem deal in illegal stuff?'

Mai walked over and bowed, 'Dinner is ready now. Can you sit at the table? You like oolong tea?'

'Oh, yes please,' Steve said.

'Mai has made my favourite dishes, Vietnamese garlic, ginger, koay teow, pak choy with soy and oyster sauce.'

'Yes, I go with my friend Tien today. We get fresh food from the market,' Mai said.

Mai served the tea and the starter, then sat with Steve and Glen.

'This is lovely Mai. You not eating?'

'I no want starter, I eat other.'

'Glen tells me you trained as a nurse in Vietnam?'

'Yes, I train in Hanoi. I hope to work in Kuala Lumpur as a nurse. Cannot work until I get a permit.' Mai bowed.

'I hope you get one soon. We can help you get a job in Malaysia. Glen and I have contacts,' Steve said.

'Yes, I like to get a job in a hospital.'

'And you are learning to use the PC.' Steve placed his knife and fork on the plate.

Glen leaned over towards Steve's plate. 'You don't like mushrooms mate?'

'No, I've never liked the texture. Since I was a boy. I can't eat them.'

'Great. Give them here mate.' Glen moved Steve's mushrooms onto his plate and consumed them just as quick.

You tosser Glen. 'Are you enjoying the PC?' Steve asked again.

'Yes, I enjoy. I want to know everything,' Mai smiled.

She retreated to the kitchen and Glen waxed on about Mai's cooking.

'Can you smell the koay teow? Mai is making this for you. It's the national dish of Malaysia.' Glen pointed at the flames leaping around the wok as Mai cooked the main course.

'Looks and smells gorgeous.'

Glen retrieved a glass jug from the fridge and poured a drink into Steve's glass. 'Try this mate. It's fresh icy soya bean juice; good for you.'

'Thanks.' *I'm not your mate. Tosser.*

Mai returned to the kitchen several times to serve a complete banquet of dishes.

Glen showed Steve a bottle. 'You want more chilli sauce mate?'

Steve smiled. 'No, I'm fine. You sure love your food.'

CHAPTER THIRTY-ONE

Wednesday 29th April

The following morning, Farid greeted Steve at the entrance to Farid's Q7 office. 'Welcome my friend, take a seat. How are you? I am sorry to hear the sad news. David was a fine man.' Farid inspected his fingernails.

'I'm doing well, thanks. It's a tragedy. David was a good friend and colleague. It's been a terrible shock,' Steve said.

'I send my sympathies to his family.' Farid nodded.

'Thank you.' Steve felt his face fall slightly.

'Q7 is going well. We increased to over two million transactions per month. I trust Roger agrees with the payments.'

'Yes, thank you.' Steve nodded.

'Did you hear I won the ASEAN Business Advisory Council award?'

'Congratulations.' Steve tried to sound as genuine as possible. 'Did you get any further with the investigations? Any further information from the police?'

'It is fine, Steve. Do not worry. We are aiming for over three million transactions next month. It is a big success.' Farid sat back.

'But David's findings. Did Boon or Rakesh take a look?'

'It is fine. Anil is taking care of that Steve. Do not worry my friend.' Farid's forced apparent nod of agreement told Steve he had failed to convince him.

'We should get more information, so the police can follow up. Do you want me to organise for Mark or another member of the Seguro team to run forensics on the system? You closed our remote access connection,' Steve said.

'Anil's team will monitor the network. We will take care of that.'

'What about access? We cannot update changes or run any of the monthly compliance reports.' Steve gave it another push.

'Anil's team will run the reports. Please send instructions over to him. The system is going well. If we need an update or find a problem, then we will give you access. It was you guys who said there were potential problems on our network. Anil has put measures in place to make our network as secure as possible. So, we must limit access to ensure its secure.'

Steve was very anxious. *This makes little sense. Why would they lock us out of the system if they have nothing to hide? We're helping them.* 'Our contract says we need to access for audit, compliance and support updates.'

'You tell us what you need to run for the audit and we will run the reports every month before our update call.' Farid made a steeple of his fingers.

Steve raised his voice. 'It's not in the contract.'

'Steve, do you not trust us? We are not stupid. We want to protect our network, so we are restricting access for everyone.'

'Our board rules and compliance procedures mean we should run the reports ourselves.' Steve tensed.

'We are a team Steve. A team together. We will give a copy of the report every month to Roger and Anthony.'

'Roger and the Seguro board will not accept that arrangement. I will have to raise this at our next Board meeting.'

'I'm sure Roger prefers to receive increasing payments as we grow rather than minor reports.'

Steve left, concerned and puzzled.

I know he's lying. But we need the money. They've cut us off from the system. David is out of the picture. He said it does not concern me. Fuck!

# # # # # #

As he left the building, he received a call from Sergeant TetLeong, who told him to walk a block to the next corner. Steve arrived at the next block and followed TetLeong into Starbucks. They sat at a vacant table. He questioned Steve about the meeting with Farid. Steve expressed his concerns.

Steve grimaced. 'I don't trust him. He wants me to stay away from questioning their network activities. They even stopped remote access for the Seguro support staff. This means we cannot access the Q7 system for updates, audit and reports.'

'Did he talk about Prem Jothi?' TetLeong said.

'No. I couldn't draw him on what the local police have done since we last met with them. I'm not happy. They're shutting shop. It makes me even more suspicious. I'm meeting with Farid and Prem Jothi next Tuesday. I'll update you.'

TetLeong nodded.

Steve handed over a copy of the mini hard drive to Sergeant TetLeong. 'Can your analysts investigate Q7? This mini drive has the forensics,' Steve said, 'There is a complete image of the Q7 system on here. I can text you the secure vault password. Do you have computer forensic ability in the country?'

'Yes, the Malaysian police have set-up a computer forensic agency.' TetLeong took the drive. 'It's called CyberSecurity Malaysia.'

Steve then sent a text containing the password, 'There you go. Can you get one of your analysts to deliver the forensics as soon as possible? Hopefully, we can prove Farid Razak and Prem Jothi are guilty.'

'Leave it with me.' TetLeong put the mini drive into his pocket.'

'I met with Cliff Lin at the Kuala Lumpur Golf course.'

'Yes, I was there.'

'Ah, sorry. OK, Cliff is a shareholder at Seguro. He's a nice guy. He said Prem Jothi could help me grow the business,' Steve said.

'Do you think Cliff Lin has any connections with illegal dealings in Malaysia?'

'No way. He is a good man, a Christian, who goes to church.' Steve rubbed his temples.

'We have no record of Cliff Lin. He is clean.'

'Oh good. I visited Glen at his apartment on Jalan Ampang.'

'Yes,' TetLeong said.

'Glen lives with his girlfriend Mai. She is a trained nurse from Vietnam, and a great cook. Glen is our sales guy. He's our local man although he also lives in the UK. He spends most of his time in Asia.'

'How long has he been with Mai?'

'Oh. A few months. They moved into a rental together. '

'Can you get her full name? She will have a short-term visa, so will have to fly back to Vietnam at some stage. She only needs two days out of Malaysia for renewal of her visa,' TetLeong said.

'Glen said a while back that he would spend a few days in Vietnam.'

'Where did he meet her?'

'At the Cuban bar. Just bumped into her one night.'

'Was she working?'

'Working? No, she was just having drinks with a friend.' Steve scrunched his nose.

'Women go to the Cuban Bar, Beach Club and other places in Kuala Lumpur to find men. They send money home and pay money to the groups who control the women in the bars and massage shops.'

'So, Mai's a prostitute.' Steve shook his head.

'She may be still paying money to the pimps. Maybe. Does she know Farid Razak and Prem Jothi?'

'Yes. Glen told me she has seen them at the Cuban Bar and Mai is in awe of Prem Jothi,' Steve said.

'Is Glen tied up in this?'

'No. Not Glen. He loves Kuala Lumpur and loves Asian women.' Steve shook his head more rapidly.

'Has he taken any bribes from Farid Razak or Prem Jothi?'

'No. He wouldn't get involved with drugs, money laundering or any other illegal stuff. He's a salesman, so he tries to influence the decision makers to buy from him. That's all.'

TetLeong nodded.

'Oh, wait a minute,' Steve paused for a moment. 'Farid gave Glen a Maybank prepaid card. Glen is spending it on local expenses. I warned him. I forgot to mention Farid also gave David and me a prepaid card each. David suspected problems in the Q7 system, so we didn't use them. We sent emails to each other, confirming our suspicions. I have the emails if you need them.'

TetLeong nodded again. He received a call and left. Steve headed back to the hotel.

CHAPTER THIRTY-TWO

Friday 1st May

Incense Master arrived at a small office on the second floor of an old shophouse near Chinatown. The huge man opened the door and another foot soldier stood next to him. Mountain Master was sitting on a leather chesterfield chair. Incense Master sat opposite.

'I have the pictures?' Incense Master spread them across the coffee table and they examined each one. Mountain Master looked up and smiled, 'Good photos. Clear pictures of Mark Farrell and no pictures of the other man's face.'

Mountain Master beckoned the huge man. 'Take these over to Straw Sandal. Tell him Mark Farrell is staying at the Concorde, floor twenty-one, room 2184. Arrest him as soon as possible.'

The huge man bowed and left the room.

Incense Master nodded. 'I met with Steve Roussos.'

'What did he say?'

'He did not talk about Q7. He wanted information on you and Farid. He said you will get him more business for his company.'

'Did he tell you about his arrest at the border?'

'No.'

'He visited the UK police. They contacted the Kuala Lumpur police. Straw Sandal controlled it.'

'Good,' Incense Master said.

'So, he didn't mention Red Pole, TetLeong?' enquired Mountain Master.

'No, why?'

'Because Red Pole has threatened to arrest him, if he does not keep him informed. Roussos will let him know what is going on in case we need to sort any issues with Q7. However, I have taken steps to put Steve Roussos out of action. Out of action for a long time.'

'Excellent.' Incense Master nodded.

There was a knock on the door and a foot soldier escorted Tien into the room. She bowed and stood at the side of the coffee table in between the two men. They ignored her until Mountain Master said, 'Did you talk to Mai?'

She bowed. 'Yes, Mountain Master.'

'What information did you get?'

'Mai said she could not listen. She was cooking in the kitchen. She talked to Glen after Steve had gone back to the hotel.'

He glared at her. 'What did she find out?'

'Glen says should not use money card Farid gave Glen for spending money. Also, Glen says he will find out more about you.'

'And Q7?'

'Steve is asking questions about Q7.'

'Did Steve Roussos eat any Cendawan?'

'No. Mai say he not eat it. She say Steve not like so Glen eats all Cendawan. Glen is sick today. She ask me for medicine for him for sickness.'

Mountain Master banged his fist on the table and jumped to his feet. 'Tell Mai she works for me. I look after her family and I make them safe. Tell her I own you both. Do you hear me?'

'Yes, Mountain Master.' Tien bowed her head forward, and stayed motionless, eyes fixed on the floor.

'Make sure you bring any information from Mai.'

'Yes, Mountain Master. I will do that. Thank you.'

The foot soldier marched Tien out of the building, into the busy marketplace.

Mountain Master walked over to the window. 'Steve Roussos is a threat which we will address. Straw Sandal will take care of Mark Farrell. He can rot for a long time waiting for his trial.'

Incense Master nodded. 'Yes, we need to complete on the real estate.'

CHAPTER THIRTY-THREE

Saturday 2nd May

Having had little sleep, Steve had spent the whole night trying to figure out what to do next. Thoughts continuously circled around his mind.

He showered, took his daily Valium and dressed before listening to a voice message from a sick sounding Glen. His message told Steve how ill he felt, so he called him.

Mai answered. 'Hello.'

'Oh hi. It's Steve. How are you? How is Glen?'

'I OK. Glen ill. I try to get him to eat remedies and food, but not work.'

'It's probably just a virus. Best let him rest and I'm sure he will be better tomorrow.'

'Glen no well. I do not think it a virus. I am worried.' Mai sounded concerned.

'Is he having Chinese medicine?'

'He not eat.'

'What do you mean Mai? Can he eat, or can't he?'

'Every day he only drinks water and two spoons of porridge or two bites of bread,' Mai said.

'If he is eating porridge and bread, and keeping it down, he should be fine,' Steve said, 'Give him plenty of water. Sounds like what Roger and a couple of our guys had in the UK. Did he go to the doctor?'

'I trained as a nurse, and he is ill. Need a doctor. Too weak to walk.'

'Can the doctor visit your apartment?'

'I can only bring him to hospital but he still not moving, so cannot get him there. He is boiling. Head on fire.'

'In the UK, you can get the doctor to visit if he cannot get to the doctors. I'll contact Cliff Chan and ask him to organise a doctor to visit Glen. Thanks for looking after him.'

'I want to look after Glen. He is a good man.'

After Steve ended the call with Mai, he immediately called Cliff Chan and left him a message regarding Glen.

CHAPTER THIRTY-FOUR

Sunday 3rd May

Cliff called Steve back first thing and apologised for the delay in responding. He told Steve that he had heard about a sickness bug that was very common at that time of year. Although it was Sunday he was confident he could arrange for a doctor to visit Glen at home at some stage during the day. Steve was relieved and very grateful that Cliff was on hand to help. Steve immediately informed Mai, who was getting very concerned.

A short time later he called Cliff again, but was greeted by Cliff's voice mail message. Steve was hoping to find out when a doctor would be visiting. He then went over to the apartment to help Mai to look after Glen.

By early afternoon, the doctor had not arrived so he called Cliff again and left another message.

Steve left several more messages for Cliff during the afternoon.

He stayed until early evening before Glen fell asleep, and as he looked relatively peaceful, Steve left him to rest, hoping that a good nights sleep would fend off the bug or whatever he had contracted.

CHAPTER THIRTY-FIVE

Monday 4th May

The hotel was very busy. Steve and Mark were sitting in the lobby after breakfast.

Mark worked on his MacBook.

Steve received a call from Glen's phone, it was Mai. 'Hello Steve, Glen in hospital. They bring here by ambulance.' He could hear the concern in her voice.

'Oh no Mai. They will take good care of him. He is in the best place,' Steve said.

'Am waiting to admit him to ICU. He no breathe. Too much water on his lungs.'

'Intensive care unit? Which hospital?' Steve cushioned the phone between his ear and shoulder, covering his other ear with the palm of his hand.

'Gleneagles in the centre of Kuala Lumpur.' Her voice was shallow.

'I'll come over right away. Does he want me to speak to anyone in the UK? Can you ask him? Or if I can do anything?'

'He not speak. Terrible. The doctor says he could die, I not know how to reach his family. I love Glen.'

'I'll ask Roger to contact his family. He will have the details. I'll come over now. The doctors will help. He's in the right place.'

Mai choked out. 'Please. Very urgent. Admitting now. Hope Glen gets better soon.'

'They will help him breathe. I'll contact Roger.' He tried to reassure her.

'He is going into ICU now. I use Glen's phone. You call me on Glen's phone.'

'OK, I'll contact Roger and meet you there.' His voice quickened.

He ended the call.

'Glen is ill. They've taken him into ICU at the Gleneagles Hospital. It sounds bad.' Steve gave a long exhale.

Mark closed the lid of his MacBook. 'Let's go.'

'I'll go. You crack on with the documentation.'

'Are you sure? Sounds serious. Poor Glen. If you need anything, let me know?' He opened his laptop.

Steve was just about to stand up and get ready to leave when three policemen approached them and stopped just over a metre away.

One officer stepped forward. 'Mr Mark Farrell.'

Mark pointed towards his chest. 'Yes, that's me.' He looked puzzled

'Please stand up, sir,' the officer said.

Mark stood up. Silence accompanied the onlookers seated in the lobby.

Steve stood up too. 'What's going on?'

'Turn to face the wall, sir.' The officer kept his eyes fixed on Mark.

As soon as Mark turned, the officer pulled Mark's arms behind his back and handcuffed him.

'What's happening? What are you doing? You're hurting me.' It filled Mark's voice with fear.

Steve stepped forward to help Mark. A second officer intercepted Steve and pushed him against the wall, causing pain to shoot from his cheekbone, across his nose and eyes.

'We will arrest you too if you don't sit down.' He pushed Steve onto the lobby chair.

Steve stood up again. 'What the fuck's going on?'

One officer read from a card, the Malaysian version of the arrest statement. 'Mr Mark Farrell, Under Penal Code 187, Section 377A. Carnal intercourse against the order of nature.

I'm arresting you. It is my duty to warn you, you are not obliged to say anything or to answer questions. Anything you say, whether in answer to a question or not, may be given in evidence. Do you understand?'

Mark had a look of fear across his face. 'I'm a British citizen and demand to speak to the British consulate. I've done nothing wrong.'

They took Mark's mobile phone and laptop then frog-marched him to the hotel entrance. Steve followed.

An officer turned and looked at Steve. 'Back off, sir. Do you want us to arrest you?'

Steve shouted, 'Mark. I'll call the embassy and Cliff Lin. We'll sort this out. Don't worry.'

The officers escorted Mark out of the building to the police car. They pushed Mark into the car and an officer sat either side of him. The other jumped into the driver's seat and they drove off.

# # # # # #

Steve contacted the British Embassy and Roger on his way to the hospital. He also finally spoke to Cliff Lin. Cliff explained that he was having problems with his mobile phone, so he had to replace it.

The taxi dropped him outside the hospital entrance, he paid the driver and called Mai to check the way to the ICU ward. She said she would come down to meet him.

He waited for her just inside the entrance. The hospital branched off into three wide and very busy corridors: Patients in wheelchairs and on stretchers accompanied by hospital porters; nurses, doctors and visitors busily passing back and forth. It reminded him of a busy Saturday morning shopping centre. He spotted Mai clearly distressed. He walked towards her. As soon as she saw him she stopped, put her hand to her mouth, looked down and cried. Steve ran to meet her. Her eyes were bloodshot and the surrounding face red from crying and lack of sleep. He put his arms around her, and she cradled her face into his shoulder, sobbing.

Steve reached for his handkerchief and gave it to her. 'You must be shattered. Thanks for everything you have done.'

She wiped her eyes and sobbed whilst catching her breath several times.

'Got here as soon as I could. How is Glen?'

Tears streaked down Mai's face. 'He now under intensive care. Hope the water in his lungs clear and he will recover. I pray for him. I phone my family and they pray for him.'

Roger called Steve back. Once he had ended the call, he updated Mai. 'Roger has spoken with Alice, Glen's ex-wife. She's arranged with his doctor in the UK to send over his medical records. Alice is contacting Glen's uncle Patrick to arrange to fly to Kuala Lumpur.' Steve consoled Mai.

'Doctor ask if Glen got insurance as he needs to go on dialysis.' Mai shuddered.

'Roger is chasing the insurance company. I'm sure they are moving as fast as they can…. Let's get a coffee.'

They walked along the corridor past a few wards, to a series of retail outlets including a pharmacy, bank, ATMs, cafes, gift shops, restaurants, hair salon and optician - all contained within the hospital grounds.

'Have you eaten?' Steve said.

'No, not since yesterday.' Her shoulders sagged.

'OK, let's get something.'

They went into the nearest cafe and ordered green tea. Mai chose chicken noodles.

'It's great that you managed to get Glen quickly to the hospital. He is in the best place now.'

'I love Glen. So worried. Who is his wife?' Mai wept.

'Let's not worry about that now. Alice is his ex-wife. I'm sure Glen will be much better tomorrow.'

'Why he get so sick?'

'No one could tell Glen would get so sick. I thought it was just a virus. He was fine when I came to dinner,' Steve said.

'I hope I not make him sick. I talk to the doctor. He not talk to me. Only family. I am not family he says.' Mai looked anxious.

'When they get his medical records, I'm sure they'll find out what is wrong and fix it.'

'Worried for him and worried for my family. Hope Glen gets better soon. They will hurt my family. He will understand. I sick every morning.' Her eyes wandered.

'Wait. You're not making sense. Are you feeling OK? If you are sick, maybe you and Glen have both caught something.'

'I have to tell Glen everything.' Mai sobbed.

A call from Mark interrupted Steve.

'Steve, it's me.'

'Are you OK?'

'Not great. I'm in a cell, in the middle of the police station,' Mark said.

'What?'

'They have only allowed me two calls. I have asked Adam to help, but I worry that he may get into trouble too.'

'What have they said?'

'They have pictures of Adam and me. Adam's face doesn't appear in them though,' Mark said.

'What can we do to get you out?'

'Can you tell the British Embassy and get me a good lawyer?' Mark's voice cracked.

'Yes, I've already contacted the British Embassy but I'll get Roger onto it as well. We'll get the best lawyer. Keep strong.'

Mark continued 'It's not what they charge you with that's fucked. It's how they do it here. They told me the police can arrest you for any reason and hold you for up to fourteen days without charge.'

'The embassy will help.'

'Tell them the police forced a statement out of me. They said they'd fuck me if I didn't cooperate.' Mark's voice cracked again.

'We'll get you out, Mark,' Steve said. *I just can't think what to say. This is so shit!*

'It's fucking awful. They are taking me to the Magistrate's court tomorrow. It's a serious offence so no bail. They'll transfer me to a remand prison to rot.'

'Prison?'

'Yes, to wait for my trial. They said they'll send me to Sungai Buloh Prison.'

'We'll sort it Mark. Keep strong.'

'Thanks, Steve.'

He closed off the call.

'Sorry Mai.' She had finished her meal.

'Let's go to the ICU ward.'

# # # # # #

Mai pressed the intercom at the ICU entrance and one of the nursing staff opened the door. They walked into the ward which contained a circular set of white chest height desks, used by the many nurses and doctors managing the patients. Each patient had their own room positioned along a half moon shape around the ward. Glen's room had a large window overlooking the car parking area and a door leading into a secluded area within the ward. They spotted several hospital staff in room six, so they waited outside. The medical team connected monitoring and lifesaving equipment to Glen by many wires. A pipe to his throat and tubes into his nostrils, connected Glen to machines that beeped and whirred. Once the staff had left the room, Mai and Steve entered. Mai kneeled beside the bed and said a prayer. Glen's face looked gaunt with yellow skin. Mai then explained that they were keeping him sedated, and he was breathing through the tube connected to his trachea. They sat for a while in silence.

'The doctors will get him back to health, then you can talk to him,' Steve said.

'I pray he gets better.'

'This is a great hospital. I'm impressed. He'll be fine.'

'Yes. Good doctors.'

'I'll go back to the hotel now. You should rest. I can call a taxi.'

'No, I stay here with Glen.'

'Are you sure?' He gave her a five hundred ringgit note. 'Take this. Make sure you eat. I will call you tomorrow.'

Mai bowed, and Steve hugged her before he left.

# # # # # #

Steve got back to the hotel room, kicked his shoes off, sat on the edge of the bed and called the British Embassy to update them regarding Mark. He then placed a call to Roger and left him a voice mail. He laid back, arms stretched above his head and legs dangling over the side of the bed. Staring at the ceiling he breathed in deeply and out slowly, his head throbbing, mouth dry, his shoulders felt like they were connected by an iron rod. Feeling hungry and dehydrated, he was trying to think and be objective, but thoughts bombarded his mind, jumping between emotions of concern, fear, anger and stress. He needed an extra Valium.

Roger interrupted Steve's thought process when he returned his call. 'How are you?'

'Not great. Malaysian police have arrested Mark.' Steve's stomach gurgled.

'What? Mark. How?'

'They've framed him. He's in a cell at Kuala Lumpur's central jail, going before a magistrate tomorrow. Looks like they'll ship him off to a prison to await trial.' His words trailed off.

'What have they charged him with?'

'Sodomy,' Steve said, 'They say they have evidence. The bastards framed him.' Steve shook his head in disbelief.

'What do we need to do?'

'I've contacted the British Embassy. He needs a good lawyer.' Steve's brow perspired.

'I'll talk to our solicitor and contact Cliff. We'll find the best lawyer,' Roger said confidently.

'I'm not sure if he will be able to cope in the police station cell let alone prison.' Steve was feeling the pressure, thoughts bounced inside his head like tiny rubber balls.

'We need to get him out as soon as possible.'

'Glen is really bad, he's sedated and in intensive care, hooked up to machines and with a breathing tube in his throat. Is Alice or Glen's uncle coming over?'

'Alice has talked to his doctor in the UK and he has sent over the medical records. They are not sure if Alice will travel or wait as they might need her consent for any emergency operations or other treatment,' Roger said.

'What about insurance?'

'I'm chasing our insurance company. He has excellent health cover under our policy, but they have to check a few things out before they release any money. Until then, I will send money over from the Seguro account.'

'Good. Can you talk to Mai? I think the hospital has already issued more bills.'

'Yes, sure. At least our bank account is looking much healthier.' Roger sighed.

'Good. There could be problems at Q7. They want to run the audit on the system. Without us.'

'But it's not in the contract.' Roger's voice was more concerned.

'Yes. I know. Farid said they are not stupid, and to protect their network they are restricting access for everyone. I said our board and compliance procedures mean we need to run those reports ourselves.'

'We cannot accept this new arrangement.' Roger groaned.

'He insisted his team will run the reports and give a copy to you and Anthony.' Steve's voice spiked upwards as he struggled to talk in a measured way.

'We must raise this at our next board meeting.'

'Farid said he is sure you prefer the payments to increase as we grow. He's got us over a barrel and could stop the commission at any time.'

'Would he do that? Should I talk to him?' Roger's voice was low and cold.

'No, let's wait. I left Farid's office disappointed, frustrated and angry — all at the same time. Let's not be hasty. Once I can think straight, I'll figure out what to do. We don't need this on top of everything else.'

'You focus on Q7 and I'll work with Cliff and the lawyers to help Glen and Mark,' Roger said.

'That's not all,' Steve said after a short pause.' I got arrested when I got off the plane at KLIA. That's just over a week ago.'

'Arrested?'

'Yes. It's complicated. UK police must have alerted the Malaysians.' Anger swelled in Steve's guts.

'But why would they arrest you?'

'The Malaysian police force are investigating illegal companies and gangs in Malaysia. Q7 is under suspicion.'

'Did they take you to jail?'

'No, I agreed to work with them to help. They took my passport. I must tell no one, otherwise they will arrest me.' Steve hung his head.

'I understand. For God's sake, please be careful.'

CHAPTER THIRTY-SIX
Tuesday 5th May

Steve arrived at the street-food centre in downtown Kuala Lumpur. Crowds of people were eating and drinking, in amongst clouds of steam rising from the street food vendors, scattered along Market Street. The hawkers beckoned him to their tables as he walked past them. He reached Tang City food court, at the back of Chinatown's no-frills food market. Unlike some city's well-known street food markets, this place was a big enclosed barn-like structure with stalls around the perimeter, cooled by huge fans. Steve found a table near the Heineken tent and sat on a stool at a red, Formica-topped table. Street hawkers took orders as fast as possible from the people sitting together on the many tables, dispersed across the length and breadth of the market square. Steve ordered a beer from one vendor and a king prawn laksa dish from another.

Adam arrived, sat down on the stool next to Steve, and ordered a cold drink. They shook hands. 'How is Glen?' Adam said.

'He's stable but will need dialysis for the rest of his life unless he can get a new kidney. Whatever it was, it affected both kidneys. I need to call Mai for an update. Let's call her now.' Steve put his mobile phone on speaker and called Mai on Glen's phone.

'Hi, it's Steve. I have Adam with me. Sorry about the background noise. How is Glen today?'

'Glen on dialysis,' Mai said, 'I find help on his blood type. In Malaysia, it is very difficult to find O negative. My friend helps me to get three donors. One thing is I am in a strange place about Glen's wife. She calls the doctor to tell everything to her and not me. My friends ask me.' Fear stretched her voice high and tight.

'Roger talked to Glen's uncle,' Steve said, 'His uncle plans to fly to Kuala Lumpur. Thank you, Mai, for helping find blood for Glen. We'll talk to Cliff and contact the embassy.'

'I will ask my friends if any are O negative,' Adam said.

'Thank you,' Mai said, 'The doctor in the UK talk to Dr Lim. He did dialysis last night. The nurse says he needs this every four hours and they have only one pack of O negative blood for him. His creatinine is 2151 means the kidneys are not working properly and could be kidney disease. This is bad, and the doctor not know what is wrong with him. My friend from Vietnam ready to give blood in case he needs extra. His red count low so I wait to see how he is later. I ask Tien to find if right blood group and tell the doctor, but they not talk as I am not family.'

'Thanks for the update Mai. I'll tell Roger and ask him to talk to Cliff Lin,' Steve said.

'Now I go to Glen,' Mai said.

'Do you need anything?'

'I not think of.'

'Let me know if there is any change and if you need anything?' Steve said.

Steve ended the call. 'Hope they can sort Glen out.'

'Yes, and Mai is under so much stress,' Adam said.

'She is great. Mai is staying at the hospital and doing everything she can.' Steve rubbed his temples.

'Yes.... And Mark. I hope we can get him released soon.' Adam nodded.

'I contacted the British Embassy,' Steve said, 'The consular representative will visit Mark tomorrow. If they send him to prison they will help with transferring money into Mark's prison account. He'll need money to buy necessities. They will also request a prison visit.'

'We need to find a way to get him out,' Adam said.

'Mark said you were trying to help. Do you have any ideas? Someone has taken photos and handed them to the police.'

Adams eyes flashed with anger. 'Mark believes someone framed him. The photos clearly identify him with a man, but they do not show any details of this man, only him, which is weird but good news for me .'

'What are we going to do? Do you think your brother could be behind this, he wants to punish Mark, but he is protecting you? Is there any way we can persuade him to help get Mark released?'

Adam considered this. 'My brother is a proud and ambitious business man with very good connections. He would not be happy if I was arrested too. I can speak to him. If he will not help I will go to the police and tell them I am Mark's lover.'

'You can't do that. You'll just end up in jail. Does your brother care for you? I figure he wants Mark out of the way because he knows about you and Mark, or because of what's happening in Q7. Either way we have to get Mark out of prison.'

'Can we work together?' Adam's shoulders flinched with a nervous shrug.

'Someone is trying to destroy my company. They murdered David, Glen is in hospital, and they framed Mark. I'm gonna be next.'

'This is terrible.'

'I raised concerns with Farid about something illegal that David had discovered within Q7 and then came David's murder. Prem is always around Farid. Could your brother be involved in a murder?' .

'My brother is a driven man, but I hope he does not have blood on his hands.'

'I'm sure Farid and maybe even your brother are trying to destroy us. Mark could get twenty years in prison.' Steve hoped he had not said too much to Adam.

'I will talk to Prem,' Adam said.

'Great but be careful. I'm meeting with Farid later today, and I have asked him to invite Prem. I'll let you know how it progresses. If my suspicions are right, then we need to be very careful. Mark is depending on us.'

Steve's phone rang as they shook hands and Adam left. It was Mai calling.

It worried Steve that there may be something wrong as he had only just talked to Mai. To his relief Mai sounded much happier.

'Glen conscious now. He is still in ICU. He is still not stable but improve.'

'That's great to hear.' Some relief came to Steve's voice.

'He is on sedation and needs a dialysis. I call my friend to donate. His type is O negative. The hospital has not enough blood and Glen's type is hard to find in Asia. The doctor said he nearly lost his life and he will try his best to save him. Glen's kidneys are bad, so they will clean them. He is breathing on his own but still with a ventilator. If his condition is better, he will go for CT scan.'

'Can he talk?'

'He is on a ventilator so still not speak,' Mai said, 'Today donors will go to the hospital. Two with same type. I hope they can donate and will help. Glen's red count, haemoglobin is around six, normal man is thirteen. Today they will give blood. Doctor say urgent need. He has bad anaemia because he doesn't have enough. Doctor say need a transfusion because danger of dying. He could have a heart attack from not enough of blood.'

'That's serious. I'm type A. Pity. I wish I could help.' Goose pimples shivered down Steve's spine.

'And creatinine dropped, so very good for Glen. Helps kidneys to work better. His lung water level lower. For kidney, the urologist will insert tube from the bladder to the kidney to clean both the bladder and the kidney. Doctor say Glen not stable yet. Sorry, this message is only overheard talk of the doctor with Alice through the phone. They send a form for Glen's uncle to sign.'

'Glad he's improving, and great your friends are donating the blood. Roger is sorting out the insurance payment. Has the hospital asked for more money? Have you received money from Roger?'

'The hospital asked me to top-up the payment. At this moment, total payment is twenty-two thousand ringgit.'

'I'm sure Roger can cover the costs until the insurance kicks in.'

# # # # # #

Later that evening Steve arrived at the Tegu Gentlemen's Club. This time the concierge asked Steve to follow him.

'Farid, Prem, thank you for sparing the time,' Steve said.

'Always time for you.' Farid ushered him to take a seat.

Steve did not waste time with formalities. 'Malaysian police have arrested Mark Farrell because he is gay. I know it's forbidden in Malaysia, but it's obvious what's happening here.'

'Mark needs to be very careful,' Farid said.

'I know who Mark's lover is. I believe you framed Mark. I'll go to the police to tell them. Do you want me to do that or will you help to get him released?'

'What can we do?' Farid raised his eye-brows.

'You should help me get Mark out of prison and cleared of the charges against him.'

Prem shook his head. 'There is nothing we can do.'

'I have a full copy image encrypted and protected in a secure vault.'

'Of what?' Farid said.

'David created the copy. It's a log of every transaction on the Q7 network. The police in the UK are investigating the murder of David. The image logs the forensics and details the transactions. I will exchange the mini drive with you, in exchange for Mark's release.'

'Do other copies exist?' Prem said.

'No, this is a master mirror image of the data. It's a full image of the servers across the complete network at Q7. I will bring this to you if you arrange for Mark's release.'

'We have done no wrong, Steve. I want to stop this paranoia. So, my friend, I will use my influence with the Malaysian government to help you with your problem,' Prem said.

I don't believe a word they're saying. They're covering up their shit and will stop anyone who gets in their way. I must get Mark out.

'I will tell the police Adam is his lover! You had better get Mark released before I go to the police.' Steve left.

# # # # # #

Once Steve was in the taxi, he called Mai to get an update.

'He still on ventilation but can breathe on his own with small oxygen. He signed a form for the operation to clear the urine from the bladder. They ask my friends to stand by for blood just in case. He not talk good at the moment. I pray for him. He is resting. Still weak and need to rest. Doctor says dialysis he need for a long time. Kidneys' terrible.'

'Wish him well from all of us,' Steve said.

Mai continued, 'Doctor suggest more operation to insert a urethral stent to help in urination to open the narrowed urethra. To open the blockage. Tube takes urine from bladder out of body.'

'You will be an expert. Thanks for explaining.'

'I am trained as a nurse in Vietnam. Glen creatinine has dropped again so very good. Tomorrow, dialysis again. For the next operation he need two more packs of blood. Heart doctor says because of the high creatinine is best to stay in ICU.'

'OK, I'll come to the hospital tomorrow.'

'I will tell him. The total bill is now thirty-seven thousand ringgit. They have asked for more money. Eighteen thousand ringgit so Glen can have more operation.'

CHAPTER THIRTY-SEVEN

Wednesday 6th May

Adam stormed into Prem's office, pushing past the huge man. 'What have you done?'

Prem stood up, arms open. 'What is wrong?'

'You are my brother and you do this!' Adam pointed his index finger at Prem.

'I would do nothing to hurt you.'

'They have moved Mark to Sungai Buloh Prison. Why?' Adam's cheeks blew.

Prem nodded to the huge man, and he left the room. 'What are you talking about?'

'The police have arrested Mark. They had photographs of both of us together. Are the police going to arrest me too?' Adam shouted.

'Why arrest you?' Prem raised the palms of his hands.

'You know why. If you don't find a way of getting Mark out, the police will be told that I am his lover and they must arrest me too.' Adam leaned on the edge of Prem's desk and thrust his head forward.

'You can't do that.' Prem said.

'Unless you stop this now!'

'My dear brother. I do not want you to be hurt. You need to forget Mark. You'll find new friends.'

'I will not forget Mark.'

'Let me try to help you,' Prem said.

'Can you call now and speak to someone?'

'It will take time.' Prem sat back down.

'We have no time. Steve Roussos can bring you and Farid to justice. What are you going to do?'

'Be careful. Do not trust Mr Roussos. He is working with the police. They are trying to gather information. This is a vendetta against me. Mr Roussos went to the police with the crazy idea that we murdered one of his guys. He is crazy.'

'Steve told me David's car explosion is a murder investigation. The UK police thought at first that it was a terrorist attack, but they've ruled that out now. I hope you do not have blood on your hands. Please help me get Mark out of jail,' Adam said.

'Why do you offend me. I will do what I can. I love you and want to protect you.'

'Then you had better help me.' Adam stormed out of the room.

# # # # # #

Once he was out of the building Adam called Steve. 'My brother says he knows nothing about Mark.'

'I spoke to your brother and Farid yesterday,' Steve said, 'They now know I have a full image of the Q7 network showing suspicious transactions. I agreed to give them the full mini drive image, if they get him released with no charges.'

'If my brother does not get him released, I will go to the police myself. Mark has done nothing wrong. If they arrest him, they should arrest me.'

'No, you can't go to the police,' Steve said, 'If your brother can get Mark out of prison, I will give him the mini drive image. I will need your help.'

'Yes, I will help. I want Mark out of jail.... There is something I need to ask you.'

'What is it?' Steve said.

'Are you working with the Kuala Lumpur police?'

'Who told you that?'

'Are you?' Adam sounded anxious.

Steve hesitated. 'Well, yes. When I arrived back into Kuala Lumpur, the Malaysian police stopped me and accused me of being part of the illegal stuff. They are investigating illegal companies in Malaysia. I told them I'm not part of anything illegal. If I help them with their enquiries, they will not arrest me.'

'So, what are you doing?' Adam asked.

'They assigned an officer, and I have been keeping him up to date with any information I find,' Steve said.

'How can I help?' Adam said.

'You can confirm Mark's release. Stay in contact with your brother and make sure he uses his influence to get Mark released without charge. Once I know he is safe, I'll give your brother the mini drive evidence.'

'I understand' Adam said.

CHAPTER THIRTY-EIGHT

Friday 8th May

Tien arrived at the hospital. She called Mai, who came to meet her at the entrance. They embraced, and Mai cried. They linked arms and went into the waiting area, found a couple of seats and sat down.

'I do not want Glen to die,' Mai said as they talked to each other in their local Vietnamese dialect.

Tien looked concerned. 'I hope he does not die too. But we work for Mountain Master. We have a job to do. Come back. Leave here.'

'No, I want to be with Glen.' Mai took a deep breath.

'Mountain Master wants you back at work.' Tien raised her voice.

'I can't. Glen needs me.' Mai's eyes widened.

'Is Steve also in the hospital?'

'No, he visits Glen a lot,' Mai said.

'Is he sick?' Tien said.

'No. Only Glen is sick. Why do you ask about Steve being sick? I only care about Glen. I love him.' Mai breathed heavily and sobbed.

'We are friends from the same village. We care for each other and we work together. You should come back. Forget Glen.'

'I cannot forget him.' Mai wiped her eyes.

'You need to send money back for your son. We must do as Mountain Master tells us.'

'I am…' Mai paused. 'I am pregnant.' Mai's words trailed off.

'A baby?' Tien pulled a face of shock.

'It is Glen's baby. He is the father.'

'You are in danger, please stop. Mountain Master wants Glen and Steve dead.' Tien shook her head.

'Mountain Master. Did he do this to Glen?' Fear clogged Mai's throat.

'He told me. I am sorry.' Tears streaked down Tien's face.

'Told you what?' Mai flinched.

'Cendawan beracun. Bad mushroom,' Tien whispered.

'Bad mushrooms. The mushrooms you gave me?' Mai trembled.

'Yes, I gave you bad mushrooms. Mountain Master commanded me. You gave them to Glen and Steve.' Tien sobbed.

'No.' Mai's eyes didn't blink as she paused in shock.

'I knew you wouldn't eat the mushrooms. You don't like them. I hoped you not sick. You are my best friend,' Tien pleaded.

Mai stood up and shot Tien a venomous look. 'Why did you do this?'

'Mountain Master gave them to me. He said I must give them to you when Steve was visiting you.' Tears streamed down her face.

'You are not my friend.' Mai's eyes flashed with anger.

Tien stood up and held Mai's hand. 'You are in danger, Mai. I am your friend. I am sorry.' Tien sobbed.

'You are no friend of mine. I love Glen. You tried to kill Glen and possibly kill me.' She walked away.

Tien sobbed. 'Come with me Mai. They own us. They can hurt our families.'

Mai did not look back.

CHAPTER THIRTY-NINE

Saturday 9th May

On arrival at the hospital, Steve went straight to the ward. Glen was sleeping, so Mai and Steve walked together towards the coffee shop.

'How are you? Glen's looking better today.' Steve tried to be positive. 'Roger told me that Glen's uncle is flying over. He arrives tomorrow.'

Mai nodded. 'The doctor says Glen will not die. He needs dialysis for a long time. I need to talk to him.'

'Roger told me the doctors have found the cause. They told Alice he ate something poisonous. So, you saved his life Mai. The poison affected his bladder and kidneys. Also, the problem with his kidneys caused the fluid on his lungs.'

'I tell the doctor. Cendawan. Cendawan beracun.' A pained look marred her face.

'Cendawan? What's that?' Steve said.

'Cendawan beracun. It is a mushroom, a bad mushroom. Sorry. I love Glen. From Tien. She is not my friend. I hate her.' Mai covered her eyes.

'There's no need to cry. It's not your fault. Just something he ate.' Steve tried to be supportive.

'I have Glen's baby. Have a child from Glen.' Mai wept.

Holy shit. Pregnant. No! Typical Glen. He's a liability. 'Slow down, Mai. Are you pregnant? Does Glen know?'

'No. When he is better, I must talk to him. I love Glen.' Mai looked forlorn.

They reached the coffee shop, and they sat down. Steve tried to console her. 'How long have you been pregnant?'

'Seven weeks maybe eight. I want to keep my baby.'

'Talk to Glen when he is stronger.'

'Who is the wife? Why does she not come here? She old wife?' Her eyes narrowed to crinkled slits.

'It's his ex-wife.'

'I hope Glen is better soon, so I tell him I am so sorry. My family is in danger if they find out.'

'What do you mean? Your family is in danger?' Steve leaned closer.

'If I stay with Glen and baby, they will hurt my family.' Mai sank into the chair.

'Who?'

'Kongsi Gelap. Mountain Master. Own me.' Mai sobbed.

'Who is Mountain Master?' His eyebrows pulled together in question.

'Bad man.' Mai looked to the floor.

'Bad man. What do you mean?'

'Prem Jothi,' Mai said, 'He is Mountain Master, very important in Kongsi. He is very bad man. Big secret. Now I tell, I am worried.'

Holy Shit. 'They're a triad gang?'

'Yes.' Mai nodded.

'He can't tell you what to do or control you! You are with Glen now.'

'Prem Jothi make me stay with Glen, and now I love Glen. He makes Tien give me the Cendawan. I cook. Now I worry he sick and not get better.' Mai sobbed.

'Prem Jothi!' Steve said, 'Oh my God! He wants to kill Glen. Hang on… Mushrooms? Isn't that what you gave both of us when I came to dinner?' Steve could not get his thoughts in line.

Fucking Hell! I could be in hospital now. I should be in hospital now. Fuck! I could be dead!

'Yes, I am so sorry Steve. Tien gave me the mushrooms. Please forgive me. I did not know it would make Glen sick.' Her words fell shaky and clipped.

'Let's go to the police together. Just tell them what you have told me, and they will help you and stop him.' It made his blood curdle.

'No, I cannot do that. They will punish my family,' Mai said.

'I'm sure the police will protect you and your family. Glen will look after you. You must tell the police. We need to stop him.' He tried to convince her.

'I am sorry,' Mai said.

'Let me talk to some people. They will help. Don't worry. You should get some rest. Shall I take you back to the apartment? You can sleep?'

Mai shook her head. 'No I stay with Glen. Make sure he is looked after. I am trained nurse, I see delays in the hospital treatment and I see drip fall out of Glen arm. I not like. I will protect him.' Steve sensed a determination in her voice.

# # # # # #

As Steve walked along the corridor to the main hospital exit, he spotted Sergeant TetLeong waiting there. 'Can you help to get Mark Farrell out of jail? They've sent him to Sungai Buloh Prison,' Steve said as he followed TetLeong to the ambulance waiting area.

'No, I cannot. You should inform your embassy,' TetLeong responded.

'I'm running out of options. What can I do?'

TetLeong did not respond.

Steve put his hands in his pockets and stopped walking. 'I've spoken to Mai.'

TetLeong took a notepad and pencil out of his top pocket and said, 'Mai is from Hanoi in Vietnam. She has a large family. Many live in a village just outside Hanoi.'

'Yes. Glen met her in Kuala Lumpur, at the Beach Club. They moved in together two months ago.'

'What has she told you?' TetLeong said.

'Where do I start? Mai is in love with Glen. She's pregnant. About eight weeks. Glen doesn't know.'

'How is he?'

'Problems with his bladder and kidneys,' Steve said, 'Mai saved his life by getting him straight to the hospital. He'll receive dialysis for a very long time. This upset Mai even more. She talked to the doctors and told them that Glen had eaten mushrooms.'

'Mushrooms?' TetLeong said.

'The mushrooms were poisonous. Mai said her friend, Tien gave them to her. Prem Jothi ordered this.'

'How is Jothi involved?' TetLeong asked.

'When I went to Glen's for dinner recently, Mai cooked us a meal including a mushroom dish. I'm very thankful that I hate any kind of mushroom. Glen ended up eating mine as well as his own. Now Glen is in here and we hope they have done enough to save his kidneys. Mai worries that Prem Jothi will hurt her family.'

'Did she give you any more information?'

'She told me he is the leader of a triad gang,' Steve said, 'Do you know Kongsi Gelap?'

'Yes, there many Kongsi in Malaysia.'

'Prem Jothi is Mountain Master. Head of Kongsi Gelap.'

'We need to gather the evidence from her,' TetLeong said.

'She is eager to protect her family and I guess she will not cooperate unless we help her.'

'If she works with us, I will allow her to stay with Glen whilst we are gathering the information.'

Steve nodded. 'I'm going back to the hotel.'

TetLeong nodded and Steve walked back towards the hospital entrance. He hailed a taxi and asked the driver to take him to Petaling Street and not the hotel.

# # # # # #

Steve arrived at Prem Jothi's old shophouse. He started a voice recording App on his iPhone. Prem's minder, tattoo man, opened the door and escorted Steve through to the room where Prem waited. 'Take a seat, Mr Roussos. How are you?'

'Not good Prem. It's my good friend Mark. I don't know what's going on. Have they released him?' Steve skewered him with an unflinching look.

'Did you bring the drive?' Prem gave a dismissive wave of his hand.

'Yes.' Steve took it out of his pocket.

'I will need to check everything is correct.'

'It's here.' Steve held the mini drive in his outstretched hand,' It's a secure encrypted vault. A complete image of the Q7 network.'

Prem nodded to tattoo man, who left the room. He returned shortly afterwards accompanied by a short man wearing a knee-length grey laboratory coat.

'Can you give the drive to my technician? He will make sure everything is in order,' Prem said.

Steve handed it over along with a set of passwords to open the vault on the mini drive. The technician left the room. Steve turned to Prem. 'I talked to Adam, and he is waiting at the police station to confirm Mark's release.'

'Green tea?' Prem sent an indifferent glance about the room.

'No thanks. Mark is in jail as if you didn't know.' Steve glared.

'I hear you have been working with the police.' Prem made a steeple of his fingers.

'They stopped me when I came back to Kuala Lumpur. They will track you down.'

'I am a respected businessman in Malaysia.' Prem raised his voice. 'And a respected figure in Kuala Lumpur.'

The technician came back into the room, stood and bowed. Prem gestured to him to come forward. He walked over to Prem, leaned forward and the technician whispered a few words. Prem nodded before the technician left the room and returned almost immediately with the mini drive. He placed it on the floor in front of Steve and Prem beckoned to the tattoo man who came forward and with a thud stamped his right foot onto the drive. He repeated this several times until it was broken into many pieces. No likelihood of being able to use it again.

'Hang on Prem. I gave you what you wanted. Is Mark free?' Anger spiralled from the pit of Steve's stomach.

'The police arrested Mark because of evidence of sodomy. I am a businessman in Malaysia and I cannot help people who commit serious crimes to go free. Mark will pay for this crime in my country.'

'But I have given you all the evidence. You murdered David, poisoned Glen and framed Mark. You will not get away with this.' Steve's belly went tight with knots.

'Steve, my friend. That has nothing to do with me. You have no evidence. Q7 is not my company, it's a company headed by Farid Razak, and he is doing nothing wrong.'

Steve jumped to his feet and raised his fist. 'You are trying to ruin my company and our families. You won't succeed.'

Tattoo man put his hand on Steve's shoulder. Steve at once reacted by pushing tattoo man's arm away.

Prem told tattoo man to step back. 'There is nothing you can do,' he said, 'Go back to the UK. Never come back to Kuala Lumpur.'

Steve held up his iPhone. 'I've recorded every word and will use it as evidence.' *I'll kill you, you fucker.*

Prem put the palms of his hands on the desk, looked at them for moment before glaring at Steve.'I could sue you for your allegations. Do you have a reputation to uphold Mr

Roussos?' He opened the desk drawer slowly and retrieved a USB stick.

Steve wondered what he was up to.

Prem put the USB stick into the PC and clicked a few buttons on the keyboard. Steve could not see the screen but heard to his horror:

"Can't do this." The sound of Steve's voice.

"What did you say Steve?" The sound of an oriental accent, a woman's voice, with a twang of an American accent.

"I can't do this!"

"But I want you."

"I can't do it."

"Come on Steve. No one will ever know."

Steve froze. *You fucking bastard.*

Prem smiled. 'What would your family think if they knew?

Steve tried to stay calm. 'If you try anything, Adam will hand himself in. He is Mark's lover.'

Prem paused and shouted, 'Get out!'

Tattoo man escorted Steve to the door. He let him out and closed the door behind him.

# # # # # #

Once he was on Petaling Street, Steve called Sergeant TetLeong. 'I met with Prem Jothi.'

'When?' TetLeong said.

'Just now. I tried to persuade him to get Mark released. I told him I was on to him.'

'You said you were going back to your hotel. Did he agree to help?'

Steve answered the last question only. 'No, it failed. He was not interested. Prem Jothi knows we need more evidence. He has framed Mark, and he knows we can't prove it.'

'He has committed a serious crime in Malaysia. No one can get him released.' TetLeong held the official line.

'Adam Jothi is trying to help.'

'Why does Adam Jothi want to help Mark? Adam is Prem's brother.'

Steve composed his thoughts. 'He is a good man, and not happy with his brother. He told Mark that family life is not good for him and the rest of his family. Prem controls them. Adam is a friend of Mark and my friend.'

'Will Adam help?' TetLeong said, 'Prem is his brother. Blood is thicker than water. You shouldn't trust him.'

'I trust him. If I can persuade Adam to get his brother to confess, can we get Mark released and sent back to the UK as a free man?'

'I have no authority to agree on a deal. They are brothers, how can this happen?'

'Look, I offered Prem the mini drive image of the Q7 system. I convinced Prem there were no other copies. He's not aware of the copy I gave you or the master image in the UK.'

'There is another copy in the UK?' TetLeong sounded surprised.

'Yes, it's with the police, although they're not interested.'

'You should hand over all copies.'

'I gave one copy to the UK police. That was before you arrested me. How are your analysts doing? Have they extracted the data?'

'I will check with the team. Let's talk in the morning,' TetLeong said.

'Hey, also, Prem knows I am working with you.'

'It is very dangerous. I suggest you stay at the hotel until I speak to you next.'

CHAPTER FORTY

Wednesday 13th May

Steve had spoken to Glen's uncle Patrick on the phone the previous day and arranged to meet. As he walked into the hospital he spotted Patrick heading towards him along the corridor. Although Steve had only met Patrick, once, when they all went to a football match together, he immediately spotted him, highlighted by the uncanny resemblance to Glen, apart from the bald head they were very similar in stature.

They shook hands. 'How is he?' Steve said

'Not too good I'm afraid. He has taken a turn for the worse.' Patrick wiped away the moisture developing across his brow.

'I thought he was improving?' Steve said as they walked back towards the ward.

'The doctor said he has Sepsis and they are trying to make sure he doesn't go into septic shock. It started last night when Glen's body temperature and his heart rate were both high, and his breathing is not good.'

'Let's hope they can get on top of it,' Steve said.

'He's not peeing. That's worrying them. Sounds as though he is hallucinating and finding it hard to breathe.'

'Do you know what they're doing for him?' Steve enquired.

'Fluid replacement, treating the infection, and other treatments. They are doing their best. I pray that he gets better.' Patrick shook his head.

'He was getting better. Do they know what caused it?'

'Because he's been in intensive care he's vulnerable to infections. That's what the doctor said.' Patrick looked pale and anxious.

As they walked further along the main corridor, Mai came running towards them. 'Glen is not good. Doctor said he has lower platelet count, his heart is pumping, and he has stomach pain. I worry he will die. I love him.'

Patrick hugged her.

Mai sobbed. 'Nurse say low blood pressure and fluid replacement is not working.'

When they got to the ward, the doctor greeted them with bad news. 'Mr Lewis has developed an infection. We are not sure if it is in the kidneys or bloodstream. We are doing the best we can.'

Mai wept, she could not control her sadness. Steve held her close to comfort her.

A tear ran down Patrick's cheek. 'What caused it?' He asked.

'Mr Lewis immune system is not good,' the doctor said, 'He is already sick, and in intensive care. The catheters or breathing tubes can sometimes cause infections. We are doing everything we can.'

Steve gave Mai a handkerchief. 'Can we be with him?'

'Yes, you can.' The doctor nodded.

As they entered the room Mai rushed over to Glen's bedside, kneeled on the floor and prayed.

Steve and Patrick sat in silence.

A nurse and a doctor came in from time to time, to check Glen's progress. His arms were covered in multi coloured bruises.

Two hours later, the doctor asked Patrick to talk outside the room. Steve and Mai followed. 'The Sepsis has worsened. It has caused blood clots to form in one of his kidneys and both of his legs. He is experiencing organ failure. There is no more we can do. He is not in any pain. We are very sorry.'

'How long?' Steve felt the tightness around his eyes and mouth with the strain of trying to keep his emotion under wraps - He wasn't sure why.

'It will not be long,' the doctor said.

Mai collapsed to the floor, sobbing.

Steve helped her up and held her close.

They went back into the room and sat in silence beside the bed. Two nurses carefully disconnected the monitors from tubes connected to Glen and then left.

Glen's expression was drawn; eyes rolled back into his head, his teeth had gnawed his lips until they bled. Each in-breath was deep and laboured. The gap between his in and out-breaths was intermittent. Steve wondered a few times if he was going to breathe at all.

An hour passed. No words were spoken other than a nurse popping her head around the door and asking if they needed anything.

Glen's breathing became more laboured, and he gasped words which Steve could not make out.

Mai was shaking, a low groaning sound bubbling from her mouth.

Glen's chest rose and fell as he took his final breath.

Patrick hurried out of the room and returned with two nurses and a doctor.

The doctor confirmed that there was no sustainable life left in Glen.

Mai screamed and sobbed, 'No, please. Cendawan beracun. Bad. I am so sorry. I love you.'

Steve walked out.

What's happening?

Everything's falling apart.

First David and now Glen.

They did not deserve this.

What have I done?

Have I caused this?
I was so focused on Q7.
Too focused.
Winning the fucking deal.
Desperate to get money.
For success.
Desperate to pay back the loans and keep the house.
To keep my family.
Desperate.
I wish I'd never got involved with Q7, or Farid, or fucking Prem Jothi.
And Mark.
Why? Why?

CHAPTER FORTY-ONE
Thursday 14th May

The taxi arrived at Sungai Buloh Prison, some forty kilometres from the centre of Kuala Lumpur and dropped Steve off outside the visitors' entrance. Directed to the front desk, he handed the visitors request slip along with his personal belongings, to a guard. The guard allowed Steve to keep his bottle of water and his ID documents. The visitor order contained strict instructions: no food items and other articles from outside unless allowed by the records office with the approval of the prison director. Visitors could not bring toiletries and items such as soap, toothpaste, shorts, T-shirts or face towels. The inmates had to buy them from the prison shop.

Two guards escorted him through a large iron gate and into a room which he found dark and cold, but only in appearance and colour. Temperature-wise it was sweltering. The dim light of the room came from two overhead light bulbs dangling from the ceiling, the only natural light seeping through the cracks of the two iron doors on either side. The place smelt like a public convenience. Not necessarily of shit, but the pungent eye-stinging chemical used to eradicate the smell of human waste, which was just as overbearing and stomach churning as raw sewage itself. He found it hard not to feel on constant alert around the guards. A fat, jovial guard conducted a pat down test and asked him if he had surrendered all his personal effects, pointing out that cameras were prohibited. He looked like he had more than a capacity to distribute some serious misery on someone. A second guard unlocked the other thick metal door and Steve was back into the sunshine, then taken through into a large, rectangular grey courtyard, a few plants pathetically dotted around the middle of the void. It was quiet; the guard instructed him to wait inside the corridor on the left-hand side. Shortly afterwards, escorted by two guards, he walked through three sets of armoured gates. Each gate was operated by an armed guard who checked IDs before unlocking the gate. He was lead into a small room and requested to sit down at a table before two officers brought the prisoner into the room. Mark was wearing an ill-fitting green uniform and handcuffs. He towered over the officers like the king in between two pawns on a chess board.

Steve tried to hide his surprise, but failed; Mark was frail, unshaven and looked dreadful. 'I'm so sorry you're in here. How are you coping?' He tried to embrace Mark, before a guard intervened. They sat opposite each other as the guards stood by the door.

'Not great. I'm still in trauma. They put me through an anal search.' Tears welled up in his eyes and his bottom lip quivered.

'Shit, I'm sorry.' Steve slowly shook his head.

Mark was struggling to hold back the tears.' A guard in a green surgical mask probed me. They do this with all new arrivals. I hope he doesn't use the same pair of latex gloves for all new prisoners, especially the drug users. They are on the lookout for tobacco, money, illegal drugs and cigarette lighters; banned in prison.'

'Did you get the money?'

Mark nodded. 'Yes, thanks. I got a toothbrush and a few other things. Before that, I had to use a brown-stained brush, few bristles left and shared by four of the prisoners in my cell. It was disgusting.'

'How are they treating you?'

Mark held his hand over his mouth and shook his head. 'Terrible. They treat us the same. There's equality for everyone, it doesn't matter, you get equal treatment and you get the same food.' Mark explained that even during roll calls, which happened several times a day and were called muster, everybody got the same punishment.

'Do they know you're British?'

'There are no special privileges for anybody. The natural reaction is that we're in it together.'

'Keep strong. We'll get you out.' Steve tried to be positive. Very difficult under the circumstances.

'What I fear most in here is that I will fall ill.'

'I know it's terrible, but you have to stay strong.'

Mark banged his wrists and the chains on the table. 'A prisoner had hepatitis C, but the guards said there was nothing wrong with him. The other night I saw him slumped on his bed with a helpless look on his face. The next morning, he died, and a guard simply erased his name from the white board. It's that brutal. It's awful.' Tears flowed from Mark's bloodshot eyes as he described the predicament of his fellow inmate.

'Do they not have any doctors?'

'The doctor checks you from six feet away, without touching you.' A pained look marred his face.

'I have sad news, Mark. I'm sorry to tell you.' A lump came to Steve's throat, and he struggled to talk. 'Glen died.'

'Glen?' Mark squeezed his eyes shut. 'What? How? Oh no!'

'He died in hospital yesterday.' Steve swallowed the lump in his throat.

'I thought he was getting better,' Mark sobbed.

'He got Sepsis,' Steve said.

'Oh no, poor Glen.' Tears streamed from Mark's eyes.

'Yes, I was there in the hospital. He drifted away.'

'I'll miss him.' Mark leaned forward, pulling the handcuffs towards his head so he could hold his forehead.

'It's tragic. But, now we must focus on getting you out. Are you eating OK? Keeping your strength up?'

'When there's a shortage of food trays, guards dump food into the dipper. The inmates eat from it, with bare hands, even those with scabs on their hands. A prisoner vomited into the dipper. As for the food, it's tasteless. You can either accept the food or go hungry for the rest of the day.'

'Fucking hell. Are you getting any sleep?' Anger spiralled from the pit of Steve's stomach.

'I had to sleep on the cement floor. In solitary confinement with no pillow, no blanket and no toiletries. There's a small window which opens to the corridor, and when they turn off the light, it's pitch black. There's a steel door. It was terrible, Steve. I'm now in a shit cell. It is a bare cell with a two-inch foam mattress placed on the floor, a bucket for bathing and a squat toilet. The jail conditions are shocking.' Darkness crossed his eyes.

'Adam sends his love. He is helping to get you out.'

'Tell him I miss him. I've tried contacting Jamie a few times,' Mark said.

'I'll ask Roger to contact him.'

'No, I asked Roger and he can't get in touch with him either.'

'We'll sort it Mark and get you out. Keep strong.'

'Thanks, Steve.' Mark's eyes clouded over with despair.

CHAPTER FORTY-TWO

Friday 15th May

Prem, Farid, and Adam met at the Sky Lounge on the forty-first floor of The Pearl Residence on Jalan Stonor. They sat in the bar overlooking the thirty-six-metre infinity pool.

Prem bought his luxurious apartment on the thirty-eighth floor three years earlier, and the Sky Lounge provided cocktail and cafe facilities to the owners. The Pearl Residence allowed Prem the sole use of the lounge on request and Prem often used it as a private meeting place.

They sat at one of the cocktail tables overlooking the city. Prem shifted his angry glare to Adam's face. 'Are you going to the police?'

Adam shrugged. 'Yes.'

'Why?' Prem shot him a sour look.

'I have had enough of your control. You framed Mark, murdered one of Steve's team and poisoned the other. And you are trying to control me and Farid.'

Farid leaned forward, and moved his face towards Adam, their noses a few inches apart. 'Prem controls no one. He is a good man. Why take the word of Steve Roussos and Mark Farrell over your brother?'

Adam stood up and shouted at Farid. 'Are you ashamed of what you did to me when I was fourteen? Are you? The police should know?' Tears welled up in his eyes.

Prem ignored Adam's revelation. 'You believe Steve and not me, your brother. You threaten my oldest friend with your imagination. I am hurt.'

'On the word of Islam, I want you to promise me you have no blood on your hands.' Adam gritted his teeth for control.

'Steve Roussos is a very dangerous man. He's trying to ruin Farid's business and ruin my reputation.'

'I do not believe you. Mama and Dewi are afraid of you. I am not. I hope you get what's coming to you. As the words of the Buddha say:

"Know this, O good one:
evil things are difficult to control,
let not greed and wickedness,
drag you to protracted misery."

You are bringing misery to our family. You are not my brother.'

Prem lurched towards Adam, pushed both hands against Adam's chest, and knocked him over. He hit the floor with a thud, as his head banged against the side of the table. Adam rushed to his feet; legs shaking. He put his hand on his forehead, took it away and saw blood smeared across his fingers.

'You're bleeding.' Prem pointed towards Adam's head.

Adam fled the room making a beeline for the pool changing area. He grabbed a towel, held it against his forehead, and rushed down the corridor, slamming the door behind him.

Farid followed Adam and came back minutes later. 'He has left.'

Prem did not respond.

# # # # # #

Steve heard his hotel room doorbell ring. It concerned him, Prem or one of his men might arrive to put pressure on him. 'Who is it?'

'It's Adam.'

Steve opened the door and immediately spotted blood, caked and hardened, clinging to the side of Adam's face. He led him straight into the bathroom to clean his wounds. 'What's happened?'

Adam gingerly touched the wound near his temple and winced slightly on contact. He flicked a few flakes of dry blood from his fingers. 'I had an argument with Prem and Farid. Prem pushed me to the floor.' Adam left the door ajar whilst he washed away the congealed blood. 'My head is throbbing Steve. I hate him. He is not my brother. He wants to control everyone.'

'Will you tell the police?'

'It's difficult.' Adam came out of the bathroom.

'What about Sergeant TetLeong? He is helping us?'

'I am not sure.' Adam shook his head.

'I have some bad news.' Steve bowed his head.

'Is Mark OK?' Adam asked.

'No it's Glen.' Steve coughed. 'Glen caught Sepsis and passed away on Wednesday.'

'Oh no! I thought Glen was getting better. Oh poor Mai.'

'It's terrible…' Steve tensed. 'I've just returned from visiting Mark in prison. He's struggling to cope. We need to get him out.'

'Yes, we do,' Adam said with a determined look.

On hearing his doorbell ring again Steve shouted, 'It's OK, I need nothing tonight.'

'It's TetLeong,' a voice came from behind the door.

Adam gestured to send him away. Steve shrugged his shoulders and whispered, 'I must. I know you don't want to talk to him. Just go into the bathroom and I'll get rid of him.'

Steve let TetLeong in and he brushed past Steve as he walked into the room. 'The analysts have completed the forensics on the mini drive and they have a few questions to ask you. Can you come to the police station to help?'

'That's great. Now we might get somewhere. When do you want me to come?' Steve detected some hope.

'Now.'

'OK. I'll change. Give me a few minutes.' Steve joined Adam and turned on the sink taps and allowed the noise of the water to drown the whispered conversation. 'I'll go with him. You stay here. I'll touch base with you when I get back. Don't worry, I'll not mention anything. The forensics might be enough.'

'Thank you, Steve. I will figure out where I will stay tonight.'

'Look. We still have Mark's room in the hotel. I'll sort you out a key when I get back,' Steve said.

'Thank you.'

Steve left the bathroom, took off his t-shirt and grabbed a shirt from the walk-in wardrobe.

The sergeant retrieved a pair of rubber gloves from his pocket, put them on and pulled out a piece of a plastic strip from his back pocket.

Steve pulled on a clean pair of trousers and bent forward to put on his shoes. TetLeong walked into the changing room. He held the plastic strip in both hands, looped it across Steve's head and moved it down to his neck. As he tightened the noose, Steve felt immediate pain as though a knife had slashed his throat. He gasped and struggled for breath, his face becoming contorted and eyes bulging. Losing consciousness, his breathing became shallow, as the sergeant tightened the strip even further. After a brief murmur and struggle, Steve dropped to the floor.

# # # # # #

Kongsi Gelap thirty-one congregated in the penthouse of the Tun Sambanthan building, central Wilayah Persekutuan district of Kuala Lumpur.

Mountain Master sat at the head of the oval table. 'Is the money flow on track?'

Incense Master nodded. 'Yes, we are on track for the real estate.'

Mountain Master looked towards White Paper Fan and nodded.

'Transactions from Q7 have increased over two hundred and thirty percent this month. It is going well.' White Paper Fan delivered the good news whilst still retaining a deep-set frown on his face.

Vanguard interrupted. 'Flow out is good. Farid has removed Seguro from Q7.'

Mountain Master nodded. 'Have we moved Seguro payments to Grithos?'

'Yes, we moved the payments last week,' Vanguard said.

'We destroyed a copy of the Q7 network. Red Pole has a copy, but Steve Roussos told us he gave the UK police a copy. This is dangerous,' Mountain Master said. 'Glen Lewis is dead and Mark Farrell is out of the way.'

'I talked to Red Pole.' Incense Master plucked at the cuff of his shirt. 'We have problems with Steve Roussos and Mai Le. She told him about the group, Mountain Master and the cendawan. He knows everything.'

'Tell Red Pole to take out Steve Roussos and Mai Le, to stop the threat now.' Mountain Master shot him a venomous look.

'Yes, I have already told Red Pole.' Incense Master crossed his legs and continued to pluck at the cuff of his shirt.

'Yes. Do that. We need to ramp up the offshore flow as much as possible. Take out any risks, however small.' Mountain Master leaned his head slightly to the right and raised his eyebrow.

They nodded and carried on with the rest of their agenda.

# # # # # #

Adam shook Steve and slapped both sides of his face to wake him. 'Steve, Steve.'

Steve stumbled back to the floor as he tried to get to his feet. 'What happened? Dizzy.' He held his forehead.

'Are you all right?' Adam kneeled beside him.

217

Steve rubbed his throat. 'Head's spinning. Feeling fuzzy.'

'He tried to kill you. I hit him over the head with the marble lamp-stand.' Adam pointed to TetLeong, lying on the floor.

Steve turned his head and spotted the sergeant. 'Oh my God.'

'My brother told me you are working with the sergeant, and now he is trying to kill you,' Adam said.

'What happened?' Steve looked up, dazed and gulped.

Adam pointed to the lamp on the floor. 'I hit him.'

'My God. Is he dead?' Steve asked.

'No, he is unconscious. I can feel his pulse. We must get away. Before he wakes.'

He stumbled again, trying to get up off the floor.

Adam tried to support him. 'Are you all right? Can you walk?'

'I'm fine. 'Thanks for your help.' Steve shook his head and rolled his shoulders. 'I'm OK now adrenaline has kicked in. I must grab my stuff.'

'We must go now.'

Steve got to his feet and put his laptop, iPad and cables into his briefcase, opened the room safe and grabbed his wallet, the Maybank prepaid cards and personal items. Picked up his phone and staggered towards the door.

Adam looked at the sergeant. 'He is waking. Let's go.'

Steve put the Do Not Disturb notice on the handle and the door snapped shut. They took the elevator to the ground floor, walked as fast as possible through the lobby and out to Adam's car parked outside the Planet Hollywood restaurant, a short walk from the hotel.

Adam grabbed Steve's arm to support him. 'You look pale.'

'I'll be fine.' He looked upwards and breathed deeply.

They set off, heading east on Jalan Sultan Ismail towards Jalan Ramlee.

The sunlight made Steve's eyes sting. 'How long to the embassy?'

'It is not far but it depends on Kuala Lumpur traffic.'

Steve's neck started hurting, with a dull ache increasing rapidly to severe pain.

Adam turned left onto Jalan Raja Chulan. 'I can try a shortcut. You need to go straight into the embassy once I drop you off. This is Sovereign territory for you. You will be safe.'

'And you, Adam?'

'I will find a safe place.'

'Be careful.'

'I will get Mark out of prison, somehow.' Steve had a determined look.

His phone rang and to his surprise it was Prem Jothi. 'Steve my friend, how are you?'

He put the phone on speaker. 'OK, thanks.'

'You have left the hotel. Where is my brother? Tell him to come back. I hope he is not in danger.'

Steve did not respond.

'I can help you if you work with me. Come over and we can discuss,' Prem said.

'You tried to kill me. I don't want to meet you.' A fine sheen of sweat shone on Steve's upper lip.

'I want to help. I know they will stop you leaving the country. I can help you.'

'You sent the sergeant over to strangle me. Why?'

'I can protect you. You can become a rich man.'

'I have to go.' Steve ended the call. *I'll kill him. If it's the last thing I do.*

'My brother is a dangerous man. You will be safe at the embassy.' Adam focused on the road.

Steve nodded.

'He said he has a video of you?' Adam said.

'Yes, he'll blackmail me. Just like he did to Mark. He is evil.' Sweat erupted on Steve's forehead and he shuddered.

'We must stop him. I will call Dewi.' Adam made a hands-free call.

Dewi answered. 'Are you all right? What's wrong?'

'It's Prem and Farid,' Adam said, 'I must go. Get away.'

'Where are you going?'

'I have to sort out a problem. Will you be OK?'

'Yes, and I will look after Mama,' Dewi said.

'Thank you. Tell Mama I love her. Please do not tell Prem anything. I need time.'

'Please look after yourself,' Dewi said.

He closed the call.

'Hope your sister will be OK?' Steve said.

'She will care for my mama. Prem will not hurt them.'

'I need to convince the UK police to help. I'm also concerned about Mai. She is in danger. You could be in danger.'

'I will leave Kuala Lumpur. Mai could come with me,' Adam said.

'Can we call her?' Steve said, 'To let her know?'

'Yes,' Adam said.

Steve called Glen's phone. Mai answered. He made her aware that he was heading for the embassy, and Adam would take her to a safe place.

Adam turned off the Jalan Ampang main road into Jalan Binjai. He pulled up outside Hotel Nikko, just opposite the British Embassy.

Steve got out of the car. 'Take care. Please call me.'

Adam nodded.

# # # # # #

Steve crossed the road and entered the embassy by the main entrance. He completed the security checks before reaching the desk and talked to an assistant. 'My name is Steve

Roussos. My life is in danger. Someone has tried to murder me. I know who they are. Can you help me? This is a matter of national security, which affects the UK and other countries.'

'I'm sorry to hear that. We can help to guide you to the right people at the local police station.' The assistant smiled.

Steve took a deep breath and closed his eyes for a moment. 'No, it's a local policeman who tried to murder me.'

She nodded. 'Oh dear. Come this way.'

The assistant took details from Steve before taking him through security control and along a corridor into a side room.

'Please take a seat, Mr Roussos. I will ask the Vice Consul to speak with you.'

After a short wait. 'Good afternoon, Mr Roussos, I am Paul Reynolds, Vice Consul at the embassy. My colleague tells me you are in danger.'

Steve introduced himself, his company and explained the contract with Q7. He advised the Vice Consul of David's findings. He told him how he had confronted Farid Razak and Prem Jothi, as well as explaining the details of David's murder, Glen's poisoning and Mark's arrest. 'All arranged by Prem Jothi, head of a Triad gang'. Steve spat the final words out through gritted teeth. There was frustration and disdain wrapped up in his words.

'Sorry, Mr Roussos, slow down a little, please.'

'Oh, sorry.' Steve continued. 'Prem Jothi tried to poison me, and a policeman working for him, Sergeant TetLeong, tried to kill me.'

'What evidence do you have?'

Steve pointed to his neck. 'What evidence? Look at the marks. Is this good enough evidence? TetLeong confiscated my passport, so I cannot escape. I need your help please ' His voice broke.

'My apologies, Mr Roussos. I want to establish the background before I take the next steps,' the Vice Consul said.

'We have the evidence. David Morris captured an electronic image of the Q7 network and illegal transactions onto a mini drive.'

'Do you have the information?'

'I gave a copy to the UK police,' Steve said.

'Ah, that's good.'

'Prem Jothi is Mountain Master, head of Kongsi Gelap, the triad group. They are trying to stop us from exposing the truth. We believe the evidence shows crimes on an international scale.'

'We can help. I'm sure,' the Vice Consul said.

'They're after me!'

'This is UK sovereign soil, Mr Roussos. You're protected. I will arrange a UK emergency travel document for you to replace your passport. You can renew it when you get back to the UK.'

'That's great. Thanks.' Steve nodded.

'We have a few rooms in the embassy and I suggest we make one up for you to stay tonight.'

'Thank you.'

I will talk to the National Crime Agency. Please write down the details of the UK police officers you have already spoken to. In the meantime, I will get someone to escort you to your room and organise food. I will arrange for a doctor to take a look at the injuries you have sustained. Try to relax tonight, Mr Roussos.'

'Thank you, much appreciated.'

CHAPTER FORTY-THREE

Saturday 16th May

Adam arrived at Glen's apartment just after midnight.

Mai opened the door and as soon as she saw Adam she sobbed, face reddened, bloodshot eyes.

Adam hugged her. 'I'm so sorry. Glen was a good man.'

'Thank you,' she said.

They went into the apartment and Adam sat Mai down. 'I know it is difficult.'

'I only think of Glen. My Glen.' She wept.

'We are not safe here. Steve is at the British Embassy. They will protect him.'

'I know not what to do. They take my passport and papers. I cannot leave Malaysia.' She stopped crying and narrowed her gaze.

Adam held her hand. 'We need to get out of Kuala Lumpur. It is dangerous for you here. I will drive up to Penang.'

'I am sorry Adam, but how can I trust you? You are Prem Jothi's brother.'

'I want to help you.'

'How can I be sure you will not take me to Prem?' Mai said.

'Someone tried to strangle Steve. I hit the man over the head with a lamp-stand which gave us enough time to escape. Steve is at the embassy for his own protection. I know he rang you and told you to come with me. We both want to protect you. Do you trust Steve?'

'Yes, I trust Steve, he is Glen's friend. You are brave. Thank you for saving Steve. He is a good man.' She looked towards the floor. 'Why are you not helping your brother?'

'I am in danger myself, Mai as I have made my brother angry. Look at my head. He did this to me. I need to get away'. Adam looked at his watch. 'We should go now. Will you come with me?'

'Yes. I go to Penang, but worried about my family.'

'You need to protect yourself and then you can help your family. We need to go now.'

'How long to Penang?'

'Four hours with a stop. It is two hundred and twenty miles. I have booked into the Evergreen Laurel Hotel on Penang Island near George Town. For us both.'

'Thank you, Adam. I hope Steve is safe.'

She gathered a few belongings, and they made their way to Adam's car.

# # # # # #

Making good headway once they reached the outskirts of Kuala Lumpur, north on the E1, a four-lane motorway.

'I need to focus on the road. The motorway lighting is bad. Many drivers are tailgating, and these coaches are going too fast. I will never get used to motorway journeys in Malaysia. And I am Malaysian!' Adam smiled.

They progressed along the highway: the straight road sandwiched by endless rows of oil palm trees and rubber plants. Mai adjusted the back of her seat and leaned back on the head-rest.

'Two hours to Ipoh. We can stop for a rest,' Adam said.

'Thank you,' Mai said, 'Why are you in danger? Why did Prem Jothi hurt you?'

Adam's eyes watered. 'Because I love Mark.'

'Ah, now I know. Mark is a good man.'

'I need to get him out of prison. It is my brother who has put him there,' Adam said.

'Are you Kongsi Gelap?' Mai asked, 'With Prem Jothi?'

Adam glanced at Mai, 'Kongsi Gelap.... No.' He shook his head. 'My brother? What?'

'You know he is Mountain Master?'

'Mountain Master. No. What?' Adam paused. 'You think Prem is the leader of Kongsi Gelap?' He pushed the words out.

'Yes, I work for your brother. Kongsi Gelap control us.'

'I...I did not know.' Adam fell silent again.

On reaching Ipoh they grabbed some food and carried on the journey to Penang.

'We will be in Taiping in one hour, another hour drive to Penang.'

'It is a long way. Tiring.'

Adam looked at Mai and smiled. 'We are safe.'

'I get sick every morning. Not much sleep.'

'Are you sick?'

'No. I have Glen's baby.' She held her breath.

'You are pregnant?' Adam asked in a stuttered gasp.

'I am sad. Glen will not see his baby.'

'I am so sorry. You should try to sleep,' Adam said.

'Thank you.' She closed her eyes.

Adam focused on the road.

# # # # # #

'Almost there,' Adam said.

Mai yawned as she awakened.

'We are going over the old bridge to Penang Island and on towards George Town.'

They emerged alongside a long stretch of sea-fronted hotels, restaurants and the famous Gurney Plaza shopping mall, then on to the double frontage of the Evergreen Laurel Hotel and into the valet parking area.

'I will check in,' Adam said, 'You go into the lobby and take a seat.'

'Thank you.'

Adam entered the hotel and walked across the vast, crowded lobby to the reception area.

'Welcome to the Evergreen Laurel Hotel, checking in sir?' a receptionist said.

He handed over his passport and credit card, receiving them back along with a hotel key.

Adam walked towards the elevator and motioned Mai to follow.

They arrived at the hotel room, entered, and Adam inserted the key card to activate the electrical appliances and lighting in the room.

'I am happy to sleep on floor.' Mai straightened her dress with long, nervous strokes.

'We can share.' He handed her a phone. 'Here is a new mobile phone which has a local Malaysian number. Please turn off your own phone in case they can track it.'

'Thank you, Adam. You are a good man.'

# # # # # #

Steve made his way to a small restaurant in the embassy that provided breakfast options. He had not had much sleep since arriving the previous evening and was feeling the affects of forgetting his remaining Valium pills. He was the first to enter the restaurant, just as they opened.

The Vice Consul came into the room, sat down at Steve's table and ordered a coffee. 'Good morning, Mr Roussos. I hope you slept well.'

'Fine, thank you.' Steve lied.

'The UK police have arranged a conference call. Unfortunately the earliest they can be available is four PM today. That is eight AM UK time, today, Saturday.'

'OK. Thanks for setting it up,' Steve tried to hide his disappointment.

'Detective Chief Inspector Graham Sproson and Detective Inspector Rebecca Power will be on the call, they are part of the National Crime Agency.'

'Great. They are investigating the murder of David Morris.' Steve nodded.

'I'll get one of my assistants to escort you to the central office for the call at four PM.' The Vice Consul drank his coffee and stood up. 'And you'll have your UK emergency travel document before the call.'

'Thank you. Much appreciated.' Steve shook his hand before he left.

He slowly finished his breakfast. Steve didn't need more time to think, he needed more urgency and action.

# # # # # #

Later that day an assistant led him into the central office. The Vice Consul pointed to the chair next to his. 'Please take a seat, Mr Roussos. We have a link to the UK police using a videoconferencing unit.'

They sat facing a large screen which displayed the two policemen sitting with a recording unit and a writing pad on the desk in front of them. An assistant took notes.

The Vice Consul started the meeting. 'Good afternoon from the embassy here in Kuala Lumpur. Good morning to you in the UK, Detective Chief Inspector Sproson and Detective Inspector Power.'

The officers started to speak, and the Vice Consul interrupted. 'There's a slight time delay on the audio and video so please give plenty of time for everyone to speak. I believe you have met my colleagues from the UK, Mr Roussos?'

Steve nodded. 'Good morning.'

'Good morning, Mr Roussos, I will conduct a formal interview, 'DI Power said, 'Do you want a lawyer present?' She switched on the recorder.

Steve slumped in his chair. 'A lawyer. Why do I need a lawyer?' It concerned him.

'We are investigating the murder of Mr and Mrs Morris. You may wish a lawyer to be present. You brought to our attention details that may help with the case,' DI Power said.

'I've nothing to hide. A triad gang led by Prem Jothi murdered David Morris because he found crimes on a huge scale. Prem Jothi is Mountain Master, head of Kongsi Gelap triad group. They are trying to stop us from exposing the truth.'

'Can you take us through the sequence of events, so we can understand what has happened since you left the UK?' She made a note.

'OK. They detained me on arrival into Kuala Lumpur. They said you had alerted Interpol, and I was under suspicion. They then arrested me.'

'We contacted the Malaysian police, and they informed us there was no basis for further investigation. We didn't contact Interpol.'

'Well, someone from the UK must have contacted them. Customs stopped me at Kuala Lumpur airport. This is confusing. What on earth is going on? It was a Malaysian police officer who tried to kill me.' It was exasperating Steve.

'A Malaysian police officer tried to murder you?'

'Yes. His name is TetLeong. He came to my hotel room and tried to strangle me. If it wasn't for my friend, Adam, I'd be dead.'

'Can you explain how he tried to kill you?' DI Power said.

'Look at this.' Steve pointed to his neck and explained how TetLeong had come to his hotel room, tried to strangle him and how Adam had stepped in to save him.

'For the benefit of the tape, there are deep abrasions around the neck of Mr Roussos and signs of bleeding and bruising. Carry on Mr Roussos.'

Steve explained how Adam had saved him and they made their escape.

DI Power asked, 'Is your friend willing to support your statements?'

'Yes, but there's a problem. Adam is Prem Jothi's brother.'

'You say you left your hotel room. The policeman was dazed. Did you get medical help for him?'

'No, I called the hotel from Adam's car and told them there was a disturbance in my room so they could check. I rang the hotel, again. No one in the room, nothing disturbed. He must have been OK. The lampstand and everything else were in place, according to the hotel.'

'Where is Adam Jothi now? Can we contact him?' The officer asked.

'I think he's in danger. He will help but we need to be careful.' Steve sat bolt upright in the chair.

'Why would he be in danger?' the officer questioned.

'Because he is Prem Jothi's brother.' Steve gave him an incredulous look.

'But we need evidence, Mr Roussos. If we can't get your witness to talk to the police, how can we investigate your accusations?'

'There's a lot of information. I'm sure the local policemen are working for Prem Jothi,' Steve said.

'Do you have evidence?' She repeated.

Steve described his visit to meet with Superintendent Anwar Tempawan, 'It seemed plausible. He said his team would look into the data. It makes sense now. You must have accidentally alerted the bad guys over here. When I arrived in Kuala Lumpur, TetLeong met me and he said he would charge me if I didn't cooperate and work with them. They were just gathering information from me. Then the sergeant tried to murder me. I don't trust the police in Kuala Lumpur. Can you understand why?'

'That's a very serious accusation against the Malaysian police. The evidence needs to be in place. Then we act. We will conduct further investigations and talk again tomorrow. Can Mr Roussos stay another night at the embassy, Mr Reynolds?'

'That's fine if Mr Roussos agrees.'

'Yes please, Mr Reynolds. Much appreciated.'

CHAPTER FORTY-FOUR

Sunday 17th May

The following morning Steve was woken at four AM for a call at five AM.

It was ten PM the previous day in the UK. An assistant accompanied him into one of the side offices in the embassy. She announced, 'Good morning, Detective Inspector Rebecca Power, Mr Steve Roussos is here.' She leaned forward to speak to the conference phone positioned at the centre of the desk.

'Thank you. Good morning, Mr Roussos,' DI Power said.

'Good evening,' Steve said.

'We contacted the Royal Malaysian police. Sergeant TetLeong has no recollection of any meeting at your hotel or any struggle. At the time you said he was with you, he was meeting with a superintendent, at the Kuala Lumpur police station.'

Steve thumped his fist on the desk. 'He is lying. And the superintendent is lying.'

'Calm down, sir,' DI Power said, 'You have no witnesses prepared to back up your story. The policeman in question says he wasn't even there and has made no accusations of any struggle with him.'

'He works for Prem Jothi. I repeat what I told you. They murdered David Morris and Glen Lewis, framed Mark Farrell, and tried to murder me.' Steve crossed his arms in front of his chest.

'I'm sorry, but with no evidence, how can we corroborate your allegations?' She repeated.

'So, you might drop this? This is crazy!'

'We need more evidence. If it concerns you, we can organise with the embassy to fly you home.'

'Does TetLeong know I'm here?'

'Yes, he knows you are at the embassy, but he is not suggesting he will press any charges or contact you,' DI Power said.

'Press charges. This is crazy. He's lying.'

'I suggest you work with Mr Reynolds to organise a flight back to the UK. When you're home, gather your thoughts. If you get more evidence I may be able to help you.'

'Look, I gave you data which exposed them. Guess you've done nothing with it? I'll get more evidence. You'll listen then. Thank you for your time.' A ball of fear formed in Steve's stomach.

'Thank you, Mr Roussos. Safe journey home.'

# # # # # #

Steve waited until just after nine AM before he entered the Vice Consul's office. 'Mr Reynolds, thank you for your hospitality and for arranging the calls.'

'I'm sorry you've had difficulties in Malaysia,' the Vice Consul said.

'The UK police are not interested. My life is in danger. These bastards have murdered my colleagues. We know criminal stuff is going on here and nobody wants to help.' Steve shook his head.

The Vice Consul handed Steve a large envelope containing the official UK stamp and the words "British High Commission Kuala Lumpur." 'Here is the temporary passport. I'm sorry I can do nothing except help you get back home. I can organise a seat on the next available flight to Heathrow if that helps?'

'Thank you, but what about my colleague Mark Farrell? I can't just leave him. They framed Mark, and he is in prison.

Glen has lost the fight for his life. I can't help Mark if I'm in the UK, and no one is listening from the UK police.'

'Has Mr Farrell engaged a lawyer?' the Vice Consul said.

'Yes, one of Mark's friends who lives in Kuala Lumpur has organised one.'

'Then you should be able to return home knowing Mr Farrell is in good hands.'

'He's not safe in a Malaysian prison. I will talk to one of our shareholders here in Malaysia, Cliff Lin. If he is OK, I will return home. I would like to get my laptop and mobile phone to make calls and read emails if you don't mind?' Steve was determined to help Mark.

'That's fine, I will have your things brought to you in the public reception area.'

'Thank you, Mr Reynolds, and thanks again for your help.' They shook hands and Steve left the room.

# # # # # #

Steve retrieved his iPad, notepad, chargers and emergency travel document, leaving the rest of his belongings in the room. He left the room and walked along the corridor, down two flights of stairs into the security area where UK border control personnel manned the X-ray and scanning machines. Once he had reclaimed his briefcase and mobile phone, he signed the release document and walked past the scanners into the public area where many people were waiting their turn to see one of the embassy assistants. He took a seat at a table, turned on his laptop and mobile phone, which beeped several times with text, voice mail and WhatsApp messages. Also, some phone calls; two from Roger, and three from Beth.

Steve received an incoming call. He rarely answered unrecognised calls but thought he should answer the local Malaysian number on this occasion. 'Steve Roussos.'

'It's Adam. I am in Penang with Mai. We drove up yesterday.'

'Are you both safe?' Steve said.

'It is safer here. How are you?'

'I got nowhere with the embassy or the UK police. They checked out TetLeong, but he denied everything, even denying he was hit over the head.'

'Can you stay at the embassy?' Adam said.

'No, they said they can help me get home, but they don't even think there's a problem. I'm coming up to Penang.' Steve thought on his feet.

'You should go back to the UK. It's safer,' Adam said.

'They'll stop me at the airport. The embassy will escort me but they have no jurisdiction if the Malaysian police arrest me. I'm sure Superintendent Tempawan and Sergeant TetLeong will have KLIA airport covered with police.'

'That is a real problem,' Adam said.

'I'm coming to Penang. I'll disguise myself and get a pay-as-you-go phone. Hire a car and drive up.'

'Are you sure?'

'Yes, I'll be there in a few hours. I have this number. I'll call you en route to get details of where you are staying in Penang.'

'OK. It's easy. We are staying at the Evergreen Laurel Hotel.'

'Great.'

He ended the call and turned to a woman sitting nearby in the reception area. 'Can you tell me where I can find the nearest shopping mall, please?' She looked confused, raised her shoulders and talked to him in the local language, Malay.

'There is a mall close by,' said a man sitting next to him, 'One minute away in a car.'

'Oh, thank you. Can I walk?' Steve asked.

'Yes, if you turn left and walk up to Jalan Binjal, you will see it across the road. You will need to use the subway which takes you to the mall.'

'Perfect. Thank you.' He packed his briefcase and exited. As he walked away from the embassy, he could see the large illuminated sign of the Ampang Park Shopping Centre. He tried to look as inconspicuous as possible. Although a short walk, he felt the strength of the sun on his eyes, shoulders and arms, coupled with the humidity, this made him very uncomfortable. He reached the centre and entered the mall via an entrance next to a KFC takeaway. He welcomed the pleasant air conditioning as he viewed an electronic guide to look up men's fashion shops.

His phone rang.

'Steve, it's Mark.'

'Mark, are you OK?'

'It's great to talk to you. It's terrible here. I have to get out. It's frightening.' Mark's voice was hoarse.

'It won't be long. We'll get you out of there.'

'It's horrible. The guards love to beat the crap out of inmates. Won't touch me as they're afraid of western embassies,' Mark said.

'Oh, good. At least they'll leave you alone.'

'The only thing that matters to the embassy is if you are being beaten, otherwise, it doesn't care what happens.'

'They will help.' Steve did not know what to say.

'The guards are crazy if a prisoner fights back. They throw them in the hole for weeks and only give them milk and stale bread to eat three times a day. Two guys got into a small scuffle during the lunch handout yesterday. The guards broke it up and threw them into the hole.'

'Are the other prisoners OK with you?' Steve could not think of anything positive to say.

'I'm keeping myself to myself. They tried to steal my stuff when I wasn't looking, but no one bothers me. Guards beat the shit out of inmates if they get out of hand or complain. I upset a Chinese Malay guy who went mad at me just because

I asked him not to tear apart a newspaper a guard had handed to us in the cell, so he showed me his fist.'

'We'll have you out soon.' *What can I say? Not sure what to do.*

'Not sure how I can carry on. The scary thing is I have no idea what is happening outside the prison. You get to talk to no one and you're cut off from all communication.' Mark's voice jumped to a higher pitch.

'Is it corrupt?'

'The local Chinese are here for drug possession. Most take ice. The guards are selling drugs to the inmates.'

'What's ice?' Steve said.

'Crystal, crystal meth. Ice is the purest and strongest form. So, they tell me.'

'Jesus. And are the conditions any better?'

Mark's voice turned to a lower, angry tone. 'They're fucked up in here. In some parts, it's fifty people per cell, just one blanket, crackers for breakfast, with porridge, and tea, or hot water. Sardines and rice for lunch and dinner, with a bread roll, a piece of chicken to replace the sardines if you're lucky. Only one hour a day in the exercise yard. Besides roll calls and feeding, we're locked in our cell. I daren't get sick in here. There is no medicine. Shit overflows out of the toilets.'

'Are you in that cell?'

'No, I'm along the way, in a low-medium level prisoner cell, as it's called. But I'm sleeping on a hardwood floor, and the shitty food is taking its toll on my physical health.' Mark said.

Steve decided not to tell Mark that he was on his way to Penang. 'We'll get you out, Mark. Keep strong.' He closed off the call.

# # # # # #

The escalator took Steve up to the second floor where he found the menswear shops. He spotted a store called Kirei

Fashion, where he tried on a pair of DKNY jeans, and a multi-coloured shirt. He left the jeans and shirt on, so the assistant packed away his existing clothing into a bag. Once paid, he left and walked a short distance to a sports outlet called "Foot In" to buy Nike trainers and a baseball cap, leaving the shop wearing both items. He went up the escalator to the fourth floor, and into Suntec Mobile/Celcom where he purchased a pay-as-you-go SIM card and cheap phone. He used Google Maps to find the car rental, eight minutes' walk along Jalan Ampang. The shaded bus shelter acted as a long tunnel, stretching a good distance along the Jalan Ampang walkway. Once at the Advantage car rental, he hired a Proton saloon, set the SatNav GPS device to the Penang address and set off to meet up with Adam and Mai.

En-route, he rang Beth. 'It's me, sorry I missed your calls.'

'Is everything OK?' Beth sounded anxious.

'Same shit, different day. Problems at Q7. That's all. You ok?'

He tried to sound as confident as possible.

I'm glad Beth doesn't know what's going on. This is falling apart.

'Yes, I'm fine love. Will you be able to sort it out?'

I hope so. 'Yes, we'll be fine love. Kids OK?'

'Yes, they are fine, and Millie is getting bigger.'

'Ah…'

'And…' Beth said, 'I've finished the lounge… ceiling, walls and skirting boards. Look's great even though I say it myself.'

'That's brilliant love. Well done. I'm proud of you.'

'I'm proud of you too, love.'

'Send my love to the kids,' Steve said, 'Got to go. Will ring you tomorrow. Love you.'

Beth sighed, 'Love you too. Take care.'

# # # # # #

The dulcet tones of the American voice on the SatNav gave a blow by blow direction at every point of the non-stop four-hour journey to Penang. Steve crossed the bridge from the main island to Penang Island and towards George Town. The SatNav instructed, 'Take the third Exit.' The Evergreen Laurel was ahead on the right-hand side of the road and the deep blue sea on the left. The SatNav took the car along the dual carriageway, past the Hotel. It then instructed a U-turn just beyond the restaurant complex.

'You have reached your destination,' the SatNav instructed.

\# \# \# \# \# \#

He drove into the parking lot right out front and paid the very expensive hotel parking rate. He got his briefcase out of the car, and as he walked towards the entrance, Steve spotted the welcoming smiles of Mai and Adam.

'Oh, am I glad to get here,' Steve said.

'How are you?' Mai asked as they embraced.

'I'm good,' Steve lied.

'Let us get you booked in and get a cup of tea to refresh you.' Adam shook hands with Steve.

'A beer for me. Boy, that was a long journey. I'm so glad you drive on the same side of the road as we do in the UK.'

Once Steve checked-in to the hotel they made their way to the coffee bar.

'Why is your brother doing this?' Steve asked Adam.

'My brother was not always an ambitious man. When my father was alive, Prem was a caring person. As a Muslim, he went to the mosque every Friday for congregational prayers. Prem prayed every day at home and loved to come together with the Islamic brotherhood. Now he does not attend the mosque, and I do not think he prays. He has ruled the family for the past eleven years... and his business.'

Mai's eyes narrowed, and her face reddened. 'But he is the head of Kongsi Gelap.'

The sad look on Adam's face prompted Steve. 'Did you-'

'Mai told me everything.' Adam stopped Steve in his tracks. 'In Malay it means Dark Partnership. It's an underground criminal group in Malaysia.'

'I know it is the truth, I worked for him,' Mai said.

'My brother is ambitious, but I cannot believe this. They control drugs, gambling, prostitution and protection for many businesses in Malaysia.' Adam looked dejected.

'Oh, my God. And your brother manages this?' Steve said.

Mai nodded. 'He is Mountain Master. Are you part of the group Adam?'

'I told you already, I am a Buddhist.' Adam looked to the floor.

'Is Farid involved?' Steve said.

'He is close to Prem,' Adam said.

'Prem Jothi is dangerous,' Mai said.

Adam looked up and fixed his eyes on Mai. 'Prem does business with politicians and businessmen. But he cannot be part of the gang.'

Mai's nostrils flared as she became even more emotional. 'He uses women for prostitution and the government do not bother him. How could you not know?'

Adam shook his head. His shoulders sagged.

'So, he must have support from the government and the police,' Steve said.

Mai's cheeks blushed. 'We told to work same hours every day, so they do not arrest us.'

'They are dangerous, 'Adam said, 'criminal men, but they are businessmen. I hope he is not part of this.'

'He is the leader,' Mai said.

'The police officer Farid took me to see must have been corrupt. Superintendent Anwar Tempawan. Do you know him?' Steve enquired.

'No, I do not know him. I am devastated,' Adam said.

'I wonder how Farid and Q7 got involved?' Steve mused.

Adam gazed at the floor. 'Many companies in Malaysia need help from the government to grow. They need help to gain permissions from government officials and protection. Prem and Farid have been friends since childhood. They have helped each other over the years. It could be Kongsi who protect Q7. It is possible.'

'Ah I see, so Q7 run the network for the Kongsi Gelap activities.' Steve nodded. 'Farid funds the network servers, data centres and people. Anil must be the mastermind behind the network. Everyone benefits,' Steve said, 'Now I understand how a very successful company such as Q7 works with the triads, or at least individuals from that company. It's a perfect cover.'

Adam's face soured. 'Prem is not my brother and I need to stop him. I must get my mother and sister to a safe place. He will not hurt them, but he is unfeeling and cruel.'

'How do we stop him? Will you go to the police and tell them Adam?' Mai said.

'No, I can't do that Mai,' Adam said, 'You know. My family will be in danger and they will arrest me for being part of his family. If Prem has so many people working in government and the police in his group, we cannot stop him. He probably gets other people to do his dirty work, and they protect him.'

'Your brother murdered David and Glen, and tried to poison me. When that failed he ordered my death, and Mark put away in a F-ing stinking prison. He has to pay for what he has done.' Steve shifted his angry glare to Adam's face.

'Why are you helping us?' Mai glared at Adam.

'Why are you asking that question?' Adam held his hands out in front of him, in submission.

'He is your brother and you are putting yourself in danger,' Steve said.

'There are many reasons. I did not know he was involved in Kongsi. Since my father died, he has become a furious man. I disappoint him because I am gay, and I am a Buddhist. Prem is ashamed of me. His friends detest me.' Adam seemed to accept the inevitable.

'He has hurt you,' Mai said.

'I love Mark. I told Prem I will tell the police I am gay, if Prem does not get him released. If the police arrest me in Malaysia for being gay it brings shame on him, the family name and the family. He will not allow me to give myself up, he will use his influence and contacts to hunt me down.'

'Would he do that?' Mai said.

'It looks like he will stop at nothing to protect his empire,' Steve said.

Mai shook her head. 'He made me poison Glen. I never forget and never forgive him for that. I am worried for my family, so I told my family in Hanoi to move to my uncle's.'

'That is good. They are safe, I hope. Will you go back to Vietnam?' Steve said.

'They take my passport and arrest me at the airport,' Mai said.

'You are safe here. We will stop my brother and protect you,' Adam said with a determined face.

'Thank you, Adam.'

'Is there anyone in Kuala Lumpur you can trust to give you any information about Prem?' Steve said.

Mai paused then shook her head. 'I not trust Tien and I think other women will tell Tien and Prem. They are afraid.'

'I understand.....I suggest you rest Mai, and we meet up this evening. We could talk over dinner,' Steve said.

'Let's meet in the lobby at say seven thirty?' Adam said.

Mai nodded, and they made their way to the hotel elevators.

# # # # # #

Steve could not rest in his room, so he went for a walk to clear his head. He was feeling very anxious, irritated and was experiencing a slight fever. Thoughts bombarded him. Across the road from the hotel the sea looked turquoise as gentle, rhythmical waves rolled in towards the beach, breaking and lapping on the shore. David's death, Glen's death, and Mark all played on his mind.

Prem must pay for this.

He changed his focus for a few minutes to dream about moving the whole family over to Penang, spending time with Beth and the kids. An escape. The pressure was taking its toll. *Ridiculous thoughts.* He wanted to stop time. Find a gap in which to think. *What the fuck am I going to do?*

After a while, he headed back into the hotel and spotted Mai and Adam emerging from the elevators disguised as lovers. Steve waved.

Adam responded. 'Hello. Where have you been?'

'I needed to clear my head. I walked.' Steve tried to put on a brave face.

'That is nice,' Mai said.

'Yes, across the road, by the sea. Nice breeze, a cloudless day. The fresh air helped me to relax a little.'

'Let's walk down to the left along the front to the restaurants just before Gurney Mall,' Adam said.

They walked along the crowded Main Street, towards the main shopping mall. The spicy scent of nutmegs, a strong smell of belacan shrimp paste and bursts of fragrances wafted along the road. They passed street cafes, restaurants, and even a small funfair. Several market stalls sold what probably are fake clothes, shoes and movies. They spotted a group of restaurants just inside the Gurney Plaza, next to the Go Hotel.

Adam paused. 'Look, my favourite restaurant, Din Tai Fung.' Adam pointed towards the mall. 'Good food and a good price.'

'Let's go there,' Steve said. 'I'm starving.'

They walked to the lower ground floor of the Gurney Plaza, through the food court and into the busy restaurant. The waitress seated them at their table in a matter of minutes.

'I love the interior decor. The wood gives me a calm and Zen vibe.' Adam rubbed his hand along the wood.

Steve looked at the menu, put it down and asked Adam and Mai. 'Can you order a selection for me?'

Adam smiled, and Mai nodded in agreement.

'But we must have Xiao Long Bao, that is Shanghainese soup dumplings with pork filling and Chinese hand-pulled noodles,' Adam said.

They ordered drinks. Mai and Adam chose from the vast list of dishes on the menu.

'Let's work out what to do.' Steve could think of nothing else. 'The UK police are no help. They say there's not enough evidence. It's dangerous. Looks like many of the Malaysian police are corrupt and controlled by Prem. TetLeong denies even visiting the hotel. He's back on the job. I'm sure they'll try to find us.'

Adam paused for thought. 'It is dangerous to stay in this hotel. They may trace our credit cards.'

'Do you think Prem knows you are with us?' Mai asked.

'I doubt Prem knows where I am,' Adam said, 'But I am not sure. They may have alerted border control to stop us leaving the country.'

Steve steepled his fingers and tried to think clearer. 'Leaving the country is out of the question until we bring Prem to justice. I'm sorry Adam.'

'It is dangerous if you stay in Malaysia,' Mai said, 'What can we do?'

'I understand you will not go to the police. And we don't know who is corrupt. Who we can trust.' Steve looked towards Adam.

'We cannot trust anyone,' Mai said.

'Can we find another way of stopping him?' Steve said.

'It is difficult,' Adam admitted.

'The only way we can find proof is to use the mini drive images David created,' Steve said, 'We use forensic tools to trace specifics of every transaction and every movement to follow the money.'

Steve paused whilst he thought. I'm sure we can create enough evidence. But one big problem, I gave the corrupt police an image. Prem destroyed his copy and the UK police have the final one. We're stuffed unless we can get the mini drive from the UK police. Or, we try to get safe passage back to the UK and Vietnam for you Mai. We then go to the police and convince them to give the evidence back to us. A tough task when we can't even leave the country.'

'Hmm.' Adam sighed.

'We could hack into the Q7 network and do a live probe on everything.' Steve sat upright.

'What is a live probe?' Mai said.

'Helps to prove live transactions are fraudulent. Mind you I would have to buy the probe software on the illegal market. Ironic!' Steve shook his head.

'How can you do that? Do we have enough money?' Adam said.

'Yes. A big problem. It'll be difficult using my laptop, and Q7 are not allowing us to access the Seguro system,' Steve paused for thought. 'We need to move out of the hotel as they could trace us to here.'

'We can find somewhere,' Adam said.

'Can we rent an apartment? Is that possible?' Steve looked towards Adam. 'We have two Maybank prepaid cards Prem gave us. They have fifty thousand ringgit prepaid on the cards. As long as I use an ATM away from here. Somewhere in George Town and disguise my face, we should be OK.'

'I know a couple of people in Kuala Lumpur who have friends here. They may be able to help us to find an apartment,' Adam said.

'Sounds good. We could buy the kit we need, and I should be able to hack into our own system.' Steve felt more confident. 'The cards are traceable but unless Prem has registered the user against the card number, we might just be lucky, and our spending will go unnoticed. The irony of spending Prem's illegal money to stop him. What do you think, Adam?'

'We should do this,' Mai said.

We can go to Gurney Mall tomorrow which has a floor dedicated to computers,' Adam said.

'OK. Let's do that,' Steve said.

CHAPTER FORTY-FIVE

Monday 18th May

The following day, Steve, Mai and Adam met in reception. Adam opened some photos on his phone. 'I have found an apartment, close to this hotel, just next to Starbucks. Pictures look good. Mai likes it.' He showed them to Steve.

'Does Prem know the people that own the apartment? We need to be careful,' Steve said.

'No, my brother does not know them.' Adam shook his head.

'Great,' Steve said.

'It's a three-bedroom furnished apartment,' Adam said, 'We must pay a three-month lease in cash, with one month extra to cover any damages. Total cost is four thousand, four hundred ringgit.'

'Looks very nice,' Mai said.

'That's reasonable,' Steve said. 'I'll draw the money out of the Maybank card. Excellent. When can we move in?'

Mai smiled.

'It's ready now so I guess as soon as we pay the money. We could target tomorrow,' Adam said.

'Do they have broadband and Wi-Fi?' Steve asked.

'Yes, I remembered to ask. It is Time Fibre Home Broadband.' Adam read a note containing the details.

'That should be fine, thanks.' Steve smiled and held up a card. 'The concierge has recommended a shop - "TECH GEAR IT HYPER HUB", it's on Jalan Penang in George Town.'

'We can take my car. It is parked only twenty metres away,' Adam said.

'We need quite a few pieces of equipment. Do you have plenty of room in the car?' Steve asked.

'Yes, it is an estate car. We should be okay. Otherwise we can make two trips,' Adam said.

'OK. Great.' They walked towards the hotel entrance doors and headed out towards Adam's car.

Adam set the SatNav, and they drove to the IT shop. He made a hands-free call whilst driving. 'Hello, Dewi, it is Adam.'

'Adam, where are you? I tried to call you. How are you?'

'I am fine. I changed my phone. This is a new number. I need to spend some time away.'

'Mama is anxious.'

'How are you?' Adam said.

'I am fine. We are just worried about you. Prem worries.'

'Prem is not my brother, he has changed.'

'He loves you Adam, and he is sorry. We love you.'

'I do not want Prem to find me,' Adam said, 'Please do not let him have my new number. I need time. I will call you again soon. Give my love to Mama.'

'Please take care and please come home soon. Prem is sorry,' Dewi said.

'We will talk soon. Please do not call me unless it is urgent. Give me time.'

Adam closed off the call.

'I hope they will be OK,' Steve said.

'Yes, so do I.' Adam looked away.

# # # # # #

Mark had tried to ring Steve and also his UK boyfriend Jamie several times, without success. The same happened when he called Adam. He got through to Roger, and he said he was also trying to contact Steve.

Struggling to get through each day, his toughest battle in prison was to maintain emotional balance and not to lose hope. At seven o'clock every morning, hundreds of prisoners in green shirts and shorts poured out of the three-storey, whitewashed cell blocks into the courtyard for the first roll call of the day. Leading the procession were dozens of prisoners carrying black night-soil buckets into which prisoners had relieved themselves overnight. They dumped the contents into a stinking open sewer in a corner of the grounds. The daily schedule made life for inmates as hard as possible.

Sungai Buloh Prison was a terrible place; the most bitter experience of his life. The Malaysian government trained their prison staff and jail police to be as harsh as they could be. Even though the only punishment permitted for misbehaviour was putting a prisoner into an isolation block, the punishment prisoners feared most was being whacked on the bottom of their feet with a guard's nightstick. This caused blood to rush to a victim's head, precipitating a thundering headache and making it extremely painful to stand upright for several days. Every day, the guards greeted prisoners with a mixture of rudeness, hate, torture, beating and kicking. There was no natural light, poor sanitation with few working toilets, poor hygiene with no pure drinking water available, not enough food… and what food was offered was rank, and it was also really difficult to access the telephone. The overcrowding, constant noise, putrid smells and regular fighting between the various groups drove Mark mad.

Once in prison, you are nobody, and you have nothing; no house, no car, no job, no money, no friends or loved ones, no dignity, no freedom. One of Mark's biggest adjustments to confinement was the lack of privacy. Never alone. There were even no doors in the toilets. It was deeply humiliating to come down with diarrhoea and have to relieve yourself in full view of cellmates. Lights kept on all night meant it was hard to sleep.

They shifted Mark into the working block during the day so he had a little respite. Communication was also a big problem. It worried Mark that if he got sick, there was no emergency treatment in the block and the hospital unit was seven security gates away.

The Sungai Buloh Prison guards were ruthless and never listened, so Mark kept as low a profile as possible, following any instructions obediently, with no complaints. International rule prevented the torture of foreign prisoners, but he heard it happening, often without reason. Malaysian guards and fellow prisoners tortured foreigners out of sight, inside their cells. Special forces beat and kicked prisoners, wounding randomly and maliciously without warning. Mark saw four or five guards beating a foreigner because he had a rape case against him. He thought he would be next. Just a matter of time. He was sure he would be a target because he was gay.

Malaysian criminals dominated, ruling the whole block including cell allotment and food distribution. Malaysian guards took bribes from prisoners in return for drugs such as heroin, ice and other narcotics.

Mark was struggling physically and mentally, not sure how much longer he could cope.

# # # # # #

Steve, Mai and Adam arrived at the IT shop. Adam parked just outside the entrance.

'Can I help you, sir?' The assistant looked about fifteen, with child-size hands and a soft complexion.

'Yes, I want to buy computer equipment,' Steve said. 'Hmm, let's start with two Linux boxes. The highest spec you have, please. Two large monitors, two keyboards, and a quality printer.'

'We pre-build Linux systems to a high specification for memory, processor, graphics and storage. Here are the monitors we have today, and I recommend this printer.' The assistant pointed to the components.

'We'll take two monitors, two Linux specification and this printer.' Steve pointed them out. 'Do you take Maybank prepaid cards?' He handed over the card.

'Yes, sir. They use Visa, sir.' The assistant said.

'Do you give discount? We buy many things,' Mai said.

Steve was impressed, and even more impressed when they were given a ten percent discount.

The assistant ushered his colleagues, who emerged from every crevice of the shop, to help gather the kit. The packaged items were then brought out and loaded into the car. They struggled to fit the kit into the car. Adam guided the assistants to put the boxes in the boot and on the back seat. Steve placed a monitor on his lap.

# # # # # #

They arrived back at the hotel and parked in one of the prime spots out front. Adam gave the concierge fifty ringgit and asked him to keep a keen watch on the car.

'We may as well set one of my Linux systems up in the room.' Steve carried a monitor, keyboard and Linux box into the hotel, and up to his room. They unpacked the kit.

'So, what are you going to do next?' Adam asked.

'I'll buy the hacking tools online and download them. It will cost us over ten thousand ringgit. David wouldn't approve as the tools are banned. But it's the only way I can quickly find the information. Otherwise it would take weeks, or even months to find anything.' *Could have done with Mark.*

'The idea is to use the hacking tool to run a deep dive transaction log to trace specifics of every transaction and every movement. I'll drill down with a live probe to everything, encrypted and de-encrypted. I'll use an audit tool to follow the money to get the evidence. The hacking tool does all this. Make sense?' Steve smiled at Adam.

Adam gave a nervous smile. 'Are you going to be able to break into the Q7 system?'

'I should get into the Seguro system OK. Once in, the fun starts. I will then jump onto the onion router as an administrator and drill down from there.'

'Great,' Adam said.

'Using the Wi-Fi in this hotel is risky for the payment and downloading the hacking tools, but I need to crack on. We'll need to use the fibre broadband at the apartment for the actual hacking.'

'I see,' Adam said, 'We should be able to move into the apartment tomorrow. They will confirm with me later today.'

CHAPTER FORTY-SIX

Tuesday 19th May

The following morning they checked out of the hotel and moved into the apartment. Although overlooking the sea, and positioned further along the main road, Steve was happy that they were far enough away from the hotel. He looked out of the window. 'Great view.'

'Adam has found a nice place.' Mai smiled.

'The owner is a friend,' Adam said, 'He is happy to receive the rent money in cash and will keep our location secret. And two minutes' walk from Starbucks.'

'Great!' Steve exclaimed.

Mai helped Adam to connect all the cables under instruction from Steve. Once they had set-up the computers and got online, they had lunch in the flat, before Steve started the investigation process.

'I'm rusty, but I've downloaded the hacking tools and we're ready to go,' Steve said.

Adam asked Steve, 'Is the Wi-Fi working well?'

'Yes, it's not too bad. Not as fast as the UK. I'm setting up the systems, so we can hide our location and our IP address.'

'Great. How will you get into the system?' Adam asked.

'What I'm planning on doing is to make a dummy payment request to the Seguro system on the Q7 network. This is a legitimate request by our system, the firewall should let it through,' Steve explained.

He started the second Linux computer.' I'll be able to trace specifics of every transaction, every movement and deep dive into the log. I'll set myself up with administrator rights which means, with luck and good use of the hacking tools, I'll be able to move around the Q7 onion router.'

'Can we do this without getting spotted?' Adam asked.

'I hope so. I'll use a fixed line VPN or public Wi-Fi deep packet inspection to find anything of interest. It delves into the data to find the information we want to analyse further, even if encrypted. That's how the big cloud services track child pornography on their encrypted platforms and tip off the authorities.'

Adam went out for a short walk. Steve focused on the job in hand. Mai spent time observing Steve's progress.

He remained in the same position for a few hours before he stood up, placed his hands at the base of his spine and stretched. 'Mai, I'm making good progress.'

When Adam returned he asked Steve, 'Did you get to the Seguro solution?'

'Yes, I've set myself up as an administrator, so I have root privileges. I'm capturing the audit log and system log which looks fine to auditors. Live probe to everything on the Seguro system, encrypted and de-encrypted. The plan is to get trails of transaction origins and terminations. I'll focus on getting details of bank accounts, credit cards and bitcoin flow and using this information to look for laundering payments. Follow the money to find the evidence.'

'Can I help?' Adam asked.

'Lots of data crunching required at the moment. I'll then use the penetration tools to hack into the Q7 network server across their onion router. You can help soon.'

After another few hours of probing and number crunching, Steve was struggling to find any information other than standard transactions.

I hope we can find something. We need to nail the bastards.

Adam and Mai had gone to bed. Tiredness was creeping up on Steve; he hoped he had made no mistakes.

I know you wouldn't approve of me using the hacking tool David. But I have to use it.

If only Mark and David were here! I need you both!
Exhausted, he retired to bed.

CHAPTER FORTY-SEVEN

Wednesday 20th May

Steve woke after a restless night of cold sweats and stomach ache. Mai was already up, studying one of the manuals that accompanied the computers.

Steve made them both a coffee. 'You enjoying reading that? It's a bit boring.'

'No, I like to learn as much as possible. Glen was teaching me about PC and Windows.'

'This is Linux. A different kind of Microsoft... How is your reading? I don't mean to be offensive.'

'No, I learn English at school and when I train to be a nurse. I try to learn when in Malaysia,' Mai said.

'That's great... Are you feeling OK?' Steve asked.

'I get sick every morning.' Mai said.

'Do you need anything?' Steve added.

'No. You OK Steve? You sweat and look pale,' Mai said.

'I'm struggling. Insomnia, cold sweats, stomach ache, muscle pains - you name it.'

'You have fever?' Mai asked.

'To be honest, the doctor prescribed me Valium. I left my pills in Kuala Lumpur.'

'Valium?'

'Yes, it's a muscle-relaxant drug to relieve stress,' Steve explained.

'Valium?' Mai shook her head.

Steve opened a browser on one of the computers and looked-up Valium. 'It's call Xanax in Asia.'

'Ah, yes, Xanax. Cold turkey is bad.'

'Yes.' Steve nodded.

'I know. You can buy CBD oil to help,' Mai said.

'CBD oil?'

'Yes. It is drops. Put in mouth. Helps. Very good.'

'Oh that would be wonderful,' Steve felt some hope.

'It is cannabis, but will help.'

'I'll try anything,' Steve said.

'I get for you today.'

'Thank you. You could really help by supplying coffee at regular intervals,' Steve said.

Mai nodded.

Adam entered the room looking as though he had not slept.

After a short time, Mai and Adam decided to go to the local shopping mall to buy food and drink.

Steve returned to the task, changed a few settings and tried an alternative approach to get onto the Q7 network.

On their return Mai said, 'We have shopping. She followed Adam into the kitchen to put the food and drink away.

'Also I have sandwiches,' Adam said.

'Oh, thanks,' Steve smiled.

'I hope you do not mind but these are from Starbucks,' Adam said.

'I love Starbucks,' Steve mocked, 'When in Rome and all that.' Steve carried on with his investigations whilst he sipped his coffee and ate his sandwich. Steve felt a burst of adrenaline. 'Boy, are we on to something.'

Mai picked up her glass of water from the coffee table and pulled up a seat next to Steve. Adam sat on a chair next to Steve.

'OK, I've jumped onto the onion router at Q7.' Steve focused on his computer screen. 'Lots of proxies. Powerful hardware including FTP servers containing content available to buy. It's logging their addresses and it's configured at the deep web level of the internet which supports more advanced sites containing stuff to buy. It looks like stolen identities.' Steve made notes.

'I do not understand. Stolen identities?' Mai said.

'Yes. For sale. It's easy. David was spot on with his findings. Q7 is a marketplace for secure undercover transactions including stolen or created credit cards. Oh my God. David was right,' Steve jotted down more notes. 'Q7 is the trusted network controlling these dealings. They appear to be using a special proxy, TOR browser, encrypted USB/ flash devices to store files, a special password manager programme and VPN to hide their identity. They prefer payment using bitcoins because it's an anonymous way of paying for goods or services. Well, I should say that bitcoin can be tracked but they use the TOR network to conceal the owners. We need to dig much further.'

# # # # # #

Later that evening, Adam had fallen asleep on the chair and Mai had gone to bed... Steve exclaimed loudly, 'Got it. It's here. It's all here!'

'What, what?' Adam jumped up startled.

'They are selling illegal drugs and guns. Wow. Are you listening up there David?' Steve pointed towards the sky. 'Can't believe what we've found.'

'Can we get the evidence without getting caught?' Adam asked anxiously.

'Yes, I jumped onto the other servers across the network and nobody spotted me. However, if they do a system or user log check they will find something odd, so we need to be careful. The penetration tool is flaky so I'm having to use live probes, which could alert them.'

'Can you download the information and then analyse it offline?' Adam asked.

'No. I think we need to do more. Mai, wake up! We have news,' Steve shouted and stretched back in the chair.

Mai came into the lounge, blurry eyed and sat beside Adam. 'What have you found?'

'This is a complete onion router illegal marketplace.'

'Marketplace? You mean buying and selling?' Mai was trying to understand.

Steve displayed a list on one of the monitors. 'Let's go through the sites.' He clicked on the first item and the other monitor displayed the results. 'Right, the first one I found is a hidden site for stolen identities and forged signatures.' He pointed to the second screen. 'Includes stolen or fraudulently created credit cards and prepaid cards. It's a dream. You can buy credit cards with thousands of dollars' credit limit on them for a pittance paid in bitcoins. It's crazy!'

'Is this where the Maybank prepaid cards came from?' Adam asked.

Steve clicked on another item in the list and the other screen changed its display. 'Yep. The irony, eh? That's big business. I found a site which sells illegal drugs including LSD, Heroin, Cocaine, Ecstasy and Meth. Delivered to your bloody door. It's frightening.'

'How does it work?' Adam asked.

Steve stretched his aching back again. 'The buyer changes money into bitcoins, held by Q7 until goods are received, the buyer pays for the stuff, and the seller delivers the goods. Q7 pays the seller in bitcoins and the seller exchanges the bitcoins for money. Easy and you know the best of it, Q7 gets a cut of everything. So Q7 are not selling actual goods, they are the eBay of the dark world.'

'Wow, and your system is helping to complete the payments and give them their commission,' Adam said.

'Same for all stuff for sale. You can buy machine guns and there's also an arms trafficking exchange.' He listed the site options. 'There's bad stuff here. I found a site for trafficking humans, children and slaves. Even a paedophile exchange and hard-core child pornography. Sickening!'

'I am worried. Would Prem Jothi know this?' Mai asked nervously.

'He must know,' Steve replied, 'That's why he is trying to get rid of us Seguro directors and Glen – we know too much. There's big money involved.'

'And Prem makes money from this?' Mai sounded shocked.

'Yes, vast amounts. You can even buy counterfeit money. Look! Crazy! It goes from the sublime to the ridiculous, you can buy banned movies and chemical explosives, even hire assassins and buy content relating to assassinations. Bloody hell, I can buy untraceable machine guns, children and slaves. There's even stolen art and computers, forged signatures, porn, fireworks and other illegal products delivered to your bloody door. Unbelievable!'

'How do they do this? ' Adam shook his head in disbelief.

Steve puffed out his chest. 'It's an onion router using software that acts as a security socket proxy. Their proxy server makes it very difficult to crack the encryption. Every user has to go through this.'

Adam nodded.

'The encrypted proxy is using the public key of each selected node. Look here, by bouncing from one relay to the next, every layer of encryption lifted off for the next relay. Until it reaches an exit node and the unencrypted request can then travel to its destination.'

'I do not understand, but it must be smart,' Mai said.

'This onion router looks weird to a newcomer; most savvy internet users find this tool an easy way to get access to the dark net. The privacy solutions mask your internet identity by encrypting your data and bouncing your access through a myriad of worldwide IP addresses,' Steve explained.

Adam exploded. 'How could Prem allow this to happen and make his money in this awful way?'

Steve and Mai tried to calm him down.

'What's the plan with all the data? Will we catch all traces of the transactions?' Adam asked.

'Yes, as soon as I have gained access to all areas of the network, I'll pull back the data images, so we can record the transactions and follow the transaction trace logs. I can print them off for hard evidence to a hard drive?'

Adam retired to bed that night, looking totally drained and full of anxiety. He did not sleep.

CHAPTER FORTY-EIGHT

Thursday 21st May

The CBD oil had helped Steve to work throughout the night although he nodded off a few times.

He felt the tiredness in every sinew of his body, his brain begged for sleep; sleep overcame him a few times in fitful phases until black coffee and adrenaline kicked in once more, keeping him awake, urging him on until the task was done.

'Bloody hell! This is big.' Steve shouted.

Adam rushed into the room. 'What is it?' He asked hazily.

Mai woke up too and got out of bed to see what was happening.

Adrenaline pumped, Steve explained. 'They're holding mercenary contracts, hidden wikis, and a hidden video archive for paedophile exchanges.'

'Paedophile videos' Adam looked disgusted and quizzical.

'Yes, I've found a lower level location used by black market dealers to sell hard-core child pornography. Men and women sexually molesting babies. Content from assassinations and illegal game hunting. And below that chemical testing on humans and decentralised terrorism orders.'

Adam looked horrified.

Steve continued, 'Looks like you can trace the buyers and the sellers and follow the transactions?' Steve was very focused. 'Lots more work to do. These companies and individuals leave a transaction trail including laundering to offshore bank accounts.'

'I hear about Kongsi getting paid from prostitution and they hide money. The women talk about this,' Mai said.

'Yes, and I think they are doing this on a very big scale. This is huge!' Steve said, 'We need to be very careful. We need to act now.'

'Well done Steve,' Adam said.

Mai nodded.

# # # # # #

'Detective Inspector Power?' Steve said.

'Yes, hello Mr Roussos. What can I do for you?' she said.

'I'm still in Malaysia. When we last spoke, at the British Embassy, I said that I believed a businessman, Prem Jothi, the master of a Triad gang, was responsible for the deaths of two of my colleagues and that he had also tried to murder me. You wanted more evidence. Well, I've gathered more evidence. I want to share it, so it helps to bring these guys to justice.'

'Mr Roussos, I'm working on the murder case of your colleague, David Morris and his wife Patricia Morris. If you have specific evidence that will help us in this matter, please send it over.'

'I have evidence that Q7, the company we have been dealing with over here, is at the centre of a black market for buying and selling, with vast amounts of money raised funding the triad gang that Prem Jothi heads.' He listed the things he had found. 'Buyers and sellers worldwide.'

'If you have evidence connected to the murders, I will help. From what you describe this comes under one of my colleagues at The Fraud Office in the National Crime Agency. I can get somebody to contact you.'

Steve found it hard to conceal his frustration. 'That's disappointing. I aim to prove Prem Jothi murdered David Morris. Once I find concrete evidence, I'll be back on to you. Meantime, yes please get the Fraud Squad to call me on this local Malaysian number.'

He ended the call and walked from his bedroom back into the lounge to update Adam and Mai.

# # # # # #

'I've spoken to the UK police and they don't want to know. They've palmed me off to the Fraud Squad. Someone will contact me. What about the Malaysian police? Can we find anyone, not in the pockets of Prem? Or Malaysian Government officials through the embassy?'

'We must be careful,' Adam said.

Steve pursed his lips together in a faint smile and shook his head. 'I can see why they chose us at Seguro. Converting any currency into another is a dream to Q7. We played right into their trap. We are protecting the thieves. Crazy! In the wrong hands, every payment system or any secure system can be open to abuse. We have security and payments with an active audit. However, Q7 cut Seguro support staff off from the system so we couldn't see what was going on. Couldn't do this in the UK.'

'Yes. This is Malaysia,' Adam mused.

'Let's figure out how we can use the evidence,' Steve said. 'How can we make the most impact? Several things we can do. We've got to be careful. If they rumble us, it'll be difficult to get back in.'

'What can we do?' Mai asked.

'Right, we can send out alerts to the buyers and the sellers saying the police are on to them. Also alert the authorities about the stores, run by the mafia in several countries,' Steve said, 'But as soon as they get wind of this they'll stop us. We only get one shot at that. Stop a lot of buying and selling for a short while. We could close down one or more of the sites. Create havoc and lose them lots of business.'

'Yes, but that would just be temporary,' Adam said.

'Well, if we delete the databases and anything else we can find, it would shut them down, whilst they restore from their

263

backup. Again temporary. As we are an administrator on the Seguro system, we can divert payments or set-up new payment options,' Steve explained, 'That would be another temporary solution, but they would be back...We could take bitcoins. As a percentage, like Grithos.'

'So, move money into another account?' Adam said

'Yes, we could do that, but it's illegal,' Steve answered hesitantly.

'If it's illegal, we become like them. Like my brother.' Adam shook his head.

'Nobody seems bothered, here or in the UK. They are up to bad stuff, so would they be able to chase us down?' A million thoughts rushed through Steve's mind, though he couldn't snatch and hold on to any single one. *Think. Think.*

'But it is illegal, Adam repeated.

'Maybe divert buyer's payments from sellers to us,' Steve continued, 'Now I'm getting carried away. What if we divert funds into Prem's account? Even the seller's payments into Prem's bank account. Authorities and gangs would be after him. We might be better tracking the money flow for Grithos into the offshore accounts. Find out who's behind Grithos. Then we have a case.'

'How does this help to get Mark released and bring my brother to justice?' Adam enquired.

'We need to force your brother to release Mark. Let's focus on the buyers and sellers' transactions, on the Seguro system. We can check this out without getting caught. OK, look here.' Steve pointed to the computer screen. 'Buyers. Most pay in bitcoins. They're not exchanging bank or card details to buy the bitcoins, they must exchange elsewhere. I can't find many who pay by debit or credit cards. Anyway, they're probably stolen cards.' Steve tried to settle on an action.

'What reliable information can you get?' Adam asked Steve.

'We can get the country. We must do a live trace of each transaction, to get their IP address, which gives us their location. There are millions of transactions though, so not practical.'

'What about sellers?' Mai enquired.

'They receive bitcoins and keep them as bitcoins. Can't find the sellers locations,' Steve said.

'Can you get delivery details of the buyers who ordered goods?' Adam asked.

'No, I need to go onto the onion router network to get information. Hey. Odd?' Steve paused.

'What?' Adam said.

Steve released a sarcastic laugh. 'Guess the name of the company who are receiving the commission on the bad stuff?'

'Q7?' Adam guessed.

'No. Grithos PTE Limited.'

'Can you trace the company?' Adam asked.

'I've got the IBAN for the payment which gives me the bank account number and location, plus a postal address in Singapore. What about Lloyd Dodd?' Steve thought aloud.

'Lloyd Dodd?' Adam questioned.

'Oh, sorry Lloyd, is a friend. He works at Goldman Sachs in Kuala Lumpur,' Steve said.

'Yes, I know Lloyd. He is a nice man. Good friend of Glen,' Mai said.

'I'll call him,' Steve said.

Steve called Lloyd and after they had shared a few words about Glen's untimely death, Steve explained the situation that he now found himself in. Lloyd told him that a guy who resembled tattoo man and a police officer had visited the Cuban bar and questioned Lloyd about Steve and Mai. Steve was very concerned and chose not to tell Adam or Mai.

Lloyd offered to help in any way he could, and Steve asked him to get back to him as soon as possible.

# # # # # #

Later that day, Lloyd called Steve.

'Hi, Lloyd, I'll put you on speakerphone, Mai and Adam are here.'

They gathered around the phone.

'Hi,' Lloyd said, 'I am so sorry to hear about Glen. My deepest sympathies, Mai. I can't believe he has gone,'

'Thank you, Lloyd. I miss him so much,' Mai said.

There were a few moments of silence before Steve said, 'What did you find?'

'Grithos PTE is an offshore business based in Singapore. They run the location from a serviced postal address, so no real detail. But, it gets interesting. It's owned by a Shell company based in the US called Columbus Properties NYC.'

'A US firm, eh? How is a Shell company different?' Steve drilled down.

'It's a company which does business transactions but has no assets or operations in the US. It's basically the same as the offshore business in Singapore.'

'So, they are taking the money out of Malaysia to Singapore and then out of Singapore to the US. Perfect,' Steve said.

'It gets worse,' Lloyd carried on. 'Columbus Properties NYC own condominiums in New York, including The Plaza and The Warner Centre.'

'So, they must be worth millions of dollars,' Steve said.

'And they avoid any lawsuits or double taxation because they are a Shell company,' Lloyd advised.

'How can you tell who the owners are? Are the owners names hidden?' Steve leaned forward.

'These companies help avoid taxation in the US. But importantly, they don't use nominee directors in these types of company. So they reveal who the real owners are.'

'Oh, so they don't use a stand-in director. They can't hide, like the old offshore companies?'

'They have registered directors, but they can hide by creating a chain of shell companies,' Lloyd explained.

'Wow. The perfect way to avoid any corporation tax and move money?' Steve smiled and shook his head.

'Yes, South Mounthill LLC another US Shell company own Columbus Properties NYC,. A Singapore Offshore business called Schrader Investments PTE Limited own South Mounthill LLC.'

'So, there's a trail of money flow from Malaysia, via Singapore, on to the US and back to Singapore. And they pick up a ton of US real estate along the way. Perfect.' Steve was aghast.

Lloyd coughed, 'The Schrader Investments PTE Limited directors are ....Prem Jothi, Cliff Lin..'

Steve interrupted,' Cliff Lin? Did you say Cliff Lin?'

Lloyd confirmed, 'Yes, Cliff Lin and the son-in-law of the Malaysian Prime Minister, Ariff Samahon, who works for the government.'

A bug-eyed Steve's mouth gaped. 'Oh my God. No wonder they're trying to shut us up! Cliff Lin.' Steve turned away in an attempt to hide his shock, but his eyes glistened with the pain of the betrayal. 'Prem Jothi and Cliff Lin. Oh fuck. I'm floored by that Lloyd. What do we do next?'

'I'll email the evidence to your new email address. Just let me know if I can help further,' Lloyd said.

'Thanks, Lloyd. Thanks for finding the info. Can you keep this to yourself?'

'No problem, talk soon.'

Adam fell back slumped in the chair. 'Wow. What now?'

Mai looked forlorn, the mention of Glen evoking grief.

Steve stood up, walked over to the window and gazed out. 'Cliff Lin and Prem Jothi hmm. Now I understand.' He turned around. 'Small company with exactly the right solution and commission structure that could be hidden from the rest of

Q7. It must have been a dream find for them. We need to put him off our scent.'

'How will we do that?' Adam said.

'I will call Cliff using Skype and tell him we are in Hong Kong. To put them off the scent? What do you think?' Steve tried to think of the best option.

'They need to believe you have left the country. Yes, Hong Kong. Who is Cliff Lin?' Adam asked.

'He's a Chinese Malay, living in Kuala Lumpur and a shareholder in Seguro. We met him two years ago when we were working with the UK Trade and Industry department in the UK. They hooked us up with the embassies in Singapore and Malaysia. They helped us find partners in Asia. That's when we met Cliff Lin. He invested in us.'

'I have not heard Prem mention him.' Adam shook his head.

'I do not know his name.' Mai shook her head too.

'Now it figures why Q7 awarded us for the payments' solution contract. Cliff Lin knows us well. We must have been the obvious choice. Cliff must have informed Sergeant TetLeong and Superintendent Anwar Tempawan. They fabricated the Interpol alert. Bloody Hell!!' *It all makes sense now.*

Adam sighed. 'What are we going to do? I trust no one anymore.'

'OK, let's look at options,' Steve said, 'We could change the Seguro system to pay as many of the sellers' money into Prem Jothi's account. Do you have the details of Prem's bank account?'

'I can get the details,' Adam said.

'The Mafia groups go crazy, throw a wobbler and go after Prem or Farid or Anil or who knows.'

'What if Prem just leaves the country, with the money?' Adam said.

'Good point. Could we alert a journalist to expose this? We could even use social media to get the story out there.'

Adam leaned forward. 'I have a friend, Eileen Yeong, she is a reporter at The Malaysian Daily. Based in Petaling Jaya, Selangor, west of Kuala Lumpur. I am sure she will agree to visit us.'

'Can we trust her? Does she know your brother? Sorry to be paranoid.'

'I think we can.'

'OK, don't say too much. If you get her to come up to Penang, we can fill her in on the details. Try to get her to come quickly. It's urgent.'

Adam nodded.

CHAPTER FORTY-NINE

Saturday 23rd May

Steve had spent the previous day and night aligning the right timezone combinations to catch up with Beth and the kids. The CBD oil was helping him enormously. The stomach ache and cold sweats had subsided. Although concerned about taking cannabis, he was consoled by the fact that the consensus seemed to conclude that it was not addictive.

He had made further headway going over all the forensic data but needed more computing resources and time to get down to the level of detail required to unlock the data sources.

Adam answered his mobile phone. 'Hello Eileen. Thank you, I will be right down.' He slipped his shoes on. 'Eileen has arrived, I will go and fetch her.'

'Excellent.' Steve smiled.

Eileen followed Adam into the apartment and shook hands with Mai and Steve. 'Steve, it's good to meet you. I recognise you from your LinkedIn profile.'

Eileen Yeong, a confident, slender and well-dressed woman, was sub-editor and head of politics at *The Malaysian Daily*. She had been in the role for over four years, having begun her career covering Southeast Asia politics for a local publisher more than a decade ago.

They sat down.

'What have you got for me?' Eileen asked.

'We have uncovered something big. How can we be sure we can trust you?' Steve said.

'Trust me with what Steve? I'm a reporter. I will report the truth.'

'We don't trust the Malaysian police, and we suspect important government officials of illegal actions.'

'The Malaysian Daily is one of the few press organisations who are not government controlled in this industry. We will report on Malaysian culture even if it involves the police and the government.'

'We are in danger. Will you keep our anonymity and not disclose our location?' Steve enquired further.

'Yes, if that's what you need,' Eileen said.

'Where do we start? Malaysian government officials and businessmen are making money by illegal means, and syphoning it off through Singapore, to the US. They are sending millions of ringgit through shell companies in the US who are then buying real estate, in New York.'

'Who are these people? How are they making money?'

'The businessmen are Prem Jothi, Farid Razak and Cliff Lin. They are from Kuala Lumpur and they are involved with the son-in-law of the Prime Minister of Malaysia.'

'Well, that's big. What proof do you have?' Eileen asked.

Steve explained the background to Seguro's contract with Q7, and the role played by Farid Razak, Prem Jothi and Cliff Lin. 'They set us up to win the contract. We installed our secure payment system, and they now use it for hiding criminal transactions.' He explained the dark net and the syphoning of money to an offshore company in Singapore.

'How did you find the information?' Eileen was writing notes.

'Let me show you.' Steve turned on the large monitor, 'OK, I am on a connection in Penang. I use a piece of software to hop between thousands of servers. We change our connection, and our location, every couple of minutes. This is so they can't track us. Q7 have created an online criminal community using an onion router as a dark net. They use bitcoins, in the main, for online anonymous currencies. The huge scale of the operation suggests it's the hub of an international dark market.'

'So, you are on the Q7 dark net?' Eileen made more shorthand notes on a small pad. Steve could not make out the words. She listened to him, moving closer to the edge of her seat as he progressed his explanation.

Steve showed how he had gained access via the Seguro payment's system and then the Q7 dark net, making sure he was not spotted on their system when they run their security checks. He ran through a transaction flow showing how the bad guys hopped onto a hosted dark net site and paid their fees. He explained the money trail and US shell companies. Eileen made copious notes.

'Schrader Investments' directors are Prem Jothi, Cliff Lin and the son-in-law of the Prime Minister of Malaysia.' Darkness crossed Steve's eyes.

'Have you reported this?'

'We reported our initial concerns to Q7's CEO, Farid Razak. He introduced us to Prem Jothi. Our Chief Technical Officer, David Morris found the first evidence of the dark net. Prem Jothi murdered David,' Steve said.

'Murder! Did you go to the police?' Eileen was shocked.

Steve told her about his arrest at the airport when he had arrived back from the UK and how they had taken him to the police headquarters in Kuala Lumpur to be interviewed by a corrupt superintendent. He also explained Mark's arrest.

'And are you and Mark together?' Eileen looked at Adam.

'Yes, we are partners.'

Eileen sighed. 'Crazy outdated laws here.'

'Prem Jothi killed my Glen.' Mai said, 'He poison him. He died at Gleneagles Hospital.' Mai's eyes watered.

'Oh my God, that is awful!' Eileen gasped.

'They murdered Glen. Tragic! A great guy and a big loss to all of us and especially Mai,' Steve said.

'I'm so sorry Mai,' Eileen said.

Steve was determined to get the story out, 'My guess is Q7 needed us for our secure payment system, and this was set-up by Cliff Lin, one of our investors. However, once David found what looked like suspicious transactions on the system, they tried to silence us...'

Eileen made more notes.

Steve continued, 'One of the Malaysian policemen tried to kill me. Adam saved my life, and I escaped to the British Embassy in Kuala Lumpur. The UK police keep saying there's not enough evidence to arrest Prem Jothi for David's death. They're not interested in drug crimes and money laundering in Malaysia. However, as they are investigating David's murder, which happened in the UK, I need to show them evidence to connect his death to the dodgy business dealings he found, to show why he was killed.'

'Why have you not left the country? You'd be safer,' Eileen said.

'We're not sure if the bad guys have alerted border control, and we can't risk getting arrested as we try to leave,' Steve said, And anyway, we owe it to David and Glen to find enough evidence to convict their killers and get them justice.'

'I can help.' Eileen smiled.

'Can you publish this story and create enough bad press to stop this?'

'I hope so. It's a big story.'

'Great. At last! Someone is on our side!' Steve exclaimed.

'You should talk to the Malaysian opposition party. The wife of Ahmad Rozhan, former deputy Prime Minister of Malaysia. The current de facto opposition leader, and leader of the PKR, her name is Dr. Sarimah Rozhan.'

'She is a good person,' Adam said.

'Where is she based?'

'Their headquarters are in George Town Penang, but I think she is based near Penang Hill. I will arrange for you to meet her. She is head of the opposition party, standing in for her husband. He was the opposition party leader until they sentenced him to five years in prison for sodomy with one of his aides. It is common knowledge and belief that this was a set-up by the government to stop the opposition party's progress. Dr. Rozhan is making great progress opposing the current Prime Minister. Good timing.'

'She sounds as though she might help.' Steve nodded.

'I know her daughter,' Eileen said. 'Arrul Izzah Rozhan. She is a Malaysian politician and the current Member of Parliament for Lembah Pantai, a district of Kuala Lumpur. I am sure she will make an intro to her mother.'

CHAPTER FIFTY

Tuesday 26th May

Mai, Steve and Adam were early for the meeting with Dr. Sarimah Rozhan at her home in Bukit Bendera, located in the north of Penang. They had overestimated the time to drive the ten kilometres, so took a short detour en route and stopped at a tea terrace restaurant. Steve felt oddly familiar with the place, David Brown's on Strawberry Hill Penang, a quintessential colonial restaurant which reminded him of how the British of the past, tried to create their country abroad.

Mai looked worried, 'Can we trust her?'

'Do we have any choice?' Steve shook his head in resignation. 'You are a local, Adam, what do you think of her? Could she be corrupt?'

'No. She has a very good reputation and defends the rights of the people.'

'Do you think she can help?' Mai said.

Adam sipped his water. 'She is in opposition and her husband is in jail. I am not sure how much power she has to do anything.'

'Let's find out.' Steve breathed out heavily.

They left the restaurant and drove the short distance to Dr. Rozhan's house. As they drove along the private road leading up to the house, a grand white edifice stood to attention in the distance. The large entrance gates were opened after they had shown their ID's to the security guards and as they passed through them, Steve spotted a trail of yellow powder running along the perimeter. 'What's the yellow stuff?' Steve peered out of the window.

'Trails of sulphur to keep out the snakes,' Adam answered.

'What?' *I'd like to get hold of some and kill the snake, Prem Jothi!*

As they approached the perfectly cut green lawn leading to the magnificent house, it felt like going back in time to a colonial past.

The assistant ushered them through the main hall and into a large drawing room to meet Dr. Rozhan. For a person in high authority, she looked serene. She wore a striking green and purple head veil which extended to make a complete dress covering her body, except for her hands and face. Dr. Rozhan looked studious in her spectacles. Born in Malaysia, educated in the UK and a mother of six. Her parlimentary seat was in the northern state of Penang, which was vacated after her husband was jailed for five years on sodomy charges against a former male aide. Her Party knew the government had fabricated the evidence, so Dr. Rozhan was elected by the political party to step in for her husband during his controversial imprisonment.

They shook hands, exchanged pleasantries, and sat around a large oblong table.

Steve looked around. 'Thank you for seeing us so quickly. This is a beautiful place.'

Dr. Rozhan smiled and bowed. 'Yes, very British. I love it. Amongst the butterflies, mosses and ferns the colonialists came to escape the fierce heat of George Town below.'

'I can see the attraction,' Steve said.

'Eileen Yeong tells me you bring serious allegations. How can I help?'

'It's good of you to meet with us. Our aim is to get justice for our two murdered colleagues and the release from jail of another colleague. We have found enough evidence to prove corruption within the Malaysian government, Malaysian police and it also involves high profile businessmen in

Malaysia. Can you help us to expose it and get justice?' Steve said.

'You are making serious allegations. We need to be sure of our grounds. The Interior Minister can arrest any Malaysian without trial. No one can challenge convictions. The government has control of the media. They can only operate if licensed by the government. I must be careful. Eileen Yeong must be careful. You need to be sure.'

Steve felt like a broken record explaining yet again the background to the illegal activities and money trail. 'They own condominiums in New York's richest areas. We're sure.'

'Who is responsible?'

'There are at least three prominent Malaysian businessmen and the son-in-law of the Prime Minister of Malaysia. They have at least two high ranking Malaysian policemen in their group,' Steve said.

'If you have the proof, the best way to get justice is to present the evidence to Dr Laksana. He is Malaysia's ex. Prime Minister, in his mid-eighties and longest-serving minister. Dr Laksana has gone on a tirade against Ariff Samahon in recent months, urging the Prime Minister to step down from office because of many scandals. Last week, Dr Laksana again called for him to step down.'

'Could you arrange for us to meet him?' Adam said.

'I will contact him and explain the background to your accusations. Although he has retired, he holds great power and influence in Malaysia. He is a statesman of the Malay ruling party UMNO. He is a leader that the Malay people will listen to. I support the opposition party to UMNO, called PKR. There have been hostilities between the parties, and my husband arrested and imprisoned by the ruling party. I hope he is a just man and will listen. I will try to meet with him and contact you when I find news.'

'Thank you. Much appreciated.' Steve nodded.

# # # # # #

On the way back from the meeting Adam received a call. 'Hi Eileen, yes thank you. We had a good meeting with Dr. Rozhan. She will introduce us to Dr Laksana, who she thinks will help us... Yes, thanks. Why? Who wants to stop the publication? Please let no one know where we are staying. Thank you. Goodbye.'

'What's the problem?' Steve asked anxiously.

'That was Eileen Yeong. The paper stopped the publication. This is a major concern.'

'We need to be careful. We are not safe,' Mai cried.

'That's fucking shit!' Steve said. *What do we do? Who can we believe? Have I caused this? Fuck! Think! Think!*

CHAPTER FIFTY-ONE

Wednesday 27th May

They arrived back at the apartment just after midnight. Steve went straight to bed but could not sleep. Anxious, sweating and heart thumping, he could not shift the adrenaline or the thought of whether they could trust Dr. Rozhan. He decided to call Beth. 'Hiya.'

She replied, 'Hello you, what's the time?'

He brushed his hand through his hair whilst the other hand covered a yawn. 'Two in the morning.'

'Can't you sleep?'

'I'm fine,' he lied, 'Thought I'd give you a shout.'

'We got another letter about the mortgage,' Beth said, 'We need to sort it out Steve, I'm worried.'

'I'll call them tomorrow, don't worry,' Steve said.

'I'm doing my best but it's a struggle. Trying to stretch to cover the bills. Working part-time just doesn't cut it. I'll have to find something full-time. Credit card is nearly at the limit and the house insurance, building content and water bills are all due,' Beth's voice tailed off.

'I'll talk to Roger and get him to send some money over.'

Fuck. Roger won't send any over. That's for sure. Now they have cut us of from Q7, we must be near the overdraft limit again. The pot's empty.

'I'm going to talk to a few contacts about getting back into my old job again; full time. We need the money,' Beth said.

'How can you juggle a full-time job, the kids and everything else including Millie?'

'We've got no other choice, Steve,' Beth said, 'I'll have to get help.'

'As soon as I get sorted here, I'll be back home,' Steve said, 'It'll be OK, Beth. Don't worry.'

Fuckin hope so!

They chatted about the kids and Millie's progress during her pregnancy.

Steve missed home so much.

When will this nightmare end?

CHAPTER FIFTY-TWO
Thursday 28th May

Accompanied by three of her staff, Dr. Sarimah Rozhan travelled to Kuala Lumpur from Penang arriving at the home of Dr Laksana, Malaysia's ex. Prime Minister. They were greeted by an assistant and taken into a large drawing room. They sat at the dining table and the assistant served them tea and coffee. Dr Laksana and one of his staff came into the room. Dr. Rozhan and her colleagues stood up and bowed to acknowledge Dr Laksana as he and his aide sat at the table.

As this was a meeting between two opposition groups, both parties were diplomatic and cagey in their mannerisms and speech, mainly discussing non-political current events. After several topics' Dr Laksana gestured to his aide and assistant, and they both left the room. He nodded towards Dr. Rozhan who asked her own staff to leave the house and wait in the car.

Once they were alone, Dr Laksana held her hand. 'Sorry to hear your husband is in prison.'

She bowed her head slightly. 'Thank you. He is innocent. The Prime Minister framed him. I will carry on in my husband's name whilst he is in prison. I know we are from opposing parties, but you are a good man and Ariff Samahon is an atrocious man.'

'We lobbied for Ariff Samahon to become Prime Minister because of our gratitude to his father, Tun Abdul Samahon,' Dr Laksana said, 'he was my mentor and idol. He paved the way for his son, Ariff Samahon to take over as Prime Minister later. When you are thankful to someone who has died, you want to repay them through their children.'

'I understand.' Dr. Rozhan nodded.

'So, we ensured Samahon's son became Prime Minister. I don't want to betray Samahon's memory, but I cannot keep silent any longer, because of Ariff's terrible actions. I thought I was choosing a good man. Absolute power corrupts even the greatest leaders. He doesn't have to ask the permission of the Cabinet before he does or decides anything.'

'I have information which will help you to remove him from his position.' She pointed to a folder on the table.

Dr Laksana looked across and nodded. 'I know we are on opposing sides but we both have the interest of our country at heart. Thank you for your help and loyalty to our country.'

'The evidence in here proves corruption within the our government, the police and some high-profile businessmen in Malaysia. The corruption is making millions of ringgit for the Ariff Samahon family.' She pushed the folder towards Dr Laksana, keeping her hand on top.

He nodded.

'I need you to help me too,' she said.

'How can I help?' he asked.

'Help free my husband from prison, get the charges dropped. Our parties have differences, but we have Malaysia in our hearts.'

'I will try to help you.'

'One more request. This evidence has been found by a British citizen, together with the brother of one of the corrupt Malaysian businessmen and a Vietnamese subject. Another British citizen has been framed and is in prison. I need you to pardon him, and help all four of them with safe passage back to the UK or any other country of their preference?'

'If they can help to remove Ariff Samahon, we must help them,' Dr Laksana said.

Dr. Rozhan pushed the folder further across the table to Dr Laksana and removed her hand... 'This folder has the details of the bank accounts and companies involved in Malaysia,

Singapore and New York. The shareholding shows details of the ownership trail. The documents also detail the real estate held in the US.' All the evidence is captured electronically on the disk drive included.

'Is there any involvement in drugs?' he asked.

'Yes. The British subjects are computer experts. They found a lot of corruption,' she answered.

'Can you estimate how much they laundered?' Dr Laksana opened the folder carefully.

'The estimate is one point two billion US dollars in sales and eighty million US dollars in commission, so far.'

'When I was in office, I recognised the need for computer forensic ability in the country. I asked the Ministry of Science, Technology and Innovation to set-up CyberSecurity Malaysia under its control for computer forensic matters. I will need their support and to involve our military commanders.'

'I hope this evidence is sufficient for your needs and that we can reach a mutually beneficial and positive outcome. Contact me again if you need any further assistance' Dr. Rozhan said.

'Thank you', Dr Laksana smiled.

They both stood up, bowed to each other and Dr. Rozhan left the room and joined her staff for the journey back to Penang.

CHAPTER FIFTY-THREE

Monday 1st June

A representative of Dr Laksana had called Steve the previous day and asked to meet. Steve was fearful of going back to Kuala Lumpur, but he felt they had no choice but to trust Dr Laksana.

After the long journey, they reached the city. They headed along the handsome tree-lined avenue of a large private house and diplomatic residence, past the Royal Selangor Golf Club in the north area of the city.

Steve narrowed his gaze. 'I hope this journey is worth it. It's dangerous for us being anywhere near Kuala Lumpur.'

'Yes, I hope so too. Dr Laksana is a very important man in Malaysia,' Adam said.

'Should I to come to meeting or stay in car?' Mai asked nervously.

'No, we are a team.' Steve smiled.

'As a woman from Vietnam?' Mai said.

'Yes, you should be with us,' Adam endorsed Steve's answer.

They arrived at the entrance to Dr Laksana's very expansive property and stopped at the sentry point. A soldier in full uniform, with an assortment of weapons, including a rifle, asked for their ID's and radioed the house. He opened the barrier and Adam drove his car along the road, and up to the house.

Steve looked at the house set in a tropical landscape. 'Reminds me of colonial British India.'

'Yes, a colonial house owned by the British before Malaysia's independence,' Adam said, 'A long time before

Malaysia and Singapore split as countries, with riots here between the Malays and Singaporeans, back in the sixties.'

'I didn't know you were a history buff?' Steve smiled.

'There are many things you do not know about me. This part of Kuala Lumpur is one of the most sought after addresses in Malaysia,' Adam continued.

On arrival at the house, a well-dressed concierge directed them to a parking spot just beyond the entrance.

'Nice motors,' Steve remarked as he looked at the parked vehicles.

'Those are diplomat limousines.'

Once out of the car, the concierge ushered them into the house. A magnificent hallway with antique furniture and an enormous crystal glass chandelier hanging over the opulent double stairway greeted them.

They were shown into a large sitting room, which featured a grand stone fireplace, and a Persian rug centre piece. Dr Laksana was sitting on a plush camel-back sofa positioned opposite two identical sofas on the other side of a large mahogany coffee table.

'Good morning. I am Dr Laksana. Good to meet you.'

They reciprocated before they sat down next to two men regaled in striking Malaysian official uniforms.

Dr Laksana pointed to the army officers. 'May I introduce Sri Khalid bin Abu Bakar, Inspector General of Police at the Commercial Crime Investigation Department – CCID. Tan Sri Kassim, Chief Commissioner of the Malaysian Anti-Corruption Commission – MACC.'

They completed the formalities and Steve gave the officers a complete update, and a breakdown of the technical investigation and findings.

Dr Laksana opened the conversation. 'We thank you for the information you have provided. I have asked Inspector General Bakar and Chief Commissioner Kassim to form a joint operation to investigate Prem Jothi, Cliff Lin and the son-in-law of Ariff Samahon. We will also investigate Sergeant TetLeong and Superintendent Anwar,'

The two officers nodded in agreement.

'Perhaps it would be useful if you could give us some background on your dealings with Q7 and how this has all unfolded?' Dr Laksana said.

Steve summarised the events to date.

'Thank you, Mr Roussos,' Inspector General Bakar said. 'We will set-up a covert investigation room in George Town.'

'Would you be willing to wear a wire?' Chief Commissioner Kassim said, 'I know it is dangerous, but can you do this?' He directed the question to all three of them.

Steve thought for a few moments. 'We have forensic data which should prove them guilty, but I understand if we could get a confession that would help enormously.'

'Can you provide the forensic data?' Chief Commissioner Kassim said.

'OK, we have a complete copy of the data across two Linux computers back at the apartment,' Steve said.

'We will collect the systems from you.' Chief Commissioner Kassim nodded.

'Great,' Steve said.

'Tomorrow,' Chief Commissioner Kassim said.

'Do you want to move to the operation centre at the police station in George Town for your protection?' Dr Laksana said.

'Thank you. Let us discuss this and get back to you,' Steve said.

Dr Laksana nodded.

# # # # # #

Although they had a four-hour journey ahead of them, they were glad to be heading away from Kuala Lumpur.

'Can we trust them?' Mai asked.

Steve raised his eyebrows. 'I trust no one, but I guess we have no choice. I'm not sure about moving to George Town. What if they are corrupt too?'

'Dr. Laksana has a good reputation, but I am worried,' Adam said.

'I would trust them more if they found further evidence from their own forensic investigation,' Steve added.

'Dr Laksana can protect us if we can trust him, but can we trust the Police?' Adam looked pensive.

CHAPTER FIFTY-FOUR

Tuesday 2nd June

It was mid afternoon before Chief Commissioner Kassim had sent two of his officers, from the newly set up operational HQ in George Town, to the apartment to collect the Linux computer systems. Earlier that morning Steve had taken three full copies of the findings before he released the systems. He made a mental note to send one of the copies back to Roger for safe keeping.

Early evening, he went for a short walk to clear his head, crossed the road onto the path and stood for a moment, enjoying the nice breeze on a cloudless day. He took a deep breath in and a long breath out, trying to calm his mind. Watching the waves and breathing in the fresh air, helped him to release the tension, stress and anxiety racing through his body. Many thoughts cascaded through his brain. He remembered he had promised to call Beth back.

'Beth, it's me. Sorry I can't use FaceTime as I'm on this local Malaysian number.'

'Thank God you called. We had a terrible day yesterday.'

'What's wrong? Are you OK? Are the kids OK?'

'It's Millie, she has died.' Beth sobbed.

'Millie?'

'The kids are distraught, as you can imagine, although they have gone to school today. I thought it best if they go, to take their mind off Millie.'

'Oh no. Was it the pregnancy?'

'Someone poisoned her.' Beth held her breath for a moment.

'Poisoned!' Steve proclaimed.

'The vet found pieces of beef in her stomach with slug and rat venom, sewn inside the beef. The slugs caused Millie to dehydrate to death, and the rats caused internal bleeding. It's awful Steve.' She sobbed.

'Oh no.'

'Millie was in great pain and distress for hours. She died in my arms. The puppies died.'

'Oh, God. Poor Millie. I should be there with you. And the kids.'

'We're all in a state of shock. Please come home Steve.'

'Oh love. I'm sorry. I'll be home as soon as I can. There are problems over here. Q7 stopped paying us. They are crooks.'

'Why are you doing this? You should be here. I'm trying to keep everything together. I've stepped up, but I can't do this alone. They'll take the house. And the kids are distraught.'

'I have to do this Beth. They murdered David and Glen.'

'Oh my God! You are not in the army now Steve for God's sake. And Roger's been trying to find you.'

'I'll talk to him.'

'This is dangerous. If they murdered David and Glen, they could murder you. We need you. I need you. Come home.' She found it difficult to talk as she sobbed.

'I have to do this Beth. I'll be home soon.'

'So, you let your family and your house fall apart. Your children and I need you.' Beth disconnected the call.

Steve's head was spinning as he made his way back to the apartment.

I should go home.
I should be there for Beth and the kids.
I'm responsible for Glen's and David's deaths.
How can I leave Mark?
Fuck. Fuck.
Somehow, I could have changed things.
I can't think.

Let me think.

# # # # # #

Steve headed straight back to the apartment.

Mai met him at the front door in a state of distress. 'Prem Jothi has called Adam. Adam, Steve is back,' she shouted.

Adam came out of his bedroom.

Steve looked puzzled. 'How did he find you?'

'Prem told Dewi to speak, and she handed over the phone.'

'What did he say?'

'He said you are trying to destroy Farid and Q7.'

'That's nonsense. As you know.'

'Prem knows about Eileen Yeong. I asked him why he had stopped the newspaper from releasing the story if he had nothing to hide. He claims it is all lies, and he is a respectable businessman. He wants to protect his reputation and you, Steve, sleep with prostitutes.'

Bastard. Shit. He'll let Beth know. Shit.

'That's nonsense. So, he has stopped the newspaper. Does he know you are with us in Penang?' Steve asked.

'Yes, he knows. He knows we were at the Evergreen Laurel Hotel.' Adam nodded.

'Credit card and maybe GPS location. They traced the card and located your mobile, which pinpointed the hotel,' Steve said.

'He wants me to come home and get away from you. He believes I am not safe.' Adam looked anxious.

'We need to ask Dr Laksana to help us. We should move to George Town. If they know we are near the Evergreen Laurel Hotel, it won't take them long to find out where we are. We are only ten minutes' walk from the hotel and they can check when we left.'

'Yes, I am very worried,' Adam said.

'He wants you home Adam, so he can come after us,' Steve said.

'I am not leaving. He is not my brother.' Adam looked determined.

'How do we stop him?' Steve shared his thoughts aloud, 'We can't do any more, we've told Dr Laksana. Can we leave the country now? Dr Laksana must get us out.' For Steve, a bucketful of thoughts needed to go, to make room for new ones.

'He said your wife, lovely children and handsome dog are not safe.'

'He what?' Steve had to suppress a wave of nausea.

'Your family in the UK. The name of your wife, Elisa,' Adam said.

'No Beth, Elisabeth.' A ball of fear formed in Steve's stomach.

Adam nodded.

'He has killed my dog.' Steve cupped his forehead in the palms of his hands.

'What?' Mai said with a horrified look.

'Yes, I just talked to Beth. They have poisoned Millie with rat poison.'

Bastard, Bastards.

I need to go home now.

I'm gonna kill him.

Where do I get a gun?

What shall I do?

'We need to move to George Town, get their protection and then figure out how we get you back to the UK,' Adam said.

'I agree, but in the meantime I have to get Beth and the family to a safe place. How do I do that?' *Think. Think.* Angry bile stung Steve's throat.

'Can she go to stay with family?' Mai asked.

'I'm gonna call my brother and get him to take Beth and the kids over to Mallorca. He lives out there.' Steve nodded.

'I am worried about Mark. I cannot stop thinking about him. Hope he is safe…in prison.' Adam looked pale.

'Prem could have men anywhere, even in prison,' Steve shook his head.

I don't know which way to turn. Poor Beth.

'Adam, can you talk to Dr Laksana?' Mai asked.

'Yes, we need to leave now.' Adam nodded.

# # # # # #

Steve left the room to call Roger. 'Hi, it's Steve.'

'Where the hell have you been? I've been trying to contact you.'

'Sorry.' Steve held his forehead.

'I called you many times. I even called Beth. What's go—' Roger said.

Steve interrupted, 'There's a big problem at Q7.'

'They've stopped making any payments to us. What's happening? We are in dire straits. I haven't been able to pay any wages or ex—.'

Steve raised his voice. 'Roger, let me speak please, let me speak! They tried to murder me?'

'Who tried to murder you?' Roger asked.

'Prem Jothi and Cliff Lin, yes Cliff Lin.'

'What do you mean?'

Steve tried to explain. 'They run an empire which uses Q7 to help sell illegal stuff, launder the money out via Singapore into the US. Cliff invested in us because he wanted to use our secure payment system to hide the details. David found out and he was killed. Glen was poisoned, Mark's been framed, and I've had to flee for my life. Adam threatened his brother to get Mark out of jail.'

'Yes, Mark told me about Adam,' Roger said.

'Then you know Adam is Prem Jothi's brother. Prem Jothi and Cliff Lin are in cahoots with the son-in-law of the Malaysian Prime Minister, this is big stuff!' Steve gasped.

'Bloody Hell! You need to come back to the UK. You are not safe over there.'

'We are in Penang.' Steve grimaced.

'Penang? Mark couldn't get in touch with you either. He's in a bad way.'

'I'm trying to get him out. I know he is struggling. Has Glen's family got him home?' Steve asked.

'He's still in Kuala Lumpur, in the morgue. I'm helping the family fly him back to the UK, under our insurance,' Roger said.

'Very sad. A corrupt policeman tried to strangle me. If Adam hadn't been there, I'd be dead too. I need you to help me Roger. It's urgent.'

'I'll do whatever I can.' Roger's voice sounded focused and forceful.

'Beth and the kids are not safe. Prem Jothi has threatened me with their safety. Prem poisoned our dog as a warning. Can you arrange for my family to fly over to Mallorca to stay with my brother Brian?'

'Yes sure, I'll pay for the flights. I'll go over to Beth and sort out the flights as soon as possible.'

'That's great Roger. I'm so worried about them. I really appreciate it.'

'When are you coming home?' Roger asked.

'The British Embassy are a waste of time, but we met with the ex-Prime Minister of Malaysia. He will help us get back.'

'What can I do?'

'Can you tell Mark we are doing everything we can to get him out and remember, make sure you don't tell Cliff Lin anything?'

'Please be careful. I'll arrange the flights with Beth.'

'Thanks, I'll phone Brian now and tell Beth you will contact her.' Steve ended the call.

# # # # # #

After Steve had contacted Brian to arrange for his family to travel over to Mallorca, he called Beth, 'Hi, it's me. I'm sorry.'

'When are you coming home? We need you. You missed Kate's appointment. What are you doing out there?'

'Oh no. Sorry. Is she OK?'

'The consultant has increased her dosage. She's had more attacks, one was severe. I'm worried.' She sobbed.

'I'll get back as soon as I can. Give her a hug and tell her I'll make it up to her when I get home.'

'When? When Steve? What are you doing?'

'Beth, listen. We're certain the people who gave us the deal are corrupt. Even Cliff Lin, who invested in Seguro, is part of this.'

'Part of what?'

'They set us up.'

'So, come home.' Beth's voice cracked.

'No, it's not that simple. They will stop us at the airport. They're murderers, and we must stop them.'

'Please come home,' she pleaded.

'I'll be home soon. We have told top brass Malaysian Government people, and we need to hand over everything to them.'

'I'm worried,' Beth said.

'Please don't. I've been thinking. Until it's over, it'll give me peace of mind if you and the kids go and stay with Brian and Hazel in Mallorca for a while. That will also be good for Kate.'

'No, we can't do that Steve. How can we? They'll go to school today. I'm working, and people are still shouting at us to pay our bills. How can I leave? Why aren't you coming home now?' Beth started to cry.

'I need you and the kids to go to a safe place. And when I come home, we will meet up in Mallorca for a romantic holiday. Hey, let's sell up and go live in Spain.'

'I'm not staying with Brian and Hazel. And anyway, Kate has another appointment with the consultant.'

'There's plenty of room. The kids love it by the sea. And there are good doctors in Mallorca and the climate will help.'

'No, Steve. What about school? What about the cost?'

'Beth, it's important that you leave the house and go stay with Brian. I've spoken to him and it's all fine with them. Roger will pay for the flights and he'll call you about it later.'

'Now you're scaring me.'

'You and the kids are the most important people in the world to me. I want you to be safe whilst I sort out things over here.'

'Are we in danger?'

'I don't want to take any risks.'

'We're safer at home, and I'm worried about you.'

'No, Beth. You need to get out today.'

'You're scaring me,' The tone of her voice changed.

'Look - I need you to be a hundred percent safe.'

'I'll think about it.'

'Beth, I need you to do this. Please. I'm sure the bad guys arranged for Millie to be poisoned. I'm worried Beth. I don't want to take any chances.'

'It's you who should worry, and I'm worried for you. This bad lot are in Malaysia. Not here. Come home.'

'Let me make a few calls and I will ring you later. Please make arrangements to leave and I will call you and explain to the kids.'

'OK, but please come home love. Let's forget all this. Get away, as a family together.'

'Talk later, love you.'

'Please be careful. I love you Steve.'

# # # # # #

Adam picked up his mobile and made a call. 'Dewi it is me.'

'I am so sorry,' Dewi said, 'Sorry Prem talked to you, but Mama and I worry.'

'Is Prem threatening you and Mama?' Adam's voice suddenly lowered as if there was someone else in the room who might overhear.

'No, he wants you to come home. He is missing you.' Dewi wept.

'No, he wants me out of the way.' Adam choked out the words.

'What do you mean? Come home. He knows you are in Penang,' Dewi said.

'Look Dewi, Prem is a bad man. He is doing bad things. He wants to hurt my friends. I must protect them.'

'What about Mama and me?' Dewi raised her voice.

'What do you mean? Do you need protecting?' Adam panicked.

'No Adam. I mean you should be home with your family.'

'Prem is ashamed of me.' Adam's words tailed off.

'No, he loves you. We all love you and worry about you.'

'I am fine. There is nothing to worry about. The problem is my friends found information about Prem and the dreadful things he is doing. They are not safe.'

'Adam, you are wrong.'

'You tell Prem to keep away from my friends and me. If he does not, then I will do whatever I can to protect them. Tell him I will go to the police and tell them I am gay. Prem believes his reputation is more important than anything else.'

'I love you Adam. Please take care.'

CHAPTER FIFTY-FIVE

Wednesday 3rd June

It was her neighbours turn to take her daughter along with Beth's twins to school. Beth waved them off before she left the house, holding Jake's hand. She opened the rear passenger door of her car, and Jake jumped in. Beth backed off the drive, and they set off on the morning school run.

Although most parked cars sat on their driveways, a few dotted the tree-laden, quiet suburban street. A broad oak tree across the street prevented the black Audi from being seen. The Audi passenger nudged the driver with his elbow. 'Hey. Wake up, they're moving.'

'OK.' He sat up straight, raised his shoulders, moved his neck in a circular direction and lifted his cap off his eyes. He started the engine, and moved off, keeping enough distance behind not to attract any attention. 'Get this done and go eat? I fancy a full breakfast.'

'Focus on the job. So, like the dry run yesterday.'

'I know what I'm doing.'

They followed the Citroen along the busy Monmouth Parkway and left towards Tudor Hill.

'Remember, once she drops the kid off, we trap her when she gets to Parkhill.'

'How many times do you need to tell me? I know.' Tapping his fingers on the steering wheel he drummed and sang to the rhythm of a song playing on the car radio. 'Tragedy,' Tap, Tap, 'Tragedy,' Tap, Tap, Tap, 'Tragedy,' Tap, Tap, 'Tragedy,' Tap, Tap.

'Shut the fuck up.'

The driver sang with a wry smirk on his face. 'Tragedy. Tragedy.'

The Audi passenger leaned forward and turned the radio off. 'Focus! Let's get the job done, and you can fuck off to your breakfast.'

This did not prevent the driver continuing to tap to an imaginary tune. He threw his cap onto the back seat and moved his head forward. 'No problem. You're in too deep.'

'Focus. Once we've finished this job, we should both get out.'

'Too damn right. I'm too old for this game.'

Beth turned left into Nursery Road and found a parking space amongst the daily ritual of the urban tractors, dropping their kids off as near to the school entrance as possible. Jake jumped out, waved and Beth set off on the horseshoe-shaped Nursery Road, and back on to Tudor Hill.

The Audi tracked Beth as she took a right on to College Road.

'She's going right. Follow her.'

The driver nodded, keeping his eyes fixed on the road, whilst he tapped at a more rapid rate. The windscreen clouded up, despite the two men trying to stay calm and focused.

'Where's she going?'

'Not sure, forget the park entrance.'

The traffic flowed slowly. The Audi, a few cars behind on New Oscott Road, Beth took a left into the shopping centre car park. The Audi followed.

'It's too busy here to do anything.'

'We have to do it today.'

'We can't do it here.'

'Let me think. If she goes home, she won't go by Parkhill, so we have no cover.'

'It's getting busier here and they'll have CCTV.'

'Yeah. Let's go back to her house. I want you to drive past the house, and park by the care home next door.'

'What's the plan?'

'I wait for her. I'll jump her and bundle her into the back of her car. You follow me to the forge.'

'Wow, isn't that risky?'

'Look we need to get her to the warehouse and take the photos before we detonate. You know the deal, we get the final payment and we're out of here.'

'You're the boss.'

# # # # # #

The Audi arrived back on the road, close to Beth's house.

'Down there, drop me on the left and stay further down the road. Once you see the target arrive, get ready. I'll grab her, I take her car, you follow.'

'OK.'

'Drop me here.'

He jumped out of the car, walked past the side entrance of the care home and into the rear car park. Scaling the fence into the neighbouring garden, he unlocked the side gate and emerged at the front of Beth's house. Hiding behind the tall hedge which contoured the front garden and drive, he pulled on a black woollen balaclava.

He waited.

# # # # # #

Beth arrived back at the house. She reversed the car onto the drive, grabbed two plastic shopping bags and her handbag off the seat, got out of the car, opened the front door of the house and went inside to turn off the alarm. As she walked back to close the front door, he rushed towards her, grabbed her blouse with his left hand and thrust the palm of his right hand into her face, pushing her back into the narrow hallway. The plastic bags dropped to the floor and the contents; toiletries, sun-cream, wet-wipes and sweets were strewn across the hallway. He flicked the door closed with his right ankle. Beth tried to scream, but he pushed his right palm with force over her mouth, and pushed her down to the floor, landing on top of her, knocking her handbag and keys onto the floor. She could not breathe and instinctively thrust her knee between his legs. Beth's action caused him to roll off her, writhing in pain. She turned onto her front and spotted an umbrella and one of Jake's action men. Beth tried to get up off the floor and lurched towards the umbrella.

Quickly composing himself, he jumped on her, pinning her to the floor and put his left hand over her mouth. She tried to bite his hand. He reached into his pocket and retrieved his flick knife, and held it against Beth's neck, drawing a small amount of blood.

'Shut the fuck up or you're dead. Do you hear me?' He moved himself up to sit on Beth's back, looking like a jockey crouching forward in the home straight. Pressing on the back of her head, he kneeled on each arm, pinning both arms down to the floor, placed the knife on the floor, grabbed a tie and a roll of tape from his pocket. He pulled Beth's neck back by her hair, wrapped the tie around her head covering her mouth and tied it around the back of her head in a double knot. She tried to scream as he wrapped the tape around her nose, ears, and eyes.

He picked up his knife and yanked her hands together behind her back and wrapped tape around her wrists, then pulled Beth to her feet. 'Do as I say.' Grabbing Beth's keys he tipped the contents of Beth's hand-bag onto the floor, spotted a travel money envelope, opened it and pocketed the Euro notes. He opened the front door, marched Beth out, opened the tailgate and bundled her into the boot of the Citroen, covered her with the dog blanket, jumped into the car, pulled off his balaclava and drove away. The Audi followed.

He made a call. 'Follow me. If I lose you, meet at the Forge as planned. It'll take us about an hour.

# # # # # #

The cars arrived together at the derelict industrial estate. They drove past two rundown units and stopped outside the third. The driver of the Citroen got out, engine running, unlocked and opened the large wrought-iron gate. Jumped back in the car and drove into the industrial unit. The Audi followed.

'Your balaclava, put it on,' he pointed to the Audi driver as they got out of the cars. 'Let's get her out.'

They dragged her out of the back of the estate, holding her by each arm, and marched her around to the front of the car, before wrapping more tape, this time around her ankles. He untied the gag covering her mouth which drew her expression in agony, but not over her own pain.

'What do you want?' Beth tried to compose herself and waited for a response... 'Who are you? What do you want with me?' She tried not to cry. Blood caked her knife wound, forming smudged streaks down her neck.

One of the men stood back and took photos using his iPhone before they re-gagged her mouth, dragged her along the concrete floor further into the derelict workshop and planted her against a pillar.

'Let's go.'

The Audi driver backed out of the unit, followed by the Citroen. The Citroen driver stopped outside, closed the unit's wrought-iron gate, jumped back in the car and followed the Audi over to a patch of waste ground. He got out of the Citroen and walked over to the boot of the Audi, took out a silver-cased box and opened it, pulled out a small electrical device, retrieved a second metal box and opened it to reveal two sticks of dynamite. He connected the two items, placed the device on the back seat of Beth's car and jumped into the Audi. They drove about a hundred feet away and stopped.

'She's a good-looking bird. I'd shag her all right.'

'Shut the fuck up, you idiot.' He took two pictures of the Citroen and switched to another app on his phone.

'I'll give it ten seconds.' He pressed on the screen of his iPhone. The Citroen exploded, and fire consumed the car.

He took another couple of photos. Then using WhatsApp he composed a message containing the pictures of Beth and the Citroen in flames. He sent it off then placed a call, 'It's done. I've sent over the photos? How long do you want us leave her? - OK, we will wait to hear from you.'

He turned to the driver. 'Right, done. We leave her. Let's get out of here, we're done for now.'

CHAPTER FIFTY-SIX

Thursday 4th June

It was just after midnight when he heard Adam call out. Steve was trying without success to get some sleep, so immediately jumped out of bed, slipped on some shorts and tee shirt and ran into the lounge.

Adam looked concerned, he showed Steve his phone. It contained a photo of a person standing next to a car, hands and legs tied, and read: "They have taken Mr Roussos's wife. Do you want my help?"

Steve could not contain his anger. 'Oh no. It's Beth. What have they done?'

Adam shook his head. 'It is a blocked Malaysian caller ID. Prem must be behind this. I am so sorry. What can I do?'

Mai came into the room and looked at the picture.

'Let me think. Send the photo to my phone? I must go home to find her.' Steve's chest was thumping, and it felt like a clamp was crushing his skull.

'Oh no.' Mai welled up.

A bombardment of thoughts hit Steve. 'Need to find the geolocation.' He opened the photo, saved it and looked at the metadata.

'Shall I call my brother? I can do as he says if he releases your wife.'

Adam's phone beeped again, and he opened the message. This time it contained a picture of Beth's car and another of the car with flames exuding from all sides. This time the message read - "She is next. Do you want my help?"

Steve raised his arms above his head and screamed. 'I'll kill him. I'll fucking kill him. If it's the last thing I do.'

Adam looked horrified. 'I am so sorry. What can I do?'

Mai found it difficult to stop the tears. 'I hope your wife will be ok. Your brother will pay for this Adam.'

'What can we do?' pleaded Adam.

Mai composed herself. 'I do not know but he must pay. He must pay for what he has done.'

Steve froze. He could not speak.

Beth. My Beth. How can I save her? I must do what he wants. My kids! Are they ok? What have I done?

Steve composed himself and opened the picture that Adam had just sent him. He opened the metadata on the photo and looked at the details. He could see the location timestamp - 11:49:16 UK time - over four hours ago. This caused him to experience a panic attack; he could not breathe.

He pulled himself together. 'I need to contact the police and Roger.' He left the room.

# # # # # #

'Detective Inspector Power, it's Steve Roussos. Help me please. They've taken my wife, and my kids are not safe.'

'Your wife?'

'Yes, I need you to find my wife and protect my kids. I'm still in Malaysia, trying to help you prove they murdered David Morris.'

Steve used his phone to email the GeoLocation information he had gathered from the photos.

Detective Inspector Power, the details – it's a location near
Dagenham, Please help!
Map Link: 53.354880,-4.366942†
SceneCaptureType: Standard
SceneType: Directly Photographed
Altitude: 51.38259833134684m
AltitudeRef: Above sea level
DestBearing: 90.56474820143885
ImgDirection: 90.5648°= East
ImgDirectionRef: True North

Latitude: 53.35488
LatitudeRef: N
Longitude: 4.366941666666666
LongitudeRef: W
Speed: 0
SpeedRef: km/h
TimeStamp: 11:49:16
FileName: IMG_5492.JPG
FileSize: 2.74004 MB
Thank you, Steve

'It looks like Beth is indoors in the photo, in some kind of factory unit,' Steve said.

The Detective Inspector took details of the children's school and Steve's home address. Steve also provided Roger's details so that he could help with the children.

Steve paused to think once off the call.

'Adam, contact your brother. Tell him we will meet him in Penang,' Steve said.

'Are you sure? This could be a trap,' Mai said.

Steve nodded. 'I need to do something. I'll be back soon.'

Steve felt numb. He chose not to tell Mai or Adam his intentions.

Where is my Beth? Prem will not get away with this. I'll fucking kill him! Meeting is dangerous. But I need to do this.

# # # # # #

Steve left the room and made a call. 'Can I talk to Chief Commissioner Kassim?'

'Who is calling please?'

'Steve Roussos.'

After a short wait. 'Kassim.'

'Chief Commissioner, it's Steve Roussos.'

'Mr Roussos, what can I do for you?'

'I'll wear a wire.'

'Are you sure you want to do this?'

'Yes, I'm certain. He has taken my wife.'

'Your wife?'

'Yes, in the UK. He has kidnapped her.'

'Have you contacted the UK police?'

'Yes they are searching for her. I know it's dangerous but I have to meet him. But I want backup from your team at the meeting.'

'Yes we will. It is a one-way wire. We will give back up, but you understand it is very dangerous?'

'I'm fine with that,' Steve said.

'We will be able to hear you and respond as needed.'

'I understand. I want to stop them. I have asked to meet with Prem tomorrow morning. Can you fit the wire as soon as possible?' Steve said.

'I will send one of my men to you. It's a belt transmitter. You just wear it as a normal belt. The wire is concealed behind the buckle, and activated by a micro switch concealed within the buckle. My man will show you how to use it. He should be with you by seven AM? '

'OK, thanks.'

'Thank you, Mr Roussos.'

Steve ended the call.

What have I done? My Beth. My poor Beth. I'm so sorry. Please forgive me! I love you. I'll always love you. I can't believe this is happening. It's all my fault.

Roger rang a short time later; he had spoken to the police and to his relief, his kids were at school. Roger planned to go straight over to Steve's house to meet the police and get his kids to a safe place.

# # # # # #

Adam made contact with his brother and agreed to meet him the following morning at nine AM. Steve called Chief Commissioner Kassim to let him know the time and location of the meeting. Although it was just after three AM, Kassim told Steve that one of his men would be with him within the hour, and he agreed to mobilise his team in preparation for the meeting.

Detective Inspector Power called him. The local police had found the burnt out car on a derelict wasteland. Although it was just after seven PM UK time the police had questioned some occupants of a row of local houses on the opposite side of the road to the entrance to a yard containing a group of industrial units. In addition they were trying to locate the landlord to gain access.

Steve was relieved that the police confirmed that no one was in the burnt out car although it was confirmed as Beth's Citroen, but he was concerned that the police had not broken into the units. DI Power could not give him any reassurance that Beth was alive and well.

# # # # # #

At just after five AM, one of Chief Commissioner Kassim's men arrived to fit the wire. The officer had agreed to message Steve on his arrival. Steve met him in the corridor adjacent to the apartment entrance. Mai and Adam were in their bedrooms; Steve decided not to tell them about the wire.

He showed him how to turn it on and they agreed to a call just before Steve was due to arrive at the meeting place, so they could test that it was still transmitting.

# # # # # #

Pitch black, a cold breeze flowed through the unit. The rancid oil and petrol overpowered any other lurking smells. Helpless; mouth, wrists, legs bound, her knees, ankles and back aching, her legs cramping. Trying to ease her aching body, Beth adjusted her position at regular intervals to try to get into the most comfortable position. Mouth dry, she found it increasingly hard to breathe; panic made it worse and she realised she had to stay calm if she had any chance of surviving. Wrists hurting, she shivered as a bitter raw chill crept up from the concrete floor. Steve will find me, he won't let me die, she recycled this thought continually to give her a sense of hope. She was trying to keep alert, but at the same time struggling to stay calm as each thought about Steve, the kids, rescue made her panic and affected her breathing.

She heard the wrought-iron gate clang open and an engine running as a car entered the industrial unit. Her heart pumped rapidly with anticipation. The engine noise stopped and she could hear footsteps moving towards her, and a person pulled the tape off her eyes and gag off her mouth. The headlights pierced Beth's eyes, causing her to close as pain hit the back of her head. Her skull felt like an eggshell. Pain funnelled into her heart. He held the back of her head and drew a bottle of water to her lips. She coughed as the water hit the back of her throat. A balaclava disguised the face of the tall man.

Her wrists and ankles still bound by tape, she said, 'Who are you? Let me go… Please.' Her voice was hoarse and faint.

The man did not respond but retrieved a plastic-wrapped sandwich from a bag, pulled off the wrapping, and pushed a sandwich triangle towards her mouth. 'Ham and cheese.'

The smell was inviting but nauseating at the same time. She was starving, but closed her mouth, refusing to eat. She bowed her head.

'Suit yourself.'

Chills chased up her back. 'My children need me. Why have you kidnapped me?' *What can I do?*

'I'll let you go.'

'Thank you… thank you. I need to go to my children.' *I don't believe him. Why is he here? How long will he keep me here?*

He crouched down before her. 'I'll let you go, but what will you do for me?'

'I can get you money. How much do you want?'

'I don't want your money. You're stunning.'

'Let me go.' She tried not to cry. *Will I ever get out of here? I hurt. My knees. My hands.*

'Don't cry, you're so beautiful. I've got money. Love to take you with me.'

Her eyes watered. Fear clenched like a tight fist around her chest. 'I'll get you anything if you let me go. Please let me go.' She gasped, short of air.

'One shag. That's all. Then you can go home.'

He wants to rape me. Beth sobbed. *How do I stop him? I can't run. He is too strong for me. I can't defend myself.* 'No.'

'You might enjoy it.'

'Please don't do this.' *Bastard. Enjoy it! Fuck you. I'm scared. Let me think.*

'Do you want to get out alive bitch?' He grabbed her shirt and pulled her towards him.

'How do I know you'll let me go?' Beth said.

I can't do this. Be strong. I must survive for my kids. What's around me?

'Well, I haven't killed you yet. Got money and I'm leaving. I'll just let you go, jump in the car and leave you.'

'No, I can't.' She inhaled sharply.

He pulled her head back using her hair as leverage. 'You do it nice, or you do it rough. You choose, bitch.'

Beth's chin hit her chest as he pulled her head forward. 'Please don't do this.'

He grabbed her by the arm, raised her to her feet and dragged her towards the car. Her shoe fell off, and she felt intense pain as her foot dragged across the concrete. Once at the car, he stood her up and faced her towards the bonnet, her shins touching the bumper.

'Stand there you bitch.' He thumped his fist on the bonnet of the car, stood behind her, reached around her waist and untied her belt, undid her button, unzipped her jeans and pulled the jeans down onto the ankle tape.

She was rigid. *I have to do something.*

'Nice arse.' He kneeled behind her and slapped her right buttock.

'Please don't.' Panic engulfed her as she wet herself.

He yanked the tape to release it from her wrists, and pushed her forward pinning her down onto the car bonnet. Leaning on her, he spread her arms out and pushed her head against the bonnet. Her left cheek thudded against the metal.

'Shut the fuck up bitch.' He reached either side of her waist, to pull down her panties.

Frozen rigid. *My kids. I need to do something.* She wilted.

'Lift your right foot bitch.' He yanked her jeans and panties off her leg, breaking the tape at the same time.

Adrenaline kicked in. Beth screamed and raised her right arm and leg twisting towards the man. She caught the side of his face with her elbow and kicked him in his thigh.

He lurched back, held his hand against the side of his face, smudging a trickle of blood. 'You fucking bitch.' She tried to get away, but he pulled her back and slammed her back down into position on the car bonnet. Her nose and left eye were bleeding.

'Open your legs bitch.' He put his hand between her legs in a downward motion, pushed her shoulders on the car bonnet and pushed his left elbow and hand into her back. Beth was silent, rigid and numb.

'Wow, I love it, bitch.' With one hand he opened his belt, undid his button and zip, pushed his jeans and pants to his ankles.

Beth held her breath. She felt weak and numb but she could struggle no more.

# # # # # #

A screeching sound of tyres and sirens cascaded outside the unit gates. Within seconds the metal gate crashed open. As the man looked up, Beth raised her right leg as hard as possible, smashing between his legs. He dropped to the floor. Three police officers ran towards them, a policewoman grabbed Beth, took her away, helped pull her panties and jeans back on and wrapped her up in the officer's police blazer. The two policemen jumped onto the man, cuffed him and read him his rights.

'You're safe now. We need to get you to the hospital.'

'Thank you. I need to see my children. 'Blood flowed from her eye and nose. She could not control the shivering which started at the back of her legs and spread up her body.

'They are fine. We are with them now.'

'Thank you. How did you find me?'

'You are safe now. We will take care of you.'

'I need Steve.' Beth sobbed and shivered.

# # # # # #

The taxi stopped outside the Go Hotel and Gurney Shopping complex. Mai looked towards the restaurant. 'I am worried. We cannot trust Prem. I am sorry he is your brother, but I hate him.'

Adam did not respond.

They jumped out of the taxi and Steve paid the driver. As they walked through the busy mall, Steve detoured into the public toilets. Mai and Adam waited outside. Once in the cubicle he made a call on his mobile and whispered. 'Can you hear me?'

'Yes. We are ready Mr Roussos, We can hear you from the wire and this call,' was the response, 'Remember, we will have our men watching the restaurant and monitoring the wire. If we suspect any problems we will move in. If you get into difficulty please say the signal words - "I am not feeling well. Give me a minute." - We will move in.'

'I am not feeling well. Give me a minute. Got it. I'm on my way.'

# # # # # #

Detective Inspector Power called Steve and was greeted by voice mail. She left a message letting him know the great news that Beth was safe and sound.

# # # # # #

Steve's phone pinged with a message. He chose to ignore it, turned his mobile phone to silent mode and left the cubicle to rejoin Mai and Adam.

They mingled with the chaotic flow of busy morning shoppers and headed for the restaurant.

Prem Jothi and Cliff Lin sat at a table in the middle of the restaurant. Tattoo man stood by the entrance, and another man stood on the opposite side of the restaurant, watching as the waitress placed drinks on the table.

Steve stopped before they got to the restaurant. 'There's no one else in there. I'm not happy with this.'

Adam carried on walking towards the entrance. 'Prem has cleared it.'

Tattoo man opened the restaurant door. He frisked Adam. Mai walked straight past tattoo man. He tried to stop her but Prem gestured to let her go. She walked to the table, stood opposite, held her palms together as though praying, and bowed towards Prem. Steve pushed ahead of Adam to the table not giving Tattoo man time to frisk him. Tattoo man approached Steve but Prem gestured him away, so he took his position on guard at the restaurant entrance.

Prem beckoned them to sit, ignoring Mai. 'Mr Roussos, Adam, my dear brother. Please sit down.'

Steve pulled a chair over to the table, so that Mai could also sit down.

Prem held out his arms towards Adam. 'I am worried about you my brother.'

Adam levelled a glowering look.

Cliff sat motionless.

Steve leaned forward, closer to the table. His heart pounded hard in his chest. 'What have you done to my wife?'

Prem smirked. 'I want to help. There are bad people. I want to protect you and my brother.'

Steve wanted to kill him there and then. Clenching his fists, he tried to stay calm. 'Have you taken my wife. What do I need to do to get my wife back?'

Prem shook his head. 'They are bad people, who could harm your family. I can stop them.'

Steve moved his chair closer to the table and jabbed his finger towards Prem. 'What do you mean? What do you want?'

'I want you to keep away from Q7 and destroy any information you may have. If you do this, I will make sure they do not harm you and your family.' Disapproval gleamed in Prem's eyes.

Steve found it difficult to contain his anger. 'It's you who has taken my wife, you murdered David and his wife, and you murdered Glen.'

'She murdered Mr Lewis.' Prem pointed towards Mai.

Mai stood up and shouted expletives in Vietnamese. Tattoo man moved forward quickly and pushed Mai back into her seat, squeezing down on her shoulders to keep her seated.

Adam stood up and tried to push Tattoo man away. 'Leave her.'

Prem gestured to Tattoo man, to go back to his position.

Steve looked towards Cliff Lin with distain. 'Is my wife safe? Will you let her go? I thought you were a good guy. You invested in us. This was a set-up all along?'

Cliff remained emotionless, his eyes fixed on the wall beyond Steve.

Steve banged his fist onto the table. 'Where is my wife? Look at what you've done. Please tell me my wife is safe?'

Shit! The fucking belt. They won't be able to hear the wire if I keep banging the fucking table.

Cliff did not respond, remaining motionless and emotionless.

Prem sat back in his chair. 'Bad men have taken your wife.'

Adam stood up trying to control his temper. Tattoo man moved quickly to restrain him. 'Stop playing games. I am going to the police to tell them I am gay, and that Farid is gay. He raped me many times right under your nose. I will ruin you and your reputation, and your best friend too. Our father would be ashamed of you and not of me.'

Cliff remained static, his unseeing eyes staring into space.

Prem looked to the ground, shook his head and fixed his eyes on Adam. 'Do not talk about our father. Our father was a great man. He was ashamed of you.'

Adam met Prem's unrelenting stare. 'You are Mountain Master, head of Kongsi Gelap. I am ashamed of you. You have changed. You are not my brother. Look what you have done to Mark and my friends.'

'You are not safe my brother. I care about you.' Prem leaned closer.

'You only care about yourself. Only you.'

'We are a family. I love you Adam, Mama and Dewi. I don't care about Malaysia or the mosque. We're moving to America. Cliff will help us.'

'You do not care about Mama or Dewi.' Adam's eyes flashed with anger as Tattoo man's hold hardened.

Steve pulled Adam back into his seat and said, 'You own shell companies and real estate in the US.'

'Mr Roussos, Steve. You will have enough money to make your family comfortable forever.'

'So, you're not denying it. You are the head of the triad group and you're moving vast sums of money out of

Malaysia, into Singapore, then on to the US to buy real estate. You and Cliff are both owners.'

'Why are you asking me all these questions Mr Roussos?' Prem cast only the slightest of glances to Steve before focusing back on Adam.

'I want to know,' Steve demanded.

'Why? If you say you already know?' Prem took in a deep breath.

'You murdered David. Admit it!' Steve said.

Adam stood up again. 'You have blood on your hands. How can you sleep at night?'

'I can protect you from bad people.' Prem's face twitched

Cliff broke his silence. 'Are you wearing a wire?'

Steve continued, 'I want to know. I need to know for my own piece of mind. So, you set this up from the start Cliff, when you bought shares in Seguro? There is blood on your hands too.'

Cliff and Prem exchanged glances. Prem gestured for Tattoo man to come to him. Prem whispered in his ear, which prompted Tattoo man to walk back around the table, stand behind Steve, and put his hands on Steve's shoulders. 'I am sure you won't mind if we check you are not wearing a wire.'

Steve stood up, shaking off Tattoo man. 'Back off, don't touch me. Where is my wife.' His heart beat was thumping double-time.

Mai fidgeted and stooped forward on her chair, sounding as though she was about to vomit, making a moaning sound distracting Tattoo man for a moment. She reached down and grabbed a gun concealed under her full-length white cotton dress, tucked inside one of her knee-high patent-leather boots, stood up, and held the gun in both hands. Shaking, she pointed it towards Prem. Steve looked over and everything seemed to move in slow motion. Words came out of her contorted face like the cries of a pod of whales. Shock covered

Prem's face, his eyes expanded and his mouth gaped wide. Cliff jumped up, lunged at her, pushing the table over to the right as glasses shattered on the floor. Tattoo man pulled out a gun.

Adam jumped up. 'Stttttooooppppp. Noooooo.'

Mai pulled the trigger and a bullet shot towards Prem. Cliff crashed against the floor. The bullet missed the target and ricocheted off a nearby wall. Adam dived towards Prem. Tattoo man pounced, fired his gun, piercing Adam in the neck, his head falling to one side as he dropped, blood spurting across the floor. The other foot soldier rushed forward and aimed his gun at Mai. Steve lurched towards him trying to protect her. The foot soldier fired a shot hitting Steve in the left shoulder, the bullet penetrated his arm causing him to fall back, knocking Mai to the ground. She hit the table with a thud; blood seeped from her head and leg. Adrenaline helped Steve to crouch down and protect Mai, pinning her to the ground. He grabbed her gun and shot Tattoo man in the chest from close range, forcing him backwards onto the floor. Blood jetted in all directions, hitting Steve in the face. Prem rushed over to Adam. Steve fired two shots towards Prem. Prem dropped to the floor. As Steve tried to get up the foot soldier fired a shot at him; this time the barrel jammed. There seemed to be no life left in Mai, so Steve lurched forward, knocking the foot soldier over with the weight of his own body. Something knocked the gun from Steve's hand as he hit the floor; he rose to his feet almost immediately, desperate to escape and ran out of the restaurant, blood bubbling up through his wound. The foot soldier jumped up in pursuit, grabbed Tattoo man's gun off the floor and fired a shot which missed Steve by some margin and ricocheted off a car passing along the road.

Steve knew from his army days that the best way to avoid getting shot was to keep calm and stay focused on survival.

Natural instinct was to run away from the attacker in a direct line as this was the shortest route to get furthest away. However, his army training kicked in making him fight this tendency, as he made random cuts in his flight pattern. He knew a moving target was hard to hit, but running in a straight line made it much easier since the shooter only had to slightly adjust the aim if he missed. He also remembered that he should not run in a simple zigzag pattern, or in any other predictable way as to hit a moving target a shooter would lead with the gun, swinging it ahead to where they thought the target was going to be next. He looked for concealment and cover as much as possible; any trees, shrubs, buildings, vehicles or anything else around, to work into his flight pattern and get them between him and the foot soldier. He grabbed his shoulder as a surge of splitting pain pounded within and blood sprinkled from the wound. He aimed to find a place of safety, any government building or a corporate or public centre, which might have security or an accessible space he could access and secure behind him. The foot soldier stopped twice to fire shots at Steve. Passers-by screamed as they heard the gunshots and spotted the gun. He was catching up with Steve, who by now had lost a lot of blood. Steve ran up an alleyway towards the entrance to the mall, people around him screamed in panic and two security guards rushed to close the doors, blocking his entry. Steve was trapped. The foot soldier stopped running, now only about twelve feet away and slowly took his aim. Steve desperately ran towards the foot soldier in a zigzag motion, trying to make the inevitable shot more difficult. A sudden and forceful tremor sent him sprawling on all fours as a bullet struck the foot soldier in the back of the head, and shot out of his forehead, taking with it most of the left side of his face. He dropped and bled his life out on the floor. Three Malaysian

Police officers ran up to grab Steve as he fell, unconscious, on the body of the dead man.

CHAPTER FIFTY-SEVEN

Sunday 7th June

Steve opened his eyes. A stream of light from the window flowed across his face forcing his eyelids to snap shut. He listened to a consistent beeping sound before he raised his eyelids again. Disorientated, dry throat, difficult to swallow, the room spinning, the memories flooding back. A woman walked over to his bedside and said a few words that Steve missed. He struggled to get up; excruciating pain in his arm, shoulder and chest, caused him to shout out. The room came into focus: monitors, oxygen bottle, beep, beep. The nurse eased him up and helped him to sip a drink.

He found it difficult to swallow. 'Where am I?' He whispered.

'Hello, Mr Roussos. You are in Pantai Hospital here in Penang. A doctor will visit you soon.'

Shoulder and arm strapped to his body and his hand connected to a drip, causing great pain whenever he moved. He remembered the shooting. It played in slow motion in his mind. He felt a deep pain in the pit of his stomach.

Where is my Beth, oh Beth, I'm so sorry. What have I done?

My kids. I need to get back to them. Hug them all and take care of them.

My Beth… Is she alive?

I should have just co-operated.

I have caused this! I don't think Adam has made it, nor Mai.

A single tear flowed across his cheek. 'How long have I been here?'

'This is the morning of your forth day, Mr Roussos.'

'Oh no, I need to find Beth and talk to my kids.'

A tall man in a white gown entered the room, followed by his support team. 'How are you today, Mr Roussos? I am Doctor Pasupathy. I operated on your arm and shoulder.'

He nodded. 'Thank you doctor. Did you fix my shoulder?'

'The bullet hit the joint between the humeral head and the glenoid fossa, with damage to the humerus. We replaced the humeral head, that's your collarbone, and repaired the fractures to the upper arm bone or the humerus.'

'How long before I'm back to normal?'

'The proximal humerus fractures will take four to eight weeks to heal well enough so you don't need external support. Good strength will be back by twelve weeks, but full healing with bones may take six to twelve months.'

'When can I go home?'

'You lost a lot of blood and suffered damage to the tissues, tendons and nerves. You also have a wound infection.'

'I need to get home to find my wife and protect my kids.'

'You cannot travel yet Mr Roussos. You were lucky, there was no paralysis and minimal tendon and muscle tear. The projectile was a full metal jacket bullet which did not expand in diameter when it hit you, the destroyed tissue was limited to the path of the bullet, this was larger than the actual bullet diameter. The bullet turned sideways when it hit the bone but left a clean exit hole out of your shoulder.'

'I don't feel lucky.'

'The bullet didn't hit the perforated aorta or femoral artery, so there was no catastrophic loss of blood pressure. You were very lucky, Mr Roussos. You should rest.' The doctor bowed and left the room along with his followers.

Steve turned to the nurse. 'Can I call my kids? Where's my phone?'

The nurse looked, without success, amongst the few items, in the cabinet beside his bed. 'Sorry Mr Roussos, you can use a hospital phone.' She left the room and returned wheeling in a prepaid landline unit. She loaded credits and assigned them to the room bill.

Steve called home only to be greeted by the answering machine. The sound of Beth's light-hearted message hit him harder than the bullet, bringing tears to his eyes. He was desperate to speak to his family. He was so full of drugs that he could not remember Beth's mobile number. Neither could he recall Roger's home or mobile numbers, nor Beth's sister's number. His mind was suddenly blank. There was no need to remember any details when your phone kept all the details.

Steve was desperate to know how Mai, Adam and Mark were doing and feared he would be questioned by the police for his part in the murders. He tried home once more, unsuccessfully thirty minutes later, after the nurse had administered further pain relief via the drip. Beth's voice ripped him apart and he sobbed loudly, releasing pent up anguish, before eventually exhaustion led to sleep.

CHAPTER FIFTY-EIGHT

Monday 8th June

Although shivering, sweat emerged from every crevice of Steve's body. He opened his eyes and jerked his head back. The nightmare had rolled in and out throughout his fitful sleep, replaying the shootings', the chase, about to die, the blood, the explosion, Beth kidnapped. Are his kids safe? He planned to get out. Go home.

He pulled the call rope.

As the door opened, he could see a silhouette entering the room. Steve struggled to focus as he tried to force his upper body up off the bed. He was just about to ask for the doctor to visit him.

He heard, 'Hello my love, it's me.'

He collapsed back onto the bed, unsure how long he had been asleep or unconscious. He felt light-headed as he opened his eyes.

'Steve it's me, Beth. Are you OK?'

He wondered if he was still dreaming. She leaned over and kissed his forehead.

'Beth?' *Am I dreaming?*

'It's me.'

'How? How could? I mean. You're here.'

'Yes, love. I arrived today.'

'You're not. You're OK. Are you alive?' His heart thudded louder and louder. 'I thought…' Steve gasped for air.

'I'm here. I'm fine.'

'But…' He tried to sit up.

'Everything will be fine my love. I'm here. The children are safe, and you will be OK. We'll call the children later today when it's breakfast time at home.'

She embraced him, and he whispered, 'I love you. I thought I'd lost you. I love you.'

'I love you too, more than words can say.'

Steve's heart leapt like a wild stag in his throat, overwhelmed to know that Beth was alive and well, he held her as close as possible, feeling no pain. Beth evaded Steve's questions about the cut next to her eye; she chose not to talk about her own experience.

She picked up the newspaper. 'It's in the paper, Steve. It's over love. The headline in the New Straits Times read. Joint Raiding Operation on Q7 and Grithos PTE. Underneath it continued – 'A covert joint raiding operation was conducted on Q7 Berhad and its affiliates by the Royal Malaysian Police; Ministry of Domestic Trade, Cooperatives and Consumerism; Companies Commission of Malaysia and also Bank Negara Malaysia for suspected offences under the laws administered by the respective enforcement agencies. Singapore's Commercial Affairs' Department has also conducted a similar operation against Grithos PTE in Singapore. Prominent businessmen have been arrested by the Royal Malaysian Police in Kuala Lumpur, in connection with the activities.'

'Great news.'

Steve tried to find out as much information as possible from Beth about her kidnapping, injuries and incarceration. She evaded most of the questions. They talked about Adam, Mai and Mark. Steve feared the worst, and prayed that they were ok and was trying to get an update. He also hoped that Prem was either behind bars or dead.

They waited until after nine AM UK time before calling the kids and then Roger.

By this time Steve was exhausted and drifted off to sleep.

CHAPTER FIFTY-NINE

Tuesday 9th June

The hospital had set up a bed in Steve's hospital room, so that Beth could stay the night. She was helping Steve to eat a yoghurt when the door opened. Steve looked up and saw Mark standing in the doorway. His gaunt face and thin frame shocked Steve. 'Mark!' He tried to smile.

'They've released me. The embassy arranged a driver to bring me here.' Mark burst into tears and wiped his face with his hands.

Beth rushed over to console him. She wiped the tears from his eyes with a tissue, led him over to a seat next to Steve's hospital bed, pulled another chair up and sat beside him.

Mark explained, 'The police returned my mobile phone and laptop, and I visited the Concorde Hotel to get the rest of my things before they drove me up to Penang.'

'I'm so glad you're OK,' Beth said.

'It was terrible. Don't know how much longer I could have taken it in there,' Mark said.

Steve reached out to Mark. The intravenous drip, tube and cannula restricted his movement. 'Glad you're safe now.'

'Not sure how I'll get over this. I keep getting panic attacks,' Mark said.

'We'll look after you. You and I can start again.' Steve tried to comfort him.

Beth put her hand on Mark's shoulder. 'Steve and I will help you put this in the past.'

'Thank you,' Mark said.

'Do you know how Adam and Mai are?' Steve asked.

'No, when I was released, I was only told that there had been a confrontation which had turned violent and they would leave me at the hospital where you were being treated. The embassy is sending someone over to see us apparently,' Mark explained, 'So, how are you?'

Steve winked. 'I'm fine. A few bumps and bruises.'

'He got shot in the shoulder and arm; more than a few bruises. Don't let him kid you.' Beth laughed.

Steve smiled, hearing her cheery voice in real life was just so amazing, the best pain relief in the world.

Shortly after, Paul Reynolds arrived. The Vice Consul of the British Embassy had travelled up to Penang. 'Mr and Mrs Roussos and Mr Farrell.'

Steve did his best to smile and try to raise himself up on the bed with his one good arm. 'Thank you for coming, Mr Reynolds,' He gestured to Beth. 'Mr Reynolds is in-charge at the embassy in Kuala Lumpur.'

'Mr Reynolds, nice to meet you.' Beth smiled and shook hands with the Vice Consul.

'Please call me Paul, good to meet you.'

Mark and the Vice Consul shook hands. 'Thank you, Paul. I'm so happy to be out of prison.'

'Dr Laksana asked me to say how grateful he is for your help in these matters, Steve. I am very happy to confirm that due to Dr Laksana's intervention, he has ensured Mark's release; all charges dropped.'

Mark took a deep breath in… and out again.

Steve nodded. 'Thanks Paul. I'm glad he listened to us.'

'Yes, he is very grateful. By the way, the embassy will take care of any expenses in the hospital.'

'Thank you.'

Paul nodded.

'What happened to Adam and Mai?' Steve asked, 'We don't know how they are - and I've not had the chance to talk to someone about it, until now?'.

'I am sorry to have to tell you that Adam Jothi died at the restaurant. His family have made arrangements for his funeral.'

Mark's eyes watered, and he turned towards the wall.

'Adam was trying to protect Prem from being hurt, when he was shot himself. The brothers did love one another after all,' Steve mused, remembering the harrowing scene.

'What about Mai?'

'Wounded in the leg, Mai Le also suffered a head injury causing a severe concussion. She is in a stable condition at the Loh Guan Lye Specialists Centre in Penang. She is pregnant. They are not sure if the baby will survive.'

Beth raised a tissue to her eyes.

'Let's hope they are both OK.'

Steve felt weak and nauseous. *Oh my God! If I had known Beth was OK, maybe Adam and Mai would be here today. Have I caused this?*

'Prem Jothi and Cliff Lin?' Steve looked at Paul.

'Prem Jothi was wounded and taken to a hospital in Kuala Lumpur. He is in a stable condition. Cliff Lin sustained a head injury and a flesh wound. Also, two bodyguards, Wei Zhang and Tony Situ were shot dead.'

'Have they arrested them?'

'Once they have recovered, they will be arrested and questioned,' the Vice Consul said.

Steve frowned. 'He deserves to pay for what he has done. Death would be the easy way out.'

As a result of a covert operation by the authorities, 'Farid Razak, Anil Krishnan and Anthony Suppiah were arrested and are being questioned. Q7's assets have been frozen by the Malaysian government. Their business is now under the day to day control of Axiatel. They are a large company based in Kuala Lumpur.'

'What about the triad gang Kongsi?'

'It's a constant battle in Malaysia. Jothi is the head of Kongsi thirty-one who run the Kuala Lumpur central area. Information sources say Kongsi seventy-seven, who control the northern suburbs have taken over the Ampang district? It looks like Kongsi seventy-seven will try to take over Jothi's Kongsi thirty-one.'

'And the corrupt police officers?'

'Yes, they arrested Superintendent Anwar Bin Tempawan and Sergeant TetLeong, along with several other policemen based in Kuala Lumpur. They will serve long sentences.'

What about me? I killed someone. I caused the killings. Are they going to arrest me.

Steve nodded. 'Do the police need me to give a statement?'

'Unless Prem Jothi or Cliff Lin want to press charges, which I doubt. And I am very pleased to say you helped to bring down the government, Mr Roussos,' the Vice Consul said.

'The Malaysian government?' Steve expressed surprise.

'Yes, the Malaysian Prime Minister, Ariff Samahon, resigned and left with his wife and extended family, including his son-in-law. Rumour has it they negotiated a safe passage to the US.'

'Yes, with the money!' Steve shook his head.

'The Malaysian government named Dr Laksana as the interim Prime Minister, and they have released Dr. Sarimah Rozhan's husband; charges dropped. It all happened very quickly,' The Vice Consul said.

'That's great progress, but at an awful cost,' Mark said ruefully.

'And also Alan Kam, Chief Executive of Axiatel has asked if he can come to see you both tomorrow? And Dr Laksana may visit you. He has arranged for a doctor and nurse to travel back with you to the UK to make sure you have a comfortable flight.'

# # # # # #

After the Vice Consul left the hospital, Mark went for a coffee and some fresh air, allowing Steve and Beth a private call home. Steve and Beth called their children as soon as it was seven am in the UK. They were staying at home with Steve's brother Brian and his wife Hazel who had flown over from Mallorca. They had police protection whilst everything was settling down. Jake told his dad all about how he was beating the police officer on his FIFA game. It overjoyed Steve to hear his children's voices, and he could not wait to be with them again.

# # # # # #

Mark arrived back at the hospital a short time later, 'It'll be great to soak in a bath and sleep in a bed tonight,' Mark said.

'We will develop a successful business again, together Mark. We're a team.' Steve tried to smile despite the surging pain.

Mark smiled, 'sure we will' and Beth kissed him on the cheek. Mark left to book into the same hotel as Beth.

Steve and Beth talked for a while. Exhausted, Steve was struggling to stay awake so Beth said she would go back to the hotel and come back first thing in the morning. They held each other and kissed. Even though he was in a lot of pain, he didn't care now that he knew Beth and the kids were safe.

CHAPTER SIXTY

Wednesday 10th June

Mark and Beth arrived at the hospital. Mark seemed a little fresher than the previous day, but still looked pale and thin. Beth leaned over and kissed Steve before taking a seat by the bed.

Mark shook Steve's hand and sat down. 'I checked Alan Kam on LinkedIn.'

'What time is he due?'

'Eleven o'clock this morning. He's the new Chief Executive of Axiatel. Ran NTT, Avaya and Lucent, Asia regions.'

'So, the top man eh? I thought it was Kee Yeow.' Steve looked puzzled.

'Kee Yeow has moved on. Alan Kam is new in from NTT.'

'You never know. They might want to discuss a new contract.'

Beth glared at Steve. 'I think you both should take a long rest. This has been traumatic for all of us.'

'It will do no harm in talking to him.'

'But you shouldn't be working.' Beth wagged her index finger at Steve.

'As soon as I can get out of this hospital, we'll be on the next plane home.'

'First class.' She smiled.

Mark received a call from Paul Reynolds. He put the mobile on speaker, so Beth and Steve could listen.

'Mr Jothi recovered enough to talk to the authorities.'

'Have they arrested him?' Steve said.

There was a short silence before Paul said, 'I'm sorry to inform you that the authorities arrested Mr Jothi and then released him due to lack of evidence. He is not pressing any charges against you, Steve and is planning to leave for the US.'

Steve was aware of his heart beating against the inside of his chest and his dry mouth made it difficult for him to speak. 'You're joking. He must have done a deal. Are we safe? If they release him he could come after us.'

Mark shook his head. 'That can't be. He's the reason I went to jail.'

Many thoughts came flooding back that worried Steve. *Bastard. We need justice.*

'He is still in hospital. I will keep you informed of any developments,' Paul said before he hung up.

Steve was very uncomfortable. The pain in his arm and shoulder meant he could not get into any position which enabled him to rest. Beth expressed her concern that he should rest. Eleven o'clock came with no sign of Alan Kam.

'It's midday. Where is he?' Mark walked over to the window and looked out.

'The Malaysians have a relaxed attitude to turning up on time. 'Steve was ratty and frustrated.

Beth suggested they should leave Steve to rest. Mark gathered his things just as three men entered the room. Alan Kam introduced himself and his colleagues, Vincent Wong and Gillian Chan. There were several uncomfortable moments. They surrounded Steve's bed. Beth left to go back to the hotel. Nursing staff appeared with three chairs.

Alan's jet-black hair, black-framed glasses and a red dickey-bow made Steve smiled to himself; although he was feeling shit.

Alan started the meeting by explaining how he made Avaya and Lucent major players in Asia. Then quoted high growth numbers and described in great detail the fantastic job he did at NTT. Steve was trying to look interested but was finding it difficult to concentrate. He was in pain, bored and frustrated. Alan Kam took them through his vision for Axiatel and the improvements he had presided over during the first few months in the job. He introduced Vincent Wong who described his role as Head of Services responsible for all mobile services for Axiatel's one hundred and seventy million customers in five countries across Asia. Steve was struggling, and Mark looked bored.

Gillian Chan introduced herself as the Head of Solution and Project Management. She explained how pleased they were with the Seguro system launched in Malaysia and Indonesia targeting over sixty million customers.

Steve focused on what they were saying. He could not believe what he heard. *Wow!*

Gillian carried on. 'We plan to expand the service across Malaysia and Indonesia.'

Mark interrupted. 'Have you isolated the dark net?'

'Yes, the government have brought in security specialists,' Alan Kam said.

Mark nodded.

'The government have taken over Q7 and split-up the company. Axiatel have taken over the services division of Q7 which includes the Seguro secure payments system.'

'Beyond Malaysia and Indonesia,' Gillian said, 'We are planning Singapore, Cambodia and Sri Lanka.'

Mark gave an immediate positive response. 'Yes, we can scale up to cover all one hundred and seventy million Axiatel subscribers and beyond.'

Vincent interrupted. 'We need your assurance that Seguro can support the solution at Axiatel.'

Steve looked towards Mark and nodded. 'Yes, we have a team who can support you. We need full remote access to the system. In addition, we would suggest local support,' Mark said.

'That's great. We can draw up a service level agreement,' Vincent smiled, looking over to Alan and nodding.

'And the commercial contract. Will you honour our contract with Q7?' Steve looked over towards Mark who was grimacing.

Alan opened a folder and looked at the paperwork. 'Procurement will draw up the agreement based on our standard contract.'

'And the terms we agreed with Q7?'

'Yes, we can duplicate the terms.' Alan nodded.

Mark smiled.

Although Steve felt dizzy, in pain and disorientated, he was determined to be business like. 'Perfect.'

'I'm sure you will be pleased to know,' Alan said, 'Although Q7's assets have been frozen by the Malaysian government our new leader, Dr Laksana has issued a directive to the government administrators. They will honour the contract with Q7 to date. It is difficult to apportion the number of legal transactions at Q7, so he suggested a one-off payment of two million US dollars. Dr Laksana asked me to convey the gratitude of the government for your service to Malaysia.'

Two million dollars! Steve gulped, mouth dry, the words stuck inside him, as he tried to pull himself up on the bed, dizzy and disorientated. He couldn't believe what he had heard. He fell back onto the pillow and passed out.

CHAPTER SIXTY-ONE

Thursday 11th June

The following day Steve woke up and the room was spinning. A sudden pain shot through his arm, along his shoulder and deep into the crevices of his brain. Beth helped by offering him a glass of water. He tried to pull his head forward and vomited. It was bile. She cupped tissues below his chin. The nurse came in to attend to him.

'I'm sorry. Shooting pain and dizzy.'

The nurse adjusted the drip. 'I have increased the morphine level Mr Roussos. I'll get you something to stop the sickness.'

Steve forced a smile as Beth kissed his forehead.

'Where's Mark?'

'He's at the hotel phoning Roger.'

'Oh good. Did he tell you about Axiatel?'

'Yes. It's wonderful. Mark is over the moon.'

'I thought I might be dreaming.'

'You deserve this Steve.'

'We can sort the mortgage and go on holiday.'

'When you are better! You need to rest now.' She smiled.

A buoyant Mark arrived at the hospital, frailty had diminished. 'I've talked to Roger. He's onto it.'

'Ah great. What about the contract?'

'Axiatel have already sent across the commercial and support framework agreement. Roger will respond. The support team are getting organised.'

'That's good. Can you apologise to Alan Kam?'

'Sure, he was fine. Concerned for you but fine.'

'Great. What about the two million dollars?' Steve said.

'They will transfer it this week to go into the Seguro account. It's already cleared with HSBC Bank. Roger is still in shock.' Mark looked as though he was about to burst with excitement.

'Wow, that's fantastic. If only David and Glen were here to witness this,' Steve said, 'not forgetting Trish and Adam.'

'Yes, nothing can ever make up for the terrible things that happened to them.'

'Can you print out a copy of the framework agreement?'

Beth overheard and stepped into the conversation. 'Steve. You're not in a fit state to do anything.'

'It's all in hand,' Mark said, 'We need you back, but only when you are fit.'

'Thank you,' she said.

'I have more great news,' Mark said.

'Not sure I can take any more good news.' Steve smiled.

'I visited Mai in hospital. She will be fine.'

'Ah, that's great.'

'And. The scans show the baby is well. Mai had a few problems but she is fine.'

Tears swelled in Beth's eyes. 'Oh my God. That's great. Thank God.'

'She sends her love.'

'Little Glen.' Steve smiled. 'What about her hospital bills?'

'The administration are taking care of the bills?'

'Good. And her family?'

'She has talked to them. They are safe.'

'Ask Roger to arrange return flights for Mai's mother, sister and son. They should be with Mai.'

'Brilliant.'

'We owe it to Glen to look after Mai, the baby and her family. So, we will support her as much as we can.'

Tears welled up in Mark's eyes.

Beth sobbed and hugged Steve.

CHAPTER SIXTY-TWO

Monday 15th June

Four days later the hospital discharged Steve. They visited Mai on the way to the airport, met Mai's family and discussed plans to visit Hanoi. It moved Steve when Mai thanked him for all they were doing and will do for her and her family.

Accompanied by a private doctor and nurse, they travelled from Penang and arrived at Kuala Lumpur airport. The nurse pushed Steve along in a wheelchair. Beth held his hand. Steve smiled to himself as Mark had wasted no time in engaging with the handsome Malaysian doctor.

Paul Reynolds, Vice Consul of the British Embassy was waiting at the gate with passports for Steve and Mark and to wish them a safe journey home. He pulled Mark and Steve to one side. 'Dr Laksana asked me to update you. As you know the Malaysian authorities arrested Mr Jothi but released him due to lack of evidence.'

Steve frowned. 'That's crazy. He was a director of the Shell Company. The evidence is all there. What the hell.'

Paul nodded. 'He left hospital two days ago. The car that picked him up was ambushed and gunned down in Petaling Jaya, fifteen miles outside Kuala Lumpur. Shot at close range with several gunshot wounds to his face and chest. Police found him in a pool of blood in the back seat of the car. They also murdered the driver.'

'Who ambushed him?' Mark asked.

'Witnesses who heard the shots saw two suspects entering separate cars before driving away. Both vehicles parked in front and behind Mr Jothi's car. The police believe the suspects intercepted the vehicle before firing shots. We know Kongsi seventy-seven has taken over the Ampang district and are moving towards Kongsi thirty-one's district. Kongsi thirty-one have no Mountain Master now. Police suspect the rival gang murdered Mr Jothi.'

'Wow. Do you think Dr Laksana released him to his fate?'

'I couldn't comment.' Paul nodded.

Everything flooded back, Steve felt relieved and somehow this justified the action.

They said their goodbyes and moved through customs and into the first-class lounge. The departure board showed that flight BA34 to Heathrow was on time.

Steve and Beth could not wait to get back home to see the children.

A fresh start.

I will never forget my dear friends David, Trish and Glen.

And poor Adam. He was a good man.

We will always support Mai and her children.

I hope they can have a great life.

A tribute to Glen.

A bright future for Mark.

I love Beth. Thank God she is OK.

Can't wait to hug the kids.

A fresh start.

PART FOUR

SIX MONTHS LATER

CHAPTER SIXTY-THREE

Wednesday 9th December

The head of Kongsi Gelap thirty-one, Mountain Master, arrived at the penthouse of the Tun Sambanthan building in the central Wilayah Persekutuan district of Kuala Lumpur, flanked by two foot soldiers both wearing black suits. Born in Malaysia of Chinese origin, his fine grey shoulder length hair clashed with his smart black trousers and tailored white shirt. The receptionist bowed as they walked straight past her into the boardroom.

The large fan worked overtime booming out air from the conditioning unit. Mountain Master sat at the head of an oval table and the two men stood motionless in front of the pillars.

Incense Master arrived. Although wearing his usual expensive suit, shirt and tie, his small frame supported a large gut due to many extravagances over the years. His thinning hair on the crown of his head and dark black stubble, made him appear much older. Mountain Master clicked his fingers. 'Two oolong,' he said to one of his foot soldiers, who left the room to organise the tea.

A petite woman entered the room, bowed and placed the oolong tea on the table in front of them, bowing again, walked backwards and left the room. Other gang members arrived. Vanguard, a skinny, weasel-like face, slight-framed man, above average height for someone from Malaysia, accompanied by White Paper Fan, a plump man with glasses and greying hair.

White Paper Fan, the money man summarised income for the month.

Mountain Master stood up, walked over to the window and looked out. He turned and focussed on Vanguard. 'Do we have the child?'

'Yes, Tien Nguyen called me this morning. A boy. Born just over a week ago at the private French International Hospital in Hanoi. There was security but no issues. She moved it to a location just outside Hanoi.'

He nodded. 'Any communication with Mai Le?'

'No. She had complications with the birth. Was due to leave hospital tomorrow.'

'Good. We move forward with the plan.'

They nodded and carried on with the rest of the agenda.

# # # # # #

Steve could still not believe how times had changed. As a regular passenger in the exclusive first-class cabin of the Boeing 787 Dreamliner aircraft, he loved travelling on the flight to Kuala Lumpur. The seat together with the ottoman transformed into a comfortable lie-flat bed, the soft mattress topper, thick pillow, comfortable blanket, and the lightweight, dark green pyjamas meant he had no problem in falling asleep for most of the flight. About ninety minutes before landing the cabin attendants served tea. Mark sat in the seat across the aisle. 'How are you doing?'

Steve stretched and smiled. 'Brilliant. Slept like a baby. Only way to travel.'

These days Steve preferred to stay in a suite at The Grand Millennium Hotel, a far cry from the Concorde. The chauffeur pulled up outside the hotel, the bell boy greeted them as they stepped out of the car, gathered their suitcases from the boot and moved them into the lobby.

As they entered the hotel, the concierge stepped forward and bowed. 'Mr Cliff Lin and Mr Farid Razak are waiting in the atrium.'

The blood drained from Steve's body making him light-headed. He froze, trying to comprehend the situation. Mark's face was ashen.

Cliff Lin and Farid Razak.
Steve felt sick.

THE END

About Leo James

Leo began writing during his recovery from a serious fall into a storm drain whilst on business in Singapore. To this day, he has not solved the mystery of who pushed him. Stuck in hospital, Leo found it cathartic to write. It helped with his recovery, both mentally and physically. That was the start. Once back to work, and travelling internationally, he would write everywhere: on planes, trains, staying at hotels, basically at any given opportunity.

Leo worked for over 20 years in global information technology. He is an expert in cryptocurrencies, blockchain and cybersecurity. In addition, Leo is a practicing therapist in clinical hypnosis and cognitive behaviour therapy.

Born in the UK, he graduated from Illinois State University in America. He has a postgraduate qualification in behavioural therapy from the University of West London in the UK.

I hope you enjoyed reading my novel.
It would be great if you could leave a review on the site where you bought the book.

Please sign up for my email list at
http://layersofdeception.info

Thank you.

Printed in July 2019
by Rotomail Italia S.p.A., Vignate (MI) - Italy